Time and Again

Ian Weaver

TIME AND AGAIN
Copyright © 2009 Ian Weaver

First Published in the UK by
Paul Mould Publishing
p.mould@yahoo.com

In association with
Empire Publishing Service www.ppeps.com
P.O. Box 1344, Studio City, CA 91614-0344

A CIP Catalogue record for this book is available from the British Library or from the US Library of Congress.

Simultaneously published in
Australia, Canada, Germany, UK, USA

Printed in Great Britain
First Printing 2009

US 13 ISBN 978-1-58690-104-2
UK 13 ISBN 978-1-904959-37-3

Introduction

Ian Weaver was born in Louth, Lincolnshire in 1960. Educated in Grantham he joined the Royal Navy in 1979 as a Seaking Observer in the Fleet Air Arm. In 1989 he transferred to the Royal Air Force flying as a Navigator in the Tornado F3. He left the service in 1997 following a flying accident and continued to work for the RAF in a flight simulator. He now resides in Lincoln working on his writing career.

Time and Again is his first novel and draws on some of his many experiences in the Armed forces. Although a work of fiction and fantasy, much of the book is true to life and factually accurate. Readers may be surprised to learn that the first few chapters were written before his flying accident and yet there are striking similarities between the fictional and actual circumstances, events and injuries. Now working on the sequel, he is far more wary in the way he 'treats' his hero!

Chapter One

The sea rolled past on its never-ending journey and Sub Lieutenant Tony 'Harry' Harrison had been watching it, as if in a trance, for about half an hour. He leant against the highly polished wooden rail mounted on steel stanchions and stared into the depths. The ocean was a deep green and the turbulent waters thrown up by the ship's massive screws were, in contrast, pure white; the bubbles spewing up to burst onto the surface and split the sun's rays into all the colours of the rainbow. He watched as the albatross that had followed them for days floated lazily just above the surface, hardly needing to beat it's 7ft long wings as it effortlessly and endlessly rode the ship's wake for reasons known only to itself.

Harry wondered if this trip was ever going to end, and his mind wandered back to the night before he had flown from his base, Royal Naval Air Station (RNAS) Culdrose, in Cornwall to join the Ship in Portsmouth. That had been six weeks earlier and he'd had a bit of a bust up with his girlfriend of three months. Twelve weeks he mused, that's almost a record for me. With his square jaw, clean complexion and piercing steel grey eyes topping his 6'2' frame he never had trouble attracting women, he just couldn't seem to maintain a relationship for longer than a few weeks. It wasn't the slight air of arrogance or even the aura of power about him that drove them away, rather the feeling that they couldn't live up to the extremely high standards he set for himself and anyone with him. Laura seemed to be going the same way, he thought, added to which she could not control the insane jealousy she felt every time they were apart. He didn't even know if she would still be there for him when they finally got back to Port. Still only two more weeks to go and then he would see where he stood with her when they got home. He hoped...

'You gonna stand there all day or are you coming flying with the rest of yer crew?...Oiy Harry I'm talking to you.'

'Christ, sorry mate, I'll be up in the briefing room in a couple of minutes,' said Harry looking at his watch. 'Just give me a few minutes to get my thoughts together.'

The interruption had come from 'Smokey' Jonston, his 1st Pilot. Harry rubbed his hand over his rugged face and thought about the approaching sortie. Should be a fairly run of the mill trip. He had been flying as an Observer or 'backseater' in the Fleet Air Arm for about four years and in that time had participated in a number of NATO Exercises. At last he was beginning to feel that he had a grip on the job; no longer just mayhem from the beginning of a sortie to the end. He felt confident enough to sit back and enjoy the feeling of command as he vectored his and other Seaking Anti-Submarine Helicopters round the skies, ordered ships into the fight and dropped his simulated weapons onto the unseen steel monsters below. A different man from the one that had joined the ship straight out of training just three years ago, carefully treading his way through the mine-field of his advanced continuation training, working up to his certificate of competence.

He also had time to access the ability of the various pilots that he flew with, all of which bought him back to Smokey. Not a bad pilot and a good friend. Smokey was only about 5'6' with ginger hair and a face that had grown old before its time. At 27 going on 40 he had pock-marked skin and extremely high cheek bones which gave him the look of a predator, and as a Qualified Helicopter Instructor this often gave him the edge he needed when dealing with a difficult student. Harry glanced idly at his watch again and saw that another 5 minutes had passed.

'Shit!' he exclaimed, causing the others on the quarterdeck to peer round with some amusement. Now he would have to hurry to make the briefing time and he hated everything getting bunched up just before takeoff. He rushed off the quarterdeck and onto the main drag of

HMS INDOMITABLE, the Navy's newest in a brand new line of Through-deck Cruisers. At a pinch over 540' it was not dissimilar to the older Invincible class, except the briefing room was forward!

'Jesus H Christ Sir, don't you know you're not supposed to run in the walkways?' yelled the somewhat taken aback and definitely grumpy Chief Stoker he'd almost bundled over in his haste.

'Sorry Chief,' he called back whilst painting a picture of the Stokers face in his mind so he would be able to buy him a pint next time he got an invite down the Senior Rates Mess.

At last he arrived at the briefing room; a stark, oblong room with cream bulkheads and a green tiled floor. Along the tops of the bulkheads and deck-heads ran pipes of varying diameter, each with metallic tape identifying its contents. Most were fresh or salt water whilst others carried steam. One of the lessons learnt during the Falklands crisis in 1982 was how easily fire and smoke spread from one section to another via electric cabling. These were now also encased in steel pipes that would offer some protection to the wiring and would limit the spread of smoke throughout a stricken ship. The monotony of the walls was broken by the various tote boards and intelligence briefings on the latest phase of Exercise Stop Gap. Harry knew well the concept of the exercise, having been involved in the planning phase as far as the anti-submarine effort went. NATO forces would have to escort friendly convoys through the Iceland – Faroes gap whilst 'Red' forces would oppose them. Quite who the Red forces were supposed to be in these days of peace between the two main super powers remained a mystery.

'Ah there you are,' sighed Lieutenant Commander 'Stormy' Peterson. 'Now, perhaps, we can begin.'

Just my bloody luck thought Harry, trust me to be late when the sortie's being led by the Senior Observer (SOBS). He settled down into one of the surprisingly comfortable airline style seats and started to concentrate on the job at hand. He gave his full attention to Lt Cdr Peterson who started to cover the domestics of the sortie. It was going to be a fairly standard mission; departing as a pair and sitting in an active sonar search about 20 miles ahead of the task force that clung to INDOMITABLE like chicks to a mother hen. The Seaking's job was to set up a screen that any Submarine intending to attack the fleet would have to pass through. On this occasion they would be using active sonar, which, working on the same principle as radar, involved putting sound into the water and waiting for the returning echo from any targets within the beam. To achieve this aim the Seaking has a variable depth dipping sonar, which when lowered up to 600' below the aircraft would set about the job of finding submarines. Although very accurate it has one big disadvantage; the targets could hear the sonar long before you were in range to receive their telltale echo, and could take action to steer around the defence and maybe still get to their targets. However by randomly 'jumping' about in their assigned sector, and with the backing of shipborne sonar, the active screen is still a good way to defeat the submarine threat, and also advertised their presence to the enemy thus possibly warning them off from attempting an attack that might prove fatal to the submarine.

'Okay' said Peterson. 'I'll be Dipboss for the first hour and then we'll go through the swap procedures and you can take it for the rest of the trip Harry. Any questions?' finished SOBS.

Silence greeted him and so with a slightly self-praising smile he turned and left the room, heading for the changing rooms. Harry thought about brushing up on the procedures for handing over 'Dipboss' but then thought the better of it. There may well be 4 or 5 Seakings involved in the active screen, each arriving and leaving at different times. One of the Observers would sit in over all tactical command and once contact was gained with the enemy he had the responsibility of prosecuting any attacks. When the Dipboss was due to go off task he handed control to another aircraft. Harry had done it many times before and pretty well knew the procedures inside out.

'That's what gets me about this job,' murmured Smokey interrupting his thoughts. 'The number of times we have to change clothing in a day.' He wandered off still grumbling to himself, but he had a point. This would be the fourth change of the day and it was still only 1400.

Harry reached the cluttered changing room that contained the Squadron's flying clothing and was greeted with the familiar smell of sweat and rubber. Opening his locker he looked at the photo of Laura pinned to the inside of the door. Quickly looking away he put all thoughts of home out of his mind and concentrated on the job at hand. He changed into two layers of thermal underwear and a knitted bunny suit before pulling on his 'Goonsuit'; a bulky and uncomfortable garment, not unlike a diver's drysuit; it was an essential addition when flying over cold water. In the unlikely event of ditching into the sea the fabric of the suit and the rubber wrist and neck seals combined to stop any freezing water from reaching the body. In the water temperatures of about 3-4 degrees centigrade that they were sailing through it would increase survival time from about 1 hour maximum to somewhere in the region of 12. This figure would obviously be greatly extended if the survivor managed to board his single-seat life raft, which was connected to his life jacket as part of his strapping in procedure once he boarded the seat in the aircraft. All these things together would give ample time for any rescue operation to be mounted.

This was the last thing on Harry's mind as he finished off by quickly grabbing and donning his life jacket. He picked up the bulky flying helmet and navigation bag, containing overlays for the radar and anything else he may require for the sortie. With a friendly nod to Smokey he darted out of the door hoping to make up for the preparation time he'd lost before the briefing.

'Do the walk round for me,' called Smokey after him. 'I'm having a bit of trouble with me boots.'

'Lazy Bastard,' came the good-natured reply from Harry.

Arriving on the flight deck he pulled the heavy water-tight door shut behind him and spun the wheel that threw the six retaining bolts into place. He was surprised by the cutting wind and salt spray that slammed into his face. The quarterdeck he'd been on earlier was sheltered and gave a false impression of the weather conditions and here he judged that the Ship was making about 20 knots into wind, giving about 40 kts over the deck. The sea was also getting up he observed as he bounded down wind to 5 spot where his 'cab' sat waiting. Once in the lee of the ship's huge super-structure he started to get some shelter, though the wind eddied around the 'island', becoming gustier in the turbulence forming downwind.

'Should make for an interesting take-off,' he muttered to himself as he started walking round the helicopter looking for the tell-tale signs of a leak that could lead to an engine failure or, God forbid, a main gearbox seizure in flight.

'What was that?' asked Sub Lieutenant Paul Spencer, the 2nd Pilot for the sortie.

'Oh nothing,' returned Harry. 'I'm just doing a walkround for Smokey.'

'Don't worry I've just finished. There's a bit of oil on the Starboard side, but as they say, if it's not leaking - it's empty.' He gave Harry one of his best youthful smiles and disappeared through the front door of the aircraft.

Harry carried on with his walkround. Paul had been on the Squadron about 3 months and in Harry's opinion showed a dangerous trait in any Pilot however experienced - over confidence. In Paul's case this was combined with inability borne from *inexperience* and this made him doubly dangerous. Harry knew that as Captain of the aircraft he would have to keep an eye on him. His thoughts were broken by the arrival of Smokey and the Aircrewman who would operate the sonar.

'You know my feelings about Paul,' Harry confided to his Pilot once Leading Aircrewman McKilroy was out of earshot. 'Just watch him will you, especially on take off; it could be pretty bumpy with this wind.'

'Don't worry, it's my skin too and Mandy ain't gonna put up with damaged goods when we get home in a couple of weeks.' With this he treated Harry to his dirtiest leer before getting back to reality and continuing. 'Anything on the walkround?'

'There's a bit of fresh engine oil on the starboard side that I think we should get the Crew Chief to take a quick look at it.'

'OK I'll check it out - you get your gear sorted out in the back.' Smokey ducked under the tail and motioned for the chief of the deck crew to join him.

Seeing that the possible mechanical problem was in good hands Harry entered the aircraft through the split front door, the bottom of which dropped down to form steps into the interior. Gaining entrance the familiar smell of stale hydraulic fluid that had soaked into the grey, sponge sound proofing that lined the inside of the aircraft hit him full in the face. Not altogether unpleasant it held with it many memories both fond and fraught. He made his way aft through the narrow passage between the starboard bulk-head and the sonar winching gear and ended up in the rear cabin. What used to be a spacious area that could seat 21 people was now jammed full of equipment. Radar, teardrop sonar displays, magnetic anomaly detection equipment along with rows of passive sonar buoys, all helped to give the appearance of a high tech environment. After a cursory glance at McKilroy, who was checking the safety equipment and secure stowage of any potential loose articles, Harry dropped himself into the left hand seat and started running his fingers over the familiar controls. As he worked he ran through a mental check list; Radar to standby, Tactical Air Navigation System (TANS) initialised and Ships Position and intended Movement (PIM) entered along with the current time. As he was selecting the radios on he heard the engines starting to wind up and Paul was calling to the Ground crew as he started spreading the rotor blades.

'Everyone on intercom?' asked Smokey, and continued before anyone had the chance to reply. 'And confirm you're all strapped in or holding on.' Having received an affirmative from the whole crew he let the rotor brake off and the cab lurched sideways, rocking on the oleos as the blades started to rotate. Soon the bouncing settled down to the usual high frequency vibration as the rotor disc reached its operating speed. Harry finished off in the back as Smokey and Paul went through the challenge and response pre take-off checks.

'Flyco this is W6Y ready for take off spot 5,' called Smokey once the checks were complete.

'Flyco roger, relative wind off the clock is red 20/45 knots, cleared non-standard departure to the left - launch on the green,' came the staccato reply.

'OK Paul, that'll be your take off - you happy?'

'No snags' Paul replied enthusiastically. 'Got the green light and the Flight Deck Officer looks happy, starting to pull power...torque's coming in together...lifting off...'

'Jesus Christ,' shouted Smokey. 'Control malfunction, tail rotor failure.' As the Helicopter leapt into the air it rapidly yawed to the left and had completed a full pirouette by the time it reached ten feet from the deck. Just as suddenly the aircraft rocked sharply and came back under some semblance of control.

'What the hell happened there?' gasped Harry as the aircraft lurched away from the ship and cleared the flight deck to the left. The sheepish reply came from Paul:

'Sorry about that guys, I put the wrong boot in as we lifted off.'

'Too bloody right you'll be sorry,' came the seething reply from Smokey.

Paul had made an elementary mistake. The force of the turning rotor blades has an equal and opposite reaction, which those of us conversant with Newton's laws will appreciate, and this causes the body of the aircraft to spin. To overcome this, a side mounted tail rotor is fitted and by varying the pitch and therefore the lift of the tail rotor blades by use of the 'rudder' pedals, the rotating motion is controlled. Paul had kicked the wrong pedal in as he lifted the cab off the deck and in so doing had compounded the effect instead of compensating for it. Harry broke the lengthening silence.

'Flyco, W6Y airborne, chopping to operational frequency.' After a short pause he said. 'Dial up frequency 274.2 on your box please Paul.'

'Yeah, let's see if you can get that right,' added Smokey caustically.

'Alright, cut it out,' snapped Harry. 'Leave it for the debrief. Let's just get on with the job at hand. Right, it's about 18 miles to the first dip position, we'll let the flight control system (FCS) take us down into the hover, set the height hold at 40 feet.' Thinking for a moment and referring to the water temperature charts in his kneepad he said to Leading Aircrewman McKilroy. 'Ok Tom, set up for an all-round sweep, 4 pings per sector. I make the optimum body depth around 240 feet,' he finished. His reference to 'body depth' was the depth to which they would lower the sonar transmitter to achieve the best detection range. Sometimes there were pronounced temperature layers in the water and a submarine could hide above or below them. In that case the helicopters would carry out a sweep above and below the layer. McKilroy studied his own crib sheet of figures and agreed with Harry that they would only need to search the one depth on this occasion.

The rest of the transit was in relative silence as each member of the crew went about setting his equipment up for the tactical stage of the sortie. In the front Paul set up the Flight Control System (FCS) ready for the first transition to the hover. Smokey watched his every move, still annoyed after the take-off. McKilroy set up the sonar displays and double-checked all his figures. Harry had nothing more to do and so studied the radar picture carefully, hoping to get the small return from the Submarine as it raised it's periscope above the surface for a sneaky look at it's targets. With the sea state as it was he had little hope but it would make their job a lot easier if he did spot something.

After following SOBS for the first part of the transit they were cleared to act independently and Harry vectored his aircraft to the centre of their nominated sector and instructed the Pilots to 'mark dip'. Hitting the 'transition down button on the FCS the aircraft flew itself to the hover on an estimated into wind heading and the Pilots set about their never-ending list of checks. They started by getting the hover sorted out; ensuring the cab was facing directly into wind by sliding their windows open and feeling for any draught that would indicate a cross wind. Then it was onto the FCS; confirming the hover height and parameters for leaving the hover, before finishing with a ditching brief to the crew.

'We're pulling 76% matched torque's.' Paul's voice droned on. 'If we loose an engine in the hover the other engine will not be able to sustain rotor speed, and we will be making a positive water landing. With this sea state we'll turn over immediately and it will be everybody for himself. Any questions?' There were none; they'd heard it all before.

For the next thirty minutes they worked, methodically searching their sector, jumping to a new position about every 5 minutes, maintaining relative position in sector about 20 nautical miles ahead of the ship. Where the hell is that Submarine thought Harry, probably gone home and forgotten to tell anyone; it had happened before. Harry dropped the blind from the window by his left shoulder. The dark grey sea was still building up, showing the occasional white horses dancing over the waves. His mind was starting to wander back to Laura. No other woman had affected him like this and if the truth were known he wasn't sure whether or not he liked it. He pictured her face in his mind. She could only be described as beautiful with classic bone structure, deep brown eyes, a face set off by her multi-coloured and somewhat spiky hair and a smile to die for. With an effort he dragged his mind back to the job

- he'd be taking over from Stormy shortly and he wanted to make a good job of it especially after turning up late for the brief.

'What do you make of that Paul?' asked Smokey.

'Dunno, maybe lightening, could even be the Northern lights.'

Harry didn't like the tense edge in Smokey's voice; he wasn't one that normally got flustered. Unstrapping his harness Harry struggled his way past McKilroy, who carried on with his methodical search of the ocean without showing any interest in the current proceedings, and made his way forward. As he appeared between the pilot's seats Paul pointed about thirty degrees starboard.

'What do you reckon then Harry?'

'Search me.' Harry looked over to the horizon where the sky had started to darken. At first he could see nothing out of the ordinary and was about to return to his seat when suddenly the sky lit up with an orangey-green flash. It was over in a moment, but was quickly followed by another and yet another before dying away, leaving just a faint impression on the retina. Harry had never seen anything like it before in his life. As he watched, glued to the spot, the lights burst again and this time seemed much brighter and maybe a little closer than before.

'Er..Sir, those lights, 30 right would you say?' So McKilroy had been listening all along.

'Yes, why?' Harry's reply was very short. He could feel the hairs on the back of his neck rising and he watched yet another conflagration light up the inside of the helicopter.

'Well...'

'Come on man, spit it out,' returned Harry through gritted teeth.

'Sorry Sir, It's just that I've never seen anything like this before. From about 15 to 45 degrees right the sonar display is full of noise, but it's not just normal wide band noise; it seems to be modulated in some way. It's as if somebody's put some kind of message on top of it, and it's getting closer Sir; it's on the nose round to 90 degrees now.' As he finished the lights burst again, this time bright enough to light up the cockpit as clear as day.

'I don't like this one little bit,' said Harry. 'McKilroy raise the sonar body, let's get the hell out of here and see what's going on. Smokey, give the Ship a call and see if they are recording any of this. Oh and while you're at it give them an accurate position.'

Smokey didn't like the hidden meaning of the last command, but complied all the same. Suddenly Paul gave a warning shout.

'Torque split, call NR.' The worst had happened. On the torque meter the left power needle had fallen to zero and the right was hovering at its end stop at 140%. The screeching sound of tortured bearings said it all - the right engine could not produce enough power to maintain rotor speed (NR)

'NR is 96 percent...94...90 percent, shit...Brace, brace, brace!' cried Smokey as he anticipated the inevitable outcome.

Harry never had a chance of making it back to his seat. He could physically hear the rotors slowing down and with the rotor speed went their lift. He clung onto the back of the two Pilots seats and spread his legs awaiting the impact. The next second all hell broke loose.

As the helicopter impacted with the sea it pitched forward. Harry's knees buckled and he was thrown into the Pilots seats. His helmet took the first blow but was rapidly followed by his left shoulder. He heard rather than felt his collarbone break and although not conscious of the pain he would feel later, if he survived, he was aware of growing warmth around his left shoulder. He tried to push himself off his knees but in the next moment the cab rolled viciously to the left and he felt a sickening jar as the rotor blades made contact with the sea. Water was pouring in through the open cockpit windows at an alarming rate and Harry was vaguely aware of a pair of boots disappearing out of the port window before the rush of water pushed him towards the rear cabin.

Miraculously Harry was carried along the passage past the sonar without becoming snagged, however he was rapidly becoming disoriented and grabbed out with his good arm to retard his progress and get his bearings. He opened his eyes in the stinging salt water and found himself looking into the dead face of Tom McKilroy at close quarters. The shock of it nearly killed him, but also gave him the best chance of survival. He let go of his anchor point and instinctively drew in a breath. Freezing cold water was sucked into his trachea before being checked by his choking; the air expelled from his lungs forcing the water out ahead of it. He realised he was drowning and felt the flow of water and the buoyancy given by the air trapped in his goon suit pushing him to what he assumed was the far rear of the aircraft. It was the air in his suit that saved him as he had floated up to where the rest of the trapped air had accumulated. As his head broke surface into the small pocket of air he drew in a huge, sweet mouthful and immediately started choking again.

As he took stock of his position he began to feel the first bolts of pain in his left shoulder. He explored it with his good hand and immediately knew that it was a compound fracture; the exposed bone pushing hard against the inner fabric of his waterproof suit. He was also aware of the numbing cold that was starting to affect his exposed hands and face.

'Well I can't stay here all day,' he said aloud into the eerie silence. There was no telling how deep he was but the wreckage appeared to have stopped moving violently. The only clues were the light filtering into the cabin and the rolling motion that could only have come from the wave action of the sea surface. Taking a large breath he pushed himself under the water and peered about. It quickly became obvious what had happened to Tom McKilroy. On impact with the water the momentum of the main gearbox had pulled it through the roof, striking McKilroy on the head and breaking his neck before coming to rest on the backs of the two seats. Had he been in his seat at the moment of impact Harry would have met with the same fate. Harry broke surface again. Poor Bastard he thought, however it had revealed a possible escape route through the gaping hole ripped in the roof of the cab where the gearbox had come crashing through. Harry had correctly guessed that he was at the tail end of the aircraft, which was suspended nose down by the air in the tail and the external flotation bags that had automatically deployed on contact with the salt water.

Harry took 5 or 6 deep breaths, purging the CO_2 from his lungs in preparation for his final escape attempt. The pain in his left shoulder was becoming unbearable and was rapidly spreading all down his left side. In addition he was losing the use of his fingers due to the cold. Too bad he wouldn't be able to collect his single man life raft on the way out; that was still snugly sat in the seat pan below tonnes of gearbox and other wreckage. With a final breath he pushed himself down towards the source of light. He almost made it as well. It was a struggle grappling his way against the buoyancy of his suit that had only two minutes ago saved his life, but he made it to the 'exit' with plenty of breath to spare. He took some time to clear some soundproofing material and control run cables that were blocking his way and then made the final push for freedom. He moved about a foot and then felt the excruciating pain as his left shoulder rammed into the torn remains of the radome. He felt consciousness slipping from him but fought it back, only to realise that he was now snagged in the exit. He started to struggle; panic setting in. He felt the fabric of his goonsuit tear, saw a red cloud of his own blood blossom in front of his face, and realised that cold water was flooding into his suit. In probably his last lucid moment before blind terror set in, he fired his life jacket in the vain hope that it would free him from the snag and carry him to the surface. Shortly thereafter the panic left him and he calmly slipped into a black void.

Chapter Two

So this is what it's like being dead thought Harry. He had the feeling of floating and he felt warm and safe. As yet he had no recollection of the crash that had occurred some time earlier, he just felt happily content to be floating in limbo awaiting the unknowns that death might hold.

In fact Harry had survived the crash and was drifting in and out of consciousness. It was his last, almost futile action that had saved his life. Unbeknown to him the jerk that had ripped his emersion suit had freed him from the snag, and the action of inflating his life jacket had carried him safely to the surface. After that his survival was in the hands of the inflated stole of his jacket that supported his neck, and kept him floating on his back with his head forced up, well clear of the water.

Just before the darkness closed in on him again Harry saw that the sun was low in the sky, and he realised that he was not dead but floating in a calm sea. At least the rescue helicopter should be here soon he thought as he peacefully drifted into the comfort of unconsciousness once again.

He was dreaming now - one of his favourites - a flying dream. Not in one of Her Majesties noisy, rattling, smelly old Seakings, but freely and effortlessly like a gull on the up draughts at the top of the Rock of Gibraltar. It exhilarated him so much that Harry had even taken a course in free-fall parachuting to try to re-enact his dreams. Although it had been fun it didn't come close to the feeling of ecstasy he was now experiencing. Harry was slowly approaching consciousness again and as often happens his dream changed tack. Now he *was* parachuting, but there was no joy, only a deep fear of the unknown; some terror just out of reach of his grasping mind. He looked down and saw that he was approaching the water much too fast, but there was nothing he could do to slow his fall, in fact every time he pulled on his rigging lines he seemed to spill more air from his chute and increase his rate of descent. Just before impact with the water Harry instinctively braced himself and squeezed his eyes tightly shut.

He jerked awake, his heart pounding and his breath coming in short bursts. He was completely disorientated; unable to associate his surroundings with anything his confused mind would recognise. Suddenly the events of the accident flooded into his head and with a sinking feeling he noted that the sun had risen and was now high in the sky. Why hadn't he been picked up? Wildly he twisted about, searching the horizon for signs of the rest of his crew or the helicopter. All he could see was the calm still ocean, not even any wreckage from the crash.

'How long have I been here?' he said out loud, more to convince himself that he wasn't dreaming than anything else. His voice died strangely in the still, lonely air. He lifted his left arm and tried to focus on his watch and would have had more joy had it still been there. Instead all he saw was a livid gash on his wrist. There was no blood, only the jagged, sea washed curtains of skin gaping slightly to reveal the dark red flesh beneath. He naturally assumed that the injury had occurred in his struggle to leave the doomed aircraft. It didn't even dawn on him that the black rubber wrist seal was also missing. His mind was slowly starting to function, however, and he remembered that at the time of ditching the sun had been setting. As he looked up into the clear, azure sky he noted with increasing trepidation that the sun was reaching its zenith. His befuddled mind finally grasped the fact that he'd been in the water over night, which meant that things had gone badly wrong somewhere down the line. They had only been about 20 miles ahead of the Task Force at the time of ditching and had passed their position to the Ship just beforehand. There was no way that the rescue teams would have called off the search for a missing crewmember this early. There had to be some logical explanation but Harry couldn't see it at the moment.

He pondered his situation. If only he had taken the time and effort to grab his life raft on the way out of the aircraft. Apart from the protection it could give him, tucked away in it's fibre-glass container was a bag of survival aids that comprised of extra clothing, distress flares, glucose sweets and most importantly five bags of fresh water and a de-salting kit, capable of producing 2 litres of disgusting black but for all that, drinkable water. Other items included a saw, fishing kit and spare batteries for the personal locator beacon (PLB) that was tucked away in the left pocket of his life jacket. Thinking back to his escape he knew that had he tried to retrieve it he would probably never have made it out.

The PLB was his best location aid. Triggered automatically on immersion into salt water it transmitted a radio signal on 243.0 and 121.5 MHz, the aeronautical distress frequencies in the UHF and VHF bands. Rescue helicopters could home onto the signal, which bleeped away for about 48 hours, and then with the flick of a switch the PLB could be used as a two way radio to assist in the location of the poor unfortunate using it. A theory as to why he hadn't been rescued was forming in Harry's head. If for some reason his beacon wasn't operating and the rescue team hadn't arrived until after dark, he could easily have been missed. From his own experience of rescue operations Harry knew the difficulties of spotting a life raft in the water, let alone the unconscious body of a man with only his head protruding from the dark sea. The search would also have been centred on any survivors that had been found, and with its flotation bags deployed acting as sails, the half-submerged wreckage could have drifted for miles before Harry had even got out. But surely they would have found the wreckage he thought to himself. The helicopter itself was also equipped with a homing beacon for both radio and sonar. Maybe it sank just after he got out, wouldn't that explain why he couldn't see the aircraft now?

'You're starting to sound like a desperate man clutching at straws,' he said aloud. The fog that had been clouding his brain ever since coming round was finally clearing, and although his theory was a bit thin in places it did have its good points. He had been a fool not to check his PLB straight away. Don't forget the basics. He reached across his body to the left-hand side of his jacket. He fumbled about but couldn't find the pocket.

'Come on, where the bloody hell is it?' He shouted as he started to feel the frustration boiling in his mind. He started thrashing wildly about, twisting his body in an effort to reach further around his side and locate the pocket. Eventually he stopped and was surprised at how weak and breathless he felt. The experience of the last few hours had taken a lot more out of him than he realised. He felt around to the right side of his jacket, to the pocket containing mini-flares, first aid kit and heliograph. He couldn't locate that pocket either. For some reason it didn't come as a surprise to him this time. Nothing seemed to have gone right since he was late for a briefing for the first time in his life. There was obviously a logical explanation and once again he made an assumption to explain away an otherwise puzzling discrepancy in his situation. He thought back to the changing room on HMS INDOMITABLE and realised that his mistake had been in grabbing a drill life jacket in his rush to make up lost time, and a drill jacket, of course, contained no survival aids.

He actually started to feel a bit better; he was getting his breath back and at least he had an explanation for why he hadn't been picked up. Now he just needed to sort out what the hell he was going to do about it. He put himself into the shoes of the rescue Commander; given the same circumstances how would he conduct the search? Well, by now he would have half the Squadron airborne conducting an expanding square search from the datum; be that the last reported position or the sighting of any survivors or wreckage. It was, therefore, only a matter of time he thought confidently, before he was spotted; however, deep down he was getting more and more concerned that he hadn't seen or heard any aircraft. Surely the search area couldn't be that big.

Harry tried to relax and force his mind away from his present predicament. He thought of Laura and the first time he met her. He was based at Royal Naval Air Station Culdrose in Cornwall and she worked in a school for special needs children, as a British Sign Language (BSL) translator for a handicapped boy in Helston, a small market town a couple of miles away. It was only chance that he had gone out with her at all. Harry had been in town with Pete Hancock, another Observer on the Squadron. Pete had dragged him into just about every school in town looking for a suitable place to educate his little boy, who suffered from ADHD. Pete had been left the task of bringing little Ben up alone after his wife had died some two years earlier in a car accident. When they finally arrived at Laura's school Harry was bored and clowned about, pulling faces, whilst Pete chatted to Laura about the facilities available. Laura kept glancing up at Harry and had to cover her little giggles behind the back of her hand. Pete naturally assumed she was reacting to his witty banter and so asked her if she was free that evening.

'Only if I can bring along my best friend,' she responded and then looking up at Harry she continued. 'How about you bring your friend here?'

It was then that Harry first looked at her seriously and noticed just how attractive she was. Apart from the models profile, she had the body to go with it. Her slender neck led down to well-defined collar bones and onto her smallish chest that was shown off to the best advantage by a skimpy white top that contrasted so well with her even tan. His eyes continued down taking in the perfectly flat tummy that struggled to remain covered as she moved in the seat. In fact just at that moment he caught sight of the small jewel mounted just above her naval on the top of the pin that passed through the flesh. At this point his view was interrupted as her hips and long legs disappeared under the desk. He dragged his gaze back to her face only to find her staring straight back at him. He expected her to look away as their eyes met but she just smiled back at him. Harry was immediately attracted to her.

'It's a deal,' said Pete wondering what was going on between the two of them. 'We'll meet you in the Angel at 8 o'clock.' She looked back to Pete and smiled, confirming the arrangements.

From there it had been a bit of a whirlwind affair; Harry and Laura hitting it off immediately finding that they were both studying the same course on the Open University. Pete and Laura's 'best friend' Heather, a rather plain looking and serious girl were left to pick up the pieces as Harry and Laura delved into the possibilities of getting together for some serious studying the following evening.

The evening had finished with the four of them driving down to Mullion, and Harry and Laura had walked hand in hand along the coast with only the moonlight to illuminate their way. They had finally stopped and turned to look across the deceptive calm of the sea. The stars reflected on the surface had thrilled Laura, as had the regular sweep of the unmanned lighthouse far out to sea. Harry put his arm around her shoulders and had tried to explain the attraction that he felt for the ocean to her; how at first glance it could be calm, as it was now, but underneath there was a cold fury that could at any time quickly turn into a violent killer of those that didn't respect it. Finally, lost for words he had given up and turned to her, pulling her closer. She yielded to him completely; leaning into his strong arms and turning her face up to offer her full lips to him. He bent down and kissed her, gently at first, then...

'Jesus Christ, the water,' he shouted as his mind catapulted back to reality.

It was blindingly obvious now that he thought about it, yet it had only just come to him. The water was warm. He thought back to when he had struggled for his life in the back of the doomed Seaking. The water had been so cold as to deny him the use of his hands within minutes. What possible explanation could there be to explain that he was now bobbing about in water warm enough to be a cool bath or a public swimming pool? Harry's mind struggled to maintain some grip on reality, but the more he thought about the problem the more unlikely it seemed. Yet the water *was* warm. Could he possibly be in something like the Gulf Stream? He couldn't accept that and his mind was beginning to notice the other oddities he'd denied in an attempt to set his mind at rest. It was all adding up to something very weird or very sinister. The simple fact staring him in the face was that he was no longer in the same area that he had ditched. It would certainly explain why there was no wreckage, no search party. But who would have rescued him, only to transport him to a different climate and drop him back in the sea.

Could it also explain why his jacket was devoid of survival aids? Yes he supposed it could. But who, who would have gone through all this trouble to, what, get rid of him? If that were the case then why not just kill him. Christ what am I thinking? He tried another train of thought. What else was different? He thought through the last sortie from the time that Smokey found him on the quarterdeck until he came to in the water. Apart from the discrepancies he had already discovered everything seemed to be in place, right up until he recalled the pain and shock of breaking his collarbone.

Automatically he lifted his left arm. There was no pain, no loss of mobility that he would have expected, just as there hadn't been when he had checked for his watch. Harry's breathing was starting to become laboured, coming in short fast gasps and he felt a huge rush of adrenaline purge through his body. Slowly he brought his right hand up to his 'injured' shoulder, praying that he would feel the protruding bone pushing against his torn goon suit. What he felt sent a cold fear running through his heart. Instead of the abrasive material of his immersion suit, his hands slipped over the smooth waterlogged surface of a leather-flying jacket. His shoulder underneath was in one piece; as far as he could tell it was not damaged in any way.

'No! I couldn't have imagined it,' he cried out between his rapid breaths. Unable to control it now, the fear welled up inside him, his pulse rate was increasing rapidly and his breathing was so fast that his body was receiving an over-dose of oxygen. He felt extremely light-headed and with it the fear magnified. He thought that he was having a heart attack at first, and by the time he recognised his symptoms as hyperventilation it was too late - it was out of control. Harry once again slipped into the comfort of unconsciousness.

Chapter Three

Lieutenant Commander Peter Rogers sat thoughtfully in front of his laptop computer in his cabin on HMS Indomitable. Since his recent promotion he was lucky enough to have his own cabin down on 5 deck, away from the noise of Sea Harriers suffered by the occupants of the other cabin spaces on 2 deck; just below the flight deck. He looked around the small compact room. There was no daylight to brighten the smooth magnolia walls, only the harsh blue-whiteness of the neon tube shining over-head, for there were no windows down here below the water line. The room appeared even starker than it might have due to the clinical tidiness. There was no bed cluttering up the place; this was folded away into the wall to afford more space to the already cramped environment. All the shelves and table-tops were bare except for the items ready for immediate use and these were kept to a bare minimum. It wasn't that Peter was fanatically tidy; indeed it used to be just the opposite. It was more the need to have everything stowed away for when the sea played one of its tricks and in a matter of moments became the random track for a roller coaster ride that would leave a badly kept cabin looking like the victim of a Police search.

Peter's eyes finally came to rest on a small group of photographs blue-tac'ed to the wall above his desk. Most were of his family and as his eyes flicked from picture to picture he felt a deep sense of homesickness. This was his last trip before leaving for the New World of Civil Aviation with Cathay Pacific and it seemed to be lasting forever. Finally his gaze lingered on a photo of his youngest daughter's Christening. It had been taken just before the Ship sailed and had arrived in the last mail drop. It showed his six-year-old daughter Katy in a white Christening dress standing in front of the font. Next to her was her sister Beth whose long blond hair contrasted with the mass of dark curls surrounding Katy's pretty face.

Behind the two girls stood Peter himself. At six feet four in his socks his tall frame dominated the picture. He studied his face; with the dark tanned skin, smiling eyes and tightly cropped beard. He smiled. Couldn't complain he thought; though he was a little peeved about the premature grey that was rapidly taking over the otherwise black hair. Beside him in the photo stood his wife Donna, the woman that featured in his best dreams. Her red hair and green eyes never failed to excite him and as his eyes lingered on her face he felt his heart swelling with emotion. The last two characters in the portrait were Harry and his new girlfriend, Laura. Peter was delighted when Harry had agreed to be Katy's Godfather- he wasn't so sure about Laura, but Donna had been spending a lot of time with her and had confided to Peter that she considered Laura to be more than a flash in the pan where Harry was concerned. Anyway she too had been thrilled to be involved, though Harry had thrown some funny looks around when Donna had broached the subject of Godmother!

Peter dragged his thoughts away from home and back to the task at hand on the computer. His last shot had put him straight into the bunker just short of the 17th green at Gleneagles. It was going to need a pretty good shot and all his 'golfing' skill if he was going to make the green and stand a chance of making par. He chose his club, considered the wind, then judging the power required committed himself to the shot. He never saw whether he made the green as his concentration was shattered by the loud metallic voice on the tannoy: Proceeded by the screeching of the emergency siren the message sent adrenaline coursing through his body.

'Do you here there, launch the Search and Rescue (SAR) helicopter...'

Peter bolted out of his chair and the cabin in one fluid movement. As duty SAR Pilot he was on 60 minutes readiness, however they would normally make better time than that, especially in daylight hours. As he ran up the corridor he listened out for any more details he could get from the tannoy, though he knew he would get the full message on arrival at the helicopter.

'...of 814 Squadron ditched in position 270 degrees by 22 miles.'

'Shit!' exclaimed Peter as he heard that it was one of his own Squadron aircraft that had ditched. He doubled his efforts and as he burst onto the deck he headed for the cab already spread on 1 spot. As his co-pilot, Nige Crawford joined him his years of experience took over.

'You flash her up Nige, I'll give her a once over and join you in a sec.'

By the time he was halfway through his walk round the engines were starting and the Aircrewman and Observer had arrived and were sorting out the gear in the back. Peter scrambled through the front door, pulled it shut and clambered into his seat. As Nige's hand came across and rested on the rotor brake Peter gave him a thumbs up and Nige released it allowing the rotors to engage. They were ready to go as he finished strapping in and he took control of the aircraft so that Nige could strap in.

'All set in the back,'

'Yeah, the Diver's just securing his gear...we're ready to go.' Peter checked he had a green launch light and started pulling power with the collective lever.

'Hang on Sir,' Came a cry from the back. For God's sake what now thought Peter and was just about to put his thoughts into words when the same voice continued: ' Ok clear to take off.'

Peter pulled the aircraft into a hover, moved to the left over the water, did a quick check left and right and then transitioned into forward flight. Once the cab was safely climbing he asked no one in particular. 'What was all that about?'

The answer came unexpectedly from a voice he didn't know. 'It's Doc White Sir, I thought you might be able to use me on this trip.'

'I hope we won't need you, but thanks for getting ready so quick, we're normally airborne before you guys are even half dressed.'

Peter then keyed his radio switch. 'Flyco this is Rescue 1, airborne, request sitrep and instructions.'

'Flyco, roger standby,' came the metallic reply. Moments later the voice continued. 'Rescue 1 this is Flyco, Seaking W6Y transmitted a ditching call and position at 1527 zulu time. Search datum established 22 nautical miles bearing 270 degrees true from mother, timed at 1527z. Rescue 1 is to proceed to datum and establish search; Rescue 2 is being brought to readiness and should launch in approx. One Five minutes. Rescue one to act as Scene of Search Commander until this unit arrives to take over.'

'Rescue 1 acknowledged, request tide conditions and number of persons on board.'

'Flyco roger, standby.'

'Any other info you need Dave?' asked Peter.

'No, that's fine,' replied Dave Hammersmith, the Observer. 'Turn left 260 degrees, 14 miles to the datum, we'll be there in about seven minutes.'

'Rescue 1 this is Flyco, W6Y has 4 souls on board and the tide is 340 degrees at 1 knot, good luck.'

Dave cut in and acknowledged and then continued to the rest of the crew. 'Ok guys, we'll carry out an expanding square search on the datum at 100 feet and 60 knots whilst the light holds. We'll adjust that if necessary as it get dark. The spacing between legs will be 1/4 of a mile.'

'Isn't that a bit close between tracks?' asked Nige.

'Not really,' replied Dave. 'Remember we could be looking for as little as a head protruding from the water.' He continued: 'Peter and Nige search from the 9 o'clock to the 3 o'clock, Sharkey and Mike from 2 o'clock to 6 o'clock and I'll cover what I can out to the left, any questions?'

'Yes, anything I can do?' piped up the Doc. 'My kits all sorted out and I've a good pair of eyes.'

'Sure, if you can go up front and look out of the left hand window it would give us more coverage, but don't lean on the door...we don't want any more casualties!' replied Dave.

Between them Sharkey Ward the Aircrewman and Mike Lowther the Diver opened the main cabin door and hung out on dispatcher harnesses, searching the dark water that rushed past below. Although they weren't yet at the search height and speed, in fact not even at the datum, it was worth searching because positions passed in emergency calls were not always accurate.

'Any idea who was in...' began Nige.

'Shut up and listen.' Interrupted Dave. 'I think that's a PLB transmission.' They could all hear it now, the two-toned homing signal of the distress beacon. Peter switched the receiver to homing mode and called. 'Ten degrees to the left.'

At the same time he brought the cab round onto a heading of 250 and centralised the homing indicator needle.

'Christ I hope that means they're all right,' sighed Nige, echoing everybody's thoughts.

Peter was pleased, but he needed to keep his team working in top gear if they were to complete the rescue in good order. 'We haven't found them yet so keep on your toes and keep your eyes peeled,' he barked.

With growing enthusiasm Mike finished climbing into his diving equipment, fitting the complicated harnesses with an ease brought on by familiarity and practice. He checked his regulator and the contents of the single air bottle before sitting in the doorway and giving Sharkey the thumbs up.

'Red flare just left of the nose!' shouted Nige. 'And another.' As the Helicopter adjusted heading towards the flare there was a burst of red smoke just beneath the horizon. The aircraft continued to close on the smoke until at last the Pilots could make out the orange fabric of the single man life raft. Designed to sit in the seat pan and connected to the crewman's life-jacket, the small dinghy was made up of three inflatable compartments. The main was a black rubber, coffin-shaped hull that was inflated by a carbon dioxide charge activated by the aircrew once clear of the stricken aircraft. The floor of the 'boat' was then inflated orally as was the orange covering that pulled up around the sitting crewman, protecting him from wind and spray.

'Visual one survivor at 12 o'clock about 3 miles,' said Peter in a steady voice. He started to position the cab to make a visual approach into wind. As the dinghy started to move to the right it soon became obvious that there was more than one survivor.

'Running in,' called Peter.

'Roger, Dave's on the con, Sharkey's in the double man lift harness.' Dave concentrated on the aircraft's approach and commenced his commentary. 'Height line and speed all good with fifty yards to run...thirty yards, reduce speed and height, line good...fifteen yards height now good.' Dave raised the winch that pulled Sharkey up and swung him out of the doorway. 'Lowering the double lift man now...Ten yards, five yards easy, easy, steady.'

During the later stages of the procedure he lowered Sharkey into the water and used the motion of the helicopter to 'drag' the winchman to the survivor. By pulling him through the water it cut out any swing that might build up. The helicopter had arrived in a twenty-foot hover over the survivors and Dave continued to con the aircraft, keeping it in a steady hover as Sharkey got the first man ready for recovery.

'There's only two guys down there so keep a good look out for the rest of the crew,' Dave told the Pilots who could not see the rescue and relied solely on the con to keep the aircraft steady.

The rest of the rescue went smoothly. The two survivors were bought to the cabin door in turn and bundled into one of the spare seats in the back. The engineers had fitted out the cab as dedicated SAR and much of the ASW equipment had been temporarily removed. Smokie was the first in and having secured himself in the jump seat he ripped off his sodden helmet and indicated to Mike that he wanted to talk to the crew. Mike found him a spare head set and Smokie quickly pulled it on.

'Thank God you guys came along,' he gasped. 'That lightening storm didn't get in your way then?'

'What storm?' Queried Peter.

'The one that...Oh it doesn't matter, look me and Paul got out very quickly but we haven't seen anything of Harry or Tom McKilroy.'

Peter felt his heart sink. He'd had a sense of foreboding ever since lift off, and when Dave had reported that the first survivor was Smokie he knew it was Harry's crew. Then it was a matter of hoping that the 2nd survivor was Harry. It wasn't that he had anything against Paul, in fact he felt the first pangs of guilt for hoping it was Harry instead of him, it was just that Harry was like a brother to him and the feeling of loss was already starting. Peter wrenched his mind back to the commentary coming from Dave as the helicopter started to move left and forward at an increasing rate. He was tempted to hand over control to Nige but thought the better of it; preferring to keep his mind on the job rather than it running riot with speculation.

Smokie was talking again. 'I last saw the aircraft drifting down wind but it was sinking quite quickly. It was tail up and it looked a bit smashed up I'm afraid.'

Peter looked over his shoulder as Paul was bought into the rear cabin. He was deathly white and even from that distance Peter could see he was shaking uncontrollably. Dave had stowed the winch and was wrapping Paul up in blankets having deflated his Mae West lifejacket.

'Paul's going into shock,' Dave reported. 'I think we need to get him straight back to the Ship.'

Peter's first reaction was to shout 'NO' and to continue the search, but he checked himself again and considered his options. He couldn't endanger Paul's life further just because his best friend was still missing. With rescue 2 about to launch logic and common sense demanded that he get Paul back to medical care as soon as possible.

'Doc, check Paul over and see what you can do,' said Peter and then continued on the radio: 'Flyco this is Rescue 1, have recovered 2 survivors, 1 suffering from shock. No sign yet of the wreckage or other missing persons. Standby for intentions.'

'Flyco copied, for information Rescue 2 has just gone unserviceable on start up, they're running for the spare now.'

'Oh shit!' exclaimed Peter. 'What do you think Doc, it's your call on this one.'

'Carry on with search for the time being, I've got a drip into him and he's stable at the moment. I'll continue to monitor him but if he shows any signs of getting worse we'll have to get him back on board.'

'I'm glad you came along Doc, thanks.'

Doc White smiled to himself, glad to be appreciated. He didn't think it worth mentioning at this stage that the only reason he'd made it in time was because he'd been locked away in his office trying all the kit on. When the alarm went up he was trying to set the self-timer on his camera to get a snap shot for his girlfriend. No I'll save that story for the bar later, he thought.

Peter flew the aircraft out of the hover and commenced a square search controlled by Dave. Smokie's and Paul's PLB's had been disconnected and the emergency channel was all quiet; not a good sign. The light was also fading rapidly and soon it would be impossible to see anything other than a light in the water. For the next 10 minutes very little happened. Doc White reported that Paul's condition was improving and that he'd even had a smile out of him. Peter certainly wasn't smiling. Things were not looking too good for Harry and Tom. His thoughts were interrupted by the radio.

'Rescue 1 this is Rescue 2, proceeding to datum at 200 feet, request sitrep and instructions.'

'Rescue 1 roger, two survivors recovered, Rescue 1 carrying out expanding square search at 100 feet. New datum established at 035 TT 3.5 based on recovered survivors.' The observer in Rescue 2 held Rescue 1 on his radar and carefully plotted the datum 035 degrees 3.5 miles from its transponder return. Dave continued on the radio, 'Rescue 2 climb to 400 feet and conduct a radar search out to 20 miles from datum.'

'Rescue 2 roger.'

The search continued without bearing results for another 20 minutes when an excited voice broke the silence.

'This is Rescue 2. I have a small radar contact bearing 150 degrees at 12 miles. Rescue 1 that's about 4 miles due East of you.'

Dave searched his radarscope, adjusting the gain and contrast controls to give him the best picture. Nothing. He was too low and all he could see was the clutter of sea returns.

'Rescue 1 no contact, heading 150, vector me to the on top.'

The Observer in Rescue 2 used his radar to control the other cab over the small contact he had found. To be honest he wasn't very confident of it turning out to be the stricken helicopter as it was some 15 miles from the datum where the two Pilots had been recovered, and with little wind and only 1 knot of tide there was no way it could have drifted that far. He was more than a little surprised then when Rescue 1 reported that he had the tail of the lost helicopter visual and was going in for a closer look. Rescue 2 arrived on the scene shortly after and commenced a search of the immediate area whilst Peter positioned his cab ready to dispatch the diver.

In the cabin doorway Mike was sitting ready to drop the 15 feet or so into the cold, black water. This was what he was trained for but he was still apprehensive when doing it for real. You never really knew what you would find when entering an overturned ship or crashed aircraft. In this case he was hoping that it would be a fruitless search. The aircraft was in a steady hover with the wreckage about 30 feet down wind. Sharkey gave him two taps

31

on left shoulder and without hesitating Mike held his mask to his face with both hands and launched himself into space.

Landing feet first Mike was plunged into a dark cold world. A couple of kicks with his flippers brought him to the surface and having again checked the operation of his regulator gave Sharkey a thumbs up and disappeared beneath the waves.

'Divers gone' said Sharkey.

'Roger.' The simple reply. It was now just a matter of waiting, bad enough during any rescue but doubly so when your friends were involved. Peter thought about what Mike was going through and found he didn't envy him at all. It couldn't be very pleasant swimming around in the dark in zero visibility and suddenly finding yourself face to face with death. Peter felt a shudder run through his body from top to bottom. Donna would have said that a goose had walked over his grave. Peter knew the real reason and tried to think of more pleasant times. Again his train of thought was shattered by real events. It was Dave's voice on the intercom and it sounded choked, as if he were being strangled.

'Mike's up Peter, and it looks like he's dragging something heavy.' He couldn't bring himself to say body, but everyone knew that that was what he meant. Peter felt his spirits sinking even lower as he positioned the aircraft for the recovery. He couldn't look over his shoulder as the heavy body was pulled into the rear cabin.

'It's Tom McKilroy, Sir, it looks like his neck was broken on impact. Doc you'd better come and take a look at him just to be sure'

The young doctor moved to the rear cabin and knelt down to find himself looking into the dead eyes of Tom McKilroy. The head was pushed over at an impossible angle and as he moved it he saw that the back of his helmet was completely smashed revealing a massive trauma to the brain.

'Something heavy hit him it seems,' said the Doc in a low voice. 'The only good thing I can say is that he would have died instantly feeling no pain.'

At least there's still a chance for Harry, thought Peter but it didn't make him feel any better about McKilroy. He tried to think what the next step would be whilst Mike was winched back into the aircraft. Once he was back on intercom Peter asked:

'Are you Ok Mike, I know he was a good friend of yours.'

'Yeah...' and then he continued in a subdued voice, 'He was still strapped into his seat. It looked as if the gearbox had come down onto the rear seats.'

Peter could picture the scene. There had been a similar accident overland some years ago and he had seen the wreckage after it had been recovered to Culdrose. The only reason the rear crew hadn't been killed in that crash was that they had both been in the cabin doorway. The significance of what he'd just thought hit him like a thunderbolt. As if reading his thoughts Smokie suddenly piped up:

'Harry was standing between the pilot's seats when the engine failed; I doubt that he made it back to his seat.'

'Well he's definitely not in that aircraft,' responded Mike with certainty.

Peter was still undecided as to their next step so took things one step at a time. The night was almost fully upon them and the first thing was to transfer from a manual hover to a system hover. His fingers moved deftly over the Flight Control System (FCS) panel setting the hover height and the parameters for the move to forward flight. Nige monitored the flying controls and when Peter was ready called:

'Re-engage down.' Nige hit the 'engage down' button on the FCS and the computer fed itself the correct settings. At this stage the aircraft stayed exactly where it was, however, had they not gone through this laborious procedure, upon selecting the automatic transition mode the cab would over-torque itself by trying to climb from the hover to 'system height' instantaneously.

'Engage up,' said Peter, and then monitored the controls as the 'system' flew the aircraft out of the hover to 200 feet and 100 knots.

What happened next was pure luck. Doc White, having finished checking McKilroy was moving back to his position by the front door. The movement of the aircraft as it went into a turn at the top of climb caused him to stumble and fall against the starboard window opposite the sonar body. As he tried to right himself something caught his eye. A small white light was drifting down the right hand side.

'There's a light in the water over there,' he screamed pointing at it.

'Where's 'over there',' asked Nige, craning his neck round to see where the Doc was pointing.

'Over there, over there.' Then realising his error 'Er...it's on the right hand side...just by the little window.'

Nige flew the aircraft round in a hard right turn and Sharkey soon reported that he was visual. The team now functioned like a well-oiled machine. Nige flew the cab to the 'on top' position and Dave plugged it into the TANS computer. The FCS was then engaged and the system flew a circuit to end up in the hover with the light in the 2 o'clock at about 100 yards. From then on it was just a matter of moving the cab to the on top and sending Sharkey to pick up Harry. The small light on his lifejacket had been his saviour. Although only tiny and often ridiculed by aircrew during survival drills, it automatically lights up when the battery cell is immersed into salt water and can be seen for miles on a dark night. Consequently it didn't matter that Harry was unconscious; the light still came on.

As soon as Sharkey and Dave had manhandled Harry's inert form into the cabin the Doc got to work on him. Realising the anxiety of the crew he reported quickly on Harry's state.

'He's still alive guys, though he is unconscious...and he appears to have a broken shoulder. Apart from that he seems to be in reasonable shape.'

'Right lets get him back,' said Peter.

They reported to the Ship and flew back to the waiting medical team. Harry and the rest of his crew were bundled away and the rescue team was left to tidy up the helicopter and reflect on their evening's work. They all felt much the same; a feeling of pride at what they had achieved, tainted by the sadness of Tom McKilroy's death. Peter was still running things through in his mind, mentally debriefing the mission to see if they could have done things any better. By the time he reached his cabin he had decided that things had gone pretty well on the whole. With good teamwork and a little luck they'd achieved the best result they could have in the circumstances. Entering his cabin he glanced at the computer sat on the desk, but felt no satisfaction in seeing he'd chipped straight into the hole for a birdie.

Chapter Four

Harry awoke to the feel of warm water lapping gently against his face. His eyes blinked open against the bright sun that shone directly into his face. Once his eyes had painfully adjusted to the conditions all he could see was a white beach stretching for miles. He lifted his face from the sand that was so fine he didn't feel any abrasive qualities, and tried to take in his surroundings; to orient himself in this unexpected environment. Slowly his eyes became accustomed to the glare of the sun that was high in the pure blue sky. He brought his hand up to shield his eyes and brushed against his mouth. As he felt the swollen, cracked lips that hurt out of all proportion to their damage, he was suddenly aware of the raging thirst deep within him.

'Where the hell am I?' he asked himself, and was a little surprised at how strange his voice sounded. The strain of talking had opened up the myriad of small cracks in his lips and he realised that his first priority must be to find a supply of fresh water. He remembered from his training that the body couldn't survive long without it and he had no idea how long it had been since his last drink.

By now he was on his feet and he swayed about drunkenly. He continued to survey his immediate surroundings as he staggered away from the water line towards the dense growth of trees about twenty yards up the beach. The first trees he came to were impossibly high palm trees and he was vaguely amused at how much like cartoon trees they really were. He lent gratefully against one and looked up into the fronds high above. At the base of the leaves he could just make out the immature nuts in their green cases. He quickly dismissed any thoughts he'd had of coconuts as a supply of liquid refreshment. He looked past the first row of trees that skirted the beach and into what he could only describe as jungle. He vaguely remembered a Desmond Bagley novel set in South America where the jungle was described by the depth that you could see into it, and he decided that this was probably about five foot jungle. One thing was for certain; he would not be able to penetrate it without the aid of a good axe or knife.

Harry staggered back onto the beach and as he left the shade he was once again hit by the full strength of the sun. He looked up and down the long stretch of sand and was met by the same uniform line of palms in both directions. The shimmering heat reflected off the white sand seemed to blur his mind as he tried to sort out what the hell was going on. His thoughts returned to his last conscious thoughts in the water.

He talked aloud as much to satisfy himself that he was awake than anything else and smiled when he thought that he'd been doing it quite a lot lately.

'Right, let's get this straight. One, I'm on a routine training sortie and ditch into the cold waters of the Northern Atlantic. Two, I survive but when I come to I'm in warm water and the injuries that I sustained, or thought I sustained are healed or at least not evident. Three, I'm washed up on a desert island in some sort of fancy dress.'

As he finished the last sentence he looked down at himself and the unfamiliar clothes he was wearing. His boots were made of leather, including the soles, and were heavy and cumbersome with lightweight khaki trousers tucked into them. His blouse top was of a similar material and covered in medal ribbons that meant absolutely nothing to him. Finally the leather jacket, that he now discarded, finished off the feeling that he had been dressed up as an American World War Two pilot. Having inspected the uniform Harry took the opportunity to methodically search through his clothes. He turned every pocket inside out and even felt behind the lining of the blouse top and flying jacket. He found nothing at all which struck him as a little odd.

'But then what's odd at the moment?' He paused to think about that and a little laugh escaped him. He bit down on his tongue aware that he could easily lose control. Fighting off the urge to laugh he moved back into the shade and started to think about his next move; certainly his priority must be in finding water. His only course of action was to walk along the tree line in hope of finding an opening into the jungle. Stepping back onto the beach he studied the long line of palm trees in both directions but could distinguish no discernible difference, and so putting his back to the sun Harry set off along the beach, as much as possible keeping to the shade offered by the tall palms.

Half an hour later he was still walking and starting to believe that he was in desperate trouble. His tongue seemed to be too large for his mouth and the splits in his lips had opened further causing him to wince in pain every time he opened or closed his mouth. He felt desperately weak; the effort of moving his feet through the sand was rapidly becoming insurmountable. But this wasn't what was really worrying him deep down; he wasn't sweating - he was desperately hot but there wasn't a bead of perspiration on him. Harry tried to think back to the survival lectures he'd received during his training but naturally it had concentrated on sea survival. The only thing he could remember from the two-hour desert survival lesson was that if you had plenty of water you should drink it all at once rather than small sips every now and again. Come to think of it, did he have that the right way round?

Harry sat down with his back against a tree and started to ponder the question anew. His mind was becoming confused and the questions of what to do with the water spun round and round in his head until:

'You haven't got any bloody water, you idiot,' he shouted.

In fact the shout was more of a croak but it served to pull him out of the spiral that threatened to endanger his sanity. He almost let out a giggle as the words echoed in his ears but again managed to stifle it before it got the better of him. The pain caused by shouting also contributed to the control of his mirth and he gently felt his swollen lips and stared at the blood on his fingers as he pulled away. Looking up he saw that he sun was a little lower in the sky than when he'd first come round on the beach. Harry rearranged his position in the shade and decided to sit it out until the temperature dropped as the sun lost its power. Once more he set his mind to the mystery of what was happening to him. As much as anything else this was an effort to fight off the sleep that was threatening to creep up on him, from which he was afraid he might never wake up.

However much he mulled it over in his mind Harry could not make head or tail of what was going on. He still thought it must be some sort of dream, but it was like no dream he'd ever had before. For a start it was definitely in colour which was contrary to what he had been led to believe. He pinched himself on the leg and felt another giggle trying to break its way to the surface. He rubbed his lips and the pain stopped any hint of laughter, as he knew it would. He decided that he wasn't dreaming and so his mind started to explore other avenues. He hadn't got any further before he lost his battle against sleep and he fell into a dreamless abyss.

Harry jerked awake, but unlike his last awakening he was immediately aware of his surroundings. The sun was huge and much closer to the horizon, and he judged that he'd been out for at least a few hours. There was still plenty of light, enough to see that his situation hadn't changed whilst he slept. But something had woken him. As he struggled to his feet he was painfully aware of the pounding in his head brought on by dehydration. He was also aware of something else, something familiar to him. The welcome sound of a helicopter reached his ears and despite the strange happenings of the last few hours? Days? Or whatever, he felt everything would now be OK. He scanned the horizon as the noise got louder. It isn't a Seaking, he thought to himself, the sound was too deep, too uniform, and in fact it didn't sound like a helicopter at all. The sound was more like the Spitfire's engine he'd heard at a recent air show and it was now reaching a crescendo. Harry looked up and down the beach but there was still no sign of an aircraft and he thought that maybe it was another figment of his over-active imagination. He ran out onto the beach and was seriously starting to doubt his sanity when the noise suddenly became a roar and an aircraft appeared low, very low over the jungle canopy.

'What the...,' exclaimed Harry as the aircraft flashed close aboard down his left-hand side. He stared in disbelief as the old fashioned aircraft started a hard banking turn to the left, contrasting against the deep blue ocean. Small vortexes of moisture formed at the tips of the low mounted single wing as the pilot applied G to tighten his turn. Though he had never seen one before, Harry knew what he was looking at: The nose appeared blunt behind the single propeller, the huge, black engine cowling clashing with the mottled grey and green fuselage that tapered away to a point below the tail. The glass canopy sat high on the fuselage, sheltering the solitary pilot from the elements. But what gave it away for Harry was the large red circle, trimmed with white, painted on the wings and body of the machine. He was staring at a Second World War Mitsubishi Zero.

Still an aircraft's an aircraft thought Harry as he started feebly jumping and waving to the approaching Zero. The pilot had obviously seen him as he rolled out with the nose pointing straight at Harry. Unable to stay on his feet any longer and sure he'd been spotted anyway Harry slumped to the sand just in time to hear the supersonic crack of a bullet passing just over his head. This was followed quickly by the explosive roar as the sound of the twin 0.303-inch machine guns reached him. He reactively twisted away and saw the spurts of sand leaping up behind him. It was as if the beach had come alive, the twin tracks of destruction marching towards the tree line before disappearing with a rattle of leaves. The air was full of noise, the rattling of the guns suddenly stopping, to be replaced by the howl of the aircraft as it passed directly overhead pulling out of the shallow strafing dive in order to clear the tree line.

The Zero disappeared behind the canopy and Harry sat in shocked silence, unable to believe what had just happened. He started shaking all over but was still unable to move. He felt physically sick and could feel his heart pounding in his chest. That pounding was echoed in his head and added to the already thumping headache. He idly wondered if his heart could keep up the pace required of it and if not would he be conscious of it stopping dead before his life and conscious thought slipped away from him. The noise of the Zero bought him abruptly out of his morbid thoughts. It had pulled up high in some sort of wingover manoeuvre and was now heading back out to sea. Even as he watched the aircraft dropped its nose and began a spiralling dive, once more lining up on Harry's position. Harry pulled on the last reserves of his strength and bolted for the jungle. Had he looked over his shoulder he would have seen the Zero pilot making the final adjustments to his strafing run. As it was he continued on his beeline for the trees and just before he reached them he broke hard to the right to run parallel with the palms.

The Zero pilot saw the jink too late and had already committed finger to trigger. Bullets streamed from his guns, but even before he flashed over the line of palms he saw empty sand kicked up behind his quarry. Harry heard the dull thud of bullets striking the ground at his heels and wondered when the end would come, but once again all went quiet. Harry drew to a stop and considered his options. There was no way he would fool the pilot again and anyway what little strength he'd had was fast dwindling. He considered burying himself in the sand but quickly dismissed the idea knowing it would leave him a sitting duck if he hadn't finished in time. He staggered to the jungle wall and was again amazed at how thick the undergrowth was. He pushed in a foot or so but wasn't sure he would be invisible from the air. He had to chance it anyway and so dropped to the floor, pulling whatever cover he could around him.

He could still hear the Zero as it circled round for another run. The pilot had wised up and was running in at an acute angle to the trees. Harry heard him open fire and held his breath as bullets smacked into the surrounding jungle. Wood chips and leaves sprayed down on him from the trees above as the bullets tore into them. Then it was all over. Harry listened as the sound of the engine gradually faded to nothing, but he still held his ground. He was shaking again and felt so utterly exhausted that he was sure he would never manage to get up even if he thought of a good reason to attempt it. The next moment he realised he was crying, something he hadn't done since he was a child. It shook him, it really shook him, but then things really had been building up against him. He was badly confused, dying of thirst, and now some maniac had tried to kill him for no apparent reason.

Despite his resolve to stay put, Harry eased himself to his feet and stumbled off along the beach. He'd only gone about 30 yards when he thought he could see a break in the uniform jungle barrier. As he continued forward the gap widened to a definite opening that disappeared into the dark interior. The trees on either side of the gap still met above the jungle floor to form the uninterrupted canopy high above. As he neared the opening Harry could see a channel cut into the sand where a river had rent its way to the ocean. He hurried forward, a feeling of jubilation flooding through him or maybe it was just relief. His hopes were dashed, however, as he fell into the dry watercourse of a river or stream that had long since pushed its last flow of water to the sea. Feebly he dug into the dry sand hoping to find at least a hint of moisture but the fine sand just trickled through his fingers like the life force that drained from his body.

A lot of men would have given up and died in that dry riverbed, but Harry was no ordinary man. He all but crawled his way into the shelter of the jungle, not really noticing how the darkness drew around him as he entered the canopy. The light outside was fading fast, but under the cover of the canopy most of the sun's rays were cut out by the tall trees competing for light. Only the will to live pushed him on. The riverbed was slowly changing character; the dry dusty sand turning to stretches of dry hard rock, with the odd boulder thrown in for good measure. Then he was onto sand again, but harder and cooler. He stumbled and fell flat on his face. He remained prone, as he didn't have the strength to go on. He realised he was crying again; the tears sticking the sand to his face. He tried to brush the tears away with his hand, but that was also covered in sand, which struck him as odd. He sat up and dabbed his face with the back of his hand this time. There were no tears and it certainly wasn't sweat that stuck the sand to him.

Harry grabbed a handful of sand and ran it between his fingers. This was not the dry sand of the beach; this was damp sand, sand that stuck, forming clumps in his hands, sand that held water. He crawled a few paces on and felt the sand again. It could almost be described as wet. Three more paces and he tumbled over a small rise into a shallow pool of cool water. There was not enough light to see by now, but obviously the stream met its end at this point, just soaking away into the earth. He scooped water to his mouth and the pain was an exquisite pleasure as it splashed over his split lips. Passing on, the water irrigated his dry throat and he could feel its passage all the way to his stomach where it settled, causing an immediate sensation of nausea. He wretched the first few mouthfuls up, laughing as the precious water passed his lips in the wrong direction. He tried again more slowly and with more success this time. As his stomach became used to it he gulped more and more water down, anxious to re-hydrate his ravaged body.

Eventually he dragged himself out of the water and found a tree to sit against. He was amazed at how quickly he felt better. The water was like an elixir spreading through his body - mending, feeding, and transmitting goodness to all the tissues it reached.

'Now if only I had something to eat.'

He laughed - amused at just how quickly his priorities had changed. Looking around Harry viewed his surroundings as best he could in the poor light provided by the bright moon that had just risen above the horizon and luckily showed through the gap in the trees. The silver light jumped about on the sea's surface, still visible as he looked along the river's course. Animated by the sea's motion the light gave a feeling of peace, but Harry was sure that violence could erupt at any minute as it had done with the arrival of the Zero earlier. Closer in, the trees crowded over him forming a dark blanket in which he hid, but they gave him no comfort. Instead of offering him protection, the jungle appeared sinister to him, threatening to envelop and smother him. Harry expected the jungle to be full of strange noises, but it was surprisingly quiet. He could hear water trickling, as if over a small waterfall, coming from further upstream. On top of this was the gentle lapping of small waves onto the beach. Other noises - unknown animals or insects perhaps, played over the background percussion of water. Some were rhythmic, like the cricket rubbing its legs, others cut through the night, like the screech of a distant monkey disturbed by a predator.

Harry wished he had done a jungle survival course. He'd had the chance once; a place offered to him by a friend in the RAF. A few days in Hong Kong, followed by a week of lectures and acclimatisation living it up in the Officers' Mess in Brunei. Then it was out into the jungle to put the theory into practice. He had turned the offer down to go on holiday with a girlfriend who had blown him out two days into it!

He tried to recall the little gems of information his mate had passed onto him.

'Don't sleep on the forest floor,' he'd said. 'There are all sorts of creepy, crawly things that'll get into your sleeping bag with you.'

Sleeping bag thought Harry, now that would be a nice thing. Sitting, on the floor, in his wet clothes he started to feel a chill and wished he hadn't discarded his leather jacket earlier. Perhaps he would go and find that in the morning. He stood up to look around for a suitable place to spend the night and realised that he hadn't recovered as much as he thought. His head was spinning and his limbs felt like lead. He bent to the pool and took another long drink before walking upstream. He hadn't gone far before it became obvious that he wasn't going to make much progress in the dark. In fact it was becoming down-right dangerous. He turned round and made his way back to the beach. The sand still held some of the days warmth, and, by digging out a shallow depression, he thought he could make himself relatively comfortable. He collected some fallen palm fronds to pull over himself and settled down for the night. At least he would be away from the creepy crawlies!

Despite being physically exhausted he found it impossible to shut his mind down. Until now all his thoughts had been aimed at finding water but now his brain started to run over recent events, sorting, shuffling; trying to make some sense of the bizarre string of events that happened since that fateful sortie. Putting aside the fact that he was in some tropical environment miles away from where he crashed, some lunatic in a veteran aircraft had tried to kill him. It just didn't make any sense. His mind had always come up with some explanation, (even if it was as weird as someone rescuing him, healing him, dressing him in WW2 American uniform, transporting him to some tropical climate and dumping him back in the ocean,) but even in his befuddled state he couldn't come up with any justification for someone trying to kill him with a Second World War aircraft.

The theme of World War Two should have started to ring alarm bells in his mind - maybe it did in his subconscious. However, Harry never managed to put two and two together and his thoughts gradually turned to something more comforting - to Laura. The last thing he saw before dropping into the peaceful sleep of the exhausted was Laura's face gazing down on him with a look of concern. It seemed almost real; as if he could reach out and touch her.

Chapter Five

Laura hurried beside Peter Rogers as he strode purposefully along the bleak corridor of Haslar Naval Hospital. She didn't register the harsh concrete floor or the lack of windows, not even the antiseptic smell that typified older hospitals. She clung to Peter's hand as he navigated them to the Intensive Care Unit following the green-arrowed boards. She watched the lights passing above but her mind was far away. Twenty four hours ago she had been happily working, looking forward to Tony (she never called him Harry) coming home in a little under two weeks. Things had been a little strained when he had left, but the letters they'd exchanged seemed encouraging and she had certainly hoped their relationship would continue to grow on his return.

It had come as a double shock, therefore, when a Naval Captain and a Padre had arrived at her flat in Helston and informed her of the accident. The first and biggest was naturally the reaction to the news, and just how badly it had hit her was a surprise in itself. After that initial shock it dawned on her that this was an official envoy from the Royal Navy and on querying this with the Captain it transpired that she was the second nominated name on Tony's next of kin form. He was obviously much more serious about her than she had ever dared think. That of course was yesterday, in the meantime his ship had sailed to within helicopter range of the hospital and Harry had been despatched with Peter volunteering to pilot the casualty evacuation (CASEVAC) mission.

Laura was abruptly brought back to the present as Peter jerked her out of the path of a Rating pushing an overloaded trolley. As it whisked past her she caught site of the green linen of the operating theatre protruding from the white laundry sacks. Her mind saw Tony stretched out on similar materials and she felt her eyes start to mist over. She turned to Peter.

'How much further?'

'Not much,' he replied looking down at the sad face that peered up at him. She had obviously been crying on the way to the hospital, her eyes red-rimmed with dark smudges starting to form beneath them. Sensibly she had not applied any make-up that might run, but despite this she still managed to look stunningly beautiful.

'Please God, let him be alright,' she blurted out, as tears once more spilled over from her eyes and rolled down her smooth cheeks.

Peter was at a loss for words, feeling near to tears himself. He put his arm gently around her shoulders and led her through a set of double, spring-loaded doors that marked the entrance to Intensive Care. Another much shorter corridor opened up in front of them. Two or three doors led off on both sides, some to offices others to staff and visitors heads (a quaint Naval term for toilets).

'Wait here a minute, Laura,' said Peter, and with that, knocked and entered the Ward Sisters office.

Laura looked around at the stark walls, the magnolia paint scheme broken only by the odd no smoking sign. Everything looked bright and clean; clinically clean, and this time the smell clearly reached her. She had never liked the smell of hospitals, ever since breaking her arm as a child. It's amazing how the brain hangs onto details for so many years, and could evoke such strong memories. Her other senses were also picking up and storing away information. The sound of hospital machinery reached her, and the sound of a heart monitor would bring memories of this moment flashing back to her for many years to come.

'Come on, this way,' said Peter, grabbing her hand. He led Laura onto the floor of the ward through another set of double doors. Just inside a pretty nurse in a starched white uniform handed them small masks to cover nose and mouth. The noise of the medical monitors and other machinery whirring away was much louder now. They passed a number of cubicles containing seriously injured people wired up to the hardware responsible for the noise. Laura saw one individual, male or female she couldn't tell, with two or three white-coated Doctors leaning over administering some sort of aid or another. There were tubes and wires leading out of everywhere, out of the nose, mouth, back of the hand, many from the chest and even one from the abdomen. Laura was starting to have second thoughts about seeing Tony when Peter came to a halt.

After what she had just seen, it was a pleasant surprise to see him lying on his bed with just a heart monitor connected up to his left forefinger and drips set up pushing fluids and drugs into both arms. Another nurse, who had just finished taking his vital signs, beckoned them into the cubicle. Laura sank into the chair by the bed and looked into Harry's face. He looked so peaceful lying there, nothing to indicate the trauma he'd undergone except a scratch above his left eye and heavy bandaging across his chest and around the left shoulder. She reached out and stroked his cheek, but snatched back her arm at first touch. He felt so cold, or was it her imagination. She replaced her hand on his face - it was cold, but maybe that was to be expected with him being rescued from the cold sea. She ran her eyes over the rest of him. Apart from the dressing he looked reasonably unscathed. She took hold of his hand and sat watching him gently breathing in his sleep. Again she felt the sting of tears on her face.

'Why's he...' The question was left unfinished as a short, overweight man breezed into the small room.

'Good evening, I'm Commander Niall Jenkins, retired. I'm the ICU Resident Consultant, and who do we have here?' he finished, looking directly at Laura.

Laura stared back at him. Despite his short height he seemed to fill the room with his presence, and it wasn't due entirely to his wide girth. He had one of those faces that as soon as you saw it you were sure that he was a person that would be fun to know. It was a friendly face more than attractive in the classical sense. Like the rest of him it was slightly chubby, the brown beard, flecked with grey, adding to that impression. His hair was a wavy brown mop, just over regulation length and again showing the telltale signs of grey at the flanks. But it was his eyes that drew most of her attention. They were a soft brown flecked with gold and seemed to be sucking her in, making her oblivious to the fact that she was staring at him.

'Ahem,' he coughed and the spell was broken.

'Er...sorry, I'm Laura, Tony's girlfriend,' she replied. 'How is he Doctor, I mean...er...is he going to be Ok?'

'Now calm down young lady.' His voice was friendly, but authoritative. He continued in a softer tone. 'Yes as far as we can tell at this time he should make a full recovery. However, there are some things about his condition that are puzzling us at present.'

He anticipated her worried response and held his hand up.

'We've given him a thorough going over and have found very little physically wrong with him. He has a compound fracture of the left collarbone and that has been set and dressed and shouldn't cause any complications. He also has a couple of broken ribs, also on the left. Apart from those and a little water in his lungs, nothing too serious I'm glad to say, he should be fine.'

He paused before continuing. 'However, Tony is in a deep coma, much deeper than we would expect in a case like this. We can only assume that the condition has been brought on by the trauma of the accident. As I understand it he was found a long way from the others so God only knows what he went through whilst stuck in the helicopter.'

Laura was up on her feet.

'M..maybe he was knocked out, or...' Laura's words trailed off as Commander Jenkins shook his head.

'As I said my dear, we gave him a thorough check including a CAT scan and there is no damage to his brain. We even gave him an MRI scan expecting to see the brain swollen indicating oxygen starvation, but it all checked out absolutely normal. In fact,' he finished, 'the shoulder aside, I've never seen such a healthy young man.'

Laura looked totally bewildered, her eyes shifting from the Doctor's face and coming to rest on the screen of the heart monitor. The green line peaked regularly and the digits underneath registered a pulse of around 62. In addition it also showed his temperature and blood oxygen levels but it was the heart rate that kept her attention. She continued to stare for some seconds as if hypnotised. Peter gently laid a hand on her shoulder and was surprised when she flinched away from him. He was about to say something when the Doctor drew him to one side. Laura returned to the chair beside Harry and once again took his hand. She was not conscious of the low conversation between Commander Jenkins and Peter, nor were they able to hear the words she said over and over again.

'Open your eyes Tony, please open your eyes. Open your eyes Tony, please...

Chapter Six

Harry opened his eyes. At first everything was pure white, so white in fact that he thought that someone was shining a light directly into his face. He shifted his head slightly and details slowly started to form. The sun was already up quite high, the light reflecting off the white sand dazzling him. He raised his flat hand to cast a shadow over his eyes and looked about. He hoped that things would be back to normal but everything was as he remembered it.

He reluctantly climbed to his feet, feeling the stiffness in his back and limbs, and made his way to the pool he had discovered the night before. In the light he could see that this was the first in a series of pools that gradually increased in size, eventually forming a healthy looking river. He knelt and scooped up a handful of water, drinking greedily over and over. When he'd had his fill he sat back on his heels and considered his next move. He became aware of a hollow rumbling in his stomach.

'Christ I'm hungry,' he said aloud. 'What the hell do you do for food around here.'

He got up and walked over to the nearest tree. He didn't have a clue what type it was; only that it was tall, and covered in some sort of creeper that followed the bark all the way to the canopy far above. It appeared to be baren of any fruits, at least within his reach. He circled the tree and quickly became entangled in the undergrowth that was pushing almost up to the waters edge. He couldn't press any further into the jungle, and wasn't really sure that he wanted to, having caught sight of a green and black reptilian tail disappearing under a broad flat leaf. He quickly extricated himself from the area, climbing back down into the pool and decided to press on upstream in hope of finding something edible.

Ten minutes later he had covered about 200 meters and the going was getting really tough. The river was now about 10 meters wide and on average about 5 feet deep, however occasionally it opened into pools he estimated at 8 to 10 feet deep that had to be circumnavigated. To make matters worse a lot of vegetation had dropped into the stream and in places natural dams built up causing lagoons to spread into the jungle itself. These he couldn't go around and he loathed the idea of going through them. What could there be in them he thought, crocodiles, piranhas, snakes? When he actually got to thinking about it, he didn't even know what continent he was in, though for some reason he felt it wasn't South America. He saw that more as Mangrove Swamps rather than white sand beaches. Africa maybe, or the Philippines.

He sat on a large moss-covered boulder forming part of one of the natural dams and something swirled in the water just in front of him. It wasn't big enough to scare him, what with large reptiles on his mind, but it did grab his attention. He looked over the surface of the pool and saw more and more of them. They were fish rising to insects or taking seeds off the surface.

'Of course, fish,' he exclaimed. 'I can catch some fish.'

Harry immediately felt better. He was a keen fisherman in his spare time; in fact some people had described him as fanatical. Mind you this wasn't going to be like a trip down to Bolingey Lake back home near Perranporth, where he'd spent many a pleasant day pulling out carp and tench. For a start he had no fishing tackle.

He looked around his immediate vicinity hoping to find a branch that he could fashion into a simple spear. He dragged himself across the dam, pulling at the occasional stick that looked suitable. He was careful not to dislodge any major structural part of the dam, and as he reached the other side he had only two likely candidates for his weapon. He tossed one up onto the nearest bank and considered how he was going to sharpen his 'spear'.

'What I'd give for my Swiss Army penknife,' he breathed to himself after spending 10 minutes racking his brains and felt a small giggle bubbling in his throat. In frustration, but more to stop the hysteria that threatened his sanity, he swung the slender branch against the nearest tree. The end splintered and Harry was just about to toss it into the undergrowth when he paused. Drawing the damaged end closer to his face he saw that the wood had shattered, leaving just less that half thickness tapering away. Working on it with his fingernails he achieved a reasonable likeness to a point. He was ready.

He stood up on the dam and looked out over the water. There wasn't much direct sunlight penetrating the forest, but there was enough to see the dark shadows of fish just below the surface of the pool. Unfortunately they were just out of his reach. As he waited they drifted ever closer, looking for any tasty morsels that might be held up against the dam. A good size fish was just coming into range and Harry pulled the spear back in anticipation of his first strike. With his movement the structure of the dam shifted, only slightly, but enough to throw him off balance. He lost his footing and windmilled his arms around trying to maintain equilibrium. It might have worked, but as his right arm came over the spear jammed into the dam and he all but catapulted into the pool. As it was he lost his footing and stumbled into the chest-deep water with a splash that sent waves scattering across the surface, following in the wake of any fish in the local area.

Harry cursed and stumbled his way to the edge of the lagoon under the hanging branches of a small immature tree. The water was much shallower here and the footing was good. He steadied himself in the knee-deep water and settled into the long wait for the fish to return. As it turned out the wait wasn't as long as he thought it might be; the fish were obviously used to things crashing about in the water. The dark silhouette of a fish about 12 to 14 inches long came into range and, as it rose to take a large beetle off the surface Harry struck with his spear.

He thought he'd got it; he'd hit it that was for sure. He felt the jar in his wrist as the weapon struck home, saw the fish roll on its side and saw the water erupt as his quarry gave a powerful lunge and disappeared into the depths.

Over the next hour Harry had three or four more unsuccessful strikes but the makeshift spear just wasn't up to the task. The 'point' was just glancing off the bodies of the fish doing little or no damage. He hadn't even managed to stun one. Sticking the spear into the sandy bottom, he returned to his boulder and sat down for a think. His stomach rumbled loudly but he knew he could go a lot longer yet without food. He leaned over and got hold of the other branch he'd selected earlier. The point was no better, worse in fact. He looked at the thicker end, deciding whether or not he could be bothered to make a catapult.

'No elastic,' he said to himself.

Then it struck him. He'd seen a program on TV where a guy had used a forked stick to catch snakes by pushing down just behind the head with a forked tool - why couldn't it work with fish. He quickly got himself back into position and waited. As the first fish came into range he struck. The fork pinned the fish to the sand where it thrashed about, putting up an enormous struggle. Harry just pushed all the harder, leaning his weight onto the branch. The fish suddenly stopped the fight; it's back broken. Harry reached down and recovered the fish from the sand. It was slim-bodied, dark green and had a huge, spiked dorsal fin that he was careful to avoid. Flushed with his success, Harry tossed the fish onto the dam and continued fishing. After an hour or so he had another 3 fish of varying colours and sizes.

Collecting his prizes, he returned to the original pool, (base camp 1, as he called it) and laid the fish out in the shallow water.

'Now how to prepare them,' he mused, 'If only I had two Boy Scouts to rub together and start a fire I could cook up a meal.' He chuckled a little at the old joke.

'Still I've always fancied Sashimi.' With that he picked himself up and walked the short distance to the beach, scouring the sand with his eyes. It didn't take long to find what he was looking for. With only the tip showing the shell didn't look much, but as he pulled it from the sand he saw it was a beautiful conch, the bright pink at the entrance to its long since vacated and spiralling interior, almost too vivid to be real. It was almost a shame to smash it on the first boulder he came to, but smash it he did. Harry selected a couple of the sharpest pieces of shell and returned to the pool. Using the sharp edge of the piece of shell as a knife he quickly cleaned and de-scaled the largest fish and then set about the delicate task of removing the flesh from the skin and bones. He laid the results out on one of the broad leaves he'd seen earlier and pulled from the plant. It didn't look very appetising; certainly nothing like the elegant Japanese dish he was trying to emulate.

'In for a penny...' He left the old maxim unfinished as he popped a large chunk of raw fish into his mouth. The flesh was soft, almost melting in his mouth, and to his surprise tasted absolutely gorgeous (or was that just a function of his hunger.) All it needed was some soy sauce, mixed with ginger and wasabi (a paste of horseradish and water), a few fresh vegetables and he would have a banquet fit for any Japanese table. If only he had known the irony of his thoughts.

Having eaten his fill and drunk as much water as he could force into himself Harry set off along the beach to search for any useful items that might improve the quality of life until he was rescued. The beach ahead curved round to the left into what appeared to be a large bay. Across the water he noted the beach continuing endlessly, and from this distance he could see past the tree line to where the jungle climbed away to the mountains beyond. He decided to press on into the bay. He was sweating healthily now and vowed to himself that he would only push on for another hour unless he came across a fresh supply of water. About thirty minutes later, the passing of time a guess only since he had lost his watch, he rounded the point guarding the entrance to the bay. The scene looked very similar and he was just about to turn back to 'sit it out' near his water supply when something caught his eye. He stopped and shielded his eyes from the bright sun, staring into the bay. In the distance he could make out a thin tendril of black smoke curling up from the waters edge before being whisked away on the breeze.

'Civilisation at last,' he shouted, and he started to run along the sand towards the smoke.

As he got closer he could make out a structure of some type that the smoke was emanating from and it wasn't long before he was aware of the sleek lines of a sea-going vessel. He couldn't believe his luck. His rescuers would laugh when he told them he'd spent the morning catching fish with a forked stick and then eating them raw. By this time he was fairly galloping along the hard sand on the water line, waving and shouting to attract attention on the boat. It was obviously a military vessel; the silhouette of a gun now plainly visible on the bow, and it appeared to have been driven up onto the beach. Harry started to slow his pace, sure now that all was not well. The open bridge didn't look right at all; twisted out of line with the hull. He reduced speed further, to a walking pace, and took in details of the craft.

It still showed the sleek line of an old Motor Torpedo Boat (MTB), but this one had really been in the wars. The bow section looked reasonably complete; the gun pointing forward and up. The bridge not only didn't look right but was smashed from the inside out, as if something inside it had exploded. The metal of the railings and bulkheads had been twisted into tortured, impossible shapes and showed the signs of discolouring from a tremendous heat source. Because the boat was leaning away from him Harry could not see into the interior. The right torpedo tubes were intact, suffering little damage but the left side seemed to have taken some serious damage. But it was the aft end that grabbed his attention. It was clear that there had been an explosion followed by a raging fire. Most of the mahogany decking had burned away but amazingly the wooden hull seemed to have survived unscathed. A gaping black hole where the port quarter should have been was the source of the smoke, but it was the aft gun turret just behind the bridge that really mesmerised him. The smaller 50 calibre weapon was hanging on its mounting, the breech blown apart by the rounds that had ignited once the fire had got a hold. Slumped in the swivel seat behind the barrel was a charred figure that was barely recognisable as human.

Harry could not drag his eyes away from the grotesque form. The skull was bared of any flesh and through the charring that had been inflicted upon it he could see the splintering caused by the exploding rounds. It seemed to stare back at him with a sinister, empty grin; the effect caused by the exposed teeth. Some parts of the body still held patches of blackened flesh that appeared to have fused with the clothing that the victim had worn.

Harry felt the bile rising in his throat; he had seen some horrible sights in his time on the Search and Rescue (SAR) flight, but nothing he had ever experienced could have prepared him for this. He turned away and at the same time became conscious of the stench of the human remains. He retched suddenly and couldn't stop the hard-earned meal from forcing its way up his throat and onto the sand. The taste and smell of the fish helped to fuel the spasms that wracked his body; the retching continuing long after his stomach was empty.

When he was spent he dropped to his knees and cried. He sobbed like a baby; all the pain, frustration and confusion finally building up and taking him past his breaking point. He had no idea how long it went on, but when he got hold of himself at last, he felt much better. His mind had come to a conclusion of sorts: he was no longer Harry Harrison. Something had happened that had taken him to another life, another place, *another time*.

'BULLSHIT!' He shouted at the top of his voice. He continued more quietly, 'Bullshit. My name in Tony Harrison,

I'm a Seaking Observer in Her Majesty's Royal Navy. I'm dreaming, I'M DREAMING.'

Harry staggered to his feet and looked around as if searching for some proof of his existence. He was careful not to look in the direction of the MTB; he couldn't bear to see that again. He walked round the bow and saw a make-shift jetty about 100 meters up the shore. He made his way over to it and gratefully seated himself down on the splintered wood dropping his head between his knees.

He stared at his hands and became aware of a ring on the wedding finger of his right hand. He had never seen it before, though he supposed it had been present since coming round in the water. It was gold and appeared to have been made by weaving thin strands over and over, slowly building up into a band a couple of millimetres wide. He slipped it from his finger and looked at the in-side that he expected to have the same woven effect. He was wrong; it was smooth and had been engraved a long time before.

'Te amo Madre. R.M,' he read aloud. He couldn't even start to think what it's history might be or indeed what it meant, though it sounded Italian or Spanish, and he pushed it back onto his finger and began to flick it round and round with his thumb.

Again Harry lost track of time but it was only about 5 minutes before he was wrenched out of his daze.

'Hello.'

Harry jerked upright.

'Sorry I didn't mean to startle you, it's just that I...'

Harry continued to his feet, staring goggle-eyed at the apparition that had appeared before him. Now he knew he was dreaming.

'I..I...I.' The girl was completely lost for words as the strange young man stood there gazing into her eyes.

'Who the hell are you?' Harry managed to force be-tween gritted teeth. He continued looking into the hazel eyes of a girl of about 20 years. She seemed to be scared stiff, her eyes wide and pupils dilated. Her chestnut hair was long, but had been gathered up and somehow pinned to the back of her head. Her face was marked with soot or dirt, and streaks showed on her cheeks; evidence of recent tears. Around her neck hung a golden crucifix on a slightly heavy chain that looked somehow too clean against her grimy skin, however, despite all this she was fairly attractive, especially when she attempted a nervous smile.

'I..I..I'm Lucy...Lucy Fairbrother.' she stammered

'But where did you come from?'

'I was being evacuated...from Java. I was there with my mother and father, but...but they were killed in February when the Japanese started bombing.'

'Wh..what the devil are you talking about?' demanded Harry.

'They got me out just before the invasion' she continued as if she hadn't heard him. '...they're all dead you know, all of them.' Tears began to run slowly down her face but Harry couldn't comfort her; he was too concerned with the ugly pattern of his own thoughts. Things were starting to add up; the warm ocean, the jungle, the American uniform, the attack from the Zero and now the MTB. He felt his mind begin to spin as his breath becoming ragged.

'Do you know what date it is?' he asked quietly.

The girl seemed confused by the change of tack. 'I...I..'

'Do you know what the date is?' he demanded more forcefully.

'Yes...of course, it's the 5th of March; the Japanese invaded Java four days ago.'

Harry felt faint. 'Yes...' He paused for a long time before asking the next question. 'Yes...but what year is it?'

She gave him an odd look and laughed nervously.

'Please tell me what year it is,' Harry shouted.

'Why it's 1942 of course.'

Harry was convinced now that he was going to faint. Certainly the girl, Lucy, looked concerned as the colour drained from his face.

'I...it...I mean...' He gave up his effort to speak; he couldn't sort out the jumble of thoughts flying around his brain, let alone form a coherent sentence.

Lucy's attention suddenly shifted from his face, her eyes scanning the horizon. Harry snapped out of his downward spiral as he realised what was going on, but by then it was almost too late. He couldn't see the aircraft but the screaming of its engine told him it was close. He turned and started to run for the trees.

'Come on,' he shouted, and tried to grab her hand as he passed her. Lucy didn't move; she was petrified, literally rooted to the spot. As Harry looked back he saw the Zero behind her open up with its murderous machine guns.

'Come on,' he shouted again, but he knew it was too late to run. Harry dived at the girl, taking her around the waist and tumbling her to the ground. He lifted his head to see which way the attack was coming from so he could give maximum protection to her, using his body as a shield. The last thing he saw was the wing mounted machine guns spitting death in his direction. Some people say that the strike of a bullet isn't painful; more a numbing thud with the pain coming later. For Harry the pain exploded in bright lights as the bullet struck his head, and as he fell back onto Lucy his vision narrowed down with alarming rapidity as blackness swamped him.

Chapter Seven

Laura was tired, dog-tired. She had been at the hospital for a little over 36 hours and in that time she'd had the bare minimum of sleep. Harry had shown no change, but still she sat holding his hand and talking endlessly. His parents had travelled down from Inverness and had spent long periods in the cubicle with her. They hadn't met her before and were greatly impressed with her dedication, though Laura felt there was a little jealousy from his mother to begin with. But many hours had passed since then and a bond that would blossom into a long friendship had formed. She was on her own now and was starting to get the tell-tale nods of the head that indicated that she either get up and walk about for a while, or succumb to sleep. She never got the chance to make up her own mind.

The alarm sounding was nothing new; they went off quite often. Normally it was a false alarm, although Laura had seen a lot of activity around one cubicle late the previous evening following the sound. It was a few moments before it registered that the sound was much closer. Laura's heart seemed to miss a beat and she felt that she couldn't move. She was aware of the footsteps rapidly approaching from the far end of the ward. Slowly she turned to face the heart monitor.

Laura let a soft moan escape from between her lips. The screen was blank except for a thin, green, flat line. The digital readout showed zero and a red light blinked silently at her, mocking the fact that she could do nothing to alter the situation.

The first to arrive was the small nurse who had given her the mask when she first arrived. Laura knew her name to be Kate and opened her mouth to ask what was happening.

'You'll have to leave, I'm afraid,' said the nurse, as she pushed past Laura to firstly check the monitor and then feel for Harry's pulse on the side of his neck.

Laura couldn't move; she had turned to stare at Harry's face. It looked so peaceful, which was certainly a contrast to what was happening about him. Niall Jenkins was next to arrive, immediately taking charge of the situation and issuing a stream of orders to Kate and another two nurses that arrived with an assortment of medical equipment that Laura knew could only mean bad news.

'I'm sorry, but you will have to leave,' repeated Kate, placing a firm hand on Laura's forearm.

Still Laura didn't move. She watched a young doctor arrive in a hurry, and at Mr Jenkins command pushed a curved tube down Harry's throat, connecting a corrugated hose and then a black rubber bag before squeezing it, artificially breathing for him.

'Come on, out you go.' Laura was bundled out of the cubicle and was left standing alone as Kate went to assist at Harry's side. His bedclothes had been pulled back, exposing his muscular chest. A large male nurse that Laura had never seen before had started to perform an external heart massage, one hand over the other in the centre of his sternum:

'1..2..3..4..5..breath.' Two squeezes on the bag. '1..2..3..4..5..breath.' Two more 'breaths'.

Kate had prepared a syringe and handed it to the Doctor. Laura turned away as Niall leant over to inject her beloved Harry.

'1..2..3..4..5..breath.'

Her beloved Harry, beloved Harry. She was saying it over and over to herself. She realised that she was calling him Harry for the first time, but more importantly she knew then that she really loved him. She had known before that her feelings were strong, that she was becoming attached to this man. But it wasn't until this moment, with him dying on the bed in front of her, that she knew she didn't want to live without him, couldn't live without him.

'1..2..3..4..5..breath.'

Laura turned back to see another flurry of activity at the bedside. Kate had a small metal box that she opened to reveal a selection of knobs and dials. She watched in horror as Niall took hold of the rubber handled metal pads, applied some jelly and started rubbing them together.

Laura felt weak as the Doctor approached Harry. She remembered how they had watched Casualty on TV one night, and how Harry had joked when the 'pads' had come out. 'That's it then,' he'd said. 'Once they get the pads out he's had it,' referring to the poor victim on the table. He had been right too. But that's TV and this is real she thought.

'Stand back.'

She focused just in time to see the effect of the shock had on his body. The acting on Casualty had been good, but it was nothing to the way his body arched, the limbs stiffening, before slamming back onto the bed. Someone felt for the pulse;

'Nothing.'

'1..2..3..4..5..breath.'

'Stand back.'

Laura felt her knees buckle, she was falling but there was nothing she could do about it. Her vision narrowed down to a pinprick and she crumpled untidily to the floor. The last thing she was conscious of was:

'1..2..3..4..5..breath.'

'Stand back.'

Chapter Eight

Harry tried to open his eyes, but the glare of the sun forced them shut again. He lifted his head and immediately regretted the action, the blinding pain almost tipping him back over the edge into unconsciousness. Suddenly he was gripped by a tremendous pain across his chest; the muscles tightening to the stage that he thought would cause his rib cage to collapse inward. He was convinced that he was having a heart attack, but as quickly as it had started, it stopped. Gradually his breathing, quickened by the sudden pain, returned to normal and he was able to access his situation. His head was lying, slightly raised, on something warm and soft, and he decided that was good enough for the time being. Eventually he started to feel a little better and, shielding his eyes this time, he looked around at the alien environment. His head was resting in the lap of a young girl who looked down on him with big wide eyes.

'Where the hell am I ?'

'Don't worry, you're safe now,' she replied, 'the aircraft has gone and I don't think the wound in your head is too serious. The bleeding seems to have stopped,' she finished weakly.

'Do I know you, lady?' he asked.

'Well we met only a few minutes before the Japanese plane attacked. My name's Lucy Fairbrother, don't you remember?'

He closed his eyes. 'No I don't I'm afraid, in fact I don't remember anything since...well it doesn't matter now. I'm Brad by the way, Lieutenant Charles Bradshaw, United States Navy. Brad to my friends and I'll count you as one of those if I may.'

She smiled for the first time and her face was transformed from the attractive features to a pretty young girl that gave the impression of being lost.

'Can you move?'

Brad didn't really want to, he was quite happy lying there looking into her hazel eyes. It was a long time since he'd seen a pretty girl, any girl for that matter. He reluctantly pulled himself into a sitting position and lifted a hand to the wound on his forehead. It had been close. The bullet had creased a groove in the flesh, not quite down to the bone. Half an inch the other way and he would have been just one more statistic in the long list of casualties of the Pacific war.

'What actually happened here?' he asked having climbed to his feet and surveyed his surroundings.

Lucy explained how she had first seen him walking and then running along the beach towards the burnt-out MTB. She had watched him vomit, and make his way to the wooden jetty. She finished up with the attack by the Zero that had nearly ended his life.

Brad was confused, especially when she described his reaction to the carnage on the boat. He'd been in this God forsaken war long enough to become hardened to the visions of death. He'd even had one of the young sailors back on board his Ship, die in his arms; his abdomen wall shot away allowing the purple, grey mass of intestines to spill out onto Brad's legs. He brought his mind back to the present.

'But how did you come to be here?'

'I've told you...Oh of course you don't remember. I was evacuated from Java about two weeks before the Japanese invaded, but unfortunately it was completely unofficial, a favour from a friend of my fathers. I think we were due to head for Australia but the boat received new orders. As far as I could tell from the details John gave me, they were ordered north to pick up some aircraft spotters from the Caroline Islands and the Marshall Islands. That's all I really know. He couldn't call in anywhere to drop me off and so I had no alternative but to go with them.' She was close to tears as she continued.

'I don't even know where we are. Yesterday we were cruising round this Island looking for signs of life when two aircraft attacked us. One was like the one that shot you and the other was bigger, with two engines I think. They just shot us to pieces. There was something wrong with the engines and so John drove the boat onto the beach.'

There was a long moment of silence before she continued.

'He put me onto the beach first while the other men stayed at their guns, and when he turned to go back he was hit in the chest. I don't know what hit him, he just went completely rigid, his face a mask of horror as his insides seemed to burst out of the gaping wound in his body. I ran. I couldn't help him. Then...then ....' She was openly sobbing now. 'Then it just blew up...I think the big plane dropped a bomb on it and it blew up. They're all dead you know.'

Brad reached out and cradled her in his arms. He held her until she pulled away from him.

'I'm sorry Brad, I...'

The sentence was left unfinished. There was nothing either of them could say that would change anything, or make things any better. Nothing anyone could say would make any sense of this brutal war. He held her hand and started walking towards the MTB.

'No, I'm not going in there, anyway there's no need. There's a wooden cabin about a quarter of a mile into the jungle. I think it was a fisherman's long ago but more recently it looks to have been used by the aircraft spotter.'

She led him back towards the jungle and entered the undergrowth through a well-concealed entrance. Once inside they made their way along what was obviously a well-worn path that gently curved round to the right. It was only about 200 yards before the path opened into a small clearing that allowed a little more light to penetrate the canopy. At the back of the clearing was the hut. It was a very basic affair with steps leading up to a balcony or veranda. Across from the steps was an open door leading to the dark interior. To the left of the door was what appeared to be the only window, which was not much more than a hole in the wall.

They climbed the steps and entered the hut. She was right when she said an aircraft spotter had used it. The hut comprised of a single room about 10 feet by 12 feet. Along the far wall was a single cot type bed, which had a couple of Army issue blankets crumpled up at one end. The side with the window was given over entirely to shelves and cupboards, some covered in tins and a variety of other objects. The opposite wall had a bench table fixed along half its length. In the centre was a smashed radio set, probably done by the spotter when he left the hut for the final time. Above the radio, on the walls, were lots of little triangles of torn paper pinned to the walls. These had baffled Lucy, but Brad decided that they were probably from aircraft silhouette charts that had been ripped off the wall at the same time the radio was disabled. This was supported by the pile of ashes in a make shift bin made from an old oilcan. Things had obviously become a bit hot for the lone spotter; his position compromised perhaps.

Brad started going through the 'stocks', making a mental inventory of their rations. There seemed to be plenty of tinned food, a lot of it fruit that was a good source of energy and had the added benefit that it could be eaten cold straight from the can. There were also some tins of beef stew and assorted vegetables.

'We're lucky he didn't get rid of all this stuff before he left,' said Brad, as he replaced the last tin of peaches on the shelf. Lucy's voice was very flat when she replied.

'He didn't get the chance to do anything other than smash the radio. There was nothing of any use here. His body was over there,' she said, pointing to the corner in the darkest part of the room.

Brad felt sorry for the poor girl; she'd been through so much and now this. God only knows what state the body would have been in, especially after a few days in this climate.

'I dragged him into the jungle out the back and scrubbed the floor. I think I've got rid of most of the smell,' she continued in a conversational tone.

Brad reached out to hold her but hesitated when she continued: 'The supplies are all from the boat. Unfortunately a lot of the stuff was damaged in the explosion but there seems to be quite a lot here.'

Brad thought of the horrors she must have gone through on the MTB. No wonder she didn't want to go back onto it. Now Brad did reach for her and she went limp as he held her tightly against his body. He could feel the soft shaking as the silent sobs were torn from her body. Once again she composed herself very quickly. This is one tough little cookie he thought as Lucy started reorganising the tins that he'd disturbed.

'Look, why don't you have a little rest, I'll be back in a few minutes.'

She didn't object, didn't even ask where he was going. She climbed onto the bed and pulled the blankets roughly up around herself. Brad left, quietly pulling the door shut behind him. He made his way back to the MTB and had a good search round, looking for the things he could use that Lucy wouldn't have thought of. The carnage was all around him, much of it not recognisable as human remains, but it didn't affect him any more than normal.

Entering the bridge from the quarterdeck the evidence of the explosion was all around him. All the instruments were smashed beyond recognition, as were the men that had been standing in it. Thankfully the human remains had been badly burnt by the ensuing fire which meant they were less gory somehow. The radio equipment was what he had really wanted to look at, but it had been shot to pieces along with everything else on the bridge. Making his way down below it was much the same story. He searched around looking for anything that might come in handy and found two more bodies. These men looked to have died from the concussion of the blast. Reasonably intact, they had both lost blood from the nose and ears, and their skin and clothes had been subjected to flash burns indicative of an explosion. Searching throughout the vessel the best he could come up with were a few tools and a revolver that he gingerly removed from the shattered remains of one of the bodies down below, presumably one of the Officers. He couldn't find any spare rounds for it, but all six chambers were full. He tucked the weapon into the belt of his trousers and continued his search. Not finding anything else useful he returned to the hut, where he discovered Lucy sitting on the edge of the cot staring into space.

'Brad, what year is it?'

'1942 of course, why do you ask?'

'It's just something you asked me before you were shot.' She explained how he had queried her about the date, and his reaction to the answer. 'It gave me the creeps, but you seem different now, more sure of yourself.'

'I guess it must all be to do with the loss of memory I suffered. Maybe the bang on the head did me some good after all.'

'How did you come to be walking down the beach anyway?' she asked, seemingly forgetting once again that he was suffering from some sort of amnesia.

'Well it's a long story,' he said. 'And I can't remember the last part, but it all started when I was sat in the cockpit...'

Chapter Nine

Lieutenant Bradshaw was in his element. He was strapped into his Grumman F4F-4 Wildcat on the flight deck of the American Aircraft carrier Enterprise. Things had been going well lately, and lets face it, he thought, they needed to after Pearl Harbour. Enterprise was one of three Carriers in the Pacific at the time. The other two were the Lexington, and the Yorktown that had been detached from the Atlantic Fleet to replace the damaged Saratoga. Brad had seen plenty of action under the Command of Admiral William F. Halsey who had been taking the war to the Japanese since February 1942.

Today they were to join with a flight of the long-range bombers, as well as their own smaller carrier borne bombers, for a raid on Marcus Island. To Brad it was just a tiny remote Island in the middle of nowhere, but he supposed it had some strategic value, and he was generally happy with his lot.

The aircraft two ahead of him launched and his flight leader moved into position. Off down the short 'runway' he went and Brad got into position for take off. His leader was airborne and Brad gunned the throttles, the 14 cylinder Pratt and Whitney easing up to 2,900 rpm giving about 1200 horse power. He checked the engine instruments and gave a thumbs up to the flight deck team. Then he was off, the aircraft lurching off the deck at about the same time as it achieved flying speed. There was still that feeling of dropping that caused him to hold his breath until the biting prop and the aerofoil section of the wing combined to pull him up away from the sea, ever waiting to reap the benefits of poor machinery or careless flying.

Brad slid the canopy of the fighter back giving himself a much better view and quickly acquired his leader. He was in a left turn to the North, flying to join the rest of the formation that was quickly taking shape. Brad pulled some lead on the aircraft ahead, effectively cutting across the circle of his leaders turn. Once into position he settled down for the long transit, constantly searching the skies for any signs of a surprise attack.

'Close up Red two.' The tone of the radio giving his leader's voice a very impersonal touch. Brad remembered back to the briefing where the emphasis had been on keeping the formations tight, giving each other mutual support and keeping the integrity of the flight whole. He eased into position using the smallest of inputs on the flying column, then glanced in at the array of instruments, checking that the engine was running smoothly. He noticed the temperature was a little hot, but certainly nothing to worry about. Happy that all was well he pulled out the folded map from the instrument panel shroud and checked on their progress. Flying at 10,000 feet they had set about 160 knots, the max range cruise speed, giving a max range of a little over 800 miles. They still had a fair way to the rendezvous position and so he spent time thinking about the way he would approach any engagements, whilst continuing his lookout.

It was about 10 minutes later that Brad started to get worried. The temperature of his engine had continued to rise, and a fluctuating rpm and a high pitch vibration felt through the airframe now compounded this. He had sat on it for a short time, but common sense told him that a combat mission was no place for an under par engine.

'Leader from Red 2, I have engine problems and request I return to base (RTB).'

Commander Williams had known Pilots that had 'problems' on combat missions with startling regularity, only to get back to the ship to have nothing found by the engineers. These individuals didn't tend to last too long. However, if anything, Brad was just the opposite, and Chuck Williams knew the problem must be serious if he was requesting to RTB.

'Roger Red 2, clear RTB, sorry to lose you on this one.'

Brad banked away from his leader, easing the throttle forward to maintain his height. The vibration increased and changed pitch slightly, confirming his suspicions that it was tied in with the engine snag. Settling down on a course to intercept the Enterprise Brad cursed his luck, but knew there was nothing he could do about it. He felt his body begin to relax as his mind accepted that he would not be going into action, the adrenaline that had caused the tightening of his chest and shortening of breath gradually reducing to a more normal level. However, he couldn't relax too much; he still had a malfunctioning aircraft to nurse back and land on the moving deck of an Aircraft Carrier.

It was then, with some surprise, that he spotted a formation of aircraft low in his 2 O'clock. They appeared to be on a reciprocal heading, transiting over a small Island that Brad couldn't remember seeing on the way out. As they drew closer he could make out that there were only two planes, but still had no idea of the type. He stole a quick glance around him and felt the first stirrings of fear, an unfamiliar and unwelcome feeling. He was approaching a substantial group of islands that should not have been anywhere near his route. He looked in at his compass and gave it a sharp tap, but it remained stubbornly on South. As he looked out again he just saw the two aircraft disappearing under his right wing. It was at this point that he made his only mistake; he dropped the wing of his Wildcat in order to regain visual contact and in doing so caused the sun to glint off the surface of his aircraft. In the same instant he identified the smaller of the two aircraft as a Mitsubishi Zero as it peeled away from the second contact. The Japanese pilot had obviously spotted him and was spoiling for a fight.

Brad had no alternative but to turn towards the other fighter. The range was too close for him to show his heels and run, though with an over heating engine this would have been the preferable course of action. By turning to put the enemy on his nose he was cutting down the range very quickly and denying the bandit any room to turn as the aircraft passed very close, almost 180 degrees out. As he saw the Zero flash past the right hand side Brad feinted a turn to the left before pulling the aircraft as hard as he could into a right hand turn. His best option was cunning rather than relying on aircraft performance, which was somewhat degraded due to the now audibly protesting engine. He also pulled in the vertical plane, trying to force the opposition to do the same, thus slowing the fight down, enabling him to protect the engine and use his dog fighting skills. The Zero had predicted Brad's every move and was already using his power advantage to drag his nose, and hence his guns, closer to the Wildcat.

Brad knew at that moment that he couldn't win the fight and would have to change his tactics. His only option was to try to conduct the fight in a way that would allow him to separate from the Zero and then run hell for leather taking everything the engine would give him. He'd already thrown away his best chance, when the two planes had first merged with opposite headings, but there were ways and means to regenerate the same situation, or even one with more advantage, i.e. passing 180 degrees out but with him going down, increasing speed, whilst the Zero was going up and losing energy. This all flashed through Brads' mind in an instant and he was already manoeuvring to force his plan into action. Having once again passed the Zero without the opportunity for either to bring the guns to bear, Brad pulled aggressively into the vertical, rolling the aircraft off the top of the loop. He pushed the throttle forward to overcome the forces of gravity and, seeing a moment of indecision in his adversary, he dropped the nose, powering towards the Zero. He realised immediately that there was a slim chance of getting a quick kill before the Zero pilot reacted and he opened up with the six half inch machine guns as the enemy filled his sights.

It was at exactly at that moment that the engine failed. The rigors required of it in combat were just too much and with a cough and splutter it simply stopped. The speed washed off instantaneously causing the bullets to spray ineffectually into vacant space. As the Zero flashed past him Brad just stared through the canopy knowing that the end had come. He pushed the nose further down to maintain flying speed and curved to the left towards some cloud he'd noticed building up over one of the larger islands. Something made him look at the compass and he noticed it was still steady on South, even as he turned.

'This bloody Jap must think it's his Goddamn birthday.'

At this point his mind jumped back to the enormity of the situation and in the same instant he felt bullets smashing into the airframe. He didn't stand a chance; the unseen bullets cutting control runs to the rudder and elevator, continuing through the left wing smashing the aileron control linkage into unrecognisable lumps of twisted metal. The aircraft was rapidly becoming unflyable but Brad had survived that first pass and was not sitting idle. As the plane rolled to the left he slid the canopy back to it's' stops and unfastened his seat straps. Aided by gravity he was able to pull himself onto the seat and dive over the port side, mercifully missing any of the doomed Wildcats' surfaces. As he tumbled away from it he became aware of the noise over and above the windrush he was experiencing. He opened his eyes in time to see the Zero close in for the kill, saw the fuel tanks of the Wildcat explode, the structure of the airframe there one minute, gone the next. He instinctively shut his eyes against the blast and heard the Zero scream over his head.

Instinct took over now as Brad went through the drills that he had hoped he would never have to use. Without looking he quickly located the ripcord of the cumbersome parachute pack strapped to his back. Hooking his shaking fingers firmly in the metal loop he pulled in one sweeping motion across his body. He held his breath and counted to three; nothing happened. He jerked his eyes open and looked up just in time to see the white canopy snap open above him. He grunted aloud as the straps jerked his whole body, clenching his jaw in an effort to combat the excruciating pain that shot through his testicles as a badly adjusted crotch strap made itself felt. The pain, however was transitory, and was replaced with an overwhelming feeling of well being as realisation of his narrow escape hit him.

Brad started to take in his surroundings. Firstly he checked the harness and then peered again at the white chute contrasting against the dark blue sky. There was no sign of the Zero, or for that matter, of the wreckage of his aircraft that had so recently exploded. Looking down, he judged himself to be about 1500 feet over the surface of the sea, though it was difficult to assess with such a calm sea. Still a water landing should be quite easy, then it would just be a matter of waiting to be rescued when the Ship realised that he was missing. He was actually beginning to enjoy the feeling of floating down when something in his peripheral vision caught his eye. He twisted himself in the harness and stared at the disturbance on the water a mile or so away. Something was causing the water to spray out from a central point, the disturbed surface rippling outwards from the same point. At first Brad thought it was a twister like the ones back home in the States that pick up the dust in summer, as they move across the fields. But this was different. It wasn't moving across the sea for a start, and the more he looked the more that he was sure there was something at the centre, a nucleus from which the disturbance originated. The kicked up water was forming into a fine spray and as the sun caught it, its rays were refracted into all the colours of the rainbow, effectively shielding the core.

As he dropped closer to the water his sight began to penetrate the mist. He could make out some sort of craft, a small boat perhaps.

'That's no boat,' he said to himself.

The more he stared the more he was sure the object was hovering some distance above the surface of the agitated sea. He could just make out a large fan on top of the craft that appeared to be the cause of the seas' upheaval, but over all it was like nothing he'd ever seen before in his life. Apart from anything else it seemed to present a hazy image, almost as if he could see through it, but Brad assumed it was an illusion caused by the sun and the mist. In fact perhaps the whole thing was just a mirage or a figment of his imagination. But then, even as he was mulling it over in his mind he saw the object drop into the water. The fan immediately struck the sea, twisting the craft as it rolled to the left and disappeared. All that was left was the fine spray and a milky white smudge in the otherwise blue ocean.

'What the bloody hell are the Japs up to now?' shouted Brad.

The next second he was rudely brought back to his own predicament as he was suddenly submerged into the relatively cold water. Having emptied his lungs with the last exclamation he suddenly found himself fighting for his life, struggling to get to the surface before he involuntarily breathed the salt water into his body. His flying clothes seemed to weigh a ton, especially his leather flying-jacket that seemed intent on dragging him to the bottom. When he did break surface he wasn't immediately aware of it as he had come up underneath his parachute. As he continued to struggle, the rigging lines became more and more entangled around his limbs and it struck him that he had escaped death by a hair's breadth only to drown like a kitten in a sack.

The involuntary breath finally came and he was surprised to draw air into his aching lungs. He reached up and started to pull on the silk covering his head but the tangled lines made the task extremely difficult. His legs were still kicking frantically below him, barely keeping his head above water, but even they were becoming restricted and already felt like lead from the unaccustomed effort. Brad began to panic as his strength slipped away and his head more and more often dipped below the surface. Taking a large breath he made one last supreme effort to free himself from the clinging silk and twisted cord.

'...and that's the last thing I remember before waking up in your arms.' finished Brad.

'I guess that last effort did the trick; you're a very lucky guy Brad' Lucy climbed off the bed and started to arrange the stores on their shelves.

'So what do you think that contraption was, the one that was hovering over the sea,' she asked.

'I honestly have no idea,' Brad replied, 'Anyway we've got to think about our next move. We obviously can't stay here; the Japs are bound to be back once that pilot's put in a report.'

'I guess you're right,' she replied. Turning away from the shelves she dropped a tin of Bully Beef onto the floor and walked out of the door.

Chapter Ten

Brad followed Lucy out of the hut and caught her by the arm as she walked purposefully across the porch.

'Come on back inside, we don't need to set off until the morning.'

Lucy stared at him and seemed to lose all her resolve falling against him like a rag doll. Brad just stood and held her as the sobbing wracked her body over and over. Finally, when it seemed she would never stop, her body became still and the crying ceased. He lifted her face and brushed away the last of the tears and said kindly:

'Lucy, you've got nothing to prove to me; half the guys I know couldn't have handled what you've been through in the last few days. It probably doesn't mean much at the moment, but I think you're one of the bravest people I've met in this stinking war.'

Lucy's face broke into a watery smile.

'I'm sorry Brad, it's just that...well you know.' As he nodded and smiled in return, she continued. 'And yes it does mean something to me, it means a lot. Thank you.'

With this she reached up on tiptoe and kissed him gently on the cheek. Her personal crisis was on hold at the moment and she pulled away from him and went back into the hut. Brad followed her, picking up and replacing the can of beef as he went. He stood behind her for a few seconds, watching as she began to sort through the stores on the shelf. He smiled as she muttered to herself about what they would be able to carry, what was too heavy etc, and was amazed at the ability of the female mind; the way she blotted out of the horrors of the past few days as soon as there was something practical to be sorted out. He left her to it and went outside to explore beyond the immedi ate surroundings he'd seen on their arrival at the shack.

There really wasn't too much to see. He walked around the edge of the clearing, probing the jungle for any signs of an opening. As he neared the back of the hut he came across the remains of the spotter that Lucy had dragged from the room. He made a cursory search of the body, carefully peeling away the remaining rags that barely served to cover the battered remnants of the human form. The stench was atrocious, the humid atmosphere allowing the process of decay to accelerate beyond the normal rate. He hadn't died easily. The body was marked from head to foot with the signs of a severe beating. The wounds, open to the elements and the insect life whose grubs and maggots prospered amongst the rotten flesh, told the story of torture and agony that the man would never have the opportunity of telling himself. Some scavenger had eaten away at the stomach cavity, taking the soft organs and leaving a gaping wound in their place. His final deathblow had been a bullet in the brain, entering through the back of the head and taking away half of his face. Brad again wondered at the amazing courage of the woman now carrying out the mundane task of sorting their provisions.

As he knelt to search these gory remains, Brad's knee came down on something hard. Pulling away the grass and shallow undergrowth he revealed a large, rusted machete. On inspection he saw the edge was dulled and chipped; the years lying in the elements taking their toll on the already well-worn implement. Still, he considered, it was better than nothing. He continued his search of the jungle wall, slashing at the forest growth with his new found weapon and was just about to give up when he came across an area that seemed much easier to penetrate than the rest. Taking a little more time he managed to force his way through the opening and then used the machete to reveal what long ago must have been a well-worn trail. The forest had all but reclaimed the path, but even the years of neglect could not erase all trace of the hundreds of journeys made over the decades of use by local fishermen.

Having made a little progress into the undergrowth, Brad backtracked to the entrance, rearranging the undergrowth to leave it much as he'd found it. Pulling the body away from the path he covered it with some of the greenery he had hacked down; he didn't want Lucy to have to relive the horrors when they came this way in the morning. Re-entering the shack he found Lucy putting the final touches to two packs made up from one of the old blankets. He walked over to her and she passed him the larger of the two. The blanket had been pulled into a pouch sort of affair tied off at the top with thin strips of blanket Lucy had torn off.

'We need to find some way of securing and carrying them,' she said, and then looking to the machete in his hand, she added. 'Maybe Tarzan could find Jane some vines in the jungle.'

'If only I'd kept my parachute; there was plenty of cord in that. Is there nothing amongst this stuff?' He asked, indicating the jumble of stores left on the shelves.

'Nothing at all I'm afraid,' replied Lucy.

'Right wait here; there must be plenty of rope on the boat. I shouldn't be more than a few minutes.'

'It's OK,' said Lucy, 'I'll walk down to the beach with you, and I'll be fine as long as I don't go in there again.'

'Fine with me.'

They set off along the track to the beach, Brad leading the way with the machete in his left hand, service revolver in the right. At the edge of the forest he indicated for Lucy to stay still. He scanned the horizon in all directions, searching the skies and beaches for any movement. He noted that the sun was dropping towards the horizon; daylight would soon be failing and he didn't fancy being on board the MTB in darkness. Despite this he continued his search for a little longer until he was certain there were no traps or ambushes set up on the beach.

'Come on,' he said, grabbing Lucy's hand and dashing across the sand towards the wreck. He led her right up to the beached bow, where she would see nothing of the carnage aboard. It would also keep her hidden from the casual eye of any pilot flying over with the incurable curiosity that many airmen possess.

'If any planes come over stay stock still until you can't hear them, then shout for me. If anyone comes walking along stay in the shadows and try to work your way round to where you can get aboard.'

He could see that the prospect was frightening her, but he was also sure that his instructions were sinking in and that he could rely on her acting correctly if a crisis arose. He gave her one of his best boyish grins, took a quick look around and then disappeared towards the rear of the boat. Lucy sat down on the warm sand and felt a shiver run through her body. She tried to convince herself that it was the drop in temperature afforded her by the shade, and not the thought of the recently deceased sailors just above her. Unfortunately she failed miserably, her mind conjuring up all sorts of images. In her head she saw the explosion that had torn the boat apart, the Boatswain, Brian, thrown into the air, seeming to float for an instant, only to land like a discarded doll across the forecastle. She forcibly drove the thoughts from her head, thinking instead of the young man who had probably saved her life at his own expense.

A sudden crash from above made her jerk her head up, her heart pounding so hard in her chest that she thought it must surly fail. But she held her ground, scanning the horizon, unthinkingly following Brads' example. Seeing nothing she quickly pulled herself to her feet just in time to see a figure moving slowly towards her in the shadows. She opened her mouth to scream..

'It's me Lucy, are you OK?'

'Oh Brad you frightened me, I thought...' she trailed off leaving the sentence unfinished. She dropped her head and looked at the sand. She fought off the tears of desperation though she felt utterly wretched.

'Come on, It's been a long day. Let's go back, get something to eat and have an early night. You'll feel as good as new tomorrow, you wait and see.'

He gently took hold of her arm and led her back towards the hut. He was still cautious as they crossed the open expanse of sand but he didn't make a big show of it; not wanting to cause Lucy any more misgivings.

Later, after a simple meal of cold beef and tinned fruit, they sat together at the table of old crates that seemed to be the only 'furniture' in evidence.

'Have you got anybody...a girl, at home I mean?' asked Lucy without looking up.

'Not really,' he replied, 'Well there was someone, a Nurse but she was killed when the Japanese bombed Pearl Harbour.'

'Oh Brad I'm so sorry.'

'I hadn't known her that long; only saw her a few times, but it was nice just to have somebody, someone to care about.' He paused, trying to find the right words, 'Someone to give a meaning to what we're fighting for, and yet she was gone before we really started the fighting.'

He stared into space trying to conjure up a picture of her face in his mind. He failed. Turning to Lucy he forced a grin.

'And what about you?' He asked.

He noted the beginnings of a blush start on her slender neck rapidly spreading to the rest of her face.

'Mummy and Dad were very strict. I didn't really get to meet very many boys. I think Daddy was looking out for the right man for me. I've got nobody now,' she finished weakly.

Brad said nothing; he simply took her hand in his and held it as both of them sank into their own pool of thoughts. Eventually Brad got up and walked over to the pile of objects that he had salvaged from the boat. There wasn't a lot; some rope, a couple of webbing straps, bits and pieces of material and the best prizes of all, a penknife, some matches and a couple of magazines, all taken from the wrecked cabin in the bows of the vessel. He had searched amongst the tangled remains for candles or a lantern or anything to give them some light. The best he'd managed were the oil soaked rags that were now burning in the make shift rubbish bin. These not only gave off a low flickering light, but a thick, oily, black smoke that had initially threatened to choke them. Brad had finally propped the bin in the open window, relying on the cover of the jungle canopy to hide the light from any prying eyes.

Using the rope and the webbing he began to fashion some carrying harnesses for the packs that Lucy had made up. He was vaguely aware of her moving over to the bunk, and by the time he'd finished his work she was fast asleep under the only remaining blanket. Putting out the 'light' Brad resigned himself to another cold and uncomfortable night as he curled up on the floor by the bed.

Chapter Eleven

Laura came round, unable to recall where she was or why her head ached so badly. She opened her eyes and could just make out the silhouette of someone sitting beside her in the gloom. She sat bolt upright, frightened at the thought of a stranger in her room. But she wasn't in her room, wasn't even in her own flat. She was in a strange bed surrounded by curtains, with a stranger sat beside her.

'I'm in hospital,' she said aloud.

Her voice caused the mystery figure to stir and in the pale light she recognised her guardian and the details of the last few days came flooding back to her. As her mind caught up with events her last conscious memories came back to her: '1..2..3..4..5..breath.'

Her hand flew to her mouth;

'My God is he...'

'He's fine, sweetheart,' replied Mrs Harrison. 'He's stabilised and the Doctor says he's as well as can be expected. They've got him on a ventilator to help him breath at the moment but they assure me it's only temporary. Doctor Jenkins seems to think he's in the same position as before the arrest.'

'But what caused it?' asked Laura. 'The Doctor said that he was healthy, that apart from being unconscious there was nothing wrong with him.'

'I don't know Laura; I don't think that they know themselves. Everyone seems to be completely baffled.'

Harry's mother paused before continuing.

'I don't know if I should tell you this but I guess you have a right to know. They didn't resuscitate Tony, they couldn't. He just came back by himself,' Mrs Harrison saw the look of confusion on Laura's face and continued.

'After you'd fainted they continued to give heart massage and everything else including various drugs but he just didn't respond. I don't know exactly how long they kept going but eventually they gave up and were recording the time for the death certificate when the heart monitor started up at a steady 62. They thought the machine had malfunctioned but on checking Tony they found his pulse immediately and registered some weak breathing.'

'But what about brain damage?' asked Laura, feeling her heart sink.

'Well they can't be sure until he wakes up, but they said he should be OK - with the artificial respiration enough oxygen should have been getting to the brain to sustain it.'

With the good news Laura felt her strength returning. Swinging her legs over the side of the cot-like bed she lowered herself to the floor. After an initial bout of dizziness, which caused her to sway on her feet until Mrs Harrison came over to support her, she took a few tentative steps around the bed space.

'How long have you been here Mary?'

'Ever since you dropped onto the floor of intensive care.' Mary smiled and continued, 'They brought you out here to the relatives ward and they were worried you would flip out, as they put it, when you came round. Peter has had to go back to the Ship so I sat with you.'

'Mary, I can't thank you enough.'

'Well after the vigil you've kept over Tony it was the least I could do.'

Laura said, 'Can we go and see him now?'

'Yes, of course. But let's just get you checked out first.'

Ten minutes later the ward Sister had given Laura a clean bill of health and they were once again stood beside Harry's bed. The ventilator had been removed but was standing by, and he appeared exactly as he had before his last crisis.

'He looks so peaceful,' said Laura. 'Why won't he wake up? Oh God please let him wake up, please.'

Mary gently took her hand and looked down at her son.

And still Harry slept.

Chapter Twelve

Brad awoke with a start. He'd slept surprisingly well considering the conditions but now something had disturbed him. Probably the light he thought as he surveyed the room. The sun was obviously well up, its rays penetrating the canopy allowing daylight to conquer over darkness, in the clearing at least. Brad saw that Lucy was also stirring and wondered again what had disturbed them. Brad eased himself stiffly to his feet.

The shot, when it rang out, was impossibly loud. Brad dropped to the floor as if poleaxed and Lucy let out a frightened yelp, falling off the bed and grabbing Brad to see where he'd been hit.

He whispered: 'I'm OK, it didn't hit me. I think it was down on the beach.'

He was right. A small patrol of Japanese soldiers had been ordered out during the night with instructions to search the beaches for an American airman. Now bored, tired and hungry they had come across the burnt-out boat on the beach. Having searched it for anything useful or edible, and found very little, they were taking out their frustrations with a little spell of target practise. Another shot split the silence and the soldiers laughed as the burnt remains sitting at the after gun turret jerked backwards in the metal seat.

One of the soldiers quickly became bored of the game and noticing the jetty looked hard around at the forest wall. Detecting the breach leading to the path he called his colleagues and started up the beach towards it.

Of course Brad didn't know any of this; he just reacted instinctively. Grabbing the two packs, the machete and the revolver he crept to the door, staying in the shadows as he peered out into the opening. Seeing it was clear he threw away any pretence of stealth, indicated for Lucy to follow him and dashed behind the hut. It took him a few attempts to find the entrance he'd discovered the night before, but he was glad now that he hadn't enlarged the opening. Pushing Lucy through first they melted into the jungle and by the time they had travelled twenty feet or so along the path there was no sign that they had ever been there.

This was not the case back at the spotter's hut. The soldiers had arrived and cautiously approached the simple building. The junior man had been sent forward and now peered into the dark interior, his rifle held out in front of him; the viscous bayonet leading the way. Happy to find the single room empty he shouted back to the others who quickly made their way up to join him. Looking around they saw the signs of recent occupation; the remains of the simple meal, the smoke stained oilcan in the equally stained window place. The NCO barked orders to the other three men, anxious now that his Officer would react badly when he discovered the patrol had missed the American. Two of the soldiers ran down to the beach and started looking for signs that might give a clue to the airman's whereabouts. The NCO and remaining man carried out a search of the clearing. It wasn't long before the spotters body was discovered, the NCO thinking that he was off the hook. He shouted for the rest of his men to join him and then took a good look at the body. He could only assume that an earlier patrol had found him and left him for the jungle animals to take care of.

Feeling pleased with himself he set his men about torching the shack. It wouldn't be until two days later that his report was followed up and the dead mans true identity discovered. But by then it was too late, the search had been called off, the trail two days cold. The men of the patrol never saw their NCO again.

Meanwhile Brad and Lucy had heard the shouting and commotion going on back at the clearing, and had taken cover in the thickest undergrowth they could penetrate. Brad didn't actually hold out much hope of remaining hidden if the soldiers found the path. They heard the fire that took hold in the old building, the timbers cracking and the flames roaring. Before long the smell reached them, but thankfully the forest was too thick for much smoke to permeate. They waited a long time, well after the last sounds of any human activity, until, leaving Lucy concealed, Brad crept back to the clearing and looked around.

The flames had all but died away, the dry wood quickly consumed. The remains smouldered and crackled. Occasionally flames danced across the surface as small draughts moved around the clearing. Brad cast his eyes further afield, the scene shimmering through the heat haze. He saw no one but he still crept quietly when he turned and made his way back to Lucy.

'Come on,' He said, 'There's nothing for us back there, we'll move on along the path.'

'Where do you think it goes Brad?'

He almost snapped at her, how in hells name could he possibly know where the path led? Instead he smiled at her and said, 'I really don't know, but it hasn't been used for a long time so I doubt we'll meet anyone coming the other way.'

Little did he know how wrong he was.

Brad hoisted the larger of the two packs over his shoulder and fitted Lucy up with hers. Taking up the machete he started along the path, hacking the thicker greenery with the blunt instrument and pushing the lighter stuff aside. Lucy plodded on behind him collecting the occasional springy leaves and branches across the face, but there were no complaints. Even when the cans in the pack started to cut into her back she just shifted the load and carried on in his footprints. After about an hour he stopped to rest. He supposed they had covered a couple of miles and would have been surprised had he known they were not quite a mile from the clearing. Lucy flopped down onto the jungle floor, removing her pack. Not a word was spoken - there was nothing to say.

Brad realised he was very thirsty, but didn't say anything to Lucy. After she had asked where the path led he had given some serious thought to the question. The hut was originally built for a fisherman, or so he assumed, and a fisherman would need fresh water like anyone else. It therefore stood to reason that the path must lead to a fresh water supply. What he couldn't explain was why the spotter didn't use the path if indeed it led to the nearest river or stream. He also thought it would be closer than this.

He said: 'Let's press on a little further and then we'll stop and get something to eat.'

'Do you want me to take a turn at the front?' asked Lucy, 'It must be harder work than just following.'

'I'm fine thanks, but I may take you up on that later,' he replied. With that he pushed on up the trail and as he went he thought that he was going to have to change the archetypal image of women that he had held for so long. Maybe it was just the type of women that he'd met, the office girls with their perfect hairstyles and painted nails that couldn't even decide what they wanted to drink. But then again nurses couldn't be like that; he thought of Julie working away in the destruction following Pearl Harbour before an unexploded bomb detonating killed her as she tried to save the leg of a wounded Sailor. Maybe it was the way he was brought up, believing that women were the fairer, and therefore the weaker sex; his role in life therefore being to protect them. Whatever the reason he was now sure that he would have to reappraise his outlook on the subject. It also meant that any women he met in the future would have a lot to live up to.

'Brad look out!'

Her shout brought him back to the present with a splash. Swinging the machete through a screen of greenery he'd lost his footing on the steep bank leading down to a pool in a small river. Throwing himself backwards he'd managed to stop his forward motion, but not until he had ended up sitting in about six inches of water at the edge of the pool. He looked up at Lucy, his face like a thundercloud.

'Don't say a god dam word, excuse my French.'

In return she started giggling. It began as a stifled grunt but she couldn't hold it back and it blossomed into a full-blown fit. Brad tried to keep a straight face but the effort of doing so became too much and he too started to chuckle. Whether it was the relief at finding water, or just the chance to laugh, who can tell, but laugh they did, until their sides were fit to burst. Brad filled his hands with water as if to take a drink. At the last minute he diverted his hands and threw the water over Lucy, who squealed loudly and still giggling came down the bank and sat in the water beside him. Naturally it turned into a water fight, both of them receiving a soaking before Brad got hold of her wrists and pushed her back on to the bank. He looked into her eyes, her face suddenly serious. He let go of her wrists and her arms slowly came up around his neck.

'Get your hands in the air!'

The spell was immediately broken. Brad pushed himself off Lucy reaching for the revolver tucked in his belt. At the same time he rolled and looked around, trying to locate the source of the shout. A bullet slammed into the bank about a foot from his head, kicking up dirt into his face.

'I said get your hands up or next time I don't miss.'

Brad dropped the gun and raised his hands in the air. The shot had come from the other side of the stream and the voice had definitely been American.

Brad said: 'OK, don't shoot. I'm American and the young lady is English.'

'Shut up and keep your hands in the air...You, the woman...get your hands in the bloody air!' The voice had risen to a scream.

'Look I told you,' said Brad. 'We're on your side, I'm a US Air Force pilot shot down a couple of days ago. The name's Charles Bradley, but everyone calls me Brad, and this here's Lucy Fairbrother.'

Brad started to move, checking to see if Lucy was OK.

'Don't move, stay exactly where you are.'

Brad had had enough of this treatment from a fellow countryman and was turning to confront his antagonist (which thinking about it later would probably been the last thing he ever did,) when a new voice came on the scene.

'Alright, this has gone far enough.' The voice was quiet with a soft Irish accent, but for all that the command in those few words was unmistakable.

From amongst the trees on the far bank a short rotund man in an ill fitting khaki safari suit appeared. He lifted the sweat-stained, soft-brimmed hat to reveal a bald head. He looked to be about fifty years old and had a gentle smiling face. He wore a small white moustache matching the ring of hair surrounding his bald pate.

'I'm Matthew Golding, Fa...'

'Just let me handle this would you, Father.' The owner of the American voice now revealed himself. Dressed in dark trousers and a dirty white tee shirt was a man in his mid to late twenties. His skin was dark, almost Mediterranean and his head was topped with a shock of jet-black hair. He had a thin face with deep-sct eyes, and he was scowling. He was also carrying a rifle that looked far too big for him, but made him a dangerous man.

'You really ought to keep your son under control.' Brad said, addressing the older man whilst keeping a wary eye on the gun.

Golding looked confused for a moment and then smiled at Brad's forgivable mistake.

'That's Father Golding, as in a man of the cloth. But please call me Matthew.'

The Priest waded across the pool, stooped to help Lucy to her feet and then shook hands with Brad. He turned to look at the other member of his party who was still on the far side of the river, pointing the rifle at them.

'Oh for goodness sake Frank will you lower that rifle before you hurt someone.' Then turning to Brad and Lucy he continued. 'Please forgive my friend he tends to get a little carried away.'

Brad still had an eye on Frank and relaxed as the barrel of the weapon was lowered. He retrieved his own revolver and stuffed it into the belt of his trousers.

He said to Matthew: 'We'd better get out of here; we've just had a close run in with some Jap soldiers and if they've heard that shot they won't be long in finding us.'

'Right, well follow us then,' said Matthew. 'Frank here was a plane spotter and had a shack near the beach. We were going to hide up there for a while, until we think of a plan to get off the island.'

Brad turned and gave Frank a long stare. He said: 'We just came from there and the Japs have burned it to the ground.' Frank stared straight back at him, the rifle instinctively rising a few inches towards Brad. As a flush started to spread across his face he looked away, focusing his attention on Lucy whose wet dress was clinging to her body. Brad never mentioned the body of the spotter they had found at the hut but he knew that Frank couldn't be trusted. At best he was a liar and at worst a murderer.

'In that case I suggest we follow the river,' said Matthew. 'Which way would you like to go?'

'Let's go upstream,' said Brad. 'The Japs we saw went back to the beach and we don't want to bump into them.' Had he decided to move downstream he may have had some disturbing memories, such as fishing with a forked stick, which could have started off a string of revelations seriously testing his sanity.

As it was Matthew agreed and the three of them started to make their way along the bank. Frank obviously didn't like being cut out of the decision making process and started to protest loudly but Brad immediately cut him off.

'Look, if you don't like it then you can go your own way.'

Having stamped his authority on the group he turned his back on Frank and the rifle that had raised another couple of inches, and carried on along the bank. Frank stood and watched them for a few moments, and then muttering to himself he followed at a distance of about 15 feet.

Chapter Thirteen

Laura stood staring at the empty bed in the Intensive Care Unit of Haslar Hospital. There were no tears, just a look of bewilderment on her face. She turned as Doctor Niall Jenkins came up behind her. He noticed that the dark smudges under her eyes were getting bigger, but no amount of persuasion or medical advice had been able to convince her to give up the day and night vigil at Harry's bedside. The little cubicle had become like a home to her; they had even moved an armchair in so that she could get a little sleep.

But all that was coming to an end. Harry was being moved to private nursing home in Truro that specialised in care for long term coma patients. Laura and his family had objected when the decision to move him had first been put to them, but Commander Jenkins had gently explained that there was nothing more that intensive care could do for him. He thankfully didn't have to say that he could no longer justify him occupying a valuable bed, these were after all intelligent people. They had quickly come to terms with the situation and after some discussion had decided Harry should stay in the Southwest rather than travelling up to Scotland to be near his parents. That way Laura would be able to continue her work as well as visiting Harry daily and his parents, who were retired, would take it in turns to stay at Laura's flat. It was lucky that the coma clinic had been set up in the south-west and would mean that this was by far the best option. Laura, though, still had some reservations about the move.

'What if he has another of those attacks?' she asked.

'We've been through all this, Laura,' he said patiently. 'There is nothing to suggest that he will, and lets face it, nothing that we did made any difference, he just came back.' He put his arm around her shoulder and gave her a gentle hug. 'Come on the ambulance is ready to go. I've cleared it with the crew for you to ride with him. Peter is going to drive your car back.'

And so she left the ward for the final time. At the Hospital entrance she gave Niall a tearful hug, thanking him for all his efforts, and then climbing into the back of the Naval ambulance she settled down for the long ride to the clinic. She took Harry's hand gently in hers, still amazed at how cold it was.

And still he slept.

Chapter Fourteen

Brad and his party stopped for the night in a small clearing around another pool they had come across. The going had been relatively easy. The jungle had changed from the thick undergrowth he had had to contend with at the periphery. The canopy overhead was much more complete, blocking out far more light, and the undergrowth didn't get enough of the suns rays to get a really good hold. However, occasionally there were areas that took a lot of effort to get through, and apart from a little help from Matthew, Brad had been doing all the trail blazing and was exhausted. And so they had stopped early for the night.

Frank, who had remained at his station behind the party, had offered no help on the expedition, and now dropped down to sit with his back against a tree and shut his eyes. There had been little chance to talk earlier and so Brad told his and Lucy's story. Matthew listened carefully, asking the occasional question as their tale unfolded. Frank, on the other hand, showed no interest but Brad was sure that he was taking in every word. Whilst he talked Lucy prepared a simple meal from their supply of meagre rations. They ate when Brad had finished their story; Frank still refusing to move from his position against the tree.

Brad flicked his head towards Frank and said to Matthew. 'What's with your friend then?'

'I hardly know him,' replied Matthew. 'We only met up two days ago. I had to flee the mission far on the other side of the island a couple of weeks ago...' And so Matthew told his story:

Matthew Mark Golding was born in 1890 in Belfast to very strict Catholic parents. His entire upbringing was geared towards the Church; even his forenames were taken from the New Testament. Looking back in later years his only surprise was that his parents hadn't gone the whole hog and added Luke and John to his Christian names.

Many children brought up in this way rebelled against their parents' wishes; indeed some turned their back on the Church altogether, but not Matthew. Being short and fat as a child he was often the butt of many schoolyard pranks and vulnerable to more serious forms of bullying. At these times Matthew found comfort in the teachings of the Bible, turning the other cheek one could say, and before long he found that the taunting ceased and friendships formed in their place.

And so began his devotion to Christ. He followed a natural path into the Priesthood, never considering any other course on the way. He soon found that he wasn't cut out to be a run of the mill Priest, preaching to the 'respectable' congregations that attended his church every Sunday. He became drawn to the poorer areas of Belfast, finding a certain affinity to the dregs of humanity that made a living on the streets. But even this wasn't enough; he was convinced that his calling lay abroad.

In 1929 his chance came in the form of a missionary trip to China but it seemed that God was to have another hand in his destiny. Short of arriving at Shanghai the old wooden vessel that had safely transported him and the other passengers and crew half way round the world broke up and sank in a ferocious storm. Alone and clinging to life, or to be more precise, a wooden barrel, Matthew was rescued by two fishermen. He was brought back to a small settlement on the Island of Bonin on the South Honshu Ridge.

'...and I've been here ever since. Then about two weeks ago the Japanese Army landed on a beach not far from the village. The Chief insisted that I leave and find somewhere to hide in the jungle until they were gone. I wanted to stay and ensure that they weren't mal-treated, but they seemed to think they would be in more trouble if I were found with them. From what you say, Brad, I assume they are still here.'

'But how did you survive?' asked Lucy.

'Well that part was really quite easy,' he said. 'I was given plenty of provisions and camp was set up for me near to the village. Men came twice a day with food and water until a few days ago when they stopped coming.

'And what about Frank?' asked Brad. 'How does he fit into all this?'

Matthew looked over at the surly young man sitting under the tree. 'I really don't know to be perfectly honest with you. I met him shortly after the natives stopped coming. After a day without anything to eat or drink I was getting a little worried and decided to creep back to the edge of the village to see what was going on. Frank frightened the wits out of me, appearing on the path with that gun and all. By all accounts he was spotting for your lot in the shack you've just come from and was flushed out by the Japanese. We've been hiding out in the jungle waiting for the coast to clear.' Matthew pondered for a while before continuing in a conspiratorial whisper worthy of the confession box. 'I'm not really convinced that his story holds true; I don't know why and it's probably unfounded, but there's something he's hiding or that he's scared of. Last night he disappeared into the forest. He said he'd been to check his hut on the other side of the island. When he returned he said there were still soldiers there.'

Too damned right he's got something to hide, thought Brad, like the murder of the real aircraft spotter he'd left at the hut. Brad decided not to say anything at this time but promised himself that he would watch Frank like a hawk.

Some time later Matthew turned in, taking as much cover as possible from the surrounding undergrowth. They had moved away from the water as the night brought a myriad of airborne blood-suckers out from the stream looking for prey that came down to drink. Despite the move the 'little blighters', as Matthew called them, still found their exposed flesh and made for an extremely uncomfortable night.

Brad climbed to his feet and walked over to Lucy who was checking their inventory.

'Walk with me a while?' he asked, and bent to help her up when she nodded. Once they were clear of the others they stopped and Brad turned to face her.

'What do you think of our new friends?' he asked.

Lucy answered immediately. 'Oh Father Golding is a lovely man.' She seemed to be genuinely pleased to have joined up with Matthew, maybe seeing him as a surrogate father after her recent family losses. 'But as for that Frank,' she continued. 'He's another kettle of fish altogether.'

It seemed that nobody trusted Frank one little bit. Lucy went on to explain how he gave her the creeps and how she felt that he was always staring at her, his eyes seeming to see straight through her yet at the same time taking in the soft contours of her body.

'He frightens me, Brad,' she finished quietly.

'There's nothing to worry about, I'll keep a close eye on our friend Frank.'

'What's our next move Brad; we can't just keep on following the river to its source.'

'I've been thinking about that,' he said. 'I think I need to take a look at the set up the Japs have got here. There's still a war on and any information I can get now could come in useful once we're rescued.' He purposely put across a positive attitude though he wasn't that confident himself. He could hardly see her in the dim light but sensed that she could see through his optimism, but she was sensitive enough not to say anything. He continued. 'We may even be able to do something to put a spanner in the works for them; cause them a few problems.'

This time she did say something. 'Do you really think that's a good idea Brad? I mean, they've no knowledge that we're out here at the moment, why advertise the fact with what oould only be a token gesture? And we've got to think of Father Golding. He's not really up to active service.'

'Perhaps you're right,' he conceded. 'Maybe I'll just go for a recce.' They stood in silence then, both wrapped up in their own thoughts. Maybe they were both hoping to continue what had almost started on the bank of the river earlier in the day, but the moment had gone, at least for the time being. Eventually they walked slowly back to the campsite. Matthew was snoring loudly, oblivious to the chill that was setting in and the insects that 'sang' in the night. Frank, on the other hand, was nowhere to be seen as they approached, but then appeared suddenly from the vicinity of their packs and crept guiltily back to his tree.

Brad collected the remains of the blanket from his pack, noticing in the process that the contents had been rummaged through. He looked over at Frank but he was lying back as if asleep. Taking the blanket over to Lucy he made her comfortable and then stretched himself out between her and Frank. He had considered a sentry roster through the night but had come to the conclusion that if the Japs came along there was not much that they could do any way. He also had to face the fact that they were all pretty well exhausted and needed to get a decent night's rest. He thought sleep would come straight away but now that he was ready for it, it eluded him. His thoughts kept coming back to Frank. There was something about him, something sinister like a drink that left a bad taste in your mouth. There must be a reason behind his hostility, something about the group that got his back up.

Brad rolled over and looked at the silhouette of Lucy as she slept. Maybe it was something to do with her, jealousy perhaps, as he could be excused in thinking there was a relationship going on between her and Brad. But what had made Frank fire a shot at them, or more accurately at him, when they obviously posed no threat. Perhaps he was just very nervous having had a run in with the Japs, thought Brad, but more likely he was frightened that his secret, whatever it was, would be discovered. Brad continued to run things over in his mind until, at long last, he fell asleep.

Chapter Fifteen

Brad was flying. He looked up and saw the clear blue sky, whilst all around and ahead of him the fluffy cumulus clouds had edges so well-defined that they appeared almost solid. The convoluted formations created rolling hills and deep, secret valleys, and amongst these Brad played his favourite flying game. It wasn't often that he had an aircraft he could do with as he pleased and not worry about the chance of an engagement, but every now and again an instrument check would come up and he jumped at the opportunity. Now he was putting his Wildcat through its paces, 'low flying' through the clouds. Those sharp out crops of moisture giving the same effect as the ground rushing past, as he skimmed above the cloud tops. He twisted his aircraft through an impossibly tight 'valley', momentarily immersed in white light as he burst through the side before popping out into the clear air once more. Unlike the catastrophic effects had he really been low flying, the only consequence to the aircraft was a slight jarring as it picked up some turbulence from the unstable airflow that was forming the cloud structures.

Suddenly the aircraft around him was dissolving, gradually fading away to nothing. It left him floating in the vast open skies. His immediate reaction was one of panic, causing him to tumble out of control into the clouds. He was surprised at the change of temperature, a sudden drop of 10 degrees or so. He also became disorientated, losing all bearing of which way was up or down, until, at last, he burst through the bottom of the cloud and was faced with the sight of the sea's surface rushing up at him. Instinctively he stretched out his arms and was astonished when he realised that he had some control over his descent. He experimented by pushing his arms forward and was pleased to see that his body followed. By curving his arms upwards he arrested his descent and found himself flying once more.

He took himself up through a gap in the clouds and carried on where he had been forced to break off in his Wildcat. The feeling of exhilaration was something he had never experienced before; a feeling of complete freedom. As the speed of his flight swept back his hair, Brad was aware of the silence around him. He was used to noise and vibration associated with flying and yet here he was in the tranquillity that a free fall parachutist feels. But he wasn't falling, he was flying. Once again he burst into the tops of the clouds and was lost in a timeless white space. It wasn't wet or cold, as he had expected, more a comforting blanket that surrounded him, warming and calming him.

Brad let the elements take him then. He lost all track of time but was vaguely aware that he was being led somewhere. He was caught by surprise, therefore, when thinking that he was flying straight and level he popped out of cloud in a head down attitude and a left-hand turn. The contrast between what he saw and what his inner ear was telling his brain caused some severe symptoms of disorientation, often suffered by aviators flying in cloud. Before he had time to sort it out he lost control and began tumbling towards the sea.

Many dreams of this nature would have finished at this stage, before the individual hit the surface. In Brad's case he was able to apply the lessons learned earlier in the dream and during real flying, and he pulled out of the dive without any trouble. In doing so he spotted a disturbance on the sea's surface a little way in the distance. He immediately recognised it as the strange contraption he had spotted when he had crashed on his last mission. He steered towards it, eager to get a closer look and was surprised to see the vision transform into a large, blue airframe of sorts, with the propeller facing sideways and at the back and a huge rotating disc under which it hung. He noted that it bore the markings of the Royal Navy and he could make out the two pilots in the front, staring through him at something Brad was unaware of.

'So this must be the Brit's secret weapon,' he said to himself, as he circled the Helicopter. His mind quickly grasped the principles of the hover as he watched the water being thrashed about by the down flow of air. Indeed he once got a little close and was nearly forced down into the water. What amazed him were the obvious advances in technology that had been made to enable the contraption to be built.

Suddenly Brad felt that he was no longer in control of his own flight path. He had been passing over the top of the disc and now found himself being dragged around the circle with the blades. He tried desperately to 'fly' out of the perimeter but was unable to make any headway. The spinning was rapidly increasing and he realised, not without some trepidation, that he was being sucked into the disc. Try as he might, he could not divert his progress, and as he approached the inevitable collision he shut his eyes. His world was now a gyrating nightmare of noise as he came closer and closer to the rotating rotor head, until...

'Er..Sir, those lights, 30 right would you say?'

Brad heard the strange guttural voice through the bulky helmet he found himself wearing. Before he knew what he was doing he said. 'Yes, why?'

He looked around and found himself standing between the two pilot's seats in the front of the helicopter. He was amazed at the huge array of instruments in the cockpit, but his attention was quickly drawn back to the conversation that he seemed to be involved in.

'Well...' from the mystery voice.

'Come on man, spit it out.' He returned through gritted teeth. The conversation seemed vaguely familiar to him yet the surroundings were completely alien. He tried to take in some of the details; he was dressed up in a constricting canvas suit with rubber round the wrists and neck on top of which was an extremely sophisticated life jacket.

'Sorry Sir, It's just that I've never seen anything like this before. From about 15 to 45 degrees right is full of noise, but it's not just normal wide band noise, it seems to be modulated in some way. It's as if somebody's put some kind of message on top of it, and it's getting closer Sir; it's on the nose round to 90 degrees now.'

Brad knew that he had to reply and though the words didn't make any sense they flowed easily.

'I don't like this one little bit. McKilroy raise the sonar body, let's get the hell out of here and see what's going on. Smokey, give the Ship a call and see if they are recording any of this. Oh and while you're at it give them an accurate position.'

Brad realised that he had entered the aircraft in the middle of some sort of drama, and that he was taking part as one of the crew. He had no idea what the outcome was likely to be but felt that his contributions were important.

A new voice split the air, alarm obvious in the urgency of the words.

'Torque split, call NR.'

Another voice, equally agitated, answered 'NR is 96%...94...90% shit..brace, brace, brace!!'

Brad now knew what was about to happen. He'd seen the helicopter pitch into the sea when he'd been floating down on his parachute. Unfortunately he couldn't anticipate the violence of the crash, expecting to just drop gently onto the water and roll over. Instead he was thrown forward into the pilots' seat and was aware of a searing pain in his left shoulder, when he jerked awake, the echo of a scream in his head. He grabbed for his shoulder but the pain was gone. He quickly acknowledged his surroundings and looked around guiltily. Seeing he had disturbed nobody he lay down and started to analyse his dream.

Within moments he had fallen into a deep sleep, and the details of the dream started to fade in the corridors of his mind.

Chapter Sixteen

Had the Nursing home in Truro wired their long term coma patients up to equipment measuring the activity and output of the brain, they would have got a very interesting trace from their newest arrival, Lieutenant Tony Harrison, that evening. As it was, no one, not even Laura, as she sat in the very plush hospital surroundings afforded by the single room holding his hand, knew that for the first time since his accident, Harry was dreaming and reliving his recent trauma. There were no telltale visible signs. Laura was only aware that Harry still slept.

Chapter Seventeen

Brad awoke to the sound of raised voices. His dream was just a vague memory pushed to the back of his mind and he eased himself up onto one elbow to listen.

'I don't care a damn what he thinks or where he's going, and if you take his side then I don't care a damn about you either.' The voice inevitably belonged to Frank, and as Brad looked over at him he saw that Frank was red in the face and was aggressively leaning over Matthew, shouting at him. Matthew, on the other hand, was calmly sitting back looking up at the apoplectic youth.

'Calm down Frank,' he said. 'We're all in this together. It's not a question of taking sides, we have to pool our resources and, if necessary, fight the common foe.'

Frank looked up and saw Brad looking at them. He immediately turned away and said more quietly. 'I didn't ask him to come along and I'll be damned if he thinks he can order me about.'

'I've no intention of ordering you about, Frank, but so far as I can see you've not come out with any suggestions or made any contribution to our effort.'

'Who the hell asked you anyway?' shouted Frank, and without a second glance he stormed off to the river to get himself a drink.

Lucy had now sat up. 'What on earth was all that about?' she asked of no one in particular.

'Don't worry your pretty little head, my dear,' said Matthew in a gentle voice. 'It's just our volatile friend, Frank. He wanted me to split away from the pair of you and make our own way out of this mess. He seems to feel threatened by your presence, especially yours Brad.'

Frank was making his way back to the group, his eyes shifting about but not looking anyone in the face. He dropped himself down against his tree and seemed set to sulk for the rest of the day, like a spoilt child. He surprised them all then, by saying. 'What's it to be then Lieutenant?'

Something about the way he said it seemed familiar to Brad, who was starting to form an opinion on just exactly what Frank might be.

'Well first I think we all need to sit down and discuss it. I've got some ideas that I've talked over with Lucy, but I'm always open to fresh views or opinions.'

'Well why don't we start off with your thoughts then and we'll see where we might go from there,' said Matthew. And so Brad explained his ideas for seeking out the Japanese and seeing what they were up to. He felt it was important to establish whether they were preparing for any specific operations, or whether they were just using the island as a stores depot or staging post. When he came to the part about possible action to sabotage the enemy's efforts, he noticed that Frank perked up; starting to stroke the rifle that had found it's way across his knees. Matthew's thoughts on direct action were much the same as Lucy's, but for different reasons. He had never killed a man in his life and saw no reason to do so now. Privately he doubted that he could even do it in self-defence. When he put his views forward, Frank scoffed at him as if to call him a coward, but it was water off a duck's back to Matthew.

It was finally agreed, surprisingly by all parties, that they would make their way back towards the village. Frank actually contributed to the discussion by suggesting a place close to the community that would make a good hiding place for Matthew and Lucy. He and Brad would then push on and reconnoitre the Japanese positions. He surprised them further still by suggesting that as he knew the path back to the village perhaps he should do a spell of trail blazing. Brad conceded without argument, happy to hand over the machete and settle for an easy ride down the back.

They also decided that they could risk lighting a small fire. Half an hour later, having feasted on tinned fruit, they were enjoying a brew of tea made up in the empty fruit cans. Shortly after that they were on their way. Brad took hold of Lucy's arm and they fell back out of earshot of Frank.

'What do you think of that turn about by Frank?' he asked her.

'I don't know,' she replied. 'Perhaps he suddenly saw what a horse's ass he'd been.'

Brad laughed at the choice of words she had used, but then became more serious. 'No, I think it's more than that. I think he's jumping at the chance to move in the opposite direction to the dead spotter that we left behind. He knew if we went back there questions would have to be asked and his lies would come under scrutiny. I also think he's looking forward to getting into some action, to get another chance at killing; I think he enjoys it.'

Lucy looked up into his face, surprised at the picture Brad had painted of his own countryman.

'Who do you think he really is?' she asked.

'I really have no idea, but I suppose a lot of things point to a deserter. A man of his age really has no business being here that I can think of. He's definitely hiding something and being a deserter fits the bill as well as anything I can think of.'

'Maybe he really was the spotter and the other man was some intruder or something.'

'If that were the case why didn't he mention it?'

Lucy pondered this point for a few seconds and then, being unable to come up with a feasible explanation, accepted that Brad was probably right.

It was very much later in the day that they arrived at their destination. The jungle had changed again; the undergrowth building up once more, and the going had been tough over the last few hours. Earlier on in the day they had detoured from the track that Frank and Matthew had taken from the village, and now their route cut back towards the coast. Once established on the new course under the direction of Frank, who seemed to know the island surprisingly well, Brad had taken over the lead. Now his stamina was starting to fade. The blunt machete seemed to weigh more each time he swung it to smash away the forest plants that obstructed their progress. His right arm felt like lead, the biceps burning with each agonising arc of movement. He was also losing a lot of moisture, the sweat beading on his naked skin and staining the material of his uniform. He was just about to call a halt when the machete crashed against something far more solid than the foliage he had become used to. As it rang out, vibrations of searing pain ran up his arm causing him to drop the machete and grab the injured limb in his free hand. Ducking down to retrieve the knife allowed the rest of the party to catch up and draw level with him.

'What's happened,' asked Lucy allowing the concern to creep into her voice.

'It seems to be some sort of statue,' he replied. 'And it appears to be a big one.' Brad was now hacking away at the thicker woodwork with the machete, pulling large sections of foliage away from the statue.

'Stop wasting time on that old thing,' grumbled Frank as he pushed his way past Lucy and grabbed the machete from Brad's hand. 'We have arrived.'

Brad felt the ire rise in him, wanting to respond to the taunt. He felt like provoking Frank into a fight that he knew he could easily win. Maybe later, he thought to himself, we need to keep him sweet for the time being. He contented himself by rolling his eyes at Lucy who smiled at him and laid her cool fingers on his fore arm.

'Don't worry,' she whispered. 'I know what you're thinking and respect you all the more for showing restraint.'

Brad smiled back at her and then, with Matthew bringing up the rear, they followed Frank who pushed himself around the side of the stone idol, through a gap that Brad had cleared. They found themselves entering yet another small clearing in the forest, though this one had obviously been neglected for years. There were two small mounds on the far side of the open ground and these were covered in creepers much as the statue was.

'This was once a holy temple,' said Frank, and then looking to Matthew he continued: 'But not to your God, Father.' He sneered as he turned away and fought through the undergrowth across to the larger of the two mounds. It was about five-foot high and as they drew nearer Brad could see that it was a building made up from stones of the same grey substance as the statue. He thought it was probably some kind of lava that had been cut into blocks for the buildings and a far larger section carved to form the statue. By probing with the machete, Frank had located an entrance and was gently easing the undergrowth aside. Without disturbing the outward appearance too much he revealed an opening and disappeared inside. The rest of the group followed and were surprised by the deceptive size of the structure when viewed from the outside, as once inside they appeared to be in a spacious circular room. There was little plant growth inside; only pushing in around the door and a window that could just be identified in the gloom on the far side of the single chamber. The atmosphere, though clammy, was cooler than outside and the air had a musty smell, probably Brad thought, due to the bare earthen floor.

'This should keep you out of the way of the Japs and give you some protection from the elements,' said Frank. 'There's a small stream about quarter of a mile west of here that'll keep you supplied with fresh water.' With that he turned to leave them.

'You certainly seem to know an awful lot about this place considering you were stationed on the other side of the island,' said Brad, who still hadn't really got his last run in with Frank out of his system.

'Well the Japs weren't always here and I decided I would need somewhere to hide up if they did arrive. So I did some exploring a couple of months ago and bumped into old Gungadin out there. Anyway I don't have to explain myself to the likes of you.' And with that he strode out of the room.

'Well!' said Lucy. 'I've never met anyone as rude as that man in my life.'

'I think maybe I touched on a nerve,' said Brad. 'Anyway, lets get sorted out here and then we'll decide what to do next.'

As Lucy and Matthew started to sort through their meagre provisions, Brad went out into the clearing to confront Frank but he was nowhere to be seen. He had a quick hunt around the clearing, but the sun was starting to set and there really wasn't much to be seen. He found the path leading to the stream that Frank had mentioned, and again there were no signs that it had been used recently. Finally he ended up at the statue. He estimated that it was about 12 to 13 feet tall, though it was hard to judge with all the creepers twisting their way up it and into the trees that had closed in around it. The only details that he could make out were the legs, between the shin and just above the knee. They were carved out of a single piece of rock so far as he could see, and the sculptor had 'clothed' the legs in some sort of garment. Running his hand across the surface confirmed his first thoughts about the type of stone used. It was rough to his touch and as he looked closely he could make out small depressions like burst bubbles all over the surface. The light was fading quickly now and he could not see much more of the structure. Brad had no idea how old the statue was, or what it represented. He could only go on what Frank had told them, for what it was worth, and that meant it was some sort of god or idol.

Brad strolled back to the hut, his mind wondering through thoughts of ancient peoples worshipping the stone symbol of their faith. He speculated about the type of civilisation that had built this place, and was so engrossed in his thoughts that he was unaware of the movement in the shadows by the entrance to their chosen rest place. Just as he reached the door the shadow suddenly emerged to form a crouched figure.

'You want to be more careful, Brad, I could easily have been a Jap lying in wait.'

Brad recovered quickly from the shock that had gripped his body as he had first seen the movement. He grabbed Frank by the scruff of his neck and pulled his face close to his own. Talking quietly through gritted teeth he said. 'And you want to be a bit more careful who you sneak up on or you'll find yourself dead.'

Frank tried to pull away, turning his head, but Brad forced the issue and brought their faces closer together.

'And just where in hell's name have you been anyway?'

Frank exhaled into Brad's face, his breath stale and sour with overtones of tobacco. 'Not that it's any business of yours, but someone had to go down and check the water supply.'

Frank shook himself free and strutted into the shelter. Brad was left standing alone in the dark with the now familiar feeling of wanting to wipe the arrogant smile off Frank's face. Instead Brad composed himself and entered the stone building as if nothing had happened. Frank was sulking across the far side of the room and ignored him as he broached the subject about what to do next. It was quickly decided that Matthew and Lucy would stay in the 'settlement' as planned, and the other two would set off at first light to have a scout around. Frank never contributed to the discussion, but neither did he offer any objections, and the others took this as agreement.

Later, whilst Lucy prepared a simple meal from the cans they had lugged half way across the island, Brad and Matthew went out into the clearing to see what they could find to make the night more comfortable. They had not been expecting to bump into friendly company and consequently they were not prepared for it. They had already decided that one of the priorities during the reconnaissance trip was to find a food supply. Matthew had given Brad an idea of the village layout, and where he could expect to find stores and provisions that would not be immediately missed.

Brad did the best he could hacking down ferns and other broad-leafed plants, and Matthew collected them up and formed a pile by the entrance to the hut. Later Brad would fashion these into excuses for beds, which would not only protect them from the hard, cool floor, but would also turn out to be surprisingly comfortable. After a short time collecting in silence, they found themselves at the far side of the clearing, close to the statue, and Brad once again, voiced his doubts about Frank.

Having listened to the account of their last tête-à-tête, Matthew could offer no words of encouragement, in fact on the contrary he said: 'That's not the first time he's disappeared in the middle of the night without a good explanation. On the first night after we met he was gone for a couple of hours, saying only that he wanted to be sure they hadn't been followed. I was still too glad to have found an ally and was only too happy to believe him without question. Mind you,' he continued. 'I had no reason to doubt him then. In the light of things that have gone on recently, well...'

'Not to worry Father, as you said, you had no reason to disbelieve him. What's important now is that we look after each other and keep an eye on Frank.'

'You're right, of course, in fact I suppose we ought to get back and see that Lucy is all right.'

As they turned and made their way back to the pile of greenery they had harvested, neither of them saw the movement as Frank, hunched up in the shadows, silently re-entered the hut from the position by the door that he had been occupying for the previous five minutes.

Chapter Eighteen

When Brad awoke the following morning, the sun was already up, the weak influence of its rays filling the room with a dim light. Looking around he saw the sleeping bodies of Matthew and Lucy, but noted that Frank had already risen and was nowhere to be seen. Easing himself from the makeshift bed he made his way to the door and peered out at the dawn. The light was still low but he wasn't really sure how much of this was due to the forest cutting out the sun, or whether it was still early.

'You managed to drag yourself up then,' said Frank, who was sat by the statue cleaning his rifle with a dirty piece of cloth. Brad didn't rise to the bait; instead he made a super human effort, attempting to relieve some of the tension between them.

'Perhaps you could give my revolver a quick going over whilst I get a few rations together.'

Frank stared at him, and Brad was sure the answer would be no, and once again found himself wondering at the make up of the man facing him when he held out his hand for the weapon. He handed it over and watched as Frank emptied the chambers and worked the action. Brad noted the ease with which he striped down the service revolver, his sure handling a sign of familiarity. He turned back to the hut just as Lucy appeared bleary eyed and framed in the doorway. She handed Brad one of the home-made rucksacks.

'I made this up last night. It should keep you going for a few days but you do need to sort out a supply of water.'

'Water won't be a problem.' Frank had come up behind Brad and was staring at Lucy with a leer on his face. Blushing, she fixed her eyes firmly on Brad and continued. 'When do you think you'll be back?'

This time Brad got in first and said. 'This is only an initial look see; we'll probably be back before nightfall. I want to have a council of war before we take any direct action.'

'Well be careful, I...'

'How touching...come on Romeo.'

Brad ignored Frank and walked over to Lucy, gently kissing her on the cheek. 'Don't worry,' he said quietly. 'Nothing's going to happen; we're just going to have a look where we stand.' He smiled at her and turned, joined Frank and together they made their way out of the clearing.

The going was quite easy and they soon reached the river, where they took the opportunity of filling up with water. Seeing that they would be able to cross at some narrows just upstream, Brad was again surprised at the local knowledge that Frank was demonstrating. He had obviously been on the island for sometime and he was starting to wonder if he had misjudged the man. However the more he thought about it, the more it just didn't look right. Nothing innocent, in Brad's mind, could warrant the behaviour that Frank had been displaying, and he had already been caught out in at least one falsehood.

Suddenly, Brad was aware that Frank had dropped from sight. Natural instinct took over, and he followed suit, collapsing to the ground with as little movement or sound as possible. Lying in the eerie silence he started to think he might be caught up in another of Frank's little games, but then there was a burst of noise from overhead as birds and monkeys were startled into action. Brad had occasionally been aware of the commotion in the canopy as they made their way below the tree top communities, but the wildlife had quickly settled down as they had rested at the water hole. Now though something had stirred them up again. Probably a predator of some sort thought Brad, but as he listened he became aware of voices approaching their position. He strained his ears, cocking his head towards the noise, and felt his heart jump into his mouth as he recognised the language as Japanese.

Brad risked a quick look around and spotted Frank belly crawling into some thick undergrowth. Again he followed Frank's lead, concealing himself as much as the circumstances allowed. The voices were getting louder and it soon became obvious that they were approaching the river from the far side. Brad caught a quick glimpse of two soldiers with rifles casually thrown over their shoulders making their way to the waters edge. From his position, looking between two large flat leaves, Brad assessed that there was little chance of being spotted at this stage. He remained absolutely still, watching as the two Japanese stopped and bent down to fill their water canteens. They continued to converse loudly in their native tongue, showing no caution at all. Had Brad been able to understand them he might have been surprised to discover they were discussing the fate of the American Airman that had been killed at the fisherman's hut. This in fact was the reason for their nonchalance; they no longer felt that there was any threat to them on the island.

Brad continued to watch, and was surprised when the two men, having finished drinking and filling their bottles, started to cross the river. He had assumed they would go back the way they had come, having visited the river just to collect water. Of course there was nothing to suggest that this was the case, and indeed, it started to look as if they were on a routine patrol. Brad ducked down further as they approached his bank. They climbed out of the water about 10 feet left of his position, and Brad let out a silent sigh of relief as he saw them turn and disappear along the path he and Frank had recently used. He hoped that they had not disturbed the forest too much and that the Japs wouldn't notice its recent use.

A few seconds later Brad felt his heart sink to his boots as he was filled with a sudden sense of foreboding; The path the Japs were following would lead them straight to the unsuspecting and unarmed Matthew and Lucy. He was on his feet in a flash, making his way towards Frank as quietly as his haste would allow, but Frank was already one step ahead of him. Brad watched as a crouched figure disappeared down the path, a vicious looking Bowie knife held in the right hand. Brad followed, unsure of how he would be able to contribute in the narrow path. As it was, he almost ran straight into Frank who had caught up with the rear soldier. He stopped and watched as Frank grabbed the man around the throat with his left arm. As the soldier's head was pulled round Brad saw the knife flash up and slide silently across the exposed flesh of his neck. He could only stand, fascinated and yet horrified, as the flesh parted and a flood of dark red blood gushed from the wound. The only sound was a gurgling as the air from the victim's lungs took its shortest escape route and bubbled through the gaping hole that widened as the head was forced back.

Unfortunately that small sound was enough and almost in slow motion Brad saw the lead soldier turn to see what his colleague's problem was. He was speaking as he turned, but stopped short as he took in the scene. Frank still held the dying man, a look of pleasure on his face as the last struggle for life ended. As he dropped him to the forest floor he became aware, for the first time, that the second soldier was now bringing his rifle to bear, and that he had no chance to defend himself. Brad had also come to the same conclusion and, without even knowing when he'd drawn the revolver, raised it and fired off two shots. The first missed, going wide to the left; his aim spoilt by the proximity of Frank's body. He adjusted slightly before the second shot. As the soldier worked the bolt to put a round into the chamber, something he should have done before starting the patrol and the only thing that saved Frank's life, the latter fell down and to the right giving Brad plenty of room. The shot seemed impossibly loud, even more so than the first for some reason, but still he heard the impact as the round smashed into the Japanese soldier's face. His head jerked back as the bullet drove through the cheekbone, just below the right eye. There was no scream, no grabbing the wound, the soldier dead before he had time to react. Brad was horrified as he saw the right hand side of his face disintegrate and the spray of blood as the bullet exited through the back of his head. All of Brad's killing had been done at a distance, the horrors of death held at bay by the cockpit of his aircraft. This was the first time he had seen the results of his own handiwork and he didn't much like it.

Frank was on his feet in an instance, shouting to Brad who was still standing with the revolver pointed down the path. 'What the hell did you shoot for; every Jap on the God dam island will have heard it.'

The anger that Brad had been holding back for the last two days finally erupted to the surface. He marched up to Frank, grabbed him by the shoulders, and screamed into his face. 'To save your miserable skin you ungrateful bastard. You may not have noticed whilst revelling in the kill of the one you all but beheaded, but you were about to be blown away. I had no God dammed choice.'

Frank looked momentarily embarrassed but then turned away and changed the subject. 'Come on, we can't leave these two lying here. Let's cover them up and get back to the others.'

They searched the two bodies, pocketing anything useful, and then dragged them into the jungle. They carefully covered up all signs of the encounter, though they had trouble removing the blood that had spilled across a large area of foliage on the path. Nothing was said until the task was complete and then Frank surprised Brad again by saying: 'Look...back there, thanks, I guess you saved my life.' He didn't go as far as shaking Brad's hand, but nonetheless it was a change for the better.

'No problem, perhaps you can do the same for me one day.'

The moment over, Brad turned and led the way back to the others. On arrival there was no sign of either of them, and it wasn't until they called out that Matthew and Lucy revealed themselves. They had heard the shots, and thinking the worst had climbed up onto the roof of their shelter. Concealing themselves amongst the thick undergrowth they had waited to see what would transpire.

Brad quickly explained what had occurred at the river, brushing over the finer details for the sakes of his listeners. He then handed up one of the Japanese soldier's rifles, along with some ammunition recovered from one of the bodies. Matthew took hold of it and gave Brad a questioning look.

'If it comes to a fire fight, Matthew, just fire it off in the air. The more they think there are of us, the better chance we stand.'

Lucy reached out and took the weapon from him. 'I'll take it if you would be happier, Father.' Cradling the weapon in her arms she expertly worked the action and rammed a round into the breech. She looked down at the astonished faces of Brad and Frank and said: 'My father taught me the basics, the day Pearl Harbour was attacked. I guess I was the son he never had.'

Frank and Brad left them to re-cover themselves on the roof, and took up strategic positions around the clearing that would allow them to ensnare anyone entering in a crossfire, yet at the same time preventing fratricide. They all settled down for the wait. Some two hours later they had heard nothing. The sun had reached its zenith and it had become unbearably hot, even in the shade that their hiding places offered. Surprisingly it was Frank who was the first to 'break ranks'. Unbeknown to the others he had spent the last hour absolutely still as an extremely large python had slowly made its way across his right boot. At one stage he was convinced that it had settled down to sleep away the afternoon, but eventually it had moved on. Now clear of the danger the after shock caused him to burst out into the clearing.

'Well if they're not here by now they're not coming,' he declared to no one in particular. Without waiting for a reply he disappeared into the hut. Gradually the others followed him into the cooler air.

'Ok, so what's next?' asked Lucy.

'I think we should carry on where we left off,' said Brad. 'Nothing has really changed. We just have to accept that those two men will eventually be missed and the Japs will be more wary.'

'I agree with Brad,' said Frank. Everybody turned to look at him, thinking they'd maybe misheard him. He smiled back at them, amused by their reaction to his new attitude.

Brad nodded his appreciation for the support and then said: 'Right we'll get going straight away and hopefully be in a position to check the Japs out by nightfall.'

There was a general murmur of agreement and so the two of them collected their weapons and provisions and set out for the river. There progress was much more cautious, pausing at every bend in the path to check there were no Japanese patrols. On reaching the place of the morning's action Frank indicated to Brad that the bodies had not been disturbed since they had left them. Brad noted that Frank was becoming far more amiable, even chatty, so much as their situation allowed.

Crossing the river they pressed into new territory, but the jungle never really changed. The path was clearly used more often, but at least it meant there was no trail blazing to be done. Frank had given Brad a fair idea of the route and distances they would be travelling and he knew they would be approaching the village within the next hour or two. The further they went the more the tension built up inside him. He wasn't used to this sort of campaign; his war was delivered to him and his enemies (or rather targets) by machinery. This was far too personal, almost barbaric. In fact, he thought, there's no almost about it. As he walked he mused that some people enjoyed this type of combat, thrived on it, and indeed it certainly seemed to bring out the best in Frank.

For the second time that day he nearly walked straight into Frank's back. He just managed to stop himself at the last moment, and he pulled up alongside him and listened as Frank indicated for him to be quiet. Brad could hear nothing above the usual noises of the forest. As night was approaching the birds were settling down to roost but the monkeys and other primates had started to chatter and howl as they went about their business in the tree tops, foraging and collecting fruit now that the burning sun had dropped to the horizon allowing them to work without overheating.

'What is it?' whispered Brad.

'Shh.'

There was a long pause as they both listened before Frank said in a low voice. 'Come on, it's time we left this path; we're getting close and the Japs are bound to have a machine gun post, or at least a sentry, on the main entry points into the village.'

During the next hour they only covered about 200 yards. The going was extremely difficult and they were careful only to disturb the forest as little as possible. The reasons for this were two fold. Firstly they couldn't afford the noise involved with cutting a route through the greenery and secondly, although it was nearing darkness now, they didn't want their route to be visible from the path in the light of the following morning. Eventually it became too dark to safely progress any further, and they settled down for an uneasy night in the open. For the first time since landing on the island, Brad felt threatened by the jungle. The closeness of it was oppressive and he felt that he was being watched by creatures of the night that were waiting for him to fall asleep.

'How come you know the island so well, Frank?' He whispered after they had made themselves comfortable.

'Shut up and get some sleep, I want to move out as soon as it's light enough to see.'

Brad rolled over and dug around in his pack. He ate some dried Ship's biscuits and drank some water. He had hoped to get Frank talking, to find out what his background really was, but as always Frank wasn't too happy to talk about the past. Certainly what Brad had seen this morning indicated some sort of military training; the way he had dispatched the soldier would have made any Marines combat instructor happy. He also reflected that the knife Frank had used had the blade painted or burnt matt black so as not to catch the sun and give an early warning to the victim. He was about to broach the subject again but became aware of the rhythmic breathing and the very gentle snoring coming from Frank.

And so he was left alone with his thoughts. He wondered what tomorrow would bring; would he see any more action, and if so would he survive. He'd never dwelled upon such things when bedding down on board ship, even when he knew he had a big mission coming up the following day. Maybe it was the soporific effect of the sea's motion or maybe the confidence borne from being a good pilot, but it certainly wasn't with him now. As he lay there he realised that he was frightened. Frightened of the Jungle, frightened of the way he had felt after shooting the soldier earlier in the day, frightened for Lucy, and frightened for his life. However, even frightened people have to rest, and by analysing and facing his fears, he was soon drifting off into the clouds of a peaceful sleep.

Suddenly he was sitting bolt upright, the echoes of a throaty roar reverberating in his head, but he wasn't sure if it was that that had woken him. He felt as though he had been touched by something unknown, as if a spirit had passed through him. As he listened with pounding heart all he could hear was the hooting of monkeys or baboons, disturbed in the treetops by some night prowler. But, he thought, had it been something else? What had brushed his soul? He realised that he was giving himself the creeps, and put it down to the atmosphere of the Jungle. Trying to put all thoughts of ghosts and lost spirits aside and with all chance of sleep now gone, he lay listening for more sounds of the hunter that would help put his mind at ease by eliminating thoughts of more sinister night apparitions. He guessed it was a leopard or some other night stalker, and he hoped it had been successful in its hunt, and was now settling down to its meal. It was with these pictures circling around inside his head that he fell into a fitful slumber, plagued with nightmares and not giving him the sort of rejuvenating deep sleep that he so badly needed.

Chapter Nineteen

It was a dull, grey Cornish morning as Laura made her way from her flat to the red MGB GT soft top that was her pride and joy. Harry had loved that car, joking with her by saying that he might have to marry her if it was the only way he could get his hands on it. But the joy was gone from Laura's life. Each day was just a timeless drudgery during which she got up, went to work, phoned the institution to get any news and then went home to the dark, lonely flat. The only time she appeared to be happy or content was when she made her evening visit to see Harry. Every night she would spend from 6 O'clock to 11 O'clock sitting, holding his hand and talking to him. Sometimes she would bathe him as he lay in the bed, gently sponging his limbs and torso. Other times she would help the nurses to massage his unused muscles and stretch the joints in his limbs but still all the time talking to him.

It was now two and a half months since the accident. In that time she had seen very few other people. Harry's Mum and Dad would take it in turns to come and stay with her, but even that was less now as the financial burden started to tell. Her friends had been very supportive, but there was little they could do. She wouldn't go out, not wanting to miss an evening with Harry. Eventually the friends had stopped calling. The only other person she had seen on a regular basis was Peter who got over to the hospital whenever he could, sometimes bringing Donna with him. And of course Commander Jenkins had kept in touch, calling Laura once a week to see how she was.

Reaching the car she climbed in and went through the morning ritual of starting her up. It was always the same with older cars; they needed a little coaxing, especially on a cold, damp morning such as this. She gave the key a turn, giving the starter motor a quick burst, repeated it a couple of times, then sat and waited a full minute. Satisfied, she pumped the accelerator a few times, set the choke and then turned the ignition key. The engine roared into life. She smiled to herself and sat waiting for the car to warm up a little before pulling out into the narrow street. A dust truck was coming the other way and she had to pull right into her side of the road, conscious of the foot wide and 8 inch deep open drainage channel then ran the entire length of the street. She remembered well the time that she had been in a small Lotus with a previous boy-friend who had managed to drive it straight into one of them outside the Beehive Pub on the High Street. For the unwary it was a vicious trap that could turn out to be very expensive.

The way now clear she pulled out and continued along Church Street, stopping at a red traffic light before join-ing the main road. Her hill starts were pretty good now and she didn't even think about it as she left the junction that had caused anyone learning to drive in the Helston area more than their fair share of nightmares. Turning right into Coinagehall Street (The High Street by any other name.) she found a parking space opposite Barclays Bank, displayed a parking voucher and made her way over to the deli to pick up some lunch. From there it was just another short drive to the school, and so another day started.

Entering her small, austere office she waved good morn-ing to her colleagues and went through to the ladies room to check her appearance. She looked in the mirror and was not particularly happy with the reflection that stared back at her. She had to admit to herself that she was looking drawn, the face thin and the dark smudges under her eyes starting to get puffy. She felt her eyes fill with tears that spilled over and ran down her cheeks. She wiped at them with the back of her hand and then turned as she saw another reflection looking anxiously into the mirror. A hand offered her a tissue, which she took and wiped her face.

'Thanks Julie, I...' Julie stood there looking concerned, not really knowing what to say. She was a small woman, born and bred in Helston. She had a chubby, friendly face that was attractive despite the huge purple birthmark that covered the left side from temple to chin.

'What is it my Darlin, as if I didn't know'?'

'Oh God, Julie, I want him back!' cried Laura, and she fell into the open arms that Julie offered. Burying her face into Julie's shoulder she cried as she hadn't cried for a long time. Julie let her carry on for a few minutes and then gently said. 'I came in to tell you that there was a message just before you came in. You're to ring the Hospital.'

Laura jerked away from her, the crying stopping instantly. 'What did they say, is he awake...is he...'

'I'm sorry, my darlin', all they said was that you were to ring 'em.'

Laura rushed for the door and then paused, saying: 'Thank you for being there, Julie.' Then she was gone. Scrambling to her desk she reached for the phone and dialled the Truro number that she knew by heart.

'Yes, it's Laura Weaver,' she said to the metallic sounding voice of the receptionist who answered the phone. 'I had a message to ring you about Tony Harrison.'

'Oh yes, Laura isn't it?'

'That's right.'

'I have you listed here as the next of kin. Is that right?'

'Well there's his Mother and Father, but they're in Scotland. I'm registered as the point of contact in the local area.' Laura felt weak, knowing that it must be something serious if they were asking about next of kin.

'If you would just like to hold for one minute I'll put Doctor Phillips on.'

Without waiting for her reply, there was a click and some tinny music wafted out of the earpiece. Harry would have called it elevator music, thought Laura. She was kept waiting on the line for about five minutes, the music the only indication that she hadn't been cut off. She was about to hang up when a gruff voice came on the line.

'Hello Laura, it's Mike Phillips here.'

'He's dead isn't he?' burst out Laura, before the Doctor had a chance to say anything else.'

'Oh no, no, no,' said the Doctor. 'On the contrary, there's been a development overnight; you might even call it progress. However I don't want to get your hopes up too high. Can you get over?'

'Yes...yes, of course, I'm on my way, but what do you mean by progress?'

'I'll tell you all about it when you get here Laura.'

She dropped the hand-piece into its cradle and grabbed her car keys off her desk where she'd tossed them as she arrived for work. On her way out she popped her head into the Boss's office. Before she had said a word the middle-aged woman behind the desk smiled at her showing a row of perfectly even teeth that brought out the best of an attractive face. She nodded to Laura.

'Of course you can go, sweetheart, I've told you there's no need to worry about checking with me.'

Laura vaguely wondered how Mrs Fredrickson always knew what was going on, but it was soon forgotten as she left the office and ran for the car. The screech of brakes and blast of a car's horn brought her back to her senses. She hadn't even looked before dashing out into the road. Better take it easy, she thought; else I'll be joining Harry in Hospital. She held her hand up in a gesture of apology to the driver of the car, who smiled at her and waved her across in front of him. Laura felt her colour rising but still waved to the driver as he pulled away giving her a little beep on the horn. She smiled, feeling a flood of well being similar to the feeling she experienced at the end of a soppy film with a happy ending. She felt fresh tears running down her cheeks as she continued to the car. Climbing in, she took a look at herself in the mirror.

'God I'm a mess,' she laughed, and then spent 5 minutes sorting herself out and applying a little make-up. Looking in the mirror again, she felt much better. Spending those few minutes tidying herself up had settled her and she was far better equipped to undertake the short journey to Truro and actually stand a chance of getting there. As she drove she tried to think what the development might be. As far as she was concerned he was either in a coma or he wasn't. Still the Doctor had said that it was progress and that was all that really mattered at the moment. She drove the route automatically, familiar with all the curves and hills, knew when to overtake, when to stay put. She was generally an aggressive driver, but she considered herself fairly safe. Harry had joked that she'd never had an accident but she'd seen a lot in her rear view mirror. Today, though, she drove slowly; she'd already proved to herself that her mind wasn't functioning fully when she had crossed the road and she was sensible enough to heed the warning.

It was about 40 minutes later that she arrived at the small building with the sign above the door saying Bolitho's Clinic. She entered through the double swing doors and walked across the plush reception area to the elderly woman behind an ornate counter.

'Hello Laura, I'll just see if the Doctor's free,' said the receptionist, immediately recognising their most frequent visitor.

Laura went over to the window and took a seat. She looked around the room taking in the familiar furnishings that never ceased to amaze her. This was no NHS hospital. A lot of money had been spent in order to give an impression of opulence as an indicator to the kind of care that their patients would receive. The carpet was a deep, soft Axminster that was complimented perfectly by the wallpaper and curtains. The furniture was mock Georgian, or at least Laura assumed it was mock. The paintings on the walls were all originals, though Laura didn't recognise any of the artists, however she felt that the Antiques Roadshow would probably have a field day if they visited. She also knew that it wasn't just the entrance hall and other furnishings that the owners had spent money on. The Hospital boasted the state of the art equipment available on the market and Doctor Phillips was recognised as a leading figure in the field of prolonged coma. She knew that in addition to the wing containing private rooms for patients, there was also a large research laboratory in the Alio Santini Wing, dedicated to the racing driver that had spent so long here after his dreadful accident, and indeed paid for by his estate. Laura had often wondered how much per day it was costing the Navy to keep Harry here, and how long it would continue.

As she sat running these things through her mind, the swing door at the far end of the room swung open and a tall, thin man entered the room. Laura looked around and studied the lean face as he walked towards her. The deep set eyes and hooked nose gave him a mean look that had worried her when they first met, however the laughter lines around his sparkling blue eyes said far more about his character. He was dressed in a light grey suit, white shirt and pale pink tie, all very expensive though starting to look a little tired from constant use. Over the top he wore an immaculate white coat with brass buttons and a cluster of pens and other implements neatly lined up in the breast pocket. The whole effect was finished off with a mop of pure grey hair that made him look older than his 46 years. As he approached, Laura got to her feet and accepted the hand that he offered.

'Hello Laura, thanks for coming over.'

'Hello Doctor Phillips, how is he?' she asked excitedly.

'Much the same I'm afraid,' he replied dashing the hopes that Laura had. 'But it's last night that I want to talk to you about.' Doctor Phillips led the way down the carpeted corridor leading to Harry's room. Through necessity this had a much more clinical look to it. The Institute was about 3 years old, but once into his room you would think it was only finished the day before. Everything was perfectly finished and spotlessly clean. As usual Harry was lying on his back covered to the shoulders with a light quilt. He wore paisley print pyjamas, courtesy of the clinic and changed every other day, and the only things that gave a clue to his condition were a standard hospital identity band on his wrist, and the drip that was connected to his right forearm. When he first arrived they had started putting liquid food directly into his stomach through a tube down his throat. By extracting the contents at regular intervals they could gauge how much was being digested. In Harry's case it was next to nothing and they had abandoned that approach in favour of the drip. Consequently he had lost about three stone in weight. If he were conscious Harry would have called it his 'crash diet'

'I see you've changed arms for the drip,' said Laura noticing a bandage on his right arm.

'Yes,' replied the doctor. 'That was as a result of last night's episode.'

The nurse that was sat in the corner, reading a woman's magazine, got up and left the room on a signal from Doctor Phillips. There was somebody present in the room 24 hours a day, the nurses taking 8-hour shifts. Laura was aware of the scratching sound of the starched, crisp, white uniform that the nurse wore, as she passed by.

'Sandra was on last night, and as is often the case when patients come round in the middle of the night, she got the fright of her life.'

'What...he came round. What did he say?'

'Well he didn't come round as you're thinking of it. At about 2.00 am, and without any warning, he suddenly sat bolt upright, ripping the needle out of his arm in the process. He needed a couple of stitches in that incidentally. Anyway his eyes were open and he started shouting, not really making any sense. Sandra said it was about Leopards and baboons but that was all she could really make out apart from, that is, he was using an American accent.'

Laura looked at him blankly, and then said: 'Well he must be coming out of it then. You told me that initially he would only have short spells of conciseness and then...'

She stopped as Dr Phillips held up his hand, 'I know what I said Laura. I also said that I didn't want to give you

129

any false hopes and I'm not convinced that he really was conscious.'

'But Sandra said...' Again the Doctor cut her off.

'I don't doubt what Sandra saw. What's puzzling me is that we set up a brain wave monitor on him straight away and there was no sign of the activity at all. We would expect at least some residual energy, an after shock if you like, but he was immediately back into as deep a coma as ever, and as I've said to you before, I've never seen one as deep as this. By all rights he should...'

Dr Phillips stopped himself from finishing the sentence, suddenly remembering whom he was talking to.

'Well anyway, let's be positive and take it as a step in the right direction,' he said, putting his arm around her shoulders. 'I would like to move him to the research wing where we can keep a better watch over him. I admit that I am interested in studying him closer and I think this way everyone benefits.' Laura had a quick flash of one of the scenes from the film 'Coma', but quickly discounted it.

'Will I still be able to visit him in the evenings?' She asked.

'Of course my dear, of course.'

The Doctor left her then and she settled down to spend a few minutes with Harry before going back to work. She held his hand and told him all about the events of the previous night and finished by begging him to wake up, but still he slept.

Chapter Twenty

Brad awoke to the sound of crying. He was initially disorientated, but quickly came to his senses and realised that the crying was from some jungle animal as it stirred in the early dawn. He felt dreadful; the result of a poor nights sleep. Rolling over, he saw that Frank was still asleep, curled into a small bundle like a child returning to the foetal position. As quietly as he could he pulled himself upright and searched around for his water container. Before he knew what was happening Frank had leapt to his feet, his right hand holding the knife in front of his tense body.

'Jesus Christ Frank, take it easy, it's only me.'

Frank didn't say anything in return. He grabbed the half-empty water bottle from Brad, took a long swig and then emptied the remaining water over his head. Shaking the excess from his hair he turned to Brad.

'Let's go,' he said. Bending down he picked up his rifle, slung it over his shoulder and started pushing into the surrounding undergrowth.

'Wouldn't it be better to make our way back to the path?' asked Brad as he quickly gathered his provisions together. He didn't really expect a civil answer and was surprised when Frank stopped what he was doing and gave him a rough outline of the plan he had in mind. Brad was quite happy for Frank to take the lead in the present scenario as he was feeling way out of his depth. What Frank said made sense; the main paths into the village were almost certainly going to be guarded and if they were surprised he didn't want it to lead the Japs straight back to the others. This way they would skirt the village and approach from the coast. It would also allow them to get much closer to the village and hopefully give them access to more information without having to reveal themselves. It all seemed perfectly logical to Brad and so he was reasonably happy as he followed Frank into the jungle. Of course happiness is a relative commodity.

About thirty minutes later Frank called a halt. Brad opened his mouth to talk but Frank silenced him with a gesture of a forefinger across his lips. Brad drew to a halt and became aware of the noise that had alerted Frank. At first he thought it was another patrol on the way but quickly realised it was the sounds of every day hustle and bustle in a busy village. He was surprised that they were so close and wondered why he'd not heard any noise the previous night, but the jungle had a way of absorbing sound, or at least this sort of sound.

Frank dropped to the ground and started making his way towards the noise. Brad followed and eventually drew level with Frank as the forest started to open up. Together they pressed on another few yards and suddenly the vegetation stopped. This was not the edge of a natural clearing they had been stumbling into at regular intervals. This was man made, uniform and trimmed back. This was the village.

Shuffling forward on their stomachs they got their first view of the settlement. Brad was amazed at what he saw. It was like looking through a window in time. The dwellings could only be described as basic; they were single story and built out of the same volcanic rock as the hut back at the statue. These were primitive people, not at all like the Japanese of the mainland. Looking at the few he could see, they were obviously descendants of the Japanese, but their culture must have differed in many ways. Each house or hut was screened from those close to it by bamboo, not cut and woven as you might expect, but growing naturally, though regimented by pruning or more likely by harvesting. Tools and cooking implements hung from convenient branches surrounding cooking fires that seemed to be communal to two or three dwellings. Brad was reminded of the Red Indian settlements he had seen in books and at the movies.

There were not many people about; mainly women and children. They were simply but colourfully dressed in long flowing garments not unlike a sari. The women wore their hair tied up on top of their heads, held in place with long wooden pins. Their facial features were obviously Japanese but they wore no makeup and consequently looked fairly plain in most cases. As he looked around Brad saw that no one was smiling. The children were sullen, not playing as one might expect, but sitting scratching the earth with sticks or throwing twigs at the fires. The women looked sad as they went about their chores; cooking, cleaning, mending. They could only see a small part of the village from their vantage point but above and beyond the simple dwellings Brad could make out a much larger structure that he assumed was a central meeting hall or the Quarters of the Chief of these simple people. It could even be a Temple he thought.

Frank nudged him and pointed to the left. What he saw was completely out of place. A circle of sandbags did little to conceal the machine gun post that was set against the wall of one of the buildings. As he watched Brad became aware of the two soldiers that manned the weapon, sitting in the shade, smoking and conversing in low voices. Suddenly they jumped to their feet and Brad instinctively drew back, thinking they'd been spotted. He noticed that Frank didn't react at all. As he looked back on the scene he saw the reason for all the commotion. An Officer had arrived at the machine gun post, apparently without any fore warning for the unfortunate soldiers. He was tall for a Japanese and he was immaculately turned out; his uniform clean and pressed, and his boots reflecting the suns rays. He wore a pair of thin wired spectacles that seemed to enlarge his eyeballs and give him an almost comical look.

As he approached the soldiers one of them dropped his cigarette, stamped on it and threw up a sloppy salute. He was rewarded for the gesture with a vicious swipe from the cane or riding crop that the Officer held in his right hand. As he raised his hands to protect himself the Officer let forth a stream of verbal abuse that had the unfortunate individual standing to attention looking straight forward. This tirade was punctuated with an even more severe blow to the head but this time the victim did little more than flinch under the force of the impact. Brad saw a thin line of blood trickle down through his eyebrow and onto his cheek. The Officer had now shifted his attention to the other man and was screaming into his face. The soldier gave no response and the Officer turned as if to leave. A look of relief jumped onto the soldier's face and, as if sensing this, the Officer swung around, putting all his momentum and force behind the cane as it flew round in a horizontal arc. It caught the unsuspecting individual high on the cheek and flayed the flesh open to the bone. Blood erupted from the wound and the soldier collapsed, sinking to the ground in an untidy heap. The Officer barked some new order as he turned and marched away. The standing soldier saluted smartly and quickly went over to the machine gun and started stripping it down. He paid absolutely no attention to his colleague who remained unconscious in the full heat of the sun that had now risen high in the clear blue sky.

Brad had heard about the sadistic nature of some of the Japanese, but still he was shocked at the sheer brutality that the Officer had inflicted on his own men. He turned to say something to Frank but quickly changed his mind when he saw the grin on his face. Moving backwards on his stomach, careful not to make any noise, he tapped Frank and indicated for him to follow. Having backed up about 20 feet he whispered.

'Do you know the layout of the village?' Frank nodded in reply and then expanded, saying.

'The whole place is built in a circle around the large central structure. This is about as good a view as you will get without entering.'

Brad thought for a little while. 'I need to get a closer look at the Japs set up here; it could be important once we get away from the island.'

'You can stuff that,' replied Frank. 'Why should I risk my life just so some Army Intelligence boffin can quiz my brains out and then write a report.'?

'Well, because...' Brad was going to give a speech about how their information could lead to action that would save hundreds of American lives in the long run, but looking at Franks sneering features he knew that it wasn't worth the effort. He began again. 'Well, I don't give a shit what you think Frank, I'm gonna get a closer look.' With that he began to circumnavigate the village, going toward what he guessed would be the coast. Before long he noticed that Frank was following him and smiled to himself. As he started forward again he heard thunder rumbling in the distance. He thought about the clear skies he'd seen between the trees near the village. It certainly hadn't looked like rain, and he knew the rainy season was a couple of months away yet, with the really heavy stuff not due until May or June time. Maybe it's heavy gunfire he thought to himself and carried on through the undergrowth.

Every now and then he would turn 90 degrees to the right and slowly make his way back to the perimeter. He noted the positions of two more machine guns and counted at least twenty soldiers, though some of them could have been men moving around the village. As Frank had said, the village looked very similar from all angles and before too long Brad thought he was wasting his time. He communicated his thoughts to Frank, who suggested that they should continue for a while, explaining that there was a river coming up shortly that might be worth looking over.

Sure enough, about half an hour later they came across the said waterway that surprised Brad by being quite deep and slow flowing. When he queried Frank about this he explained that they were now quite close to the sea and that the river was tidal and sure enough when Brad dipped his hand into the water and tasted it, it was quite brackish. Thoughts were quickly forming in his mind.

'Does it flow like this all the way through the village?'

'Yes, the fishermen use it to paddle their boats out to sea; I guess it's why the village was built here.'

'And it goes right through the middle of the village?'

'Yes...yes I see what you're getting at. Mind you,' Frank added. 'It very quickly fades away to a small stream like the others we've seen around the island. I'm not sure that we'd be able to get all the way through without being spotted.'

'Would we be able to get clear of the village before it's too shallow to swim in?' asked Brad.

Frank hesitated before answering until he managed to come to some decision: 'Yes I think so, but if we leave it until dark anyway, even if we do get grounded we'll have the cover of darkness to hide our exit from the water.'

And so with this simple exchange it was decided to run the river through the village, getting whatever information they could on the way, and hopefully get clear away without even being noticed. In the meantime they settled down to wait for the sun to set, and to get as much rest as they could. Brad felt tense about the possibility of approaching action, still unable to come to terms with this face to face fighting, but finally he managed to grab a few hours of sleep as Frank kept watch.

It was mid afternoon when Brad awoke. Frank was nowhere to be seen but some how this didn't surprise him. He took a long drink from his canteen and climbed to his feet just in time to hear and then see Frank making his way through the undergrowth.

'Just been to see if there's any activity in the village,' he reported without waiting to be asked. He continued quickly. 'I'm gonna get some shut-eye, you keep watch for a while and call me if you hear or see anything, otherwise wake me at dusk.' With that he curled down with his back against a tree and was almost instantly asleep, or certainly seemed to be.

Brad sat watching him for a while and once again he found himself wondering what his story was. Since leaving the other two behind Frank had been different somehow; more confident and sure of himself that much was certain. But there was still something bugging Brad. He didn't like the way that he kept sneaking off without any explanation, the furtive looks he gave everybody, the indecision when confronted with a perfect way to get a good look at the Japanese set up. In fact he didn't really like anything about him at all and there weren't many people he felt like that about. He looked away as Frank rolled himself over and all but wrapped himself around the tree.

Brad changed his train of thought, considering the plight of Lucy and Father Golding. They were bearing up to the strain of the last few weeks quite well, but he was starting to worry about Lucy. Matthew was fairly wise to the World, philosophical about things and well able to cope with the added burdens that the war was bringing. Lucy, on the other hand, had a lot to contend with; the death of her parents, the deaths of those trying to take her to safety, being shot at and now having to run and hide like a hunted animal. He wondered how long she could go on putting a brave face on it before the cracks started to show. Brad considered his feelings for her and found himself smiling. He hadn't really felt like this before, not wanting to get involved in anything more than a casual relationship, especially since he had taken up a career in the Navy. But this was different somehow and he wished he knew how she felt about him. The signs had been good so far but he didn't want to rush into anything.

Frank stirred again and Brad's mind jumped back to their present predicament. He was nervous about the prospect of spying on the Japanese in the village, but at the same time there was a tingle of excitement akin to the feelings in his guts just before launching on a sortie. Maybe he was getting a taste for this type of fighting, he thought; could he really end up enjoying the killing as Frank so obviously did? He didn't think so.

Rising quietly to his feet he made his way down to the water's edge and sat with his bare feet in the river. The water was cooling and was flowing slowly towards the coast. He thought about the effects of tide and decided that later on that night when they made their ingress, the water would be flowing into the village. If their timing was right they wouldn't have to swim at all but just float along on the current. Looking around he found some old, fallen branches and tried them out in the river. The first couple were water logged and sank, but eventually he found two that would make suitable floats. Stripping his shirt off he tried out the larger of the two, walking out to the centre of the river. By keeping his head as low as possible the float also gave added camouflage should someone happen to glance at the water as they floated past. The river was shallow enough to control his speed, and to a certain extent his direction of advance with his feet that dragged across the bottom of the riverbed.

Having travelled about twenty yards or so downstream he turned and found that he could easily make way against the current with simple frog like kicks that caused little or no disturbance on the surface. Arriving back where he had started he quickly tried out the other 'float' and then dragged himself onto the bank. Finding a small patch of sunlight that managed to find its way through the canopy he lay back feeling refreshed and a little pleased with himself.

'So this is what you call keeping watch, is it?'

Brad leapt to his feet with the beginnings of an excuse on his lips but realised it would be useless. In fact, as he thought about it Frank was right; it could have been anybody sneaking up on him. He cursed himself silently, furious that he had allowed Frank the opportunity to have a go at him and be fully justified in doing so.

'You're right Frank, sorry.'

'Yeah, well forget it, the Japs won't be moving about as quietly as me and I know you were awake; I've been watching your floating log act.'

'Well it should make life easier tonight...unless you've any better ideas.'

'No,' replied Frank, indicating the logs that Brad had put aside. 'I reckon they should do fine.'

With that he returned to his tree and settled down to wait for dusk and Brad was left dripping on the river bank, wondering what the Hell the last exchange had been all about.

Chapter Twenty-One

As darkness fell Brad and Frank made their way to the water's edge. Brad was surprised at how cool the river appeared now that the day had lost the heat of the sun. Quietly he waded into the centre of the waterway and allowed the slow current to take him in its grasp. Frank followed him and as Brad looked back he was pleased to note how effectively the face camouflage broke up the sharp, pale image of Frank's face. It had been Brad's idea to black their faces using a combination of earth, water and ashes from the small fire they had chanced in order to brew themselves a hot drink. Careful now, not to splash any water onto his face, he lifted his feet from the riverbed and slowly they began to drift towards the village.

The first sign that they were getting close was the smell of burning wood, presumably from one of the campfires. There was little noise; the odd low grunt from some quiet conversation and then suddenly the loud barking of a dog. For some reason it seemed to be out of context to Brad, and he wondered if it could be a guard dog, if indeed the Japanese used such things, and if it would pick up their scent and give them away.

As if reading his thoughts, Frank whispered softly: 'Probably a descendent of some wrecked ship's dogs brought in by European traders.'

Brad didn't reply but silently hoped that Frank was right and that it wouldn't pick up their scent. They were entering the outskirts of the village now, the river flowing between two huts of a similar build to those they had seen earlier. These dwellings that backed onto the river had small bamboo jetties extending into the water. Brad could pick out the occasional small watercraft tied up to the jetties whilst others appeared to be more fence like. Something fluttered up against his leg and was gone just as quickly. Instinctively Brad pulled his legs up and felt a sharp pain is his calf.

'Damn,' he hissed. 'Something just bit me.' Reaching down he felt the flutter again, this time against wrist, and he felt the stirring of fear as his mind drew pictures of poisonous snakes and man-eating fish. Another sharp stab in the back of his hand all but sent him over the edge when the voice of reason in the form of Frank whispering in his era, said. 'Calm down will ya, they're fishing lines. Don't struggle or you'll get more hooks in you.'

Brad pushed his feet into the soft debris at the bottom of the river and anchored himself in the gentle flow. Frank did the same. After looking around to ensure they hadn't drawn attention to themselves, they went about the painful business of removing the hooks that had snagged them. Luckily most of the lines terminated in a struggling fish, hence the fluttering against his legs, but those that didn't ended in a viciously barbed hook about an inch long. The one in the back of his hand had stopped going in just before the first barb and was easily removed. The one in his calf, however, was deeply embedded and a gentle exploration told him it would not easily be removed. Explaining the problem to Frank, who had already freed himself, Brad borrowed the knife and severed the fishing line, leaving the hook in situ.

Carefully lifting their legs high in the water and making their way as near to the riverbank as possible the two men continued on their journey. They were past the first fringe of huts and gradually the dwellings drew back from the water, leaving large open spaces that appeared to have crops of some sort planted on them in semi regimented rows. Apart from the odd machine-gun post, that Brad wasn't even sure were manned, they saw little in the way of enemy activity. He felt a little let down; he had hoped to gather some invaluable intelligence. He felt that this would in some way make up for the loss of his aircraft that he was still feeling somewhat chagrined about.

Just as he was resigning himself to the fact that there was nothing going on, he saw a light appear as a door or curtain was pulled back from the entrance to one of the huts. Signalling to Frank he eased his feet into the river-bed and once again retarded his progress.

'What have you stopped for, they'll see us.'

'Not if we stay low in the water and duck behind the logs,' whispered Brad.

'It's probably some locals coming to collect water, come on lets go.'

Frank seemed to be getting edgy but Brad held his ground. He had noticed a glint of light reflected off the glasses that were worn by the Japanese Officer they had seen earlier. He was making his way towards them and was in low conservation with another, much taller man.

'Come on,' hissed Frank in a desperate tone. 'They'll see us.'

Brad brushed off the hand that grabbed at his shirt surprised that Frank seemed to be losing his nerve. He strained to hear what the two men that were now only about twenty yards away were saying. They had stopped and were looking back towards the village. The Japanese Officer was gesticulating wildly and his voice was starting to rise in volume but unfortunately he was speaking Japanese. The taller man suddenly cut him off and he too started to shout. The language, although Japanese, had a strange inflection to it, sounding almost guttural.

No it can't be, thought Brad, but even as his mind tried to dispel it the taller man suddenly switched to German and let out a mouthful of abuse at the Japanese Officer.

'Bloody hell, did you hear that?' he whispered to Frank who was now standing in the water beside him. 'That's a German Officer. What the hell are the Germans doing here?'

'No you must be mistaken; there can't be any Germans here.'

Brad failed to notice that Frank was gradually backing away from him.

'It is I tell you, there's no mistaking that language.' Brad dropped further down into the water as he saw the two men turn towards him. Frank remained standing.

'Achtung, Achtung!!'

The cry rang clear through the night. Brad remained stock still in the water unable to believe what was happening. The shout had come, not from the shore, but from Frank who had drawn his knife and was advancing on him. Frank looked over at the two Officers, who had run over to the riverbank, and let out a stream of fluent German.

Brad galvanised himself into action. He dropped down into the water and swam straight at the bank where the soldiers stood looking onto the dark surface. As he felt the water shallowing he turned an estimated 90 degrees and swam parallel to the bank, continuing with the incoming tide to put the maximum distance between himself and his enemies. Vaguely he heard the report of a weapon being fired but was not aware of any bullets coming close to him.

All hell was breaking out on the shore. The German Officer had taken his pistol from its holster and was indiscriminately firing into the dark water. This action, although not very effective against an unseen man in the water, had the effect of rousing the camp. Soldiers were approaching the scene from all directions' lining the banks and firing into the water. Frank had immediately followed Brad as he dived, lunging with his knife, but missing his quarry due to the unexpected direction that Brad had decided upon. Too late, he realised he was putting himself in danger of being shot as he splashed around in the chest-deep water. He was more shocked than hurt as the bullet from a careless rifle smashed into his fore arm, splintering the bone as it passed on its way through his limb. He grabbed the wound, knowing that the pain would be quick to follow, and cursed loudly in German. The German Officer realised what had happened and shouted out for a cease-fire, A few sporadic shots followed but these eventually dried up.

Brad felt as if his lungs were bursting; a sharp burning pain spreading from the centre of his chest becoming unbearable. He risked allowing a thin stream of air to trickle through his nose in an effort to relieve the pressure but he knew that his body was starving for oxygen and soon it would trigger an involuntary intake of breath. With his last reserves Brad propelled himself an extra few yards and then surfaced as gently as he could. The sharp inlet of air to his lungs seemed loud in the night air, but the sense of relief that it brought outweighed the dangers of discovery. Looking around he saw that he'd put about fifty yards between himself and Frank but soldiers were spreading along the bank in both directions. Torches were beginning to illuminate the surface of the river and Brad dropped below the surface once again, this time pushing out for the far bank.

Had he just continued down tide he may have made it out of the village and managed to get away, losing himself in the jungle. Alternatively he may have got shot and killed at any time during his escape. As it turned out it was the local fishermen that were responsible for his capture. In all the excitement, Brad had forgotten all about the fishing lines and their vicious hooks. The first two caught his clothes as he swam through the lines. He was vaguely aware of the scratches but by the time their meaning registered it was too late. The next hook buried itself into the flesh of his cheek just below the right eye. The shock caused him to expel some of his precious air and he automatically twisted away from the pain, which only caused the line to tighten, and the hook to tear the flesh. Suddenly it seemed as if there were lines and snags all over him and the more he tried to free himself the more entangled he became. Once again the pain was starting to build in his chest and he knew his bid for freedom was over. Making a conscious decision he twisted himself upright and in one fluid motion burst up to the surface with his hands in the air.

Taking a quick breath he shouted. 'Tell them not to shoot Frank.' A bullet 'zipped' into the water just in front of him before he heard an order shouted in Japanese.

Thankfully no more shots followed and Brad allowed his hands to drop. He looked up as Frank arrived on the bank opposite him. He inwardly smiled as he saw that Frank was wounded but didn't let it show on his face.

'Get your hands back up, Brad,' said Frank quietly. There was no sneer in his voice as Brad had expected, in fact he almost sounded remorseful.

'I'm all tangled up, and besides you know I'm not armed; we left the weapons back at the camp.'

Frank turned and talked to the German Officer who had arrived and stood a couple of yards behind him. The Officer nodded and Frank barked an order to two soldiers who removed their tunics and made their way into the water. Two minutes later Brad had been cut free and was frog marched out of the river and presented to the German Officer.

'Ah Lieutenant Bradshaw I presume,' he said in heavily accented English.

Brad ignored the Officer and turned to look at Frank. 'You filthy, traitorous...' He never managed to complete the sentence; the butt of a rifle smashing into his kidney taking his breath away. As he doubled over in pain a second blow caught him on the nape of the neck causing a bright explosion of light and pain before he slipped away into unconsciousness.

Chapter Twenty-Two

Laura sat quietly at Harry's bedside, if you could call it a bed that was. It was more like a bench in some mad professor's laboratory she mused as she looked around. Harry was lying on his back in some sort of cradle affair that was strung up to a series of pulleys. This had no other purpose than to turn him at regular intervals to protect him from bedsores and to assist his circulation. Not so much could be said for the rest of the equipment that Harry was wired up to. He seemed to have tubes and wires coming from everywhere. Some Laura recognised; the intro venous drips to nourish him, the cardiac monitor, but since moving he had sprouted electrodes from his head, his toes and just about everywhere in between. The room itself was clinically clean and three of the walls were tastefully decorated and gave it a sense of normality. They had even hung some expensive prints on the plain white walls. The forth wall had the only window but it wasn't looking out over the countryside, far from it in fact, it wasn't looking outside at all.

The long, floral curtains were drawn back at present revealing the large, double glazed and soundproofed window that looked into the monitoring room. It was difficult to make out what was happening from this side of the glass, but Laura had been into the room when Harry was first moved. Every output from Harry's body was monitored and recorded on a VDU, and under each unit was a large roll of graph paper running under a constantly recording stylus producing hard copies for future analysis and research. Two technicians in white coats monitored the equipment, but Laura knew that if there was any activity the small room would be swarming with doctors and experts within minutes. She had been staggered at the amount of effort and resources that were going into Harry's care, but as Doctor Phillips pointed out, the clinic was getting the benefit of researching a coma that was deeper than they'd ever seen before. The results of his analysis could help countless others in other hospitals and clinics, and would certainly further his standing as the leading expert in the field.

Laura looked away from the window. She didn't care about any of that; she just wanted her Harry back. She looked up as the door opened and smiled as Harry's mother entered the room.

'Hello Dear, any change?'

'I'm afraid not, Mary.' Laura was glad of the company. Mary had travelled down from Scotland two nights ago and was staying with her for a couple of weeks. It wasn't until she arrived that Laura realised how lonely she had been. Apart from work and the clinic she had not seen anyone for months. Her friends had stopped calling, though the better ones had kept in touch by writing occasionally, awaiting the time when she would be back to normal or the time when she would need them if the worst happened.

'Do you mind if I shut the curtains, I can't stand the sight of all that stuff that he's wired up to.'

'Of course not, go ahead.'

Mary went over and drew the first of the large curtains. As she pulled the second one across she paused and then turned to look at Harry.

'I think something's happening,' she said. Harry looked no different, but they both went over to the window and watched as the two technicians hovered over one of the hard copy machines. Moments later one of them broke off and went over to the phone. After a short conversation he hung up and as he went back to his colleague the tannoy crackled into life.

'Doctor Phillips and team Alpha report to Lab 5 immediately.'

Mary turned to look at Laura but she was already over at Harry's side. Mary joined her as additional staff started to arrive in the room on the other side of the window.

Doctor Phillips made a brief appearance to study the monitors and then happy to leave it in the hands of his team he made his way to join the ladies at the bedside.

'Well this is the first action since we wired him up,' he said excitedly. 'Maybe now we'll begin to know what's going on inside that mind of his.'

Mary was a little surprised at the way he referred to her son as some kind of laboratory experiment, and turned to rebuke him. Laura on the other hand was getting used to his ways and knowing he meant well put a restraining hand on Mary's shoulder. Mary seemed to understand and turned back to look at her son. She couldn't detect any difference. Dr Phillips was looking at the heart monitor.

'His heart rate is going up,' he said to no one in particular. Sure enough the machine was showing an increase from the steady 62 beats per minute and was now showing 97. Though they couldn't see them from the bedside, the styluses in Lab 5 were going berserk showing a huge amount of brain activity whereas minutes before there had been the minimum associated with keeping him alive.

Dr Phillips was now leaning over Harry. 'Look, he's in REM sleep!' he exclaimed.

'What on earth is rem sleep?' asked Mary in a high voice; the Doctor's sense of excitement becoming contagious.

'REM, that stands for Rapid Eye Movement, it's a very shallow form of sleep that a normal person experiences at intervals during the night. It's the dream sleep, but more significantly it's the sleep you're in just before you wake up.'

Laura and Mary looked at Harry's eyes and sure enough they could see the eyeballs flickering rapidly below the lids.

'He's waking up, he's waking up. Oh Harry speak to me darling,' cried Laura. But Harry remained in the same state, not even moving or twitching as one might expect with the struggle that his now rapid pulse rate indicated was going on somewhere in his dream world. Doctor

Phillips face was starting to show some signs of concern as he watched the heart monitor indicate a pulse of 164 and still rising. He picked up an intercom phone to the next room and spoke rapidly into the handset. Later he would show them that the output from every machine had gone beyond any recognisable scale, the pens moving up and down so quickly that in some cases the graph paper had torn as the stylus covered the same spot over and over again.

But that was later. Now they watched the monitor in horror as his heart continued to speed up at an incredible rate. Suddenly it flat lined. For a moment nobody reacted, the shock of the thin green line and the associated alarms stopping everyone in their tracks. It seemed like a lifetime to Laura but in fact it was only two seconds later that Dr Phillips shouted for the nurse, who had taken station by the door, to prepare 20 mils of adrenaline. As he felt for the carotid artery to check before commencing heart massage the monitor suddenly started up again at a steady 62. The Doctor stopped everything, watched Harry for a few seconds, and then spoke into the phone he was still holding.

'Everything's back to normal in there,' he said. 'It's as if nothing happened.'

'What's going on Doctor?' asked Mary, the first of the two women to come to their senses.

'I really don't know. This seems to be a similar incident to the one he had in the Naval Hospital but I've never seen anything like it before. Right now my colleagues and I are going to study the data and see what we can come up with. Can you both come to my office in an hour's time and I'll let you know what we've found out.'

Mary nodded and went over to Laura who was holding Harry's hand, gently sobbing. Once again Mary was touched by the dedication of this young woman and hoped that Harry would feel the same when he came back to them.

Laura looked up as Mary gently stroked her hair. 'I thought he was about to come round and suddenly he was nearly dead,' she cried, and the flood banks opened as Mary took her in her arms.

'There, there sweetheart, he'll be all right you wait and see. He's a fighter is our Tony, you wait and see.'

'I know he is but I just wish he'd wake up. I really wish he'd wake up.'

But still Harry slept.

Chapter Twenty-Three

When Brad opened his eyes the bright white light and the pain were still there. He shut his eyes again and tried to lift his hands to hold his throbbing head but he pulled against some invisible force and discovered that his hands were strapped behind his back. He opened his eyes again and saw that it was morning. The pain was atrocious; originating from the base of his skull and spreading radially as far as his shoulders, forehead and lower back. He was lying on his side in a large empty room, the bare earth floor cool against his flushed skin. He tried to twist around to a sitting position but the effort caused the pain to be magnified ten fold. He tried to relax and take in his surroundings without causing himself any more discomfort.

There didn't appear to be any windows in the room, the light being thrown in by the sun entering through the single open doorway. Brad saw the occasional movement just outside the opening as the guard changed position in the stifling heat. Rolling over onto his other side he was surprised to see Frank sitting at a simple table watching his every move. As Brad opened his mouth to speak Frank held up his hand.

'No one asked you to get involved Brad,' he said quietly. 'I was just trying to keep everyone out of trouble until the business here was complete. Unfortunately you had other ideas.'

'You traitorous pig, you weren't trying to help anybody but yourself; betraying your country and no doubt lining your pockets with Nazi gold.'

'You're wrong on all counts. I'm a German scientist and a Lieutenant in the German Army, though I was educated in the United States before the War. Born in 1920 to German parents my early years were spent in Berlin so I am not a traitor, I am a patriot. Lieutenant Hanz Muller at your service.'

Brad didn't know what to say. He'd known there was something about Frank but he couldn't have been further from the truth.

'But the Japanese that you killed...they're your allies.'

Frank spat onto the floor and muttered something in German before saying. 'We may have been thrown together in this filthy war but that doesn't mean I like the stinking, little, yellow pigs.' He rose to his feet and walked towards Brad. 'And now I'm going to help you again by giving you some sound advice. Tell them everything they want to know.'

'You know I can't do that,' answered Brad.

'I wouldn't have expected you to say anything else, but I wouldn't be able to live with myself if I didn't try. You've seen the way Horshima treats his own men and I'm afraid we won't be able to stop him from doing the same and worse if they start interrogating you.'

'Thanks for your concern,' Brad retorted savagely. 'How's the arm by the way?' He asked noticing the heavily splinted and bandaged arm for the first time.

Frank ignored the taunt but instead drew a pistol from the belt of his trousers with his good arm. 'There is an alternative way, of course. You could be shot trying to escape.'

'Thanks, but no thanks. I'll take my chances with Hamirosha or whatever his name is.'

'Horshima,' Frank corrected.

Brad didn't say anything further and Frank tucked the gun away. 'Well if it ever gets too much for you and I happen to be around just give me the nod.' He pulled himself up from the table and left the room. Brad was left alone with his thoughts. For a start what the hell were the Germans doing with the Japanese in the Pacific and why was Frank, a German Scientist, running around the jungle with an Irish Priest? Finding no answers to these questions he started to explore the bindings that were immobilising him. His arms were tied tightly behind his back and his feet were bound together. Rolling onto his back he tried to fold his legs and bring them through his manacled arms. He hadn't moved more than a few inches when he cried out in pain. Quickly he realised that the fishhooks had been left embedded in his flesh and the lines that remained when he was cut free had been attached to the bindings on arms and legs.

'The sadistic little bastards,' he grunted.

'Yes, one of Horshima's little touches.' Brad looked over at the unexpected reply. He knew from the voice before he saw him that it was the German Officer. 'Well I know who you are so let me introduce myself,' the German said in the accented English that had given his identity away. 'I'm Smidt, Wolfgang Smidt.'

Brad noticed that he didn't use a rank when he gave his name, nor did he appear to wear any on his uniform. In fact he wasn't wearing any insignia at all, which struck Brad as a little odd.

'Horshima has been kind enough, at my request, to allow me to question you first. I would strongly advise that you answer my questions or I shall have no alternative but to deliver you into the hands of his henchmen.'

'I have nothing to say,' Brad answered defiantly 'And besides I must insist that I am treated as a Prisoner of War under the rules of the Geneva Convention.'

Smidt laughed. 'I don't think Horshima has ever heard of the Geneva Convention, or Geneva for that matter, let alone feel that he must abide by its rules.' He paused whilst staring straight into Brad's eyes. 'Ok let me begin for you. You are Lieutenant Charles Bradshaw, erstwhile of the Aircraft Carrier Enterprise. You were shot down four days ago by a Zero on a routine patrol just to the North of the Island. How am I doing so far?'

Brad said nothing but just rolled over to make himself more comfortable. He winced as the hooks bit deeper into his flesh.

'Excuse me, I am so sorry. Let me make you more comfortable.' Smidt disappeared through the door and returned a few moments later carrying a vicious looking knife. He cut the fishing lines and then the main strands and left the knife on the table. He indicated that Brad should seat himself on the single chair.

'I trust you won't force me to shoot you by going for the knife.'

Brad saw that Smidt had positioned himself far enough away that he could draw his pistol and shoot him down before he could cover half the distance. He realised that Smidt was just playing with him and so relaxed back in the chair to see what other opportunities might materialise.

'So where were we?' said Smidt. 'Ah yes, you were about to tell me what you were doing over this island when the Enterprise was miles away; well beyond the range of the Grumman Wildcat you were flying.'

Brad said nothing but his mind was working over-time. What the German said didn't make sense. He'd taken off from the Enterprise that morning. Then it suddenly came to him. The sly Bastard, he thought, he's trying to get me to reveal the Ships' position.

The German continued to speak and his next words caused Brad to think again. 'You see, on the morning you were shot down we know that the Enterprise was conducting a raid on Marcus Island, so there is no way that you could have come from the Ship. So where did you come from?'

'You know so much, you tell me.' said Brad.

The German smiled and walked slowly over to end up behind the chair.

'So, your going to play the tough guy, are you?' Smidt hissed in Brad's ear. The next second the chair was pulled from under him and Brad fell heavily to the hard floor. Turning over he pulled himself to his hands and knees just in time to collect the Jackboot that swung maliciously into his stomach. The air was forced out of his body in an explosion of coughing and he collapsed to the floor.

'Where did you come from?' screamed Smidt.

Brad continued to cough and splutter and tried to pull himself to his knees. The next kick caught him full in the testicles, causing Brad to double up in unadulterated agony. He felt his vision greying but just managed to hold off the black void that seemed to be calling to him. He wretched a couple of times, bringing up a thin stream of bile that burnt his throat and brought tears to his eyes. Rolling onto his back he opened his eyes and looked defiantly at Smidt, who was now stood over him holding the knife.

'I'll ask you again, where did you come from on the morning you were shot down?'

'Lieutenant Charles Bradshaw, US Nav...' Brads reply went unfinished as the knife slammed into the hard ground just inches from his face. He reacted in an instant, despite his pain, reaching for the knife whilst at the same time twisting to bring himself onto his knees. Unfortunately Smidt had anticipated this move and the sole of his boot came down on Brad's hand. The little finger was bent double and trapped beneath the boot. As Brad made a grab for the knife with his other hand, Smidt transferred his weight and Brad cried out in pain as he heard the finger break.

'Oh how careless of me,' said the German as he bent down to recover the knife before releasing his hand. 'We'll talk again later. He strode out of the room leaving Brad to pick himself off the floor.

This is not going well, thought Brad, and it's going to get a lot worse. He stared down at the broken finger, the digit twisted out of shape and already beginning to swell. Sitting down and holding his hand flat on the table, he gritted his teeth and jerked the finger straight. The pain bolted up his arm but he was surprised at how quickly it dissipated. Maybe I'm becoming immune, he thought. He bound the broken finger to the adjacent one as best he could using some of the line he managed to detach from one of the hooks embedded in his flesh. Next he tried removing the hook and discovered he wasn't, in fact, immune to pain at all. Abandoning the hooks he checked out the rest of his injuries probing for any serious damage. Already there was a livid bruise in the area of his right kidney from the blow the previous night, but some fairly brutal prodding convinced him that there was no damage to the organ itself. With regards to his testicles he could not be so sure. They were swollen and painful to the touch, but at least they didn't appear to be ruptured.

Medical examination over, Brad turned his attention to the building in which he was imprisoned. Like the other buildings he had seen, this one was built of dry stone. Walking around the walls he felt for any weaknesses in the construction, but found none. He also had a quick scratch at the floor in one of the corners, but digging under the wall with his bare hands didn't seem too likely at the moment. The roof however was a different proposition altogether. It was made up from a sheet of woven bamboo secured to a frame of much thicker and stronger wood. On top of this was thatching made up of reeds or immature bamboo. Pushing at it, Brad was surprised to feel how dense and strong it felt, but he was sure that after dark he would be able to work on it and make himself a way out of the hut. For now he returned to the chair, sat with his upper body lying across the table and went to sleep.

He had no idea how long he'd been asleep when he awoke with a start. He still had a headache and his testicles throbbed with a dull pain, but apart from that he felt quite refreshed. A tray had been placed on the floor beside him. Lifting it with his good hand he found a simple meal of cold cooked fish and plain rice. There was also a drink of clear water in a simple cup and a bowl of freshly chopped fruit. He wolfed the food down quickly, realising it was the first decent meal he'd had on the island. It sure beat cold Bully Beef and beans. Finishing the meal with a drink from the cup he wondered how long he would be left alone. He could see it was still light outside but had no real idea of the time of day. Picking up the tray he walked to the open door and peered outside. The sun was still high in the sky and Brad guessed it was mid afternoon. The guard at the door became aware of his presence and barked an order at him in Japanese.

'I need to go to the bathroom,' said Brad. The order was repeated, only louder this time.

'Find me the Officer...er German.' Brad thought for a moment and then gave a Nazi salute and a beckoning to come inside. If the Japanese soldier knew what he was getting at, he certainly didn't show it. The order was repeated louder still and this time it was punctuated with a sharp jab in the leg from the bayonet at the end of his rifle. Brad got the message and retreated inside the hut, conscious of the trickle of blood running down his thigh.

Five minutes later Smidt was back. He looked at Brad, who was sitting at the table once more, inspecting the wound in his leg.

'Sorry about the guard, they have been threatened with, how you say it, a fate worse than death if you escape. Understandably, I think, they tend to be a little over-zealous. Now then, what can we do for you?'

Brad explained his needs, hoping to get a look outside to see how the ground lay. It wasn't to be though. Smidt disappeared and a few minutes later a bucket was thrown into the room by the guard. The rest of the day he was left alone. Sometime in the early evening a pretty Japanese girl; not a local by the look of her, brought him a similar meal as before, only this time served with scalding hot tea which was surprisingly refreshing. Brad sat around expecting another visit from Smidt but it never came. As the light started to fade he arranged himself as comfortably as the hard floor and fishing hooks would allow, and quickly dropped into a light sleep.

Chapter Twenty-Four

Laura found Dr Phillip's office with no trouble, following the route she had taken many times over the last few months. She entered the outer office noting the empty desk that was home to a very expensive looking computer suite. Reading the name printed in gold on the oak-panelled door opposite, she walked over and knocked. She faintly heard the shouted 'come in' and pushed the door open. Entering the office she never failed to notice that the clinic treated its senior staff as well as its patients. She stood in the doorway taking in the plush surroundings. The walls were coated with thick patterned paper and were adorned with more expensive looking painting and of course the 'mandatory' collection of Medical certificates, all with matching frames. The fittings in the room were minimal, just a few comfortable chairs and a standard lamp, but it was the desk that drew one's attention. It was a huge oak affair with a green leather top surrounded by a carved wooden frame. The carving had an oriental flavour, though Laura could not tell what story the scene depicted. Beyond and to the left of the desk was a huge bay window that looked out over the beautifully kept terraced gardens and filled the room with natural light. To add to the sense of opulence Laura felt that she was sinking into the carpet. No matter how many times she visited him she was always stunned by her surroundings. Dr Phillips pulled himself up from a chair that matched the desk.

'Come in my dear, come in.' He looked past her. 'Is Mrs Harrison not with you?'

'No, she wanted to stay with Tony.'

'Oh I see, fine - take a seat won't you and make yourself comfortable. I'm sorry my PA wasn't in the office to show you in but I've had to send her away on an errand.' Laura lowered herself into one of the chairs.

'Well has the analysis shown you anything new, Doctor?'

'How many times do I have to say it; please, call me Mike - now then, let me see. The results that we have so far are inconclusive, however I am starting to form some theories that may help to explain what is going on. Tony seems to be fighting some huge internal struggle that is linked with the state that we see him in. It probably manifests itself to him as a dream, but it's going on very deep, somewhere in the recesses of his mind that our instruments can't reach. I imagine that he is reliving the accident over and over and occasionally, when things in his dream world get too much for him, it bubbles to the surface. In fact it's more like a volcanic eruption and when it happens, our monitors pick up the results.'

Dr Phillips paused and Laura asked. 'But what about his heart stopping and starting, how can your theory explain that?'

'Again I think, and I stress *think*, it must be tied in with whatever is going on in his dream. The times that it's happened have been preceded with a rapid increase in his pulse. Let's say that this is connected to a period of increasing danger or fear in his dream. Now let's say that he is killed, in his dream and his brain shuts down the heart. The results show that his brain activity increases rather that decreases as the heart stops, and my theory is that his mind disassociates itself from the dream and kicks the body's functions back in. Of course this is all hypothetical at this stage.'

'So how is it going to end?' asked Laura. 'If what you say is true he could keep going round the loop for ever.'

'Well yes he could, however...' Dr Phillips rubbed his chin and thought for a moment before continuing. 'If those theories are correct, then at the point that his heart is restarted he's with us, completely cut off from the dream world. I think that if we can stop the heart from *restarting* we can keep his brain with us, long enough to sever the ties with the dream world completely. The brain should continue attempting to start the heart and we should be able to see on the monitors when the tie is broken. Then it's a simple case of resuscitating him.'

'And if your theories are wrong?' asked Laura.

'Well it's not without risk, I admit. However, what have we got to lose; if it doesn't work, and we would be able to tell from the real time brain activity, then we simply allow the heart to restart and we're back to square one.'

'And if you can't restart the heart, or lose him between the two worlds?'

'Laura, you have to realise that there aren't really two worlds; it's all just going on in his brain. I could stop your heart now and restart it in two minutes without you suffering any lasting damage. Tony's the same. However before we go ahead we want to study some more of these attacks, maybe even go for a dry run whilst he's still in the coma, and of course we won't try anything until we've talked it through with yourself and Mrs. Harrison.

'Have you ever seen or done anything like this before, Doctor?'

'No, even patients in the deepest comas we've seen have had some output. To be honest with you, if we saw a trace similar to Tony's in any other case, we would assume the brain had died. If that were so, the body would have to be kept alive artificially. In Tony's case the body is still functioning perfectly under its own steam and obviously the brain is capable of coherent activity as we saw during the attack. As far as I know this is the only case like it recorded. In fact I have spoken to a Dr Wiess, the leading man in this field in the United States. He's going to fly over from New York as soon as he can. He's done a lot of research with long term comas brought on by drug abuse. There are similarities, as the patients seem to keep 'tripping' whilst in the coma. He may be able to shed some light on what's going on. Anything is worth a try.'

'Well thank you for being so open with me Doctor. I'm going to get back to him now. I'll also tell his mother what you've told me if that's Ok?'

'Yes, of course. And as I said, please call me Mike.'

'Ok, goodbye Mike.'

'Goodbye Laura.'

Mike smiled to himself knowing full well that the next time they spoke she would have reverted to calling him Doctor Phillips. He gathered the papers and stylus traces on his desk and stared into space wondering if his theories were anywhere near the mark. He looked forward to meeting Doctor Wiess; just to discuss the case with a similar mind and hopefully reach some mutual conclusions. In the meantime, he thought, I'd better get back to running this clinic. He sighed and pulled his heaped in tray towards him.

Laura hurried back to Harry's bedside and explained to Mary what the Doctor felt was happening.

'It doesn't sound very likely to me,' Mary said. 'It sounds as though they just want to experiment on him.'

'Well I suppose they know best, and they won't try anything without your say so,' said Laura, careful to emphasise that Mary was the next of kin.

'Well, we'll all talk about it when and if the situation arises,' Mary replied. 'But now I'm going to get a bus home and prepare something for us to eat this evening.'

'I'll drop you back to Helston Mary, there's no need to catch a bus.'

'No you stay here with Tony, I want some time to think anyway.'

Mary paused at the door on her way out. She watched as Laura held her son's hand and spoke to him. What does she find to talk about, Mary thought as she gently closed the door and made her way out of the clinic.

Laura never ran out of things to say. She didn't know if he could hear her, though they say that hearing is the last sense to be lost, or the first to be recovered. Certainly the brain registered no different output when she did talk to him, but apart from anything else it was good therapy for her. Today she was re-telling one of the stories he had told her one evening down at the Angel. It was about the Pope of all things.

Chapter Twenty-Five

Brad was dreaming. He was in a strange car, though he couldn't work out quite what was wrong with it, driving through strange countryside. As he turned left off the main road he knew what felt strange about the car; it was right hand drive and he was driving on the wrong side of the road. Because of this and the green, hilly scenery he guessed he was in England. The road he was now on was twisting through a narrow gorge between two high hedges, or were they walls. A sign was coming up, but as he tried to read it, it became blurred. Still he seemed to know where he was going so he was happy just to drift with it. Before long he took a right turn and pulled into a small car park. From the boot he collected his equipment and made his way along the footpath to the side of a lake of about four and a half acres. The water was in the shape of a rounded capital A and Brad made his way up the left-hand leg and settled himself opposite the island. The swim he'd chosen neatly concealed him between two large clumps of Bog Iris and allowed him access to the bank of bull rushes growing on the island opposite.

Sitting himself on his tackle box, Brad carefully untied the laces on the khaki rod bag and drew out the split cane rod. Fitting the two sections together, he weighed the rod in his hand with satisfaction. It was a Richard Walker Mk IV Carp rod, the best of its kind in its day. Brad looked down the length of the rod marvelling at the craftsmanship that had gone into its making. The cane appeared amber with a gloss finish over the eight sets of maroon ring bindings and the smaller whipped rings that ran about every third of an inch the entire length of the rod. The handle was about two and a half feet of cork finished off with a rubber stopper. Fitting the centre pin reel Brad quickly tackled up with 12lb line and a simple quill float set at about eight feet. The end rig was a number 6 hook and a very small piece of split shot. Baiting up with a large piece of bread flake he skilfully cast to within about two feet of the far bank. Laying the rod in its rest he sat back and watched with satisfaction as the bread slowly sunk from sight at a natural speed. Brad knew it would end up resting gently on the bottom, which was surprising since he had never been fishing before in his life.

'Mornin' son, that'll be two pound fifty please.' Brad looked round at the short chubby man with his out-stretched hand. Reaching into his pocket Brad brought out a handful of change, sorted out the correct amount and gave it to the bailiff.

'Hi Charlie, how's it been fishing the last couple of weeks?' he said to the old man that puffed and wheezed after the walk round the lake. Before he answered Charlie reached into a pocket and pulled out a grubby handkerchief. He mopped at the sweat forming on his bald pate. Brad was amazed at the purple red colour of his face, not to mention the scowl on his features.

'Not too good son.' Charlie smiled at him and his face took on a cherubic look and Brad relaxed. 'Still you seem to do quite well however it's fishing.'

Brad shrugged the comment off with a smile and asked. 'Any sign of the Pope?'

'No lad, you won't see him in this sort of weather. He ain't been caught for the last three years as well you know. I've not even seen 'im topping of late.'

The Pope was a large Common Carp that had lost an eye due to some careless handling when he was first caught ten years ago. He wasn't seen again for seven years, after which Charlie caught him. He weighed in at 21lb 13oz on that occasion, a record for the pond, and people had been coming to try for him ever since.

'Well you never know,' said Brad.

'Now then, if you really want to 'ave a go at 'im you'd be better off with a boilie out in the deep water.'

'I've no doubt you're right,' responded Brad. 'But I like this spot and I love the old methods. No optonics for me, at least not today.'

In the light of day none of this would mean anything to Brad, he wouldn't even have heard of an optonic, let alone know what to do with one. The fact that the electronic bite indicator wouldn't be invented for another forty years didn't seem to worry whatever force was driving his dream.

'Arr well, best of luck then my handsome,' said Charlie who had recovered and moved off with his rolling gait.

As he turned back to his fishing Brad saw the red tip of his float give a twitch. He gently rested his right hand on the handle of his rod. The float twitched again but Brad waited. Over the next couple of minutes the inch or so of visible float bobbed and jigged until finally it rose up about two inches, abruptly lay on its side and then slid below the water. Now Brad reacted; lifting the rod in an easy striking motion. He felt the hook set and immediately knew he wasn't into a big fish. The bite had been characteristic of a Tench, and sure enough after a short but very worthy fight he had a tench of about 2 - 3 lbs. in the net. He wet his hands and gently held the fish, the barbless hook easily removed from the rubbery mouth. It was a beautiful specimen, the body a deep shining green, the scales too small to tell one from the next. The light caught in the red, teddy bear eye as Brad gently slid the fish back into the water.

Baiting up again he hit the same spot with his next cast and almost immediately the float disappeared. That's more like a carp bite he thought to himself as he struck and missed the fish. More bread, another cast and he was ready again. Time doesn't have much meaning in dreams but he knew it was a long wait before anything else happened; it was evening before the float moved again. It was just a small twitch, he almost missed it, and after ten minutes he thought that he'd imagined it or else the fish had got away with the bread. As he reached down for the rod he was amazed to see the top section swinging round to the left. Initially his mind could not comprehend what was happening but he grabbed the rod and struck. It felt like he had struck the bottom; there was no give at all as the hook drove home. The next second line was being torn off the reel and Brad knew he was into a big fish. He gave as much pressure as he dared, slowing the reel with his thumb.

The trusty rod was bent double; this was what it was built for after all but Brad had to back off the pressure as the line began to sing. The fish had bolted for the deep water and Brad was worried that it was going to take him round the island and smash the line on the far bank. He tried to put some side strain on the fish but to no avail, it was going where it wanted to go and there was nothing he could do about it. The fish was kiting round to the right and he thought the game was up when it suddenly changed direction, its initial run coming to an end. Brad increased the strain but as soon as it felt it the fish bolted again, this time going for some lilies in the top corner of the lake. Brad increased the pressure; straining the rod over to the right and started to wonder about the integrity of his tackle. He was in every angler's dilemma; enjoying the struggle, yet at the same time wishing it were over with the fish safely in the landing net.

Brad was starting to make ground in that he managed to turn the fish before it reached the lilies. But the struggle was far from over. He still hadn't managed to retrieve any line and now the fish was on another screaming run, stripping yet more line from the reel. Happy now that the kit he was using could stand up to anything the fish could produce, Brad increased the pressure yet again. The line was singing once more but Brad was starting to recover some onto the centre pin reel. Using the strength of the rod he started to lift the fish to the surface. Dropping the rod he would wind in a few yards and then put the strain back on. This was a dangerous time, the sudden jerk as the fish tried to go deep tested his tackle to the limits.

The give and take of ground went on for about 15 minutes but eventually the pressure started to tell on the carp. With an explosion of water the fish broke surface, Brad catching a flash of its golden flank as it rolled and made another dash for freedom. This time its head was easily pulled around and again it came to the surface, the water boiling as its tail beat the air trying to gain purchase. Brad increased the pressure yet again causing the head to come up and roll to the right. As it did so Brad saw the empty eye socket 'staring' at him and he knew what he'd suspected from the first run. He had the Pope at last.

Though there was still the danger of any last minute dashes the fight was won and moments later Brad was bringing the Pope onto the bank in his landing net. It was a beautiful fish, marred only by the missing eye. Brad gently laid the fish on his unhooking mat released it from the line and then weighed it in a dampened sack. At Twenty-seven pounds and five ounces it was a magnificent specimen and showed the weight increase consistent with living in a 'well fed' lake. As he carefully lifted the fish out of the sack, Charlie arrived, breathless and even redder than before after running as fast as his short legs would carry him from the other side of the lake.

'I thought as much, it's the Pope right enough,' he gasped, holding his chest that was rising and falling at an alarming rate. 'I was on me way round when I saw you playing him, so's I went back an' fetched me camera.'

Two minutes later the pictures were taken and cradling the Pope in his arms, Brad went to the waters edge and held the fish in the shallows, giving it time to get its 'breath' back. As he finally released it, running his hand lightly down the massive flank one last time, it gave a flick of its tail, throwing water up into Brad's face as it returned to the deep waters of Bolingey Lake.

'Wake up you filthy dog, who said you could sleep?' As Brad was coming round he received a boot in the ribs to go with the bucket of his own urine that had been thrown in his face. He quickly came to his feet, the dream all but forgotten. As he came to his senses, Brad cursed himself for sleeping so long and missing the opportunity to attempt escape through the roof. He wiped the foul smelling liquid from his face and looked at Smidt. The shorter Japanese Officer whom Brad correctly assumed was Horshima, and who had delivered the verbal and physical abuse, accompanied him. They conversed briefly in Japanese before Smidt turned to Brad.

'This is your last chance to talk to me. If you don't then I'm afraid I can't be held responsible for the treatment you receive.'

'You can't deny responsibility and you know it,' responded Brad. 'Whatever blood is spilt here will be on your hands as much as anyone else's.'

Smidt turned away, spoke briefly to Horshima and left the building. When he spoke it was in broken, heavily accented English.

'So, stubborn Yankee Airman, where you fly from?' Brad said nothing but watched as Horshima slowly circled him, swinging the thin cane that he held, against his calf. He was expecting the blow to come and easily ducked below the arc of the cane. Horshima was caught off balance allowing Brad to grab hold of his swinging arm and force him to the floor. He didn't go for any half measures but dropped with his full weight on one knee, landing on the exposed neck of the sprawling Japanese Officer. Brad heard the vertebrae under him snap. He held his position as Horshima gurgled his last breath, and then sat back on his haunches wondering what his next move should be. He quickly located the revolver sheathed in its leather holster.

'Leave that exactly where it is Lieutenant Bradshaw.'

Brad immediately raised his hands in the air and turned to face Smidt who stood in the open doorway. Brad could see a rifle, held by the guard who stood behind Smidt, pointing at his chest.

'Give me one good reason why I shouldn't have you shot,' said Smidt, looking down at Horshima. Brad remained silent. Smidt dropped to one knee and inspected the body, ensuring there was no vestige of life.

'I told him you were dangerous, that he should have a guard with him, but the arrogant little bastard thought he was invincible like the rest of his race.' Climbing to his feet he looked back over to Brad, and said: 'Well I guess you've just put me in charge here, at least until they send a replacement for Horshima.'

The German gave an order to the guard who had remained in the doorway. Turning, the guard called for assistance and a few minutes later Brad was alone in the room bound securely to the chair. Testing his bonds he realised that there would be no escape this time and so settled down to grab some more sleep.

Chapter Twenty-Six

Lucy jerked awake and looked around. In the light of the dying embers from the fire they had built earlier, she could make out the bulk of Matthew sleeping peacefully. Rubbing her aching back she climbed to her feet and started as a figure stumbled through the open doorway. Lucy quickly reached for the rifle that lay by her pack.

'Lucy wait, it's me, Frank.'

She stopped in her tracks and stared at the untidy heap in the doorway.

'Frank? What's happened? Where's Brad?'

'I'm hit Lucy.' He indicated useless right arm that had lost its earlier dressing and hung limp and bleeding by his side. 'We've got to get out of here; I think I may have been followed.'

'What is it, what's going on?' Matthew had bounded to his feet showing the agility and response of a much younger man.

'It's Frank, he's been shot,' said Lucy, and then to Frank. 'Where is he Frank, where's Brad?'

Frank looked up, his face miserable. 'I'm sorry Lucy, I really am. We were spotted in the middle of a river by a Jap patrol. The first stream of bullets cut him down. I caught this one trying to pull him to the bank but had to leave him to save being killed myself.'

'Well we've got to go and rescue him then,' she said, turning to get support from Matthew. Frank too looked up at Matthew and then dropped his gaze.

'I'm sorry Lucy, I thought I'd made myself clear. He wasn't captured by the Japs, he was killed by them.'

Realisation came to Lucy and she was shocked by her reaction to the news. Her stomach contracted in a spasm of pain and she felt the vomit rise in her throat. Her legs buckled and she dropped to her hands and knees, spewing the contents of her belly onto the earthen floor. There

169

were no tears, just an empty feeling; a feeling of utter desperation and helplessness. Gradually the heaving stopped and Matthew helped her to sit up.

Once she was steady he left her and tended to Frank, inspecting and dressing the wound in his forearm as best he could. As he worked, Frank filled in the details of their spying mission on the village. Using the truth wherever he could, he made no mention of the presence of Germans and fabricated over the areas of his involvement with the 'enemy' and of course of the 'demise' of Brad. As Matthew finished Frank looked down at the amateur job he'd made of splinting the broken limb. He smiled his thanks and then made his way over to Lucy. Kneeling in front of her he said. 'He didn't suffer Lucy, it was quick and I'm sure he would have preferred that to being taken prisoner.'

'But why did it have to happen, why?' Now she burst into tears and Frank held her. He couldn't be sure, but as Matthew went to the door to stand guard he could have sworn he saw a smile on Frank's face.

Chapter Twenty-Seven

Brad awoke to the sound of raised voices. He was desperately uncomfortable, his limbs stiff from the immobility enforced upon them. He tried to loosen the bonds securing him to the chair but just caused the rope to cut deeper into his wrists and ankles. His testicles still hurt like hell and he could feel the beat of his heart in his broken finger that he could see was swollen and black. He tried to relax and instead of struggling he strained to hear what was going on outside. Though he couldn't understand the words, which had risen in volume to a monumental level, it was obvious that a German, probably Smidt, was involved in a full-scale argument with a Japanese. As if to confirm this, the apoplectic Officer burst into the room muttering to himself in German.

Turning to look at Brad he smiled. 'You know these people are barbarians.' He paused as if waiting for a reply. When there was none he continued. 'They want to chop you up and use you for fish bait. Lucky for you I outrank them but I don't think that's going to keep them away for too much longer. Of course if I can show them that you are providing us with useful information...'

'You're wasting your time Smidt, and you know it.'

'Do not interrupt me again Lieutenant Bradshaw, or I shall invite some of them in to assist me. They have some novel ideas when it comes to interrogating prisoners.'

Brad was sure that Smidt was making empty threats, but still he felt a shiver run down his spine in any case.

'Don't dress it up with words, Smidt, you're talking about torture and you would have to be a party to it.'

'I think not, you see I am a little out of my, how do you say it, jurisdiction.'

'Yes,' replied Brad. 'I was meaning to ask what the German Army was doing in the middle of the Pacific. Even I can't see Hitler teaming up with this lot.'

'Don't let it worry you Lt Bradshaw, and besides, I will ask the questions.' Smidt paced the room for a few minutes. Having come to some internal decision he turned and left the hut without saying a word. A few minutes later a young Japanese soldier entered the room and sliced through the restraining ropes with a bayonet. As Brad rubbed his wrists and ankles trying to straighten out the rumpled skin and lay it over the weeping sores, a breakfast of steamed fish and rice was pushed through the doorway. Brad did not feel hungry but gulped the food down quickly aware that he must try to build up his strength if he were to attempt an escape. He washed the meal down with a mug of liquid that he discovered was coconut milk and then sat back on the chair feeling a lot better.

This was really the first chance he'd had to sit and think since his capture. His mind turned to Lucy and Matthew. Surely Frank would have led the enemy to their hiding place in the jungle. He thought it strange that Smidt had made no mention of them. Brad knew that a woman could make a good lever when it came to extracting information from a stubborn subject. As he thought of her, he found it easy to conjure up a picture in his mind and was surprised at how strongly he felt for her. Suddenly the thought that she might be dead jumped into his brain. She certainly wasn't the type of girl that would take too kindly to capture; she was sure to have put up some kind of resistance. Maybe that was why Smidt had said nothing. He tried to put the thought out of his mind but he was left with an empty feeling in his heart.

Brad was left alone for a long time and he guessed it was mid afternoon before Smidt returned to the hut. A small middle-aged Japanese Officer followed him into the room. Though Brad found that most of the Orientals looked alike to him, there was something about this one that made him stand out from the rest, something sinister. He stared into the wrinkled face with its thin un-smiling lips and small pinched nose, but it was the eyes that held his attention. They were dark, really dark. It was almost impossible to tell where the pupil ended and the iris started and they held ones gaze, giving the impression of being sucked into an abyss. Brad managed to drag his eyes away and looked back to Smidt.

'Lt Bradshaw, this is Captain Tongora,' he said indicating the other man. 'He is Horshima's replacement. Though we are enemies I would like to say that I do not approve of what is about to happen and that I am here as interpreter only. Tongora has no English,' he concluded needlessly.

Brad felt the blood drain from his face as he realised the meaning of his words. Smidt was warning him that things were about to get nasty.

'I understand,' said Brad looking down to the floor to hide his fear. Tongora shouted something in Japanese and the sentry came into the room taking up station in the far corner. They were taking no chances this time. And so the interrogation began. Questions were fired at Brad through Smidt. They started out simple enough; name, rank, number, and Brad answered truthfully. However it wasn't to last and the subject quickly came round to questions about his unit, his mission, Ships positions and other areas where Brad would offer no answer. He was surprised that he received no mal-treatment from Tongora and indeed after about thirty minutes the interview was terminated, Brad was secured to the chair and all other parties left the room. Later Brad was to realise it was just a tactic in an attempt to lower his guard, but for now it was a relief after the tension he'd felt earlier.

Towards the end of the afternoon another simple meal was brought to him and shortly after a medic was brought in to tend to the wounds left by the fish hooks that had now been removed. Though he was still secured to the chair, Brad was starting to feel human again and so it was even more of a shock when two guards came in and started shouting at him. As one released his bonds the other struck him across the temple with his rifle butt and so it was a dazed Brad that was half dragged out into the main meeting place of the village. Brad raised his hand to wipe the trickle of blood that was streaming into his right eye. In return he received another blow from the rifle, this time in his guts. He doubled over and dropped to his knees retching and spewing up the simple meal he'd so enjoyed earlier.

As he recovered he looked around and saw about a dozen Jap soldiers standing around the large central fire, two German soldiers keeping to the shadows, and a number of civilian women who he presumed were locals of the village. They were quite different from the petit women he had seen earlier. They were much larger in build and looked more Polynesian than Japanese. He noticed that they were all crying. As his stomach started to settle down he moved his attention to the two Officers approaching him. Tongora started to address him and he looked towards Smidt for the translation.

'In return for the murder of Captain Horshima,' began Smidt. 'Three of the village men folk, who are guilty also, of collaborating with the enemy, have been sentenced to death.' Brad looked up at Smidt as the horror of what he heard sank in. Smidt averted his eyes, unable to bring himself to look at Brad, and continued speaking. 'The first of these executions will take place immediately, the second at sunset tomorrow and the third the following day.'

'You can't do this,' shouted Brad. 'They haven't done anything.' His outburst was punctuated with yet another rifle blow, this time to the back of the head, which sent him sprawling to the dusty floor. One of the women started to whine loudly and looking up Brad saw a native in a loincloth escorted into the arena. He had the same characteristics as the women, but in the light of the fire he could make out the intricate patterns of tattoos over the chest and upper arms. This was a warrior. The woman, whose whine had now risen to a wail, rushed forward towards her man. More use of the rifle butt stopped her dead in her tracks. The warrior showed his first sign of emotion. It wasn't fear as Brad might have expected from one who was about to be executed, it was anger. The native turned to stare at Tongora and the look turned to one of pure hatred. He started to speak in a deep guttural voice that quickly increased in volume and became a chant. The women picked up the rhythm and in the distance, though muffled by the buildings, the deep rumble of men's voices could be heard joining the chant.

The reaction from Tongora was immediate, brutal and effective. Drawing the Samurai sword that hung from his waist he made one seemingly effortless strike towards the warrior. His singing stopped as a thin red line appeared on his neck. The woman who had been knocked to the floor let out a blood-curdling shriek as a gaping wound opened up in her husband's throat. Brad shut his eyes and turned away, but not before the image of a fountain of blood that erupted from the wound was imprinted on his mind. Tongora never said a word, but turned on his heel and left the scene. Brad looked around at the others around the fire. The men he correctly assumed were the firing squad started to shamble away, obviously disappointed with the outcome of what had promised to be an entertaining afternoon. The widow of the warrior that had died appeared to have fainted; lying still in the dust. Finally he looked at Smidt who returned his stare. His face said that he could not have done anything to change the events that had just occurred and Brad saw the truth in this.

Brad was roughly dragged to his feet and returned to the hut, to be bound to his chair and there he was left with his own thoughts. He found the tears came easily. He'd seen plenty of death and violence of late, even killed others himself, but this was the first time that some one had been killed for one of his actions. He felt responsible for the warrior's death and guilty as he thought of the widow left behind. He looked up as Smidt entered the room, but felt no embarrassment at the tears that continued to roll down his cheeks.

'Could you not have stopped that barbaric display?' he asked, but he knew the answer before Smidt said a word.

'I have not come to talk about what has happened, but what is about to happen. I can only advise you once again, to tell them everything they want to know.' He held up his hand as Brad was about to reply. 'Don't say anything, I know your answer. You are a brave and honourable man, Lieutenant Bradshaw. Though you are American, I have come to respect you and I take this opportunity to apologise for the rough treatment you received at my hands earlier. Good luck Lieutenant.' With those last words hanging in the air he turned and left the room before Brad had a chance to reply. They were the last pleasant words he was to hear for some time.

It was some thirty minutes later that Smidt returned, this time in the company of Tongora and another Japanese. Brad hadn't seen the newcomer before. He was a bear of a man, possibly weighing as much as 18 stone yet only about 5 foot 4 inches tall. His head was completely bald and set straight into his torso; there being no evidence of a neck. His eyes were slanted as with all Orientals but they were set very close together giving him a menacing look. He looked at Brad and smiled showing the gap where his top front teeth should have been. Brad stared back, not allowing any emotion to show on his face. Tongora started the same stream of questions as before, with Smidt interpreting and the newcomer as yet taking no part in the proceedings. It was as Brad first refused to answer a question that the role of the third man became clear. With the back of his hand he swotted Brad as if he were a bothersome insect. He was lifted clean off the floor, still secured to the chair. Over balancing, he was unable to use his bound hands to protect his face as it crashed into the floor and he felt the flesh of his lips split against his teeth and tasted the salty presence of his own blood. With one hand his antagonist yanked the chair, setting it upright again in front of Tongora.

176

Over the next hour or so Brad was subjected to a barrage of questions that he would not answer and as a result received a beating that he would previously been unable to imagine. His face felt twice its normal size and his sight was becoming badly affected as his sockets swelled and closed around the red eyes held within. His lips were swollen and bleeding, his nose was blocked with dried blood and broken in at least two places and the small wound in his cheek from the fishing hook had opened up into an ugly gash. His body had also received its fair share; his arms and legs feeling the main effects of the kicks and punches that had rained upon him. Despite all this he was amazed at how he had become almost immune to the treatment. It still hurt, but if he told himself that it wasn't getting any worse, it became bearable. It was still, however, a great relief when his three antagonists turned and left.

Brad was left alone for the time being and his thoughts turned to escape. It didn't take a genius to work out that he wasn't going to be able to put up with the sort of treatment he'd just received for too much longer. He briefly considered if there were any snippets of information, or mis-information, he could reveal that would sound like he was co-operating, but would be of no use to the enemy in the long run. Eventually he discarded this option: once he started to talk there was no telling what information might spill out or what contradictory information he might give over-time, ultimately leading to his deception being discovered. He didn't care to consider the consequences. Looking around the bare room with his distorted vision he was aware that it was starting to get dark and he hoped that he'd be left alone for the night. Thinking back to the brief talk that they'd had about torture he thought this was probably unlikely. He tested the bonds securing hio hands to the seat. They cut into his wrists as he twisted first one way and then the other and all he succeeded in doing was to aggravate the damage that had already been done. He didn't seem to be making too much progress but kept on trying; at least it took his mind off his battered face, which was throbbing atrociously. He was still trying to loosen his hands when he fell into a fitful sleep.

Chapter Twenty-Eight

Laura opened her eyes. She had fallen asleep in the chair next to Harry's bed. Someone had covered her with a hospital blanket, which in itself was luxurious, but to her no more than she had come to expect at the institute. She looked around, slowly taking in her surroundings; her eyes finally coming to rest on Harry as he lay peacefully sleeping. His breathing was regular and there was no movement in the features she could see. But Laura knew that things could change so suddenly and that there was a team of experts waiting for something to happen on the other side of the curtained window behind her. She looked round at the window but could see nothing of the lab on the other side.

She found herself in two minds. On the one hand she wanted him to be able to remain lying there peacefully. On the other she knew that this wouldn't bring him back to her and that Mike's theories were going to have to be tried at some stage. But it just seemed so extreme to stop his heart restarting spontaneously so they could break the ties with his dream world. Laura didn't doubt that they could resuscitate him when they were ready, but what would he be like once he came round? Would he even remember her? She recalled the case of a close friend whose husband had a severe car accident. He was only in a coma for about a week and when he came round everything appeared to be normal. It wasn't until he came home that Dawn started to notice changes in him. First it was small things; fanatical about security, staying up at night until she was asleep, bad irritable spells, etc. Slowly things became more sinister. She would wake up in the middle of the night with him on top of her trying to make love to her. The final straw was when she awoke on one of these occasions and he knocked her into unconsciousness and carried on. The following morning he got up as if nothing had happened. She waited for him to go out for his daily walk, then packed an overnight bag and left the house. She later found out that he had damaged the part of the brain that inhibits these sorts of actions in the normal case.

At least Harry hasn't had a brain injury she thought, but who knows what had been going on in that head of his these past weeks. She got up slowly and walked over to the door. She decided to go along to the canteen for some breakfast before heading home to shower and freshen up for the day. Entering the room, that served as a restaurant and was decorated in the same tasteful way as the rest of the building, she saw that the only other 'customers' were Doctor Phillips and Mary who were sat together by the large bay window that overlooked the gardens. Laura walked over and joined them.

'Good morning, my dear,' said the Doctor. 'We were just talking about the next steps to take in Tony's case.'

As Laura took a seat at the table, a young girl dressed smartly in a blue skirt and white blouse came over and took her order of muesli and black coffee. She felt a knot of apprehension in her throat.

'And what have you decided is your next course of action?' she asked.

'Well we wanted to talk to you before we made any decisions,' said Mary. 'I'm not blind to the devotion you have shown him and I think that you have the right to put your thoughts forward.'

Laura felt a flood of emotion surge through her and could not stop the tears from spilling onto her cheeks.

'That's very generous of you Mary, it really means a lot to me. As for what to do next...I think the only thing we can do is let Mike go ahead with his plans. I just can't think of anything...' She couldn't finish the sentence and Mary put a comforting arm around her as the girl arrived with Laura's breakfast. She pushed away the bowl of cereal and picked up the cup of steaming coffee.

'So then, we're all agreed,' said Mike softly. 'I'll get off and brief the team so that we're ready as soon as anything happens. We'll just go for a dry run the first time, just to make sure there are no unforeseen problems. I'll keep you informed.' With that he got up and left the two women to their individual thoughts.

Entering the Lab overlooking Harry's room he saw that the curtains had been drawn open now that Laura had left his bedside. Two technicians were playing a game of chess as they monitored the equipment. Dr Phillips saw that everything was quiet and left instructions that he was to be called if there was even the slightest change in Harry's condition or outputs. Satisfied that everything that could be done was being done he left and went back to his office to start the rest of the day's work.

Chapter Twenty-Nine

Lucy awoke and found herself on her own on the hard floor of the hut they had made their base. She sat up quickly, worried for the others, but then relaxed as she heard their voices outside the open door. Climbing to her feet she walked stiffly over to the opening and looked out into the still air of the clearing. Frank and Matthew were sitting about 10 yards away and seemed to be tied up in some frantic discussion. As Lucy pushed her way through the door the two men stopped talking guiltily and Matthew stood up and walked over to her.

'How did you sleep?' he asked in a concerned voice. 'I thought...'

'What are you two arguing about,' she interrupted. 'Obviously something you didn't want me to hear if you felt the need to come out here.'

'We were merely thinking of you sleeping,' said Frank as he sidled up to her.

'So what was it then, what were you arguing about.'

Before Matthew could start to say anything Frank put his arm around her shoulders and tried to turn her back towards the hut.

'Get your hands off me and answer the question,' burst Lucy with such vehemence that Matthew rushed over and forced himself between them.

'We were just contemplating what we should do next,' said Matthew. 'I think we should stay put for the time being, but Frank wants to move deeper into the jungle. Whatever we decide must include plans to get hold of some supplies pretty soon.'

'Ok,' said Frank. 'I'll make a raid into the village tonight and see what I can come up with. I won't give anything away as they saw me with Brad yesterday. In the meantime I still think we should get further away; Jap patrols are bound to drop in on this place sooner or later.

Anyway, you think about it. I'm off to get some water.'

He left the two of them alone in the clearing as he departed with the water canteen he'd removed from one of the soldiers killed the day before and of course the ever present rifle. 'I'll be back sometime after dark.' He said as he ventured onto the path. 'I want to get into position near the village as early as possible.'

Matthew fussed over Lucy for a while and when he'd got her comfortably sitting and eating the last of the tinned food, he asked for her assessment of the situation.

'I really don't know what to do for the best,' she replied. 'Brad would have known if...' She left the unfinished sentence hanging in the air. 'I just can't believe he's gone.' She stared off into space; deep in thought.

'Were you two close?' asked Matthew quietly.

'We'd only just met really,' she said in reply. 'But I felt so devastated when Frank said he was dead. I've never felt like that about anybody before.'

Matthew sat himself down next to her and gently put his arm around her. 'I could see he was something special,' he said. 'I think he was one of those few people who touch the lives of others as they go about their own.'

'Yes, but I think there was more than that, I think that I had touched him in the same way. But maybe that's just my wishful thinking.'

'No, you're right,' he said. 'I could see it in his eyes when he left you the other morning.' He looked at her as he finished the sentence and saw the glistening of tears in her eyes. He went to hold her but she pulled away. 'No,' she said. 'There have been enough tears and they didn't help any.' She sat staring into space for a short while then turning to Matthew: 'You know what?' she said, cheerfully, indicating that the moment had passed. 'I think you and I ought to have a good look round this area and see how we can best warn ourselves against an attack if, God forbid Frank is right and the Japs do show up.'

She hauled herself to her feet and offered her hand to Matthew. Smiling at the resolve of this fine young woman he allowed her to assist him to his feet.

'I would think the main area of danger is the track leading to the village.' She indicated the path that Frank had disappeared down a few minutes earlier. 'What do you think we could do to give us some early warning?' She had already thought of the empty tin cans but was aware that the male ego could only take so much, even in the case of a man of God.

'How about the empty food cans,' blurted Matthew. 'We could connect them up to some sort of trip wire mechanism across the path.'

Lucy smiled inwardly. 'Great idea,' she said. 'I'll collect them up whilst you have a hunt around for something to use as the trip wire.

They both set about the tasks they'd set themselves and in about half an hour they had finished. The cans, all five of them, had been loosely strung together and then hidden in the trees just off the side of the track about fifty yards into the forest. Matthew had fashioned some natural twine out of creepers he'd torn from the statue at the side of the clearing. These had made an excellent trip wire when connected to the cans and strung tightly across the path just above ground level. Satisfied, Matthew asked Lucy to go back to their hut whilst he tested the system. Having set off the trap he waited for Lucy to join him with her report.

'I heard it, but only just,' she called breathlessly as she ran along the path. 'I think we need to bring it a fair bit closer.'

Talking about it, they decided on halving the distance from the edge of the clearing and this time Matthew returned to the hut and Lucy set it off.

'That's fine,' he reported as he joined her back on the track. 'Now what else can we do to surprise them should they show up?'

'What about weapons?' she asked. 'If they're only expecting to come across one man, and injured at that, they may only send a small patrol. It would be a shame to warn the rest of the village with a rifle shot or two in the middle of the night.'

Matthew once again marvelled at the resourcefulness of the girl. 'How about bows and arrows,' he suggested. Lucy screwed her face up a little but then agreed to give it a go if only to keep them busy. They cut the required raw materials from the forest but however hard they tried they couldn't manufacture a working weapon. After three attempts they gave up and decided to walk down to the stream to get some fresh water. Lucy led the way with the rifle. Matthew was more than happy for her to take on this responsibility as she had seemed perfectly at ease with the weapon earlier on.

It was on the way back that Matthew suddenly stopped, slapping his hand on his forehead. Without saying anything to Lucy he cut a straight branch from a tree. She watched, fascinated, as he trimmed the stick to about 18 inches long and half an inch in diameter. He sharpened one end and put a split in the other, then searched the pockets in his safari suit and produced a piece of card. He divided it into two equal parts and pushed them into the split to form rudimentary flights on a very strange looking arrow.

'Ok, so what are you going to do with that?' she laughed. 'Throw it at them?'

'Sort of,' he replied mysteriously. He took the length of string that had been salvaged from their abortive attempt at a bow and tied a large knot in one end.

'Come on, follow me.' He pushed his way past her and almost ran back to the clearing. By the time Lucy had reset the trip wire he'd set off in his haste and entered the camp, she found him standing by the hut with his right hand containing the contraption over his shoulder.

'Quick get behind me,' he said quickly. 'For the purpose of this demonstration the tree just left of the opening is a Jap.' With that, he threw the arrow, holding onto the string, and whooped with pleasure as it embedded itself in the tree. Lucy just stared at him in amazement.

'How did you do that?' she asked as he went to retrieve the weapon.

'I remembered something I was shown at school. I think we called them Dutch arrows or French, I'm not sure which.' He paused in thought. 'Or was that French toast? Well any way the name doesn't matter. The string acts as a lever, you see.' Holding the weapon so that she could see clearly he took a turn with the knotted end of the string just below the flights, carefully taking it back over the knot and down the shaft to his right hand that held the arrow at the pointed end.' Now you just throw it and hold onto the string.' He demonstrated the technique, once again hitting the targeted tree.

'Come on, let's make some more,' Lucy shouted. 'This I've got to try. Over the next couple of hours they made another six arrows. They practised with the original until it had all but fallen apart, then salvaged the flights and recovered one of the cans from their early warning device to fashion stronger flights for their new stock. Matthew even thought of making sharp metal points with the left over metal. When they had finished they had three arrows each and could both hit the furthest tree from the hut. Content they could now dispatch an enemy stealthily, they retired to the hut to get out of the mid afternoon sun and await Franks return, hopefully with some food.

Chapter Thirty

'Doctor Phillips and team Alpha report to Lab 5 immediately.' Once again pandemonium seemed to hit the corridors of the institute, but in fact it was a well rehearsed routine falling into action. Laura was the last one to arrive at the laboratory having been caught walking back from the car park, where she had just seen Mary off. She glanced around the room with a look of consternation on her face and her eyes came to rest on Dr Phillips who was flitting from monitor to monitor. He hadn't appeared to notice her come into the room; however he spoke without looking up.

'It's Ok Laura; it seems to be the same as last time. Nothing to worry about.'

'Are you going to try to bring him back?' she asked.

'I don't think so this time,' he answered slowly. 'I think we'll just go for a dry run as we discussed. It'll give the surgical team a chance to get themselves sorted out.'

As he spoke a group of nurses and presumably doctors burst into Harry's room and started fussing around his bed. Laura watched as the two teams prepared themselves and a few minutes later the surgical team called on the two-way intercom, a far easier system than the handset they had used last time, that they were ready to go.

'Right everyone,' Mike spoke authoritatively, immediately grabbing everyone's attention. 'That took a total of four and a half minutes from the first indications of an occurrence.' He paused dramatically. 'Next time I want you ready to go within two and a half...Any questions? Good then lets watch what happens this time and be ready in case we have to step in with the planned procedure at short notice.'

He looked round at Laura for the first time and smiled reassuringly. Walking over he explained what was going on. Harry's brain output was gradually increasing in magnitude and this had been the first indication to the team monitoring the equipment. His heartbeat was also increasing and was up at 125 beats per minute. Mike stepped over to the monitor showing brain output and said to no one in particular. 'If this is going the same way as the last time he should arrest at any moment now.'

As if he were reading from a script, alarms started to sound and all eyes in the room were drawn to the flat green line on the VDU. The team in Harry's room was galvanised into action, preparing hypodermics and readying the defibrillator.

'I don't want you to do anything yet, just standby,' barked Dr Phillips. The leader of the team looked up questioningly but received no further orders and so turned back to look at Harry. Time seemed almost to stop as Laura flicked her attention between the VDU, Harry and the clock that showed the seconds ticking by. By her reckoning she lasted for about 55 seconds before she turned to Mike.

'Please you've got to do something, he'll die.' Mike Phillips held his ground and hoped that no one else had noticed the bead of sweat running down his left temple. His resolve was about to crumble when the monitor started up, faltered, and then settled down at a steady 62 beats per minute. The sighs of relief were heard clearly in both rooms and one of the technicians walked over and silently patted Mike on the back. Laura was doing her best not to cry and turned to the Doctor as he walked over to the hard copy machine.

'You would have let him die you callous bastard,' she cried. Mike looked hurt at the accusation and tried to put his hand on Laura's shoulder but she shrugged him off.

'Of course I wouldn't have let him die, but don't you see...Don't any of you see?' He turned to the rest of the team as if seeking absolution.

'See what exactly, that you were prepared to let him die?' she screamed, letting out the bottled up tensions of the past few months. 'That you, you...' Now her anger fell away from her and she seemed to collapse inwards. Mike reached out and held her up, pulling her close to him. She was muttering something about thanking God that his mother wasn't here to see this. Mike pushed her away gently and stood looking into her face with his hands resting gently on her shoulders.

'I would never have let it go on if there was any danger of not being able to bring him back; I promise you that, Laura. What I can't promise you is success in the next stage, but this episode goes some way to prove that my theories are on the right track.' He continued more positively, allowing the two teams that were watching the two of them to hear. 'He was in complete cardiac arrest and he recovered spontaneously. Something deep inside him must be causing that and it means that we may be able to sever the ties with his dream world. I want all the traces scrutinised before his next attack to give us any clues to these unprecedented happenings. We'll also check for any signs of damage to his heart or brain.' He turned back to Laura. 'But I am positive that there won't be any,' he finished.

Laura's face broke into a half smile. 'I'm sorry to have doubted you Mike.' She stood on tiptoe and kissed him lightly on the cheek. 'I didn't mean those things I said, it's just...' She left the sentence unfinished, reached into her handbag, pulled out a clean tissue and carefully wiped the sweat from the side of Mike's face.

'Don't want you being seen with my lipstick on your face,' she said for the benefit of the other members of the team. Then smiling, she winked conspiratorially at Mike and left the room.

Hours later, Dr Phillips and the main players of alpha and bravo teams sat comfortably in the main conference room. As usual Mike held their attention.

'So, we are agreed that no damage has been detected from this morning's episode.' There were mutterings of agreement around the room and so he continued. 'Right, and we're all happy that during the next attack we'll try to bring him back.' Again the mutterings of consent. 'Team B, are you happy with the way things are going to happen?'

A young doctor answered. 'Yes sir, we've had a number of practise runs this afternoon and, of course, a full brief from Dr Tarrant of team A.'

'Good. We will only let his heart stop for a maximum of two and a half minutes. After that, no matter what I say in the heat of the moment, you are to resuscitate him using whatever means you deem necessary. Is that clear Doctor Tarrant, Dr Green?'

'Yes sir.'

'Yes Mike, perfectly.'

Happy that his two colleagues would carry out his orders to the letter without fear of repercussions, Mike continued. 'From now until this situation is resolved one way or the other I will remain at the institute 24 hours a day. Your two teams will work 12-hour shifts from 7 till 7. Depending on how I feel, or my opinion of the state of the on duty team, I alone shall make the decision to go ahead or not. If there is an episode during the hand over period from 6.55 to 7.05 there will be no attempt to carry out the procedure. Is everyone quite clear on all of that or are there any final questions?' He looked around the room until his eyes came to rest on Dr Green. He was of about the same age as Mike but looked much older; his time at the cutting edge of his field having taken its toll.

'Yes, two questions Mike. One, are we going to allow his family members to be present during the proceedings?'

'Yes Ian, we are. We're only carrying out these procedures with their permission. They are fully briefed on what will happen, they're aware of the dangers and I trust them not to act hysterically.' He smiled to himself, thinking about Laura's reaction to the dry run. 'However, having said that, this is limited to only his mother and his girlfriend, Laura. Your other question Ian?'

'Just the small matter of how you intend to stop his heart restarting spontaneously.'

'Good question,' responded Mike thoughtfully. 'And I'm open to offers.'

Chapter Thirty-One

Lucy jerked awake. It wasn't the noise of the cans that disturbed her sleep, but the sounds of Matthew struggling to his feet, only to loose his balance and crash to the floor once more.

'What on earth's going on?' she hissed to the prostrate figure.

'It's the alarm,' he whispered urgently.

'Are you sure?'

'Yes, yes, I'm a light sleeper and it was definitely the cans that woke me up.

Lucy had already grabbed the rifle and thrust it into Matthew's hands. She made her way to the door and peered out. She picked up one of the arrows that leant against the wall. Everything in the clearing was quiet as Matthew joined her.

'I don't think I can use this on another human being,' he said holding up the rifle. 'Even if it is somebody trying to kill us.'

'Don't worry,' Lucy replied. 'I'll use the arrow. You've only got that as a last resort. However, I would prefer not to be caught.' Thankfully she couldn't see the look of doubt on his face in the dull light thrown by the moon above them. Slowly she eased her way out of the hut and prepared herself to launch the dart if her foe appeared. She stayed absolutely still for a few minutes and was just about to go back into the hut and put it down to Matthew's overactive imagination, when she heard the snap of a dry stick. They had been Matthew's idea, lain on the path just inside the forest.

Lucy felt the now familiar rush of adrenaline course through her body. It's probably just Frank coming back she thought, but still she tensed herself ready to throw the missile. As she stared at the entrance to the path she caught sight of a shadow slowly creeping into the clearing. She waited, hoping Frank would identify himself. The figure crouched in the moonlit greenery and didn't move. Lucy stared and could just start to make out a uniform as her eyes grew used to the dark. Unbeknown to her, the figure could also make her out and stood up to face her, swinging the rifle off his shoulder. Lucy let go with the arrow. It flew to its target as true as a bullet, but her aim was a little off, and it thudded into his shoulder.

Realising that the wound was not going to stop him, Lucy shouted to Matthew. 'Quick, hand me the rifle!'

'Lucy wait, don't shoot, it's me, Brad.'

'Brad?' She took hold of the rifle and pointed it at the figure that had now dropped to one knee. 'Brad, is that really you?'

The kneeling figure dropped the rifle, staggered to his feet and shuffled forward to where the light of the moon fell directly onto his face. He clutched at the arrow that protruded rudely from his right shoulder. 'Yes it really is me, and...and you seem to have skewered me,' he said managing to force a smile.

'Oh God, What have I done?' cried Lucy, dropping the rifle to the ground and rushing towards the swaying figure as she recognised the voice more than Brad's battered features. 'Frank told us you were dead.'

She reached him just as his legs buckled, and managed to break his fall as he collapsed to the ground. The last thing he said as he slipped into unconsciousness was: 'Frank? Frank! He's a bloody German.'

By this time Matthew had appeared by her side and helped her half carry, half drag Brad into the shelter of the hut. They laid him on his back on one of the makeshift beds and Matthew started to get a fire together. He used one of the last few precious matches and ignited the small pile of kindling he'd scraped together. He'd decided on the fire more to give light than heat, and as the fire caught he saw Lucy leaning over Brad, trying to get a clear look at the wound in his shoulder. He piled some of the bigger dry branches he'd collected earlier and the fire took hold, throwing flickering light all about the hut.

In the light Lucy clearly saw the state of Brad for the first time and threw the back of her right hand to her mouth. The man lying in front of her was barely recognisable as the man that had left her a few days earlier. His eyes had nearly closed up, his lips were swollen and split and there was a rip in his cheek that looked as if it was infected, two fingers on his right hand were crudely bound together to support the broken one and as if all that weren't enough her arrow was deeply embedded in his right shoulder. She also noticed he was wearing a Japanese soldier's uniform that was about two sizes too small for him. He was starting to stir and she called Matthew over to help her. Matthew came across from the door that he was trying to block to stop the light alerting anyone to their presence. As he saw Brad he drew in his breath but didn't say anything. He knelt beside Lucy and took stock of the situation.

'Right, lets get that arrow out before he wakes up. Do you know if it was a metal tipped one?'

'I thought he was a Jap. I didn't know it was...'

'Was the arrow tipped with the metal we cut from the tin can?' asked Matthew more firmly.

'No...no I don't think so.'

'Well thank God for small mercies,' he said. 'Go over to the remaining arrows and check would you please. There should be four metal tipped if this isn't one of them.'

Lucy got up as if in a daze and walked over to the doorway. As soon as her back was turned Matthew grabbed the arrow close to the body and with one swift motion drew it smoothly out. Brad let out a groan and jerked his legs violently, but by the time that Lucy got back he was quiet and still once again.

'No. It's Ok there's still four of them over there.' She seemed to be pulling herself together a little and knelt down to help Matthew. There wasn't a lot of blood from the wound; the arrow had embedded quite deeply, but thankfully had missed his lung and the major vessels. Between them they stripped off most of the uniform and inspected his body for any more injuries. Even by the poor light from the fire they could see he'd recently taken a hell of a beating. There were livid bruises around his arms, legs and upper torso along with the cuts and tears from the fishing hooks.

'I can't see any bullet wounds on him,' remarked Matthew.

'Didn't you hear what he said as he collapsed outside?' asked Lucy. She continued without waiting for an answer. 'He said that Frank was a German. I thought he was delirious but there seem to be a lot of inconsistencies with regards to Frank.'

'I think you're right, and I also think we'd better get the hell out of here before he returns.' Matthew crossed himself and muttered an apology to the Lord for his language.

'We can't move him in this condition.' She looked down at Brad and gently took hold of his hand. 'He's been beaten half to death.'

'We haven't got any choice. I'm only putting two and two together, but if Frank is working with the enemy, it is only a matter of time before they notice Brad has escaped, and Frank'll lead them straight here.'

'Oh Lord Jesus help us,' cried Lucy, who seemed to be on the verge of losing it again.

'Maybe He will, maybe He won't, but one thing's for sure...He's gonna need us to play our part.' Whilst speaking, Matthew was pooling together their few resources. They had no food, a single canteen of water, a rifle, a knife and the collection of home made arrows. 'Well at least we'll be travelling light,' he said with a grin. It was just the light quip that Lucy needed to take her mind off the gravity of their predicament.

'I think he's coming round,' she said, returning her attention to Brad. 'Brad, Brad, It's me Lucy, can you hear me?'

He was starting to thrash around on the bracken bed. 'No no...no more...I can't remember.' The words sounded as if they were being torn from his soul and his lips began to bleed again as they tightened in a grimace of fear.

The words wrenched at Lucy's heart and she bent and gently kissed his forehead. 'You're safe now my darling, it's me, Lucy.' The words seemed to reach him and he stopped struggling.

'Where's Frank?' he cried. As he continued his voice wavered down to a whisper. 'Where's that snivelling, traitorous bastard Frank?'

'Gone,' said Matthew coming to Lucy's side. 'For the time being anyway, but we've got to get out of here, now whilst it's still dark. With a bit of luck if we're not here when they arrive they won't chance losing our trail at night.' He dropped down on one knee. 'Do you think you can walk Brad?'

'You bet I can.' He tried to push himself up but dropped down, cursing as the weight came on to his bad shoulder.

'Oh yes.' He smiled up at Lucy. 'You speared me, didn't you?'

'Brad, I'm so sorry.'

'No need. I'm just surprised that I worried about you left here on your own.'

Lucy helped him to his feet and held on to him as he got his bearings. Having found them safe, which was the last thing he expected, Brad felt stronger. He took a long swig from the canteen that Matthew offered him, wiped his mouth with his good arm and headed towards the door. Matthew kicked the fire into oblivion, checked that the last embers were crushed into the earthen floor, and then followed the other two out of the hut.

They made good time at first. Matthew overtook and led the way back into the forest, past the silent stone guard; retracing the steps that had led them to the clearing just a few days before. Despite Brad's injuries they reached the river in a couple of hours, a journey that had taken the best part of a day when they'd had to rent their own trail through the jungle. On reaching it Brad dropped to the ground. He had to rest up even if the devil himself was following them. At Matthew's insistence they crossed the river and pushed into the forest on the far side. He then fetched water for the other two and whilst he was at the river checked that their entry into the jungle could not be seen from the watercourse. He had noticed that as things had become more desperate he was playing a far more important role in the absence of another leader; his training in leadership taking a different route from that imagined by his tutors long ago. Satisfied, he returned to the hiding place to find Brad resting against a huge tree root just starting to recount his story to Lucy.

'...and whilst I was trying to loosen my hands I must have fallen asleep.' As if on cue Brad's chin dropped onto his chest and his breathing took up the rhythm of someone in a deep sleep. It didn't really come as a surprise to the other two; his voice had started wavering a few minutes back and he had begun to repeat the odd sentence here and there. Lucy went about making him as comfortable as their conditions permitted and then sat down next to Matthew.

'He's been through an awful lot my dear, and I think there's a fair bit more to come, but he's strong, he'll get over it.'

Lucy, who had wanted to cry during the telling of Brad's ordeal but had held back, was silent now. Nothing she could say would make any difference at this stage, and so she didn't say it. Whispering goodnight to Matthew she crawled over to Brad's side and snuggled against him in an attempt to both keep him warm, and grab a few hours sleep herself before the dawn was upon them.

It seemed like only five minutes before she was woken from her sleep by a hand being clamped over her mouth. She struggled momentarily but then gave up all resistance as she heard Matthew hissing for her to be quiet.

'There are people down at the river,' he explained after he'd released her from his grip. 'I think it's the Japanese.' They listened together, straining to hear anything that would give the slightest indication they were about to be discovered. Lucy noticed that it was already starting to get light and she'd been asleep longer than she realised. Suddenly they could hear voices coming from the river. They were definitely Japanese, but they didn't sound excited, as they might if they'd discovered anything untoward. Lucy found that she had stopped breathing in an attempt to keep quiet. Now though she had to start again and it sounded like a hurricane to her ears. The voices continued for about five minutes and then she became aware of something different. The voices weren't only Japanese; there were German voices mixed in.

'I think that's Frank's voice,' whispered Matthew. Lucy was too scared to reply, but nodded an affirmative to him.

Shortly there were sounds of the party moving off, travelling downstream. When it was quiet again they contemplated what their next move should be but despite their earlier displays of courage and leadership they seemed incapable of making a decision. They looked at Brad wondering if he would know what to do. They considered waking him but decided to let him sleep on and get his strength back. Convinced now that the coast was clear Lucy eased her way down to the river to freshen up and fill the canteen. Ten minutes later she had finished and Matthew took his turn.

Lucy sat down next to Brad and saw that he was beginning to stir. She let him wake in his own time and as he became aware of his surroundings he scared the life out of her by sitting bolt upright. Remembering where he was he relaxed and settled back with a groan. His body had stiffened up with the inactivity of sleep after the mammoth effort he'd made in escaping and getting this far with his friends.

'What's happening?' he asked Lucy. At that moment Matthew who seemed in a much better frame of mind since doing his morning ablutions rejoined them.

'Good morning my son, how are you feeling after your nights rest?' he asked jovially.

'I've had better that's for sure 'Father''

Matthew grinned at him and then turned to Lucy. 'How about rustling up some breakfast, wench.'

Lucy looked at him sternly for a moment then grinning back she tossed the water canteen over to him. 'You'll have to make do with this I'm afraid.' She paused for a second. 'Unless, of course, you caught some fish down at the river.'

Brad felt the stirring of some memories deep in the recesses of his mind at the mention of catching fish. He knew it was important but couldn't recall why. Matthew interrupted his thoughts; bringing him up to date with the morning's excitement. He finished by outlining the dilemma they now found themselves in.

'Well if you want my opinion I think we should sit it out here for a while. The search party will probably give up at some stage and double back to the village. I also think that we ought to be heading downstream rather than further into the jungle and if we leave too soon we're likely to bump into them. Let's wait here until we hear them go back.'

Lucy reached out and lightly stroked his swollen face. 'Ok, I'm with Brad,' she said, glad to have him to make the decision. 'What about you Matthew?'

'Couldn't agree more,' he said, glad for the same reason. 'And as you have us here as a captive audience why don't you finish telling us your escape story Brad?'

'Sure, where did I get to?'

'You fell asleep in the hut in the village trying to loosen the rope on your wrists,' Lucy answered.

'Oh yes,' said Brad looking down at the raw flesh round his forearms. 'I was getting nowhere with the bonds anyway, so sleep seemed to be the best option.'

Chapter Thirty-Two

Brad was dreaming about flying again but this time he wasn't enjoying it. He was being chased. He hadn't seen anyone or anything behind him but he felt the presence there; a sinister, dark propinquity, slowly gaining on him, taking away any joy he may have had of floating freely amongst the cloud tops. He bent at the waist and dove into a thick cloud. The temperature dropped suddenly and the moisture seemed to slow him, dragging at his clothes, weighing him down. He glanced anxiously over his shoulder, aware that the ambient light was dropping rapidly as the entity drew ever closer. He opened his mouth to let out a scream, but no noise came.

Suddenly he was awake. He found himself still tied to the chair in the dark room but there was someone or something in the room with him. He held his breath and peered into the darkness not really aware what had alerted him to the other presence. After a while he started to think that it had just been an extension of his dream; that he was alone in the cool dark room. He let his breath out in a sigh and turned his attention to the bindings on his wrists. They were still secure and he thought that any more effort in that direction would just bring him added grief to his already desperate situation. He settled back in the chair and allowed his mind to wonder. The first thing it latched onto was Lucy and this took him by surprise. He tried to analyse his feelings and discovered that he was falling in love with her. He was also gravely worried about her. It was certain that Frank would have gone back to the camp, so why hadn't he heard anything. The only reason he could think of was that Frank had dealt out his own justice and killed them, or worse. He tried not to think any more along those lines and his mind turned once again to escape.

Brad all but died from heart failure as a cool hand clamped firmly over his mouth. He cried out in fear but the hand effectively negated any sound reaching the outside. He struggled in the chair and his anxiety doubled as another hand joined the first, this time blocking off his nose. He continued his fight but it grew weaker as his body ran out of air. Eventually he resigned himself to defeat and his body sagged into submission. Feeling the surrender in their victim, the hands relaxed their grip but held their position ready to strike again should there be any renewed resistance. Brad drew in an enormous gulp of air but decided against the cry that he'd been about to make. Satisfied that there was not going to be a repeat performance his tormentor removed his hands from Brad's face. Nothing seemed to happen for a minute. Brad tried to look around but could see nothing in the dull light that filtered into the hut through the open doorway.

'Who's there?' he whispered, as loud as he dare. There was no reply and he tried again a little louder but still not audible to the guard outside. At that moment he felt something cold against the naked flesh of his left leg. He looked down and saw the glint of a large knife. A moment later the leg was free and he felt the same movement on his other. His hands followed suit and he quickly stood and turned to confront a crouched figure. He peered into the gloom to make out who this unexpected benefactor was and stepped back in surprise when a large woman uprighted herself proudly in front of him. She stood eye to eye with him and he recognised her as the widow of the warrior that Tongora had beheaded in the village. Although it was very dark, Brad caught the hint of a crooked smile on her face and kept his eyes on the knife in case she considered that she must take his life in return.

'You go,' she whispered. Brad was caught off guard by this unexpected approach and thought quickly.

'But the consequences to your village?'

She did not seem to understand but merely repeated her simple instruction and pointed to the darkest corner of the hut. Brad laid the chair on its side and removed the ropes that had been cut. With any luck the Japanese would think he had freed himself and not suspect any of the villagers, though he thought this was unlikely having already seen the brutality of these people at first hand. With a last look at the woman he walked over to the corner that she had indicated. He could not even try to understand her motives for such an act, especially as he was responsible for the death of her husband.

In the corner he found there was a sizeable hole in the roofing and he wondered how this had been achieved so quietly. Slowly he eased himself up through the gap. Looking around he saw that the reverse of the hut backed onto the river and there was little chance of him being seen as he dropped silently to the ground. He was about to submerge himself into the water and make his way to the far bank, conscious of the dangers posed by fishing lines, when a hand dropped onto his shoulder. He spun around to find the woman had already exited the building silently and was trying to signal something to him.

'You follow,' she instructed and immediately turned and started a crouching walk parallel to the river. Without much thought as to her motives, Brad bent down and followed in a gait that soon had his calf muscles crying out in protest. She led him well away from the centre of the village, past the crop fields he had seen from the river and up to a large hut standing outside the main village circle, by itself. She dropped to the floor and seeing the two guards patrolling around the hut he did likewise. As they watched the soldiers stopped together, exchanged a few words and then continued circling the building in opposite directions.

'You look,' she said pointing towards the hut. She only seemed to know these short commands in English but he tried to get more information out of her anyway.

'What is in the hut?' he whispered slowly.

'Yes, go look,' she replied and then smiled; rose to her crouching position and proceeded back the way they'd come.

Brad watched her go and whispered a belated thank you after her. He turned his attention back to the hut. It was different from the others he had seen in the village. It was much bigger and taller than the rest, and of course it merited two guards, but there was something else. He couldn't put his finger on it though, and he tried to decide whether it was important enough to risk recapture or even death to get a look inside. The village people, or at least the widow of the murdered man, thought it warranted the danger of setting him free and so, for her if nothing else, he decided to give it a try. His next problem was the small matter of getting in and it was whilst considering this that he noticed what it was that was different. One; despite it being a large building there were no windows of any kind unlike the large building in the centre of the village. And two; the entrance, which was visible from his position by the river, had a door that appeared to be bolted.

He made his way carefully along the riverbank until he was as close as he could get without blowing his cover. As he lay considering his next move one of the soldiers left the hut and walked off towards the village. Brad watched him go and monitored the behaviour of the remaining guard. It appeared that he had arrived during some sort of hand over and there was in fact only one guard who seemed to be doing a fairly good job, circuiting the hut regularly and stopping occasionally at the door. However, as he watched, the stops at the door seemed to get longer and longer as the soldier's enthusiasm for the boring task dwindled. Brad watched him for a further thirty minutes or so and estimated that he never spent less than ten minutes stationary at the door.

Waiting for the next walk round by the sentry Brad readied himself for an assault on the building. He still didn't have a clue how he would get in but that was something he could worry about later. The soldier set off, walked round the hut and then assumed a resting position up against the door as he'd done on previous occasions. Brad proceeded quietly along the riverbank until he had the building between him and the sentry. He then ran the 15 yards or so to the hut wall and pushed himself up against it, listening for a few seconds. Hearing nothing he took a close look at the wall searching for weaknesses. The texture felt strange and as he rubbed at the surface it started to crumble in his hand. Closer examination showed that the outside was purely cosmetic; painted to match the other huts to the casual observer. Underneath was a structure built from concrete.

Brad's mind was buzzing. This was obviously some secret installation, the result of a hitherto unknown affiliation between the Germans and the Japanese. No wonder they were so keen to protect the shroud that had been carefully drawn around the island. He made his way round the wall towards the side that had been hidden to him but the edifice seemed to be uniform in composition. He could just reach the start of the roof and this too felt much more solid than the roof of his prison. He tried to use the area that he had crumbled off as a foot hole to help him get up onto the roof but this failed as soon as he started, with more of the outer surface falling away.

Brad retired to the cover of the riverbank and waited for the guard to make another circuit of the structure. It was another good 5 minutes before this happened and during the wait he formulated a plan in his mind. The only way of getting in would be to kill the sentry and try his luck with the door. In his weakened state this was going to be no mean feat he mused. Still, at least he would have surprise and the cover of darkness on his side. From the river he chose a stone that fitted comfortably into his hand and then quickly covered the ground to the hut. He took up a position with his back flat against the wall and waited. After about 20 minutes he was beginning to think the guard had finally got too bored with his patrols and given up for the night. He decided to give it about 10 more minutes or so and then retire once more and have a rethink. As he waited he realised that merely incapacitating the guard had never been an option and considered it more proof that one gets a 'feel' for this kind of combat, and shuddered at the thought. Five minutes later he heard the unmistakable sound of foot steps coming around the hut. He drew in a breath and pushed himself as flat as possible against the wall.

The Japanese soldier didn't know what hit him. Brad swung the rock in a full arc as the man drew level with him. Although fatigued it was a perfectly judged swing; the stone impacting the crown of the head with fatal force and the soldier slumped to the ground without uttering a sound. Brad was more than a little disturbed at how comfortable he was with this close quarters killing and he quickly stamped on the notion that he was becoming quite good at it. Brushing these thoughts aside he stripped the uniform off the soldier and put them on over his own clothes which were by now not much more than rags. He dragged the body down to the riverbank, collected the rifle he'd been carrying and cautiously walked round to the door of the hut. Arriving, he saw that there was no one elsc in sight but he had no idea when the dead man's relief might be due. Leaning against the door he felt it give and on inspection decided the lock was more for show than security; they just didn't expect to have people trying to break in. He used the butt of the rifle and the lock tore away at the first attempt. Brad pulled the door open just enough for him to squeeze through, and closed it behind him. The light inside was very similar to outside and looking up he was surprised to see stars through what appeared to be camouflaged netting. The building had an open top and as he looked around he saw that it was just one big room, but it wasn't this fact that held his attention.

In the middle of the vast room stood a series of sinister looking rockets. They were only about eight feet in length and fifteen inches in diameter but they gave the impression of being much bigger. There were six of them arranged in a circle and Brad made his way to the centre to get a better view. The rockets all pointed up to the open roof except for one that was laid down and was in a state of repair or investigation. They were all matt black but for the swastika painted on the tail fins. Brad had no idea what they would be used for and walked over to the prostrate rocket to get a better look. The first thing he noticed was a huge coil of copper wire mounted in the tail section. Thinking this was perhaps test equipment he looked over at one of the weapons mounted on what he assumed, correctly, was the launcher. This rocket, in fact all the rockets had the same copper wire trailing of out of the back end and on closer inspection he saw that there was also a coil mounted on the launcher. He quickly surmised that the two wires were in fact one and the same and would be free to unwind equally from both coils when the rocket was fired. Baffled as to why this was so Brad went back over to the rocket on its side. After a closer inspection he found that the four tail fins were free to move, and as they did so a motor at the end of the copper wire also turned. It didn't take him long to work out that the rockets could be steered once they left the launchers. Realisation came to him in a flash; these weren't miniature rockets but missiles that could be guided to their targets.

Brad stood rooted to the spot for a few minutes while he tried to think about the implications of what he'd found. One thing was for sure, if he was discovered with this knowledge he would certainly be killed. There would be no interrogations or torture, in fact the more he thought about it, the more surprised he was that he hadn't already been terminated. Taking one last look at the missile he walked over to the bank of desks to his left. These were the only other objects of consequence in the room. Initially he thought they were the launch consoles but then common sense told him that these and anyone standing at them would be roasted when the missiles were fired. As if to confirm this theory he noted they looked anything but permanent fixtures, and were probably for testing the systems. A bunch of thick cables ran to a panel on a small platform he hadn't noticed by the door. He had already worked out that the weapons would only be effective against a target that could be seen by the operator and the pair of extremely high-powered binoculars fixed to a pivot on the console confirmed this. He also recognised the simple pilots joystick and could see that the missile would be steered into the field of view of the binoculars and then onto the target. This could only mean that they were meant for airborne targets and although he didn't know it, Harry would have called them wire-guided surface to air missiles.

He briefly thought about sabotage but just as quickly discounted it as: a) ineffective considering his level of knowledge, and b) a dead give away of his presence in the building. Storing as much information as possible in his weary mind he left the building, replaced the lock as best he could and retired to the relative safety of the riverbank. He searched through the pockets of his recently acquired uniform and found the only item of significance was a box of matches. He tried one and found they were dry and in working order. A plan formed in his mind and though it wasn't fool proof it might give him some time. Quickly relocating the body of the soldier he gripped it below the armpits and slowly dragged it back towards the hut in which he had been held prisoner. At first the going was reasonably easy, but soon the exertion of the last few days began to take its toll and he found himself stopping to catch his breath and rest his weary limbs about every 10 yards. Eventually though he arrived back at the breach in the roof and with a gargantuan effort pushed the body through it. He heard the dull thud as it tumbled onto the bare earth and held his breath as he waited for a reaction from the guard. However, to his relief the guard was either asleep or the noise hadn't been loud enough to carry to him. In either case Brad considered that the coast must be clear after a couple of minutes and scrambled through the gap as quietly as his fatigue would allow.

Once inside he sat the body in the chair and positioned it against the wall near the hole in the roof. Climbing back through the opening he looked around and considered his best route for escape would be to head for the river. Striking one of the matches he held it to the loose material circling the rupture in the roofing and was pleased to see that it caught fairly easily. Lighting a few more matches he tossed them onto the roof and once satisfied that the fire wasn't going to fizzle out he dropped to the ground and ran to the river as quickly as his legs would carry him.

He slipped into the cool water, made his way out into mid-stream and allowed the current to take him. This time he was ready for the hooks to snag him but he felt nothing and wondered if his benefactor had also arranged this for him. The current was taking him the same way as before and he found himself travelling back through the village. It all seemed remarkably peaceful, but already he could see the light, flickering from the flames that were engulfing the hut. As he passed the outskirts of the village he heard the first cries of alarm as one of the guards spotted the fire. He submerged himself completely and swam with the current, but he needn't have worried; no one was paying the least bit of notice to the river. He hoped that the commotion caused by the fire and the remains of the charred body they would find in his chair would throw them off his scent long enough for him to get a long way away.

He paused in the telling of his story long enough to search his mind for forgotten details, then happy that he'd covered everything continued. 'Then it was just a matter of backtracking using the cover of the riverbank and adjoining forest until I reached the path that Frank and I had first cut. And the rest you know.'

Matthew and Lucy continued to stare at him until he had to ask. 'What? What is it? Have I done something wrong?'

'I just can't believe you've been through so much,' said Lucy. 'And then to cap it all, when you finally get to friendly territory I go and 'shoot' you with a...a Dutch arrow.'

207

Brad stared back at her for a moment and then burst into laughter. Matthew immediately saw the funny side of it and joined him in his mirth. Lucy stared on and the men stopped and stared back. Then, as if on some silent cue, they both lost control again. Lucy's resolve faltered and then broke all together. She let out a short burst of uncontrolled laughter, paused, and then fell backwards as she gave up completely to the feelings of relief and well being that overwhelmed her. Eventually they fell quiet.

'So what's next?' asked Matthew, turning to Brad; happy for him to take command of their situation.

'We wait,' said Brad, soberly. 'As I said before, until the patrol that passed us earlier goes back, we wait.'

Chapter Thirty-Three

'And who might Laura be?' asked Lucy, as Brad opened his eyes to be greeted with the early morning sun filtering through the canopy high above.

'Laura? I don't think I know anyone called Laura.'

'Well,' she paused for effect. 'You certainly seem to have been dreaming about her for the last 30 minutes.'

Brad tried hard to remember but nothing came to him. He shrugged his shoulders and dismissed the subject.

'We need to get hold of some food,' he said to change the subject. 'My stomach is starting to think that my throat's been cut.'

Lucy chuckled and accepted that the subject of Laura was closed. She sat and thought a while as Brad got up and made his way down to the river. She was surprised at the jealousy she had felt over the name called over and over in his sleep. Did he have a girl back home that he didn't want to talk about, or was it as he said? She wondered if she really cared and decided almost immediately that she did. The only thing she could do was ask him, but the very thought made the moths jump about in her tummy. She looked over at Matthew and saw that he was still sleeping and at that moment Brad appeared out of the trees.

'What...' She stopped as soon as she'd started when she saw that he had a finger up to his lips indicating she should be quiet. She looked back to Matthew thinking Brad was worried about waking him. Brad had arrived at her side.

'Japs,' he hissed, bypassing her to pick up the rifle. 'They're coming back along the river.'

Gently he cupped a hand over Matthew's mouth and woke him. He bent down and whispered into his ear and Matthew sat up and nodded that he understood. They sat tensely, listening for noises coming from the river. Soon they heard the first sounds of the approaching patrol. There was no talking this time, just the crunching of sticks underfoot and the odd clatter of a machete as it cut through the more persistent vegetation. Suddenly Brad was gone, ducking through the jungle without the slightest of disturbance. He had to check this was the same party returning having given up the chase. For them to continue along the river without doing so would be far too much of a risk. Catching sight of the water he dropped to his stomach and started to silently shuffle to a position that would allow him to see the enemy. A few moments later the first of the patrol, a Japanese soldier, came into view. He seemed to be much more alert than the group that had passed yesterday. Brad watched as the soldier checked all around and then signalled to the rest that the coast was clear. Having done this he proceeded to the waters edge and dropped to his knees. As he covered his head and shoulders with the refreshingly cool water and took a drink from his cupped hands, the rest of the patrol arrived in dribs and drabs. That was the way it appeared to Brad, but to an experienced ground soldier it was a valuable defensive formation.

By now Brad had seen what he was looking for; Frank and Smidt had arrived in the middle of the patrol. They seemed agitated, nervous of something, but having satisfied themselves that the area was safe they appeared to relax, a couple of them even taking the opportunity to grab a smoke, though this was put to a stop as soon as the Officers noticed. Brad was starting to feel decidedly uncomfortable; they were, after all, only 15 yards away from him. He lay perfectly still in his concealed position and, although he felt vulnerable, he would be very unlucky to be spotted so long as he didn't move.

After what seemed like half an hour, but was only 5 minutes, the group across the river were whipped into order by their leaders and departed along the path back towards the village. Letting out a long breath of relief, Brad left his hiding place and returned to the other two waiting in the jungle.

'Where the hell have you been?' hissed Lucy. 'I...we were worried sick.' She looked at Matthew for support.

'I had to make sure it was the same lot that came by yesterday otherwise we may have bumped into them further along the stream,' he replied in a tone that asked 'isn't it obvious?'

In Lucy's favour she saw the sense in his answer immediately and managed to nod her approval and look abashed at the same time.

'So what did you find?' asked Matthew.

'Well it was the same patrol, or at least Frank and the German Officer were with them.' He thought for a moment but still held their attention. 'However, they seemed a lot more on their guard than before, as if they were expecting trouble.'

'Maybe they thought we were hiding somewhere near, seeing as they'd had no luck further up the trail,' said Lucy.

'Maybe,' said Brad. 'But I wouldn't want to put any bets on it. They seemed to be in an awful hurry, more as if they were retreating from something than looking for us.'

'Could it be that something is happening back at the village?' asked Matthew.

'Again, I don't really know,' said Brad. 'But at least I think we should be clear to continue along the river. However, if there is something happening it could mean there are other Jap patrols so we must move as quietly as possible.'

Lucy wanted to ask about food but realised it was a lower priority at the moment. She also knew it would soon be much higher on the slate if nothing were done about it. Little did she know, but she was echoing Brads thoughts almost exactly, and that the subject sat quite a lot higher than she may have thought on his list. She helped collect and distribute their few possessions and weapons and decided to broach the subject at a later date.

In single file they proceeded down to the river. They each drank as much as they could hold and filled the water canteen. With Brad in the lead, Matthew next and Lucy bringing up the rear they set off along the river. The going was easy at first and they made good time to the point that Brad and Lucy had first met the other two a few long days ago.

'We might as well take a break here,' said Brad. 'It looks like virgin forest from here on in.'

'Couldn't we take the path back to the lookout's hut?' asked Lucy.

'I think they might be watching it,' said Brad. 'And besides, they burnt it to the ground. There's nothing for us there.'

'What about the boat?'

'It's a possibility,' he admitted. 'But I still think we're better off pushing into new territory.' There followed a long silence as each weighed up the various options that were available to them.

'What do you think Father?' said Brad.

Matthew was still out of breath and wheezed alarmingly. 'Whatever you think is best Brad, I'm really not cut out for this kind of thing.' With that he flopped to the ground, too tired even to make his way down to the water's edge. Brad walked over to him and offered the canteen.

'Thank you my son.' He smiled as he spoke. 'And please call me Matthew!'

Brad smiled back. Matthew opened the canteen and offered it to Lucy who took a quick drink and passed it back. Matthew took a large pull and handed it back to Brad.

'Well we're fine for water,' he said, starting to recover. 'But what are we going to do about food?'

'Good question,' answered Brad. 'Something tells me that we'll be Ok if we continue along the river. Don't ask me what or how, but I just know we'll find something before too long.'

Lucy looked at him quizzically and smiled. She was glad that Matthew had brought the subject up but she wasn't too sure about the answer. She wondered briefly if Brad was losing it but dismissed the idea as soon as it had entered her mind. Brad was studying the ground by the river and crossed to the other side to continue his examination. He crossed back and said: 'I'm no expert at tracking but it looks as if our friends crossed the river here and continued towards the hut. It gives strength to my worries about going that way, so if there are no objections we'll carry on along the river.'

Matthew and Lucy gave a general murmur of approval and they settled down for a long rest. They weren't in any hurry to get somewhere so there seemed little point in pushing themselves too hard. Matthew fell into a shallow sleep pretty well straight away and looking at him with concern Lucy moved over to sit close to Brad.

'Do you think he's Ok?' she asked.

'Nothing a good meal and some rest won't sort out, how about you?'

'Oh, I'm all right,' she said. 'But come to think of it, you're probably worse off than both of us. Does the shoulder feel any better?'

'Yes,' he lied. 'I'm just a little concerned about cutting a trail with it, but I still think we need to move along the river, if for nothing else it guarantees us a fresh water supply.

'Yes, you're right,' she said. 'I think I can lead if it becomes necessary.'

Brad lent over to kiss her forehead but at the last moment she lifted her head and their lips met. Brad opened his eyes in surprise but saw that hers were shut and so put his arms around her, drawing her close to him. The kiss grew in passion until Lucy broke the contact and looked over at the sleeping figure of Matthew. She turned back to Brad shyly and snuggled her head against his chest. Her pulse was racing and she wondered how Brad would react to her forwardness. He gave her the answer to this dilemma almost immediately; lifting her head to face him and gently kissing her again. Matthew closed the eye that had watched the two young people and smiled to himself as he tried again to get some sleep.

Chapter Thirty-Three

Mike Phillips sat at his luxurious desk holding his head in both hands. It didn't really help the throbbing deep in his skull but at least he could block out most of the light with his hands. The night before, Doctor Andy Green and himself had sat at the same desk, the only other company being provided by a fine bottle of Malt Whisky and two tumblers. They had sat until the early hours of the morning discussing the case of Tony Harrison, or Harry as most other people called him. Mike tried to recall the conclusions they had come to but realised this was far beyond the scope of his comprehension at this early stage of his hang over. He knew that he would be able to remember everything later, and more importantly evaluate the said information logically and responsibly. He just hoped that Harry didn't decide upon this morning as the time to have his next 'episode'.

Pulling himself together he sat up and decided this was the first step on his road to recovery. He talked briefly to the intercom on his desk, asking Gloria to bring him yet another cup of coffee. Releasing the transmit button he walked over to stand at the bay window and wished that he had taken the option of French windows, allowing him access to the gardens that rolled away from him. He contented himself by opening the largest window and drawing in a breath of fresh, cool air complete with the flowery smell of the late blooms.

'On the desk, Sir?'

Mike spun around to see Gloria setting coffee and biscuits on the leather surface of the desk. She was a formidable looking woman; five foot eleven inches, two hundred pounds and a face that could turn a man to stone. Many a time his associates had pulled his leg, boasting of the dolly-birds they had masquerading as secretaries, yet she was worth her weight in gold.

'Yes that'll be fine, Gloria,' he said, wincing at the effort. 'Anywhere you think fit, thank you.'

'Right you are Sir, Oh and by the way, Laura Weaver is waiting to see you. She's in the outer office.'

'Oh God.' was his only reply

'I can tell her you've been called off to an emergency,' she said.

'No no, I'll see her straight away. Show her in would you please Gloria.'

She smiled and said: 'Right away Sir and I've put a cup out for her as well.'

That woman knows me too well thought Mike as she bustled out of the door, but then, that's why I put up with her after all. He knew from previous experience that she would derive whatever advantage she thought fit from this episode later. He smiled ruefully and turned to greet Laura with his best visage as Gloria showed her into the office.

'Good morning my dear, I hope you had a good night.'

She looked him straight in the eye and answered: 'Not as good as you had it would seem.'

Mike was caught off guard by the candid response and was momentarily flustered. He turned away and looked out of the window whilst he tried to gather his thoughts. He jumped when he felt her hand fall upon his shoulder.

'Come on Mike,' she said. 'We've all got to forget about our problems occasionally.'

'If only I had done just that!' he said with feeling.

'So what have the two of you come up with?' she asked after he had explained the 'meeting' with Andy Green. He accepted the coffee she offered to him and thought about the response he would give her. She was starting to get concerned by the length of the pregnant pause, and then he started to relate the problems that faced them.

'We are happy with the whole procedure except how we stop his heart starting spontaneously before we're ready for it.'

'But surely that is the crux of the 'whole procedure',' she replied.

'Let me finish,' he said. 'We spent a long time last night considering the options open to us. Andy had one excellent idea; to cool his body right down with an ice blanket. This will slow his metabolism down and make it easier for us to stop his heart. It will of course, have the added benefit of reducing the risk of peripheral damage whilst he has less blood circulating.'

'You mean brain damage, don't you?'

'Well, yes amongst other less important areas.'

'So what about stopping his heart from restarting, and how will you restart it when the time comes?'

'Oh that bits easy,' he replied. 'With a de-fribulator and carefully administered drugs there is almost no risk. Remember Laura; we are talking about a perfectly healthy heart here, a heart that is trying to start again on its own. It's not that part of the equation that's giving me any heart ache, if you'll excuse the pun.'

'So how are you going to go about the rest?'

'Well after a lot of soul searching we've decided that to prohibit the heart with drugs which we could easily do would be potentially dangerous and, not withstanding what I've just told you, could possibly hinder the resuscitation process.'

'So?'

'So we've decided to use the defribulator sort of in reverse.'

'I don't understand,' said Laura.

'Well have you ever done a first aid course?' He continued as he saw her nod. 'If you remember, before you start external heart massage it is important to check there is no pulse otherwise you run the risk of stopping the heart rather than helping the situation.' He watched her nod again. 'Well a similar thing can happen with the defribulator. Now I'm not saying this is entirely without risk, but as far as Doctor Green and I can determine this is the safest and possibly the only way we can bring Tony out of the coma.'

Laura sat quietly for a moment running the theories, and yes she admitted to herself that this was all the ideas mounted to at this stage, through her mind. She didn't understand all that Mike had talked about in the last few days but she had a pretty good grasp of the basics and as far as she could see the only flaws in the plan were those that Mike had already brought to her attention.

'Do you want me to tell Mary any of this?' she asked.

After a moment's thought he answered: 'Yes, I think its best that she knows what is likely to happen in advance. It might save any last minute problems arising when things start happening.'

Laura saw the sense in this and she rose from the chair she had taken by the window, thanked Mike for his time and left the office. Mike remained on his feet for a few moments, surprised at how much better he felt. In fact, he discovered the more he thought about it the more he was looking forward to the chance to carry out his theories.

Laura left the office, thanked Gloria for the coffee and walked quickly to Harry's room. She too was thinking about what they'd discussed but was less keen for the procedure to start. She sat by his side and lifted his limp hand; she just wished he'd wake up now, without having to do any of the things that Mike had planned for him.

But still he slept.

Chapter Thirty-Five

Brad awoke to the sound of monkeys chattering in the treetops above. At first he was disoriented; not so much with where he was, but the time scale his mind was working to didn't seem right with the position of the sun. He quickly dismissed these thoughts though as his stomach rumbled its protest at not having been fed in the recent past. Pushing himself up with his good arm he looked over at Lucy and Matthew and saw they were sleeping soundly. He climbed to his feet and stood motionless for a few moments as a dizzy spell came and went. Pulling himself together he went over and gently shook Lucy's shoulder. Slowly she came out of a deep sleep, looked into his face and smiled.

'Hello darling, how did you sleep?' she said drowsily.

'Fine,' he replied a little shortly she thought. 'But I think we ought to get moving before we lose the whole day's light,' he continued.

Lucy let out a little laugh. 'It's dawn sleepy head,' she said. 'You've slept right through yesterday and last night. We thought it best that you got your strength back.' She looked at him seriously, wondering if they'd done the right thing and then he smiled back and bent down and kissed her lightly on the lips.

'Well I suppose we'd better get the good Father up then,' said Brad, pushing at Matthew with his foot. He was surprised by the agility shown as the older man leapt to his feet and looked around. When he saw he was with friends he explained bashfully that Brad had woken him in the middle of a sinister dream.

'Sorry,' said Brad. 'But I think we ought to make a move. I don't want to be in one place too long and besides, we've got to find a source of food or we won't be fit for anything let alone cutting our way through this jungle and possibly engaging the enemy.'

The other two nodded their consent and after gathering up the few pitiful items that they had collected they went down to the river. Crossing, they took the opportunity of freshening themselves up and filling their empty bellies with water. Climbing out on the far bank they cautiously proceeded downstream. The going wasn't as hard as they had thought it might be, due to the passing of the Japanese patrol the day before and consequently Brad led the way with Lucy bringing up the rear.

As the sun rose higher in the morning sky the jungle continued to wake up. The insects of the night were silent now and the sounds of exotic birds joined the playful calling of primates and other tree top animals. The chill of the early morning was replaced with stifling humidity that seemed to draw the very sap from their bones and it meant frequent stops to cool off in the river. Surprisingly, the water's flow seemed to be getting weaker rather than stronger as they progressed downstream; the whole character of the run changing into one of pools joined by thin trickles of clear water.

Finally they turned round a bend in the river and were greeted with the sight of the blue ocean disappearing into the distance. Brad immediately dropped to the ground and the others followed, be it a little more clumsily on Matthew's part. They lay still for a few minutes; Brad assessing the situation whilst watching for any movement. He signalled for the others to stay put and crawled gradually towards the beach. As he passed the last pool in the stream a strange feeling came over him; a feeling of familiarity with the surroundings. Deja-vu he thought to himself as he continued on his way.

Reaching the edge of the jungle he again lay perfectly still for about 5 minutes and although he didn't detect any presence he felt sure that the area held an ambience of danger that he couldn't explain. Brushing these forebodings aside he returned to the others and pronounced the all clear.

'What are we going to do about food?' asked Lucy as they made themselves comfortable yet hidden in the undergrowth. It was Matthew that provided a possible solution to their quandary:

'There's something moving about in the pool we stopped by,' he said. 'I was watching them whilst you were down at the beach, Brad.'

Again Brad had the strong feeling of deja-vu as he picked himself up and proceeded down to the water's edge. Sure enough there were fish moving about in the shallows as he knew there would be, but they were only 3 to 4 inches long.

'We need to move up to the larger pools, I'm sure we'll find bigger fish,' he said to Lucy and Matthew who'd followed him to the water.

They moved up and sure enough found a suitable pool that had been allowed to deepen thanks to the formation of a natural dam. Brad perched himself on a large, moss-covered rock and looked around.

'See if you can find a forked stick I can use,' he said, once again finding it natural to take charge of proceedings. 'And then collect some dry wood for a fire.'

Matthew passed him a suitable stick that was conveniently lying on the dam. 'Here Brad, I think this one should do the trick,' he said. 'Just you be careful up on that dam. We don't want you slipping and causing further damage to that shoulder.'

Brad turned and smiled at him, then made his way to an area of shallow water by a small overhanging tree. He wasn't sure what led him there but it was a perfect spot and he soon had half a dozen good-sized fish on the bank behind him. The other two watched in amazement as he went about the task of providing lunch as if it were something he'd been doing all his life. Satisfied with his ample catch he led the way down to the beach and prepared an area in the white sand for a small fire.

'Isn't this a little open?' asked Lucy.

'I don't think so as long as we stay close to the trees,' he said. 'And besides, any smoke from the fire will dissipate faster out here than under the forest canopy.'

Lucy conceded the point and quickly built the fire. The fish were crudely gutted, impaled on sticks and held in the flames. The skin quickly blackened, forming a barrier to protect the moist flesh underneath and it wasn't long before they were tucking into their first meal for some time.

'What do we do now?' asked Matthew after the first pangs of hunger had been satiated. Brad passed a second fish to him.

'I'm not really sure,' he said after some thought. 'I think that our main priority must be to get off this Island and into the hands of the Americans. The information we have might be crucial to the outcome of the war in the Pacific if not the entire war.'

The others nodded their agreement and then fell silent as they went about cooking their second helpings of fresh fish. Nothing had ever tasted so good they all agreed finishing their simple meal. Brad extinguished the fire and covered any signs of their presence with sand, and they all filed back to the cover of the jungle for a rest from the overhead sun.

Brad was still suffering from acute feelings of having been in this situation before and as he lay back on the cool earth looking into the treetops he tried to make sense of it all. His attention was caught by a movement far above him and his keen vision picked up the seemingly insane antics of a monkey playing in the thin branches at the very tops of the tall trees. As he watched, it came scampering down the trunk of one of the thicker trees, then stopped and seemed to study Brad's face looking up at him. With a flash it was gone along with Brad's feelings of trepidation and he rolled over and tried to get some sleep. His shoulder was still painful and he couldn't get comfortable no matter which way he turned and it was this restlessness that brought Lucy over. Without speaking she uncovered the wound checking that there was no infection and then recovered it as best she could.

'There doesn't seem to be any inflammation,' she said softly. 'But of course I'm not a doctor.'

'I'm sure it's fine,' he said. 'It's just that I can't seem to relax. Come for a walk with me and I'll tell you about it.'

They let Matthew know they'd be gone a fair while and set off towards the beach hand in hand. As they walked he started to explain about how he mysteriously knew about the fish and how to go about catching them. How he felt sure he'd been there before and the feeling that something bad was going to or had already happened on the beach. Lucy listened patiently and then walked silently as she thought about what he'd said.

'Do you remember when we first met?' she asked.

'Yes,' his reply.

'Well you were very confused and you didn't seem to remember how you got here.' She paused for a moment. 'Perhaps you had already been to the pool before and somewhere in your head revisiting it stirred the memories.'

They walked along quietly for a few moments. 'Well,' he said. 'I suppose that would explain things.' He stopped in the sand and gently pulled her towards him.

'Thanks,' he said looking into her big hazel eyes. 'Maybe I'm not going mad after all.' He bent and kissed her softly and as he tried to straighten up she clung to him, responding passionately to the kiss. Her warm body moulded to his and she felt the firmness of his muscles through his shirt as she ran her hands over his torso.

'I think I love you Brad,' she said when they finally broke from the embrace. Brad said nothing but looked down at the ring on his right hand. Rita Morgan, the nurse from Pearl Harbour, had said she loved him just before she'd been killed. He hadn't known what he felt about her, but one thing for sure, he felt different about Lucy. Taking his silence as a rebuke she turned away and started to walk along the beach. He watched her for a few paces, then made up his mind and chased after her.

'Lucy, I...' he stammered and stuttered making things even worse for her. 'I have to be honest with you, I don't really know what I feel but I feel different about you, I feel more than I've ever felt before and if that means I love you then...then...I love you,' he finished a little weakly.

Lucy's pretty face broke into a beaming smile and she flung her arms around him once more, reaching up to kiss him.

'Come on,' she laughed, and ran through the soft sand. Brad started after her and quickly cut the distance between them by half. He made a lunge for her but she anticipated him and jinked towards the jungle. She laughed again as he went sprawling onto his hands and knees. He let out a cry and rolled onto his back clutching his injured shoulder. Lucy stopped running, a look of consternation on her face.

'Brad are you Ok?'

Brad didn't reply. He writhed in agony as she came slowly back to him.

'Oh God Brad, I'm so sorry.'

As she bent to see what damage had been done Brad suddenly stopped groaning and reached up and grabbed her.

'First rule of combat,' he said. 'Always expect the unexpected.'

As she began to cry her protestations of these underhand tactics, he shut her up with a kiss that lingered, raising a fire of passion in both of them. He rolled her gently onto her back and hovered above her, uncertain whether to continue or to stop before he was unable to. As if in answer to his indecision she gently pulled him down on top of her, drawing him close so they could each feel the contours of the others body.

And so they came together, making love gently at first, and then with increasing passion as their desire grew to heights they had never experienced. Finally it was over and he moved to lie on his back beside her. Neither spoke but there was no awkwardness between them. In the troubled world in which they lived, it was the nearest thing to contentment they had felt for a long time. Brad pushed himself up on one elbow and eased the ring off his wedding finger. He reached behind Lucy and opened the clasp of her crucifix and slipped the ring onto the chain. Neither said a word, but a moment of understanding passed between them and she smiled as he gazed down into her face, softly brushing the hair from her eyes.

They could have stayed like that for a long time, maybe even made love again, but the sound of an approaching aircraft brought them rudely back to the real world. Gathering their discarded clothes they bolted for the trees, reaching cover just as the Zero roared over-head.

Chapter Thirty-Six

Mike Phillips was worried. It had been six days since Harry's last 'episode'. (That's what his attacks had become known as around the clinic for want of a better description.) Doctor Donald Wiess had arrived from New York late the previous evening and now sat in the armchair by the window in Mike's office. Mike studied him as the American sat pondering the conundrum that faced them. He was surprisingly young to be considered an expert in his field. His hair was jet black and brushed back flamboyantly from his forehead. He had silver-framed circular spectacles balanced on what could only be described as an enormous hooked nose, and his small mouth and long chin were framed by a neatly clipped goatee beard. Finally, these eccentric looks were finished off with a brown-checked jacket over a white roll-neck, and mustard-checked slacks that would be more at home on a golf course than in a hospital.

When he spoke it was with a long Southern drawl that immediately got on Mikes nerves.

'Well I can't see any holes in your theories at the moment,' he said, turning to look at Mike. 'I'm afraid the only experiences I've had with this sort of thing is with drug addicts, and they have particular problems and characteristics not really associated with this case.' He paused to consider his next question very carefully. 'I don't suppose you have any Scotch Whiskey tucked away do you?'

Mike let out a short laugh. Despite his strange looks and grating voice he was warming to his strange guest. Reaching into his bottom drawer he pulled out two tumblers and a 12 year old Malt. He poured a good measure into each and handed one to Donald as he moved his lanky frame over to the desk.

'Bottoms up,' he said tipping the neat spirit down his slender neck in one slug.

'Cheers,' responded Mike, sipping more cautiously at his own glass.

'Well I think you ought to take me to see the patient,' Donald said, placing his empty glass on the coaster provided to protect the leather desktop. Mike added his all but untouched whiskey to the other and eased himself out of his chair.

'Sure, it'll also give me the chance to show you the data we've collected so far.'

They made their way out of the office and along to laboratory 5. The usual team were monitoring the various instruments and Donald listened attentively as Mike gave him a guided tour. Although he was familiar with all of the equipment it was the way it was being used and how the resulting readings were being interpreted that kept his interest. He looked through the window into Harry's room and saw an attractive, though strained-looking young woman by the bedside. Mike followed his glance.

'That's his girlfriend, Laura. She's here every spare minute of every day.'

'Is she aware he might not remember her if he wakes up?'

'Yes, she's asked to be kept informed every step of the way. She's very sensible; understanding all that we've done and are intending to do.'

'Can I examine him or should we come back later?' asked Donald.

'No, no, come on through. I'd like you to meet her anyway.'

They left the lab, knocked and entered Harry's room, Mike motioning for Laura to remain seated as she began to rise from the chair.

'Laura, this is Doctor Donald Wiess who I told you about, he arrived from New York yesterday.'

Donald took hold of the outstretched hand and gently kissed it. 'Charmed,' he muttered holding the cool limb in his large hand. 'It's always a pleasure to meet an English rose.'

Laura glanced over at Mike, who just shrugged, and then smiled at Donald whilst trying, unsuccessfully, to cover her blushes. Giving up she turned back to the bed and took hold of Harry's hand.

'I see what you mean about him looking after his own vital functions,' said Donald. 'In most cases of a coma as deep as this we would have the patient intubated at the very least. You also say that his kidneys and bowels are functioning correctly?'

'Yep,' replied Mike. 'We were having to keep him 'fed' via intra venous drip but we've recently gone back to a central line straight into his stomach, through which we give him nourishment overnight, and his complete digestive system is operating normally. It's as if he's awake, and yet his brain output indicates that there's nothing going on.'

'Umm...the lights are on but there's no one home,' muttered Donald, placing the index finger of his right hand between his teeth.

Laura turned with a rebuke on the tip of her tongue but stopped short as she saw the American deep in thought and Mike, behind him, holding up a restraining hand.

'Right, we'll leave you in peace then young lady,' he said, as he turned on his heel. 'Come on Mike, I need another tot of that scotch to get the old brain cells working.'

Mike shrugged at Laura again then spun round to catch up with Donald who was already out of the door. Left alone, Laura took hold or Harry's hand once again and smiled at the memory of the tall American striding from the room with Mike Phillips snapping at his heels. She pushed the long hair off Harry's face and filed away the thought that she must organise another haircut for him.

'Please wake up darling,' she said softly for what felt like the millionth time. 'Please wake up.'

But still he slept.

Chapter Thirty-Seven

'Wake up Brad, wake up.'

Brad slowly surfaced from a dreamless sleep to find Lucy urgently shaking him. They had returned to find Matthew fast asleep where they'd left him and as it was starting to get dark they too had laid down together, a suitable distance from the good father so as not to disturb him, to get some rest before contemplating their next move. It was still dark as Brad opened his eyes and although he'd been in a deep sleep he was instantly alert. Before speaking he listened intently but only the usual sounds of the forest at night reached his ears.

'What is it?' he whispered.

'There's someone on the beach,' said Lucy. 'I heard voices.' Brad listened again, straining to pick up any foreign sounds. After a full minute he satisfied himself there was no one in earshot.

'Perhaps you dreamt it,' he said.

'Perhaps,' conceded Lucy, but she wasn't convinced. The dark covered her look of doubt, but it couldn't disguise the tenseness of her body as he reached out to hold her.

'Look darling, we covered all our tracks. Even if there was someone out there, what possible reason would they have to come looking in here?'

Lucy relaxed slightly as she recalled the time spent smoothing the sands with palm fronds once the aircraft had departed. She lay down by his side with her head on his chest, careful not to put any weight on his wounded shoulder.

'Tell me about yourself,' she said.

'Well,' he started. 'I'm a Lieutenant in the United States Navy, I'm serving in the Pacific and I shouldn't really give you any more details in case we're captured; it might make things worse for you.'

'No, I mean before the war,' she interrupted. 'Tell me about the real you.'

Brad was struck dumb for a moment. Was there really a time before the war? Lucy gently stoked the side of his face as she pushed herself up on one elbow and tried to see into his eyes.

'The real me,' he laughed. 'I was born back in 1917 in a place called Lorain, Ohio. Well in fact it was just outside of Lorain on the shores of Lake Erie.'

'I thought that was in Canada'

'Questions at the end please.' He smiled up at her and continued. 'Actually half of it is, but we were on the Southern shore which put me in Ohio. My parents were fairly poor; farming for a local land owner, and all I can really recall of the early years was the long hot summers playing on the shores or in the wheat fields, and the long cold winters playing in the snow or skating on frozen ponds. I had a younger sister who I played with day after day...' He seemed to drift off as if lost in the memories.

'You said *had* a sister.'

'Yes, it was the winter of '23; there was snow on the ground and we were on our way to spend some time in Chicago with my grand-parents.' He paused and this time Lucy didn't interrupt. 'Just on the outskirts of the city we rounded a bend only to come face to face with a lorry out of control, on the wrong side of the road.' He stopped again and she gently prompted him:

'And your sister was killed?'

'My father reacted instantly; braking and trying to steer away from the onrushing danger. If the roads had been clear he might have made it but we just skidded on the snow and ploughed into the truck. Beth had been crying and my mother had taken her into the front, standing her in the foot well to quieten her down. All three of them were killed instantly as the front of the car collapsed under the weight of the wagon. Beth was only four years old.' Brad paused for a minute and then looking into space he continued. 'I've never told anyone before, but I cried just about every night for two years, every night – tears for Beth.'

Lucy squeezed his hand and he smiled down at her and continued.

'After that I lived with my grandparents in Chicago. I was unhurt in the accident and for some reason they blamed me for the loss of their daughter and granddaughter. The rest of my childhood was unhappy to say the least and I ran away when I was thirteen.'

Lucy was crying and he could feel the tears dropping onto his chest, but despite this she asked him to go on.

'I hitched a lift to Detroit and lived rough for a couple of nights. There were a lot of kids on the streets back then and it wasn't long before I drew attention to myself by begging for food from passers by. The leader of the local gang took offence at me trying to muscle in on their patch. He was of mixed origin, a little older than me and 3-4 inches taller. I later found out he was called Rikko, but at that stage there were no introductions; he just began pushing me around in front of his friends. I don't know what happened, maybe the laughter of the gang or the frustrations of the last seven years, but something snapped inside me and I laid him out with one punch. His friends immediately jumped on me, pinning me to the floor, but Rikko ordered them to let me go and stood there smiling at me with blood pouring down his face from a broken nose.'

'From that day we have been the best of friends. He called me Slugger after that and we were inseparable until I joined the Navy in 1939. I haven't seen him since.'

It was a sad story but Lucy was keen to hear more. 'How did you come to join the Navy from the back streets of Detroit,' she asked.

'It was a series of coincidences,' he said. 'I managed to get myself arrested and being a juvenile I had to name a responsible adult. Rikko had an uncle whose name he'd used in court before. I named him at my hearing and I was bound over into his custody. Imagine our surprise when Uncle Paolo arrived to pick me up.'

'But that doesn't explain how you came to join up.'

'Patience my love, all will become clear. You see, Uncle Paolo was a Chief Stoker in the U.S Navy. He all but forced me to join up and although I resisted at the time, the seed was sown. We saw a lot of Paolo over the next few years and slowly the seed sprouted until the prospect of war provided the final trigger. When I pitched up at recruitment they put me through a series of tests and told me I had Officer Potential. The rest, as they say, is history.'

'I've only got one question,' she said coyly. 'Why were you arrested?'

'Well I...'

'Well if it isn't the fair Lucy in the arms of Lieutenant Bradshaw at last,' said a familiar voice. Brad obviously didn't have a chance to finish his explanation but instead rolled from under Lucy towards the rifle leaning against a nearby tree.

'Don't even think about it or she gets a bullet,' shouted Frank as he pushed his way into the small clearing they had made for themselves. To give more credence to his threat he fired a round from the revolver he was holding, which thudded into the tree trunk just above Lucy's head.

'Okay, you win,' shouted Brad, raising his hands in the air. It was still very dark but he could see that Frank now had the gun up against Lucy's head. Any false move on his part would result in her early demise and he wasn't willing to sacrifice her for the sake of a gallant gesture.

'Very wise Lieutenant, you have at least learnt something about survival these last few days. But what else have you discovered, while you were in the village for instance?'

'I don't know what you're talking about,' said Brad. 'I was held captive in a hut and escaped. That's all.'

'So whose was the body in your chair found in the smouldering remains?'

Brad said nothing as his brain raced to find a plausible explanation for the results of his handiwork in the village.

'I asked you a question,' said Frank in a sinister voice. 'This is your only warning; answer it or I shall kill the girl.'

'Don't take any notice Brad,' shouted Lucy, and received a backhand across the side of her face for her trouble.

'Don't you lay another hand on her,' said Brad through gritted teeth. 'Oh and Frank, if that's your real name, that's *your* one and only warning.'

Frank was slightly taken aback by this but he recovered quickly and gave a low chuckle. 'I don't think you're in any position to issue threats Lieutenant, do you?'

Brad didn't answer the rhetorical question and Frank didn't expect him to.

'Where is the Priest?'

Brad had anticipated this one and had an answer ready. 'Matthew died. I don't know if it was malaria or some other tropical disease, but he burnt up in a terrible fever; we buried him down by the statue.'

'I don't know whether to believe you or not,' said Frank. 'But then again it doesn't really matter. He was about as dangerous as a fly.' Had he seen Matthew creeping through the undergrowth with a machete clasped in his sweaty hand he may have thought otherwise.

'So, I ask you again, who did we find in the burnt remains?'

'I honestly don't know,' lied Brad. 'Perhaps someone tried to get me out when they saw the fire.'

'Unlikely I think.'

Brad tried to throw up a smoke screen by asking the next question. 'What are the Germans doing on an Island occupied by the Japanese; I would have thought it was well outside the Fuhrer's field of operations.'

'I'll ask the questions Lieutenant. Let me tell you what I think happened back at the village. Somehow you escaped from the hut, killed a guard who you put in your place, torched the hut and departed the scene probably using the same method as we engineered our entry.' He was careful not to mention the building that contained the missile systems. 'What do you say to that theory?'

'You're living in a fantasy world Frank; I no more had the strength to kill a guard than I do now to take you on.'

Where the hell was Matthew Brad thought to himself?

'So how did you manage to escape in the first place?'

'It was easy,' Brad returned with a sneer. 'The clown that tied me to the chair would be better suited as an escape artist's henchman. As soon as it was dark I loosened the ropes, pulled the straw to form a hole in the roof and climbed out. You were right about using the river to take me out of the village and starting the fire as a diversion appeared to work a treat.'

'With what did you start the fire?'

'Sorry?' Brad felt his heart drop as he tried to think of a believable story.

'Answer or she dies.'

'I had some matches hidden in my shoe...'

'Liar,' spat Frank. 'You weren't wearing shoes and besides, any matches you had about your person would have been water logged on the way in. I'll ask you one more time, how did you start the fire?'

Brad couldn't think straight. He was tired, wounded and scared and his mind just seemed to be full of confusing thoughts and memories. He felt the bullet before he heard the report. There was no immediate pain, just disbelief. The round had entered about halfway up his left thigh. He heard the dull thud as it hit the flesh and felt the tugging as it passed through muscle to exit his leg and drive into the soft earth. He heard Lucy scream and it was then that the pain hit him. It was like nothing he'd felt before; it was as if a burning rod had been forced into his leg and then twisted and jerked about. He felt his vision narrowing down and fought against losing consciousness. Grabbing the damaged limb he felt the copious flow of warm sticky blood pouring from both entry and exit wound.

'You will answer me, or Lucy gets the next one,' said Frank, moving the pistol back towards her head.

The next few moments were confusing to all concerned. Matthew burst from the forest wielding the machete above his head. Seeing him, Frank tried to bring his weapon to bear but was too slow. His finger involuntarily squeezed the trigger as the machete cleaved into his skull removing the left side of his face. Although he died instantly the damage, that only he could be held responsible for, was already done.

Lucy screamed again as blood from Frank's partially dismembered body splashed over her face and Matthew dropped to his knees, unable to grasp the truth of what he'd just done. In fact, he would never be able to come to terms with it and would spend the rest of his life seeking forgiveness for this one act. Brad didn't say anything. As Lucy pulled herself together she went over to treat the wound in his leg. She found him with both hand clasped to his chest trying to stop the blood that was leaking from the hole left by Frank's second shot.

'Oh my God, Matthew, help me,' she cried.

Brad never felt any pain at all this time, but he was aware that his life force was draining away. He tried to speak.

'Keep quiet my love,' wept Lucy. 'Please don't try to talk.' She turned to find Matthew still on his knees with Frank's body slumped before him.

'For God's sake help me Matthew,' she shouted. 'He's dying.'

Matthew just turned and stared, a single tear running down his cheek. Lucy discounted him, realising he was already in deep shock.

'Brad, I love you,' she said through her tears. 'I love you so much.'

'I love you too,' he said weakly, and started a spasm of coughing that caused blood to trickle from the corner of his mouth.

The sun started pushing itself above the horizon and in the first rays illuminating the clearing Lucy could see that he was very pale, but he also looked peaceful.

'I don't know what to do,' she cried in desperation.

'Just hold me,' he said, looking into her eyes. 'Did I tell you that you're beautiful?'

Lucy hugged him as best she could, her tears mingling with the blood soaking into his shirt. Grasping the chain around her neck she broke it easily and caught the ring as it fell. It caught the red of the rising sun as she held it up and looked at the inscription that was now imprinted on her heart.

'Brad you gave this to me as a way of expressing your feelings for me such a short time ago,' she sobbed through her tears. 'And I return it to you now for you to take with you, blessed with my love, so that through eternity you will know that I love you and always will.'

With that she slipped the band onto his wedding finger and gently kissed it and in those last few minutes an understanding of what was happening came to Brad. He remembered the helicopter crash, his disorientation at finding himself in the middle of the Pacific war and the reasons behind his feelings of deja-vu. He was even aware of what they were trying to do at the clinic in Cornwall. And, of course, Laura. It was whilst these thoughts were going through his mind that Lucy heard the last words muttered by Lieutenant Bradshaw, United States Navy.

'Not now Laura, please, not now.'

Chapter Thirty-Eight

'Team Alpha report to Lab 5, Operation Episode, I say again, team Alpha to lab 5, Operation Episode.'

Mike Phillips sprang up from his desk and bolted for the door. This was what they'd been waiting for. It was almost two weeks since the last episode and he was beginning to think the chance had been missed. In the outer office he just avoided bumping into Doctor Wiess who was coming in from the corridor.

'Follow me Donald,' he called excitedly over his shoulder. 'I think we're on.'

They ran together to the laboratory collecting other members of the team as they neared their destination. After pausing at the door to catch their breath they entered the room in a dignified manner. Mike was immediately given a sitrep by one of the younger doctors who was having trouble controlling his excitement.

'I don't know if it's going to continue into a full blown episode,' he said, after Mike had chastised him for his over enthusiasm. 'But we've started to pick up frontal lobe activities similar to those we've seen in previous attacks.'

Mike began drawing off paper from the roll holding the history of the last few minutes.

'This started six minutes ago,' he said irritably. 'Why weren't we called immediately it started?'

'It's in your standing orders Doctor Phillips,' replied the young man nervously. 'We're not supposed to tannoy for the team unless the increased activity has continued for at least three minutes. You added the time limit after that spate of false alarms that were disturbing the teams in the middle of the night.'

'Quite right,' joshed Mike. 'Only testing.'

The young Doctor retired to his position realising that this was the nearest he'd get to an apology. Mike thought otherwise:

236

'Sorry Andrew,' he said. 'I'm just as excited as you.' With that he turned back to the instruments and watched the progress of the increasing brain activity. He saw the second part of the team sorting out the apparatus on the other side of the window and watched as Laura and Mary left the room discreetly. Seconds later they joined him in the lab.

'This is it,' he said in a quiet voice. 'All being well he should be back with us in about 15 minutes.'

It was likely to be the longest 15 minutes in their lives thought Laura, but she didn't say anything, just grabbed hold of Mary's hand and clung on as if her life depended on it.

'The output is reaching a crescendo sir,' said Andrew, his pale blue eyes opening wide in his white, freckled face. 'If this follows the same route as the others we should have a cardiac arrest any time now.'

'Standby for my command Doctor Tarrant,' said Mike on the open intercom loop. 'The only time you can override that is if we reach two and a half minutes arrested. Is that clear?'

'Understood Mike,' said the other Doctor from Harry's bedside. 'We're ready in here.'

'Ready here Sir,' said Andrew, who had regained his composure now they were operating as a team.

'Right, all listen in,' Mike started his final briefing whilst keeping one eye scanning the machines. '...and remember that if anyone sees anything they don't like they can call it off at any time during the procedure. I would rather we had to do this all over again due to a misunderstanding than to lose the patient. Are there any questions?'

There were none and at that moment the alarms started to sound.

'He's arrested Sir,' said Andrew needlessly. 'Clock's running.' The silence in the two rooms was almost deafening.

'Thirty seconds,' called Andrew. They all looked round as they heard the door open only to catch a glance of Mary disappearing with her hand over her mouth. They all turned back as one.

'One minute.'

They all watched the heart monitor which displayed a flat line.

'How long, how long for Christ's sake?' demanded Mike.

'Seventy two seconds Sir.'

At that moment the flat line jumped, flattened and jumped again.

'Now!' shouted Mike. Doctor Tarrant immediately placed the electronic pads of the defribulator on Harry's chest.

'Clear!' He shouted, and discharged the shock in Harry's body. Laura flinched and closed her eyes as he arched on the bed as the convulsion coursed through him, but all other eyes were on the monitor. The line flattened once again and the alarm continued to sound

'Now!' Shouted Mike again as he detected another event on the green trace. Again Tarrant played his part and again the line flattened.

'My God, I think it's working,' drawled Donald Wiess.

'Two minutes.'

'Standby to bring him back at two minutes thirty.' said Mike, a sinking feeling hitting him like a hammer blow as he realised Harry's body was still trying to bring itself back. 'Just let the heart start spontaneously.' He turned away feeling the failure wash over him as he accepted they were going to have to rethink the whole procedure. The flat green line began to flicker and Tarrant looked round at the lab.

'Now!'

'What the hell...'

'Two minutes thirty.'

'Clear!'

'No...'

Harry's body bounced on the bed as Tarrant was unable to stop himself discharging the current.

'Just who in the hell do you think you are?' ranted Mike at Donald Wiess.

'Trust me.' the reply as Dr Wiess looked down his nose at the flat green line.

'Resuscitate him immediately,' shouted Mike, his face going a deep red as he tried to keep control. Dr Tarrant fiddled with the settings and applied the pad to Harry's chest.

'Clear!' The charge was administered and one of the nurses began external heart massage. Another placed a mask over his mouth and nose and squeezed the corrugated air bag twice. All eyes turned to the heart monitor.

'Nothing, clear.' The procedure was repeated a further three times.

'Three minutes thirty,' said Andrew, his voice a little shaken.

'If we've lost him, I'll...My God I'll have you struck off.' said Mike in a low voice, staring apoplectically at Wiess. 'I'll...I'll...'

'We've got an output,' shouted Dr Tarrant, dropping the pads back into their storage.

They all stared at the monitor that showed an irregular heartbeat at first but then settled down at a steady 92 beats per minute. Mike continued to stare at the machine for a full minute, then turned abruptly without saying a word and departed the room. Wiess looked around at the rest of the team, but all eyes were averted. He too then left the room. There was an audible sigh of relief broken by Andrew:

'I want a full report on vital signs and functions in my hand in one hour.' Then more to himself. 'And God help Wiess if there's any abnormalities.'

'Doctor, he's saying something,' shouted one of the nurses by his bedside.

Laura heard the report on the intercom system and rushed from the Lab to his side. She was just in time to hear the weakly spoken words that confused her yet at the same time thrilled her beyond belief. It was the same sentence over and over again:

'Not now Laura, please, not now.'

Chapter Thirty-Nine

Mike's secretary placed the report onto Mike's desk exactly one hour after he had stormed from the lab. He refused to see anyone after the incident and so it was, that Donald and Laura sat together in the outer office. Neither had said a word the whole time and Gloria would look up at them occasionally, shake her head and then get back down to her work. After another 10 silent minutes the intercom on her desk cackled into life.

'Be so kind as to send in Doctor Wiess please Gloria.'

Donald rose from his chair as Gloria crossed to the inter-connecting door, holding it open for the tall American. She closed it after him and returned to her desk.

'Now the fireworks will fly,' she whispered conspiritively to Laura. They both sat in silence looking at the door. After 10 minutes they had heard nothing and were surprised when the door opened and Donald came out of Mike's office.

'Good day ladies,' he said, touching his forehead in a mock salute, and proceeded out of the office. Neither of them ever saw him again.

'Could you send Laura in please Gloria?'

Laura jumped up, signalling that she'd get the door herself, and entered the office. Mike was sat at his desk looking for the World as if nothing had happened. She took the chair he indicated, sinking into the cushions, and sat quietly waiting for him to open the dialogue.

'How are you feeling?' he asked softly.

'Me? I'm fine. More to the point how's Harry?'

'Well, as far as we can tell at this stage the operation was a success, though I'm sure you realised that it went far from the way I'd hoped. The only risk now is whether or not he suffered from oxygen starvation.'

'Come on Mike, you know you can talk straight with me; we're talking about brain damage aren't we?'

'Yes Laura, his heart was stopped for three minutes and forty seven seconds which I think was too long. That Yankee bastard Wiess insists that he's seen people make a full recovery having been arrested for much longer periods.' He stared blankly out of the window for a few moments then continued. 'The bugger of it all is that without his intrusion we may never have got to this stage. If things turn out okay we may have him to thank. However, I will never forgive him for the liberty he took and although I will accept full responsibility for anything that has occurred under this roof, personally I shall always hold him to blame.'

'That's very noble of you Mike,' she said. 'Let's just hope it never comes to that.' She made a move to get up; she was anxious to get back to Harry's bedside, but Mike stopped her with a wave of his hand indicating she should settle back in the chair.

'Have you spoken to Mary since she left the room?'

'No, I went in to see Harry and then came straight here, why?'

'Let me speak to her first will you? At first I was going to tell her that things had gone as planned but I feel that she should know what happened and I want to be the one that tells her.'

'I think you're right,' she said. 'I don't think there should be any hint of a cover up, especially if he is brain damaged. Besides, I don't think you have anything to hide.'

'I wasn't worried about litigation or cover-ups, I was thinking of her. But then again perhaps you're right; it wouldn't look good if anything were amiss.'

'I don't doubt your motives in the slightest,' she assured him, rising from her seat. 'Now, if you don't mind, I want to get back to Harry.'

'Of course,' he said, moving nimbly to open the door for her. 'I'll see you there shortly myself.'

He closed the door and returned to his desk. He keyed the intercom through to Gloria who answered promptly.

'No visitors or calls for the next ten minutes please Gloria.' He then cut the connection before she could reply, rested his elbows on the desk and dropped his head into his hands. Then he did something he couldn't remember doing since he was a small boy; He said a prayer for Tony Harrison.

Chapter Forty

It was to be another six days before they found out whether or not 'operation episode' had been a success; six days of Harry lying on his bed as if nothing had happened. There were changes though. His brain output was looking far more like that of a 'normal' coma patient and a CAT scan had shown nothing that the doctors should be concerned about. But it was a frustrating time. Laura and Mary took turns in sitting with him, holding his hands and, in Laura's case, speaking non-stop to him.

At 0200 hours on the Tuesday morning, exactly 6 months 14 days and 11 hours after the accident, Laura was sleeping in the chair next to Harry. The room was illuminated with the dull light that penetrated from lab 5, giving it a ghostly appearance. She didn't know why but Laura suddenly jerked awake, coming immediately to her senses. Within moments the curtains connecting the two rooms were drawn back allowing more light to fall onto the stationary figure on the bed and Laura quickly rose to her feet and leant over him. Nothing had changed and she looked around at the lab assistant peering through the window, a question of what was going on written on her face. She looked at Harry and stepped back in startled surprise; Harry's eyes were open. Recovering herself quickly she grabbed his hand and looked into his face.

'Harry, Oh Harry,' was all she could manage.

As she looked into his eyes he struggled to focus on her and when he did a small smile broke onto his gentle face. A croak escaped his lips but he quickly gave up the effort to talk. Instead he mouthed four words that only Laura saw and that she would cherish for the rest of her days.

'I love you, Laura.'

The next moment the room seemed to fill with people in white coats. They crowded around the bed and Laura was pushed to the back. She didn't mind though; his simple declaration of love for her elated Laura for two reasons. Firstly, she now knew how he felt for her, but more importantly, it showed that his brain was intact; he remembered her, and was still capable of coherent thought. Not only that, but he was able to put those thoughts into words. As she stood contemplating these facts she became aware of a hand resting lightly on her shoulder. Turning she found Mike smiling down at her. He tried to speak but she cut him off.

'He spoke to me Mike, he told me he loved me,' she shouted excitedly. They both looked over at the bed and saw that Harry was lying in the same position as always, his eyes shut.

'He did speak to me,' she said, seeing the doubt spread across his face. 'He...he tried to say the words but he just croaked and so he mouthed 'I love you Laura"

'He definitely woke up,' said the assistant who had first peered through the window. 'I don't know if he spoke, but I saw his eyes open.'

'He spoke,' said Mike making up his mind. 'If Laura said he spoke, then he spoke.' He turned to look at the grateful smile on Laura's face and spoke to the team behind him:

'Come on you lot, let's leave them in peace and go and have a look at the data.'

They all filed from the room and Laura took her place by Harry's side. Mike watched her through the partition for a few seconds and then drew the curtains.

'He's a lucky man,' he said to no one in particular, and then threw himself with gusto into the piles of print outs from the brain scanning equipment.

Much later in the morning Laura started to think the faith he'd shown in her had been misplaced. Harry had not so much as fluttered an eyelid. She had been unable to sleep and was starting to feel the strain when Mary came into the room. Laura had left his side earlier just long enough to ring her and give her the news.

'You look absolutely exhausted,' said Mary pulling up the spare seat. 'Why don't you go and have a lay down. I'll call you if anything happens.'

Laura was about to resist the temptation but saw the sense in it, and besides she thought, Mary would probably like some time alone with her son. She weaved her way back to her room and was asleep as soon as her head hit the pillow. It seemed like only minutes later that she was roused from her slumber by a hand gently shaking her shoulder.

She saw that it was Mike and looked over at the clock. 1707 looked back at her in red digital figures. She sat bolt upright.

'What is it?' she asked him, concern building in her straight away.

'It's all right,' he said grinning at her. 'He's awake and wants to speak to you.'

Laura jumped out from under the covers realising too late that she'd stripped down to her underwear. Mike gallantly turned to face the door whilst she hurriedly pulled on her jeans and white roll-neck jumper.

'What has he said?' she asked as she joined Mike at the door.

'Oh, nothing much. He's only been conscious for about half an hour; he was alone with Mary for most of that. I've introduced myself and given him a quick thumb nail sketch of what's been going on and I think Mary has filled him in on the bare bones of it anyway.'

'Well what are we hanging around here for then?' she said pulling a brush through her hair and glancing quickly in the mirror to make sure she was presentable. Grabbing his arm she all but dragged him through the door and along the corridor, but on reaching Harry's room she paused, uncertain of herself. She felt like an adolescent teenager out on her first date not really knowing what was going to happen. Mike seemed to realise the turmoil her mind was in and placed a comforting arm around her shoulder. Taking a deep breath she pushed the door open and entered the room. Harry was still lying on his back but turned his head in response to the door opening. They looked at each other, neither wanting to say the first words and it was Harry who broke the silence, his voice gruff and very slightly slurred.

'I meant what I said earlier.'

Laura burst into tears, took a look at the delighted grin on Mike's face and ran across the room to hug her man.

'I love you Harry,' she cried.

'Hey,' he said. 'Who's this Harry guy?'

'It was easier to call you Harry. Tony just confused everyone when you were in the Navy environment,' she managed to say between the kisses she was smothering him in.

'If this is the way you react maybe I ought to do this more often,' he said with a grin at Mike.

'Don't you dare say that,' she said seriously. 'I know you only mean it as a joke but please don't say it again. It's been awful. She started crying again, the floodgates really opening as she felt the relief of the moment she'd prayed for all the long months.

'I'm sorry Darling.'

'Hold me Harry,' she begged between sobs.

'I can't yet,' he said softly. Laura pulled back from the bed and looked from Harry to Mike.

'Why not? What is it?'

'It's perfectly normal,' said Mike. 'He hasn't used those muscle groups for months. He needs to retrain them.'

'Promise me,' she said. 'Promise me he's OK.'

'I'm fine. Look at my fingers.' Harry wiggled the fingers of his right hand and then those on the left.

Mike said. 'Although we stimulate and massage the major muscles there is still a certain amount of wastage, but as there was no brain or spinal cord injury the physiotherapists will soon get him sorted out. It's the same with his speech; that slur you may have heard is again due to muscle wastage and should only be temporary.'

'Anyway,' said Harry. 'I don't want you worrying about that so here's something else for you to consider.'

Laura turned back to the bed and looked into his grey eyes searching for a clue as to what else might be concerning him.

'I don't want to be apart from you again,' He paused as Mike let himself quietly out of the room. 'I want you to be my wife. Laura, will you marry me?'

She felt the blood drain from her face and was convinced she was going to faint. She dropped to her knees and held his hand. This was the last thing she expected and was totally unprepared for it. She steadied herself and thought very carefully about the answer.

'My initial instinct is to say yes but I don't think it's as simple as that. We've both been through a hell of a time and I don't want to embark on a lifetime based on trauma. Still, I *am* going to say yes, as long as you promise to ask me again if you still feel the same way a month from now. If you don't ask me I'll know you've changed your mind and we'll leave it at that; there will be no need to explain anything to me, no difficult speeches or gestures, just don't mention it. A month from today, Ok?'

'Fair enough,' he said. 'I love you and I know that isn't going to change. I will take this as an affirmative,' he continued with mock formality. 'Now kiss me!'

She knew somehow at that moment that he meant every word he said. She put her hands around his head, gave him a hug and planted a kiss on his forehead.

'I do love you and I want to marry you more than anything in the world. I just want you to be sure, that's all.'

'I'm sure,' he said. 'I'm sure.' He drifted off to sleep with a smile on his face. Just before he went off he spoke to her and later she would swear it was in an American accent:

'What happened to Lucy? I hope the Japs didn't get her.'

Letting herself out of the room she went off to find Mike. Gloria was seated at her desk as usual and told her that Mary was in with him at the moment.

'I'll just let him know you're here,' She said, and spoke on the intercom.

'Send her in,' responded Mike.

Laura entered his office and found him pulling another chair alongside his and Mary's that were set looking out of the large window.

'We've only just started,' he said. 'And Mary asked if you could come in and listen. Better for me; only having to go over it once.' Mike smiled at both women and then continued. 'There's really not too much to say at this stage. You've both seen and talked to him and I think you'll agree that he seems to have all his marbles. I know this was the subject that was causing you most concern and I'm glad to report that he seems to be completely normal in that department. I thought that he may have forgotten the accident at least but this doesn't seem to be the case. He'll have to complete a number of cognitive tests as a matter of course but I don't anticipate any problems.'

'What about physically?' asked Laura.

'Well as I brushed on earlier he is weak from inactivity. We'll have him up on his feet in a couple of days and his progress will be fairly quick, though to get back to full physical fitness, as he was before his accident, could take 6 months to a year. We shall have a better idea once the Physiotherapists have done their assessment.'

'When do you think he'll be allowed home?' asked his mother.

'Well, as long as he's up on his feet, I don't see any problems with him going out this weekend.' He held up his hands as the two women jumped up with excitement. 'But I must warn you that it will be hard work and only a weekend pass at this stage.'

His words of caution did little to dampen their spirits and they cackled away making plans for the homecoming. Mike was happy then, to sit back and allow them to carry on un-heeded. Their enthusiasm brought out the best in the two women and he marvelled at the change in them, especially Laura who seemed to be positively radiating happiness. Eventually they quietened and in a gap in conversation Laura asked:

'Mike, when do you think he will be able to come out permanently?'

'Well it all depends on his progress,' he said. 'But I think it would be safe to start making plans for about 3 months from now.'

Laura looked from one to another in amazement. 'You know he asked me to marry him then?'

'Yes, Mary told me just before you came in.'

'And I suppose you knew what my answer would be,' she smiled, turning to Mary.

'I think we can both see you were made for each other,' said Mary. 'And I certainly hope you didn't turn him down.'

Laura thought it was nice to have the blessing of his mother and said: 'No I didn't turn him down. He's got a little thinking to do but he doesn't get off the hook that easily.'

Mary and Mike took it in turns to kiss her on the cheek and congratulate her. She, however, was miles away already planning the autumn wedding in her head.

'We'll just have to see what progress he makes,' she said to herself.

Chapter Forty-One

Harry's progress was nothing short of miraculous. The very next day, a nurse going into his room first thing in the morning found him sitting on the side of the bed smiling at her. After a few short words from Mike, whom the nurse fetched immediately, he lay back down to await the attentions of the physiotherapist whom, he was assured, would be around at about nine o'clock. At two minutes past he was champing at the bit, ringing the hand held attention getter he'd been supplied with. The physio turned up a few minutes later but to his frustration she was accompanied by Doctor Green who gave him a thorough examination before he would allow the Physio to get her hands on him. Finally the doctor was finished and the physio approached the bed. She made a striking figure; six feet tall, blond hair and built in a way that made men drool. Harry appraised her as she stood before him looking down. His assessment was of a beautiful woman, but that beauty was spoilt by the grim visage that looked down at him. Her hair was pulled tightly into a bun on top of her head, her complexion was fair, the skin smooth and clean of blemishes, she wore little or no make up and somehow this only went to accentuate her bright green eyes. Finally, below her button nose, her mouth was stretched into a thin line that looked as if it were incapable of breaking into a smile. As if to prove him wrong she did just that and her face immediately transformed into loveliness.

'Hello Harry,' she said in a soft, accented voice. 'You don't mind me calling you Harry do you.'

'No, not at all.'

'Good, your fiancée said that would be the case. I'm Gabrielle, call me Gabby by all means, and I shall be looking after your body for the next few weeks.'

'Nice to meet you Gabby,' he said, assessing her accent as Dutch or possibly German. 'Let's get started then, shall we?'

'Patience patience,' she laughed. 'There's plenty of time for that. First I've got to take down some details.'

He was about to object, his need to get back to his old self overpowering, but he realised she had a job to do and so lay back on the bed,

'OK, fire away.'

Pulling up one of the chairs she sat, and for the next hour, took down the particulars of accident and his appraisal of his physical state prior to it. She already had a lot of the information from the records collated in the clinic, but she thought it important to hear it from his own mouth; in a way assessing his mental attitude to his injuries. Next she outlined short and long term goals that she hoped he would achieve whilst under her care. She also explained that the Navy had agreed to allow the clinic to take care of his rehabilitation, rather than sending him up to RAF Headley Court in Surrey, which was the other alternative.

Finally she got round to starting his treatment and again he was frustrated. With him still lying on his back she began her appraisal of his condition. She checked every reflex known to man, and some that weren't. She checked the major muscle groups for tone, she checked him all over for surface sensation. She checked co-ordination in his arms and legs and even went as far as checking the muscles in his face and tongue so she could give an accurate referral to the speech therapist. Then she went on to measure the angles of movement in the numerous joints around his body and he was surprised at how much some of those joints had seized up. By the time they took a break for lunch he'd had just about enough of being poked and prodded and was glad of the interval Laura had joined them for the last half-hour and had grinned at the faces of exasperation he'd pulled.

'So what do you think of your Physio?' she asked after Gabby had left the room.

251

'She's...um...thorough,' he replied.

'Thorough? Is that really all you've got to say?'

'Well...I guess with that accent she's Dutch or perhaps a blond Swedish Goddess,' he said playfully.

'She's Irish you idiot.'

They laughed as Laura told of her and Gabby's earlier meeting in the restaurant over breakfast. Lunch arrived on a tray delivered by one of the endless assistants dressed in white coats. It was a simple affair of cold meats, cheeses, fruit and plenty of pure orange juice. Harry relished it, even though he did have a little trouble swallowing, another 'perfectly normal' reaction to his sustained period of unconsciousness. After eating they were left alone for an hour and Harry started relating details of the dream he'd had whilst in the coma.

'Have you told any of this to Mike - Doctor Phillips,' she asked.

'No. I hadn't really thought it was important; it's only a dream after all, though I must admit it felt more real than anything I've dreamt in a normal sleep.'

Laura routed around in her bag and pulled out a Dictaphone she used at work to make sure she didn't miss anything important when discussing the children under her care at the regular weekly meetings.

'Do you mind?' she asked. 'It'll save you having to go over it all twice.'

'No problem,' he said and then started the story from the beginning. Before he'd really got into it Gabby returned and Laura left them to it, promising to return later and continue where they'd left off. She kissed him goodbye and left them to get on with it. When she returned at four o'clock she was amazed to find him standing beside the bed with Gabby supporting him with a shoulder under his right arm.

'There's no stopping this man,' she said in what was now obviously a soft Irish accent.

'Tell me about it,' said Laura, with a cheeky smile on her face.

And so it continued over the next few days. Harry pushed himself like a man possessed and related his story to Laura like a man trying to rid himself of some evil possession. Mike kept himself in the background but continued to monitor Harry's progress both physically and through the amazing tales that Laura passed onto him. He even got as far as comparing the story with the printouts of his episodes and wasn't surprised to find a correlation between them. Although it would be hard to convince colleagues in the medical branch, it still went a long way to supporting his theories. Together with the facts that had been collected during Operation Episode he had enough material to submit a fairly believable thesis for publication in the British Medical Journal, with Harry's permission of course.

By Friday afternoon he had shown more than enough progress to get the weekend pass that Mike had spoken of. Mary had travelled back to Scotland and so it was back to Laura's flat in Helston.

'You're going to find this a little dull after the luxurious surroundings of the clinic,' she said after flicking on the lights. Harry eased himself out of the wheelchair they'd insisted he use and looked around the room. It was much as he remembered; functional yet comfortably decorated. He walked very slowly and deliberately over to the large sofa and turned to sink into the pile of pillows and cushions that Laura had arranged earlier. Laura carried his bag through to the bedroom and then disappeared into the kitchen to start preparing his homecoming meal.

'Yes this will do very nicely,' he said to himself looking around the room. Laura had managed to get away with putting the bare minimum into the living area. The centrepiece was a large, low, white and grey marble table on an enormous rug that covered most of the polished wood floor. He was seated on one half of a two piece suite finished in white leather, the other part being a single seater to one side of him. He was facing a large silver plastic and glass cabinet that housed both T.V and stereo CD system. The room had a lot of natural light provided by the large window and sky light, and these combined with the light-coloured paint work, tastefully highlighted with pastel stencilling, made for a bright and cheery area that some would find clinical, but which Harry liked. The effect was finished off with a wooden shelf that circumnavigated the room about 18 inches from the ceiling and joined the back wall, which was given over completely to a covering of irregular wooden shelves. On these were all the books and knick-knacks she'd collected over the years.

Laura came back and joined him on the sofa, handing him a cold bottle of Moet & Chandon Champagne and holding out two flutes.

'Mike said one glass would be fine,'

'One glass it is,' he agreed ripping off the gold foil and releasing the cork. He poured two glasses, lent forward to place the bottle on the table and toasted Laura with his glass.

'Here's to us,' he said. 'For a long and happy life together.'

'To us.' She felt the tears springing to her eyes as she raised her glass and took a sip of the sparkling wine. They cuddled up together on the comfortable seat and sat in silence for a while, enjoying the peaceful atmosphere of the room.

'Tell me the rest of your adventures in the Pacific,' she said eventually, rising to collect the Dictaphone from her bag.

'Where did I get up to?'

'You had just escaped from the village and were heading back to the Priest and the girl.'

'Matthew and Lucy, yes that's right.' And so he continued the story to its conclusion, though he did gloss over parts concerning the relationship between Brad and Lucy. Laura wept again during the sad parts and when he'd finished they both drifted off to sleep in each other's arms.

As things turned out Mike was correct when he said it would be hard work. Harry was surprised how quickly he became tired and had to rest after even the smallest bouts of activity. He had planned to go into the Wardroom for a family's Sunday lunch to meet some of his friends, but found to his disappointment that he wasn't up to it. In a way it was a relief to both of them when an ambulance from the clinic turned up to take him back on Sunday evening.

Over the next two weeks Harry continued to make good progress, surprising even Gabby, who at first had thought his efforts were part false bravado, but now saw them as sheer courage. After that first weekend he quickly improved on his walking skills and would often be seen spending the long evenings that weren't brightened by visits from Laura, walking round and round the corridors, building up strength and stamina. He was also introduced to the 'wobble board'; a simple piece of equipment that did wonders for his balance and strength in the smaller muscle groups around the ankles that were so important in walking. It was simply a square plywood board about 2 feet across and with a half a sphere of about 1 foot diameter, bolted to the underneath. The task was simply to stand on the board and keep the edges off the floor.

But his favourite was the hydrotherapy pool; a small sized pool only 4 to 6 feet deep, but filled with warm water that didn't only allow him to build up unused muscles, but contributed to a general feeling of well-being as he floated around or submerged his weary body after a strenuous work out.

'Well I reckon it's time we got rid of you,' said Mike. 'And I make that about six weeks ahead of schedule.' It was the Wednesday, the third since he'd come out of the coma, and Mike informed the delighted Harry that he would be going home at the weekend.

'I'll get packing,' he said. 'Does Laura know yet?'

'Nope, I thought we'd leave you to give her the bad news.' Mike thought for a few moments and then continued. 'But we still want to see you once a week as we discussed earlier. I want to monitor your progress throughout the recovery for two reasons. Firstly the obvious medical ones, and secondly so I can get the documentation for this medical paper finished.'

Mike had spoken to him about the idea and Harry was all for it.

'As long as you think it might be of benefit to other cases I'm happy to make medical history whilst you make a name for yourself and the clinic.'

Mike coughed and spluttered and started to explain that his motives were completely bonefide and not commercial when he saw the huge grin spreading across Harry's face.

'You bastard,' he said playfully swotting him with a file he was holding. 'I don't think I'll ever get used to this military humour.'

'I've told you before Mike, it's not the military so much as aircrew. We call it 'witty banter'; they test you for it before they let you join.'

'Yes, well anyway, I want to see you back on Wednesdays for assessment and physio with Gabby. The Navy have a physiotherapist at Culdrose, a Petty Officer Bryant, and he will look after your day to day needs, but hell, I'd love to keep in touch with you and Laura; I've come to know you both quite well over the last few months and I'd hate to lose contact.'

'The feeling's mutual Doc,' replied Harry, serious for once. 'Let's face it, but for you I probably wouldn't be back in the land of the living.'

They looked at each other for a long moment, both a little embarrassed by the others frankness, then with a simple shake of the hand Mike turned and left the room only too pleased that Harry hadn't seen the tears forming in his eyes.

Chapter Forty-Two

Laura was very excited if a little anxious about Harry coming home. Although he had been back at weekends, this was different somehow. She had briefly considered a surprise party for him but due to his relatively fragile condition had decided to consult him. He agreed to a party straight away and so it was that they now waited for the first guests to start arriving on the Saturday night after his homecoming. She had, with as much help from Harry as she would allow, moved all the furniture to the edge of the room allowing ample room for the number of guests expected. They had given an open invite to the Squadron as well as other individuals from the Station, and of course family. About 50% normally responded to these open invites but as always they had catered for the maximum number. As it turned out it was a good job they had.

Half an hour later Laura looked round the crowded room. It looked as if the whole Squadron had turned up, apart from those standing Search and Rescue duties. They had spilt over into the kitchen as always tends to happen and Laura started to relax and enjoy the atmosphere as she saw that things were going well. She couldn't fully enjoy herself though; Harry hadn't mentioned their engagement again, since that first time in hospital and the more she thought about it the more she was convinced that he *had* changed his mind. Even so she was surprised that he hadn't talked to her about it; maybe he had taken her true to her word.

'A penny for your thoughts.' Laura looked round and focused her eyes on the friendly face of Mike Philips.

'Sorry Mike I was miles away,' she said, throwing a 'professional' smile onto her face.

'Is everything thing all right?' he asked. 'You seem a little pensive.'

'No, no, everything's fine. I was just wondering if we have got enough drink in for all these people,' she lied easily.

'Yes he does seem to be remarkably popular doesn't he?' he replied. 'But I've just come from the kitchen and with the amount that people are bringing with them I reckon you'll have more at the end than you started with.'

'You haven't seen the Navy drink,' she laughed. 'I just can't believe the number of guests turning up, especially as it was at short notice.'

'There's something else I've noticed,' said Mike. 'Have you seen the number of his mates just going up and shaking his hand? Nothing odd in that really except that some are doing it more than once. I've just watched that young chap over there,' He indicated with his pipe. 'Going up four times. He didn't say anything, just shook his hand.'

Laura smiled at Mike. 'I just think they can't believe he's back.' She turned back to Mike. 'And it's you we've got to thank for that.'

'Stuff and nonsense,' he said, more than a little embarrassed. 'He's the one that's put the effort in, and don't underestimate your own contribution, without...' He stopped as she simply gave him a hug and walked away.

And so the party continued. By about ten thirty the atmosphere was beginning to take off as the alcohol was just starting to take effect, especially among the Squadron guys who seemed to making up for the fact that Harry still couldn't drink, by each doing their best to consume his share.

Suddenly the music stopped mid track and everyone looked over to where Harry was climbing onto a case of Boddingtons. At first there were jeers of 'stand up' and 'speech' but quickly a hush fell over the room as it became obvious that he was *indeed* about to make a speech.

'I'll keep this as short as possible,' he said with a strong, confident voice that had quickly recovered thanks to the exercises prescribed by his speech therapist. 'As I know every surface in the kitchen is still covered with booze;

you lot obviously need some retraining now that I'm back.' He paused for the jeering and guffaws of laughter. 'Firstly I'd like to thank you all for turning up tonight and for all the support you've given Laura and myself in the last months.' Again he paused, as there was a spontaneous round of applause. 'I'd also like to say a special thank you to my rescuers, all the medics involve with my care and especially to Mike Phillips and the clinic that brought me back to the land of the living.' Again applause. 'Mike would you come forward please?'

Mike blushed scarlet and as he made his way to Harry, the latter turning and picking up an enormous painting.

'I noticed there were no paintings of Helicopters in the Clinic so I had this commissioned by a local artist and would like you to accept it and hang it somewhere in your establishment.'

This time there was thunderous applause and Harry passed over the painting. Mike turned it to see two Seakings of Harry's Squadron overflying HMS Indomitable. There was also a brass plaque on the frame that said simply 'Thanks. Tony Harrison.' and the date of his awakening.

The room went quiet again and Mike realised that they were waiting for him to say something. He was not an accomplished public speaker but he found this surprisingly easy. 'All I can say is that I don't know about hanging this 'somewhere'; it will have pride of place in the main entrance. Thank you.'

As he walked away with the painting there was more applause and those he passed were clapping him on the back. He returned to stand next to Laura who smiled at him but still looked lost in thought.

'And finally,' continued Harry. 'I'd just like to talk to you about a very special lady.'

Laura grabbed Mike's hand as Harry continued. 'She has stood by me throughout what must have been an awful time for her despite not knowing what my feelings for her were. When I woke up I asked her to marry me and she said she would as long…' He stopped as a cheer went up from their guests. '…as long as I still felt the same way in a months time. Well Laura I'm sorry.' He paused momentarily and Laura's heart sank. 'It's a little *over* a month,' he continued. 'Laura, will you marry me?'

Suddenly her heart was in her mouth and she couldn't believe what she had heard. 'What did you say?' she all but whispered.

'Will you marry me next Saturday?' he said. The room was deathly silent as they waited for her reply. 'Yes. Oh yes,' she cried moving towards him. 'Yes of course I'll marry you.'

This time the applause and cheers were nothing short of tumultuous. In the middle of it all she reached him and fell into his arms sobbing with joy. Amongst the female guests there wasn't a dry eye in the house and although they'd never admit it quite a few of the men could be counted in that group.

Laura was busy smothering Harry's face in kisses when something he'd said suddenly registered. 'What do you mean next Saturday?'

'It's all sorted; guests, church, reception, honeymoon, everything.'

'But what about my work?'

'Sorted.'

'Bridesmaids?'

'Your mum told me who you'd said you wanted if you did get married so they're sorted.'

She stared at him in disbelief then her face broke into a wonderful smile. 'You…you…Oh just you,' she said playfully pounding him on the chest. 'It's a good job I said yes then isn't it?'

'I never doubted you would,' he said. 'I love you, Laura.'

The party carried on long into the night but neither of them could remember any of the details. In the morning they got up to find a couple of the unattached Squadron youngsters who'd slept where they'd fallen. Harry got them moving and then the two of them set to clearing up the debris.

'Was last night real?' asked Laura, picking up the Champaign bottle they'd emptied to celebrate the arrangements for the coming weekend. Harry just smiled in answer and she continued round as if in a dream.

Later Harry sat her down and went over all the arrangements in detail. He seemed to have missed nothing though there were a few guests that she wanted to add to the list.

'Who's the best man?' she asked.

'Boomer,' he said referring to Cameron Whitechapell, an old school friend whom he'd kept in touch with over the years. Laura had never met him but had heard a fair bit about him. He had followed a similar route to Harry after leaving school but instead of the Navy he had joined the Royal Air Force as a Pilot and was now flying the Tornado F3 out of RAF Coningsby.

'He's coming down for the Stag night on Thursday night and staying at Nansloe Manor until Sunday. I thought we'd have him over for dinner on Friday night if that's all right with you?'

'No it's not all right with me,' she replied. 'It's unlucky for the bride and groom to be together on the night before the wedding. You'll have to find somewhere else to stay.'

'I thought that was the Groom seeing the Bride the morning before the service,' he said.

'Well I don't know, but besides, I have my parents coming to stay Friday night.'

'OK, OK I'll make arrangements for us to stay in the Wardroom. All the talk will be about dresses and flowers and things. In fact thinking about it does your Dad want to come to the Mess for a quiet drink?'

'Good idea. Thanks I'll ask him and let you know.'

And so they carried on refining the details, enjoying each other's company and the planning of the biggest day of their lives so far.

Chapter Forty-Three

Dawn was bright and early. Laura rolled over in the expanse of her double bed and smiled the first lazy smile of what would be many smiles that day. She had slept surprisingly well considering it was her last night as a single woman. As she thought of the approaching wedding she felt the first little butterflies in her tummy and she instinctively rolled onto her side and curled into the foetal position. Again she smiled to herself and then said aloud: 'Am I doing the right thing?'

'Of course you are darling,' her Mother replied from across the room. Laura looked at the striking woman framed in the doorway. At sixty, the years had been kind to her. Her face held the same lines of classic beauty that Laura possessed; the strong cheekbones and rounded chin. She had sparkling blue eyes and her red hair, with just a hint of grey showing at the sides, was pulled back into a loose ponytail.

'I know I am mum, I'm just saying the things brides are supposed to say on their wedding day.'

'Well just in case there is any doubt I think you're a very lucky girl and that Tony is going to make you very happy - not to mention making me and your Father Grandparents!'

'Mum,' exclaimed Laura, launching a pillow at the retreating figure. 'We're not even married yet.'

Things fell into the routine one associates with wedding days; hair appointments, manicure, make-up etc. etc. There weren't even any disasters one could expect to see on 'You've been framed'. Even the video man and the photographer kept themselves very much in the background.

At about 11 0'clock Laura sat down to a light snack; she actually felt too nervous to eat but did so at her Mothers insistence:

'We don't want to hear your stomach rumbling instead of 'I will,' and mark my words you'll feel better for it in the long run of things.'

The doorbell rang for about the twentieth time and Laura's mum, Jane, went to answer it. She returned escorting an old woman of about seventy.

'Look who's here,' said Jane.

'Hello Aunt,' said Laura. 'I'm so glad you could make it.' Laura gave her a kiss on the cheek and showed the older woman to the white armchair. Despite her age she moved easily and lowered her frame into the seat. She sighed and her features relaxed as she sank into the luxuriant leather upholstery.

'I wouldn't miss this for the world,' she said, and then closed her eyes and appeared to go straight to sleep and indeed wouldn't show any signs of life until they were ready to depart for the church.

At exactly quarter to one a tall man wearing top hat and tails arrived at the door. He escorted the four bridesmaids to a black Bentley, returned to escort Laura's family to a second identical car and finally to collect Laura and her father. Laura's dad was a dark-skinned man with a balding head and happy cherubic face, and seemed to be much more nervous than his daughter. He looked very smart in top hat and tails, but Laura knocked him into a cocked hat. She stood radiant beside him. Her flowing full-length cream gown fitted her slim body perfectly despite only having a week to do the final fittings and adjustments. The skirt was plain and figure-hugging down to the calves, were it opened up into a small fish tail that pooled around the matching cream shoes she wore. But it was the bodice that made the dress special. It was tight, off the shoulder and loosely laced down the back showing just a hint of tanned flesh. This theme continued where the front drew into a point just over her navel, allowing just an occasional flash of the diamond belly bar she'd carefully fitted that morning. She wore no veil or headdress, just a simple white feather surrounded by clear crystal jewels in her hair. To finish the effect she held a simple bouquet of white lilies and greenery.

Together they climbed into the large white Rolls Royce that had just pulled up.

'Tony's certainly pulled out all the stops for this,' she gasped as her father helped her get seated comfortably.

'Actually this is courtesy of your mother and me,' he said proudly.

'Oh, thank you dad,' she said throwing her hand round his neck and kissing him on the cheek. And so they set of for the church arm in arm, on time and happy as any father and daughter in the world.

They drove through the small town centre of Helston with people stopping in the streets to watch the procession go by. Once through the town centre they got onto the by-pass to the west and picked up pace. Turning right at the top they manoeuvred onto the Lizard road and made there way down to RNAS Culdrose. Harry had explained that his first choice had been the Chapel at the Lizard, but it was fully booked every Saturday for the next three months. Instead he had arranged for the service to be held in the new church on the naval base with the reception afterwards in the Wardroom.

Passing through the main gate on the left it was an easy matter of continuing the turn to the gates of the church. De-planing they joined the bridesmaids who looked magnificent in a mixture of lilac and white dresses. The time was approaching one fifteen; spot on time.

Almost in a daze Laura, led by her father, proceeded down the isle to stand next to Tony, dressed in his immaculate Number 5 uniform. In contrast, next to him stood Cameron Whitechapell, just as well turned out but in his RAF Number one blues. From then on the service seemed to fly past and before they really knew it the Padre was announcing they were man and wife. Once the register was signed they led the way out of the main door under the most impressive arch of naval swords anyone remembers seeing. The path was lined with 12 Officers on each side, Lt Cdr Peter Rogers in charge, with swords held aloft and crossed above the bride and groom's heads. Exiting the arch they were almost drowned in confetti and rice before being whisked away by the photographer.

Before too long they were finished at the church and this time Harry escorted his new wife back to the Rolls Royce that was waiting for them. Before moving off the driver set a small table in front of the car, on which he arranged two glasses. To Laura's delight and Harry's knowing smile he opened a bottle of Champagne and poured them both a glass. The cameras flashed again as they entwined arms and took a drink, looking lovingly into each other's eyes. Taking their glasses they settled into the comfortable leather seats in the car and to their surprise, at the top of the road didn't turn left to the Wardroom but instead took the bridge over the main road to the airfield. Passing between the hangers of 706 and 810 Squadron they found themselves in front of hundreds of onlookers on the hard standing. Little did they know but these were sailors and their families who had willingly given up their Saturday afternoons to cheer the newlyweds. A newly cleaned Seaking had even been pulled out onto dispersal and along with the official photographer the crowd took hundreds of photos.

'This is unbelievable,' whispered Laura amongst the hubbub of noise and shouted 'good luck' messages.

'Yes, I wonder who's behind this,' returned Harry, who for the first time since they'd met was glowing red with embarrassment.

All too soon, for Laura at least was enjoying every moment of being in the lime light with her man, the car turned and transported them back across the bridge to the Wardroom. The Commander, yet another surprise to Harry, and the Mess Manager met them there. There were kisses, handshakes and congratulations all round and they were led to head the welcoming committee at the top of the small flight of stairs leading to the main bar. The bar could best be described as an airport lounge; it was huge. Ideal for occasions such as the Summer Ball, and indeed for the wedding, but not favoured by the livers-in as a comfy little drinking hole. For these purposes there was another bar, customised by Squadron members and other members of the Mess, downstairs.

Soon the guests started to file in. Presents were left on a large table positioned for that purpose and as the guests passed the final members in the line they were offered drinks from trays held by two very attractive Wren Stewards. After ten minutes or so, Harry's hand was starting to get sore from the tight handshakes. He had heard somewhere that it caused long term problems for the Royal Family and other Heads of State and he was beginning to understand why.

A welcome break in the long procession of guests caused Harry to look round to his right. An elderly woman was brushing off all offers of assistance and defiantly made her way up the stairs alone.

'Ah,' said Laura conspiritively to Harry. 'I don't think you've met my Aunt Lucy.'

As they waited for her to climb the stairs she added: 'In fact I only met her this morning. I've not even heard a lot about her but I found an old address and invited her on the off chance. She arrived this morning and came to the house.' Laura stopped speaking as Lucy came up to their level.

'Congratulations my dear,' she said to Laura. 'Now let's have a good look at the catch you've landed for yourself.'

With that she pulled a pair of glasses up to her face from the chain that suspended them around her neck.

'Blind as a bat without these,' she murmured as if in explanation. With that she peered up into Harry's face with hazel eyes. Every drop of colour drained from her face and she took a step backwards.

'Oh my God,' she exclaimed. 'No, it can't be!'

Harry looked on in amusement, which turned to horror as Lucy started to topple over in a dead faint. Harry bounded forward and just managed to catch her before she hit the ground. Her eyes were fluttering as he looked into her face and the first flashes of recognition crept into Harry's mind. As if to give credence to these thoughts Lucy said one more thing before she passed into unconsciousness:

'No Brad, It can't be you.'

Harry lowered Lucy to the floor, stood up and took two steps back causing him to fall through the double doors leading to the windowed bridge crossing to Keppel block. Laura, who had dropped down to check on her Aunt, now turned in disbelief as Harry went crashing to the ground. He too had lost his entire colour. More help was arriving and Lucy was showing signs of recovery. Two members of Harry's Squadron were helping Laura's father carrying her to what the Navy so quaintly call 'comfy chairs'. Seeing she was in good hands and didn't appear to be in any immediate danger, Laura crossed quickly to help Harry. She arrived just about the same time as Mike who had seen the drama unfolding.

'Darling, what is it?' she asked urgently, fighting back the tears that threatened to spoil her day.

'It's OK,' he said. 'I'm fine - I just lost my balance that's all.'

'Did you hit anything solid, like your head, as you went down?' said Mike, desperately trying to bring some humour into the situation. Harry saw what he was attempting to do and responded jovially to try and quell Laura's fears.

'Naa, just my butt,' he said. Laura was not the 'stupid female' type, and said seriously to Harry: 'I want to know what that was all about, and I want to know now.'

Harry saw that his goose was cooked and lifting himself up he took Laura's arm and escorted her to the duty steward's cabin that was conveniently situated at the start of the crossover they were on.

'Wait for me here,' he said. 'You too Mike if you don't mind.' With that he went out to the group of worried looking guests and explained that he and Laura would be back in a moment; they wanted to sort themselves out after the upset. Receiving blank or concerned looks he further said that the drinks at the bar were free before the wedding lunch. The crowd started moving away led by the boys in black uniforms. Harry watched them go and then went over to Lucy who was once again casting off any offers of help.

'You haven't changed then in all these years,' he said. 'Still as strong-willed as you were fifty years ago.'

'My God, It is you,' she said quietly. Tears started to cascade down her cheeks and Harry asked the helpers to leave them alone explaining that he and Laura would join them in the bar shortly. When they were out of earshot he said: 'Yes it is me Lucy. I'll try to explain but I want us to join Laura and my doctor before I do.'

He helped her up and escorted her to the room in which Laura and Mike were waiting in silence.

'Aunt Lucy,' said Laura getting to her feet. 'Are you all right?'

'Yes yes, I'm fine. Sit down my dear, B...Harry's got something to say.'

Harry didn't know where to start. His mind was in complete turmoil as he tried to make sense out of what was happening.

'I've got to make this as quick as possible as we have confused guests waiting for us. What I say will leave all of us with un-answered questions but now is not the time to be addressing them. What I don't want is for it to spoil our day.'

He paused, trying to think of a way to soften the blow he was about to deliver. He was unsuccessful. He looked to the faces of the three sitting in front of him on the un-made bed. Mike looked bemused, or was it amused, Laura looked confused and frightened and finally Lucy. She looked at him in wonder. She looked sad, possibly a little bewildered and yet content, as if a big weight had been lifted from her heart.

'Laura, Mike, I want you to meet Lucy Fairbrother.'

As he said it a fresh stream of tears ran down Lucy's face. 'I haven't used that name in fifty years,' she said through her tears.

Laura still looked confused but in Mike's mind a penny dropped. 'You mean Lucy from the dream?' he said, a look of wonderment on his face.

'Don't be so stupid,' scolded Laura, feeling another bout of butterflies in her stomach but this time lacking the wedding as the reason. She looked from face to face and laughed. 'You've all gone mad,' she said. 'You've had too much sun or something.'

'It appears it wasn't a dream, not in the sense that we know it,' said Harry.

'And I certainly didn't dream it.' They all turned to look at Lucy as she made this last remark; there was nothing else any of them could say.

Chapter Forty-Four

Considering the implications of their discovery, and the affects that discovery may have had on them, the rest of the day went off very smoothly. Laura was the one who most outwardly seemed to be affected by the bizarre tale that had come to light, but even she, though perhaps a trifle thoughtful, appeared to put the news behind her and get on with enjoying her day. Although he didn't show it, Harry's mind was in turmoil. No matter how he tried to explain the strange events in his own mind he could not come up with any valid explanations and finally he pushed the thoughts to the back of his head. Lucy, on the other hand, seemed to take it all in her stride, as if things had turned out exactly as she expected. Harry and Laura saw her occasionally throughout the afternoon and she'd flash them a winning smile. By the time people had been home and changed for the evenings festivities she was even more effervescent; no longer the frail old lady that had collapsed on the steps, but the real 'life and soul' of the party, dancing and laughing with all those around her.

Harry had managed to have a quiet word with his new wife, and had explained that they weren't departing on their honeymoon until late Sunday evening and they would try to make sense of things, hopefully with Lucy, on Sunday morning. Laura and Lucy were in complete agreement and they even asked Mike if he'd come along, to which he readily agreed. That settled they all enjoyed a wonderful evening of live music and celebrations, with Harry and Laura among the first to leave at about midnight. Only he, Lucy and Mike knew the whereabouts of their destination for the night, as they would join them after breakfast on Sunday.

And so it was on Sunday morning they all sat in the honeymoon suit at Nansloe Manor in Helston. Harry and Laura had woken early and gently made love before show-ering together and sneaking back into bed in time for their full English breakfast to be delivered to their rooms. Lucy was the first to arrive and this gave Harry the chance to relate his version of events from 1942, albeit in a condensed form. Lucy sat and nodded, chipping in with details if she felt it necessary, crying at the parts that had formed rigid scars in her mind. Laura listened in stunned amazement, quickly realising that there could be no mistakes; they were both retelling the same story. Mike interrupted them, apologising for being late, to find Lucy quietly crying and being comforted by Laura. Harry explained that he'd just reached the part where Brad was shot.

'What happened Lucy, after I was ki...er...after Brad was gone?' asked Harry.

Laura left Lucy and went to sit with Harry on the bed, whom she could see was having an awful time coping with the whole issue. Lucy recovered and drew a deep breath.

'I heard you, him, whatever, mutter those last word, words I shall never forget. 'Not now Laura, please, not now', and then he closed his eyes and gently exhaled his last breath.'

She explained that she would refer to the subject of the story as Brad, or in the third person, as they would be more comfortable that way. And so she took them back to a small Pacific island, 1942.

Lucy felt him go limp in her arms and knew that Brad had gone. She was so utterly devastated, heartbroken, and who was Laura? Her mind was a turmoil of emotions. Was she a sweetheart back in the States? She was aware of the tears coursing down her face and pulled Brad's body close to her. How long she stayed like that she had no idea but when she came to her senses it was too late. The shots had brought the nearby Japanese patrol running to investigate. Bursting upon the scene they found Matthew on his knees, machete in hand and the body of Frank before him. Across the clearing was a young girl cradling another body in her arms. Neither of them had moved to pick up the rifle to defend themselves, which was probably a good thing as they were heavily outnumbered and any aggression on their part would have had fatal consequences for them. As it was one of the soldiers took a rifle butt to the helpless figure of Matthew who did not let go of the machete immediately.

Things would probably have got out of hand as Lucy gently laid Brad to the floor and then flew at the guard who continued to assault Matt. He swung the rifle up only to have his shot mis-directed by Lt Smidt who burst into the clearing and used his pistol in a viscous swing to knock the over-zealous soldier to his knees. He barked loudly in German but the meaning was clear in any language. The Japanese relaxed and Smidt turned to Lucy, who had stopped in her tracks at the emergence of the German Officer.

'These people are barbarians,' she screamed, the adrenaline coursing through her veins.

'Yes, I'm sorry about that,' said Smidt, in his heavily accented English. 'Perhaps you can tell me what's going on here.'

Lucy turned to see Matthew regaining his feet, mopping at the flow of blood pouring from a nasty looking cut over his left eye. Continuing her turn she came across the body of Brad lying peacefully at the far edge of the clearing.

'I'll tell you what's happening,' she cried. 'That murdering Bastard,' she indicated Frank's body lying in a bloody heap. 'That lying, fascist, murdering piece of dung has killed Lieutenant Bradshaw, a prisoner of war at the time, and was in turn killed by our priest, Father Matthew Golding.' Her voice had risen to fever pitch and as she finished she collapsed to the floor, her body wracked with hysterical sobbing.

Lt Smidt, for all his faults, at least had a little compassion. He saw immediately that the American pilot was more to Lucy than just Lt Bradshaw. He barked some commands at the group of Japanese who were watching the exchange with some amusement. Slowly they wondered off, leaving Smidt alone with his two prisoners.

'Do I need to keep this gun trained on you?' he asked.

Matthew just continued to stare at the body of Frank and said nothing. Lucy shook her head. 'No,' she said quietly. 'I think enough damage has been done for one day.' She looked over at Matthew for confirmation, saw the blank face and turned back to Smidt. 'I don't think he will cause you any trouble now.'

Smidt holstered his weapon and surveyed the scene of destruction properly for the first time. He saw the leg wound sustained by Brad and put two and two together.

'He was questioning Lieutenant Bradshaw?' he asked Lucy. She nodded and replied. 'Yes, he asked about Brad's escape and when he wouldn't answer the pig put a bullet into his leg. He then threatened to shoot me, and was about to do so when the good Father interrupted him.' Matthew gave no response and so the Lieutenant continued.

'So what did Lieutenant Bradshaw tell you?'

'Not you as well,' she replied in a resigned tone. 'There was nothing to tell as far as I can make out, except possibly that the Japanese could do with a few lessons in how to treat prisoners. He escaped. That's all I can say to you.' She paused to consider her next words. 'He did speak kindly of you though; how you tried to warn him. He would have thanked you for the fair treatment given the chance and I do so, on his behalf. You are a credit to your country Lieutenant, and that is rare in these times.'

Lt Smidt appeared flustered and tried to work out if she was attempting to lower his guard, but looking into the sad eyes he felt he could trust her and mumbled a thank you for her kind words. It was at times like this, when he saw the hurt that war produced, that he longed for an end to the pointless slaughter of so many good men, women and children. He surprised her by dropping down to sit next to her.

'What now?' he said to no one in particular.

'I think that's up to you,' she replied, not really comprehending the depth from which his rhetorical question was dragged.

'Yes of course,' he said with renewed strength. 'You realise that I have to take the two of you with me back to the village.'

'Yes,' she said. 'But can I ask that we might bury him first.'

'Yes, I'll get some of the patrol onto it straight away.' He started to rise but stopped when he felt her hand on his arm.

'I'd like to do it myself if that's all right.' He looked into her deep hazel eyes for a long moment before replying. 'As you wish Miss...'

'Fairbrother.'

'As you wish Miss Fairbrother,' he replied. 'But I must warn you that we need to move soon. I will supply the necessary tools and offer my assistance.'

'Yes that would be acceptable,' she said, and turned to the body of Brad.

They buried him in a shallow grave and marked the spot with large boulders carried up from the riverbed. Matthew didn't help. He seemed in a trance, still trying to come to terms with the enormity of his actions earlier that day. Lucy had carefully searched Brad's clothing for any official papers or dog tags that she could return to the Americans if she got the chance, but found none. Instead she removed the rank tabs and the medal ribbons from his tunic and kept them as a reminder of the short time they'd had together.

Matthew said a few words at his graveside but he was still not really recovered from the shock of killing a man. Lucy wept quietly, said her final goodbyes to Brad and then left the clearing with Lt Smidt to join the patrol. The NCO's amongst the Japanese were anxiously pacing up and down and as soon as they appeared with Matthew they called in their sentries and got the long march back to the village underway. As they set off they passed the crumpled body of Frank that had been removed from the clearing, at Lucy's request to Lt Smidt, but not given the courtesy of a burial.

Soon Lucy was lost in her thoughts and trudged through the jungle automatically. The patrol was pushed along quickly by Smidt and the only reason she didn't walk into Matthew, two paces in front of her, was that he never stopped. It was almost as if they were running from something. Lucy didn't realise this at the time though, she was only interested in putting one foot in front of the other; her mind blank other than to thoughts of Brad and the time they had spent together.

It was even more of a shock to her then, when a shot rang out, echoing amongst the trees. She looked up to see Matthew stumbling over the body of the Japanese soldier ahead of him. He pushed himself off the struggling form who had both hands to his neck trying in vain to stem the gushing stream of bright red blood that forced its way between his fingers. His eyes were open wide in terror and his mouth formed a silent scream that gurgled in his torn-open throat. As Matthew watched in horror the struggling stopped, though even in death the face was a mask of panic and pain. More shots started to punctuate the silence that had descended over the jungle. In his disgust Matthew started to climb to his feet and was in danger of being hit until Lucy pulled him back down, and together they crawled off the track that had been cut in the undergrowth.

The Japanese were starting to return fire and the cacophony of noise that descended upon them caused Matt and Lucy to cling together, buried amongst the vegetation that gave them no protection from the flying bullets, but kept them hidden from sight thus not presenting them as targets. The battle seemed to last for hours to Lucy, but was over in a little under five minutes. It was a well-sprung ambush by a large force of American Marines, much larger than was needed to round up the patrol. The Japanese, as was proving to be the case in many of the Pacific islands, fought to the death with no thought given to surrender. They charged at the unseen enemy that surrounded them, in waves that were cut down with auto-

275

matic fire. They would have made the American's job much harder had they held their position and waited for the attack to come to them. This may have been the case had a Japanese Officer been with them but Lt Smidt neither wanted to lead them to a glorious death or would have been listened to if he'd ordered them to hold their ground.

Suddenly Lucy felt the barrel of a rifle pushed into her back.

'Git yer hands up ye yella bellied Jap.'

Lucy and Matthew both raised their hands and as Lucy turned and looked at the young, fresh-faced Marine with water-filled eyes he lowered his weapon and shouted to the rest of the American force that was sweeping the battle ground.

'Blimey you fellas, it's a Dame!'

By now Lucy was on her feet. 'You're American?'

'Yeah, course we're American, who else d'yer think could have seen off this little lot.'

'As you were Marine,' said a deep voice. Lucy looked round to see a tall, well-built man in army fatigues. He searched her face with pale blue eyes set into a rugged face. A large livid scar under his right eyes was obviously new but the crooked nose was evidence of a much earlier battle, in a bar before he was commissioned.

'Lieutenant Branson, United States Marines at your service Mam.'

'Lucy Fairbrother,' she responded weakly. 'And this is Father Matthew Golding.'

Matthew climbed to his feet, the fury of the recent gun-fight seeming to have snapped him out of his trance-like state.

'How do you do Sir?' he said holding out his right hand. The offer was about to be reciprocated when the Officer was distracted by a shout over to the right.

'Over here sir, we got one of 'em still alive.'

The whole group moved over to the Marine who'd appeared from the undergrowth.

'My God, I think you're right,' said the Lieutenant. 'Sorry Father,' he added looking guiltily at Matthew, who dismissed the blasphemy with a wave of his hand. Considering what had gone on today what was a simple 'my God'.

'I think it's an Officer,' he continued more to himself.

The man was dragged to his feet and winced as pressure was put on his shattered right shoulder.

'Lieutenant Smidt,' exclaimed Lucy. 'Your arm.' The words died weakly in the silence as all faces turned to her.

'You know this man?' asked Branson.

'Yes, he was our captor and protector from the Japanese.'

If Lieutenant Branson was surprised to see a German Officer he didn't show it, though some of his men started whispering to each other. Smidt was searched and sat on the path with his left hand on his head and his right hanging loosely by his side. The Marines checked all the Japanese bodies but found no other survivors. Lucy looked over to the German Officer and approached Branson.

'Sir,' she began. 'That man needs medical attention. I must report that he was more than fair to us and indeed to Lieutenant Bradshaw, an American pilot who was regrettably killed earlier today. If you have a first aid kit I'll gladly see to him.'

'An American pilot you say. What in hell's name was he doing here?'

'The first aid kit Sir,' she said. 'And then I shall tell you all you want to know and more.'

'Murphy, get the first aid kit over here on the double,' shouted Branson.

'Thank you Lieutenant.' She turned as Murphy arrived, took the first aid kit from him and knelt down to attend to Smidt's shoulder. In the background she could hear Branson securing the area, but she concentrated on the job at hand.

'Thank you Lucy, you don't mind if I call you Lucy?' he said looking into her eyes.

'Just because I'm tending to your wounds doesn't mean I like you,' she snapped, and regretted it as soon as the words had left her mouth. Smidt looked away and Lucy neatly wrapped the wounded shoulder as best she could with the limited resources at hand.

'I'm sorry,' she said contritely as she finished off. 'I'm not having a good day.'

Smidt smiled at her and thanked her again.

'I'm sure you'll be treated well in the hands of the Americans,' she said, and in her face he read 'Unlike Brad was in yours.'

'...and I never saw him again,' said Lucy to the hotel room of sombre-looking faces.

'And the Americans took you off the island?' asked Harry.

'Yes,' she said. 'I told them what was going on in the village and as far as I know the Marines stormed the place and destroyed the entire Pacific anti-aircraft missile operation.'

'And the villagers?' asked Harry.

'They were warned and most of them were able to get out before the covert operation took place.

'What were the Marines doing there in the first place,' asked Mike after a long pause in the story telling.

'I've done some research on this,' said Laura unexpectedly. 'Harry's story sounded so convincing I started to feel that it had really happened. I thought that if there *were* Germans in the Pacific it would be recorded in the history books. The only reference to the operation was a Marine force landed on the island to gather intelligence on a suspected submarine base on the island.'

'That's right,' said Lucy. 'Apparently the build up in the village hadn't gone unnoticed and the worst they could imagine was a submarine forward-operating base.'

'So, anyway, how does any of this explain me being there in 1942?' asked Harry. 'Or is this all just a figment of our imaginations? Mass hysteria or something.'

'No it isn't,' cried Lucy. 'I could not have imagined all

this.' She seemed lost in thought for a moment and then continued. 'When we buried you Brad,' she started, looking at Harry. 'Lt Smidt said something that I have clung onto all these years. As Matthew said a few words over the grave Smidt drew me to one side:

'Miss Fairbrother, Lucy.' He paused for a long moment. 'He's not gone you know, he's not dead.'

'What do you mean?' said Lucy through the sobs that were racking her body.

'I don't really know,' he replied in a puzzled voice. 'Don't ask me to explain but I know that you will be with Brad again.'

'...and I have lived on the strength of those words ever since.'

Everyone in the room was silently looking at Lucy who now had a steady stream of tears running down her face.

'Lucy, where exactly was Brad shot?' asked Harry.

'Well it was in a clearing...' started Lucy.

'No, where on his body did the bullets strike?'

'One in the leg and another in the chest.' said Lucy.

'Don't tell me, the left leg, yes?' said Harry.

'That's right.'

'And there was an entry and exit wound?'

'Correct again,' responded Lucy. Harry unbuckled the belt of his trousers and lowered them to his knees. Sitting back down on the bed he lifted his left leg and showed his captive audience a white birthmark about halfway up his thigh. Lifting his leg even further he revealed another, slightly larger white patch on the back of his leg.

'They're not scars,' he said. 'Just pigment changes in the skin, and incidentally I have another on my chest, but I think you'll all agree that the evidence is building for the case that Lieutenant Charles Bradshaw and Lieutenant Tony Harrison are one and the same person.'

279

Chapter Forty-Five

Not much was said after that. Laura and Harry needed to get away in order to catch a plane from Bodmin to Heathrow and onto their honeymoon destination. Lucy said her goodbyes and thank you's to Mike, who despite not having much input to the proceedings, had listened carefully and taken the odd note.

'Where are you going on honeymoon Harry,' asked Lucy when she managed to get him on her own for a minute.

'Australia. We've got four weeks touring the country before we have to return to work,' he said.

'I don't believe it,' she said. 'You'll be so close.'

'It hadn't gone unnoticed Lucy, but I don't see what we could achieve by going to the place. It might just cause more uncertainty and upset.'

'Harry I know what you're saying but would you please do one thing for me.' She reached into her bag. 'Would you write down your itinerary and fax it to this number from the airport?'

'I can do better than that,' he said. Opening the soft zip up brief case he was carrying he rooted through the travel documents and came out with a sheet of A4 paper.

'I had to produce this for the Squadron, what with the troubles in Korea and China. It's got the places, dates and even some of the telephone numbers of places we'll be staying at.'

'Thank you darling,' she said standing on tiptoe to kiss his cheek. Then she was gone.

'What was that all about?' asked Laura as he climbed into the Taxi next to her.

'Oh, just your Aunt giving me some honeymoon advice,' he said, grabbing her around the ribs and squeezing so she let out a squeal of delight. The driver grinned to himself and adjusted his mirror so as not to intrude.

'Bloody newlyweds,' he laughed, and drove off.

Chapter Forty-Six

The honeymoon was going far too quickly for Laura. Harry had spared no expense. He had always been careful with his money, not tight but careful, and a single Lieutenant on full flying pay could squirrel quite a bit away for just such an occasion. Nothing had been said between them on the subject of 1942. They just forgot about it and enjoyed themselves. Until they reached Darwin that is. It was very much the last leg of their trip before returning to Sydney for the flight home. They had booked a guide and some fishing tackle and were planning to spend two to three days roughing it in the out-back. But first they were to spend a night in the Holiday Inn.

Things changed as soon as they walked into the hotel lobby. Lucy leapt up from a sofa opposite the door and all but ran over to meet them. Laura was speechless but Harry gave her a knowing smile and said:

'And do I need to ask what you're doing here Lucy.'

'I'm sorry darlings; I just couldn't let it go at that.'

'Aunt Lucy,' said Laura recovering. 'How wonderful to see you, but what on earth are you doing here'.

'Let's go up to your room - I have a proposition to put to you both.'

A smartly dressed boy who somehow managed to carry all their bags saw them to their room. Harry tipped him generously and the three of them were left standing in the spacious room.

'Right, what's this all about?' said Laura sitting in one of the occasional chairs.

'Yep, spill the beans Lucy,' said Harry taking another chair as he saw Lucy perching herself on the edge of the enormous double bed.

'I'm offering you the trip of a life time,' she started. 'It's all paid for and you'll be back in Sydney in time for your return flight to England. Alternatively you can exchange your tickets and fly home from Japan.'

'Japan!' shouted Laura. 'Come on Auntie, what's going on.'

'Yes dear, Japan. It's all sorted with British Airways but they need to know tonight so they can reallocate seats if you decide not to go.'

Lucy then spent the next 10 minutes outlining the proposed trip. They would depart from Darwin the following morning. She had already spoken to their guide, who she tracked down through the hotel. He had agreed to accept halve the intended fee for the late cancellation, paid for by Lucy. The privately chartered jet would take them to Tokyo, where they would have the rest of the day to look around. They would stop again in the Holiday Inn before early next morning taking a taxi down to Chikawa. From there Lucy had laid on a float plane to take them to the island of Bonin, now deserted, with enough supplies to stay overnight if required. Once they had satisfied their reasons for being there it was either a reverse trip or another overnight stop in Tokyo before flying home.

'I'll leave you two to talk things over. I'll be back in an hour and then I must have your answer one way or another,' said Lucy crossing over to the door.

As the door closed Harry turned to Laura. 'Well?'

'I think your minds already made up Harry. We may have only been married for a few weeks but I can read you like a book.'

Harry laughed and then his face turned serious and he knelt down in front of Laura and held her hands in his.

'Look sweetheart, I know this whole thing is really spooky but I don't think I can let it go unless I do this thing. There is no one I'd rather have do it by my side than you but if you don't want to then we won't.'

'Well how can I refuse a man that gets down on his knees before me,' she said. Then letting out a little chuckle she carried on: 'Besides, I've always wanted to see Japan.'

He hugged her legs and laid his head on her knees. 'I love you,' he said quietly.

Chapter Forty-Seven

At last they were on the last leg of the journey. The last two days had been a whirlwind of experiences and they were glad they had decided to fly home from Tokyo as it gave them another two night's stop over in Japan. The floatplane was very basic. It was a twin engine top wing affair. Harry had no idea what type it was nor how old. The more he thought about it the less he wanted to know. They were strapped into canvas seats that ran down the length of the aircraft, not unlike the troop seats in his own Seaking helicopters, and just as uncomfortable. The trip was due to take about three and a half hours and so Harry tried to get some sleep. There was no chance of conversation due to the noise and the two women were already nodding off leaning against the bulkheads on either side, Laura next to him and Lucy on a single seat opposite them.

Harry turned and looked out of the window. They were flying quite low over the sea and in the distance he could see mountain ranges. They were very indistinct thanks to the hazy sunshine and appeared to be completely stationary in the frame formed by the window, but Harry knew this was an illusion of distance. Looking down at the water he estimated they were flying at about 140 -150 knots. This was the first time he had been flying low over the sea since his accident and he felt a knot of anxiety in his chest. The interior of the aircraft wasn't dissimilar to the Seaking. There was little or no soundproofing, and there were pipes lining the walls that he assumed were taking hydraulic fluid to the moving surfaces. There was also the characteristic smell; one that he couldn't describe that he would always associate with aviation. He found himself looking round the plane to work out an escape route should the unthinkable happen. This was a reasonable enough reaction for someone that was trained to do that every time he got into an aircraft, but deep down he knew that he was a far more pessimistic person than he had been in the past. Whereas before the accident he knew there were mishaps, especially in aviation, he felt, as all aircrew do or they wouldn't be able to do the job, that it would always be someone else; never him. That was no longer true; it had happened to him, and now it was spreading into all walks of life. He expected things to happen whether he was driving, on a train, even crossing the road and especially flying. Now he went out of his way to thwart fate by always being conscious of the dangers present in everyday life. Whether he would be able to go back to a flying career was a decision he'd not yet faced, but somehow he didn't think so.

Mulling these thoughts around in his mind eventually drove him to sleep. He was jolted back to awareness by the first bounce of the seaplane as the pilot lowered the floats onto the calm water. Unknown to him they had circumnavigated the island and, with Lucy as a guide, had landed adjacent to the beach by the aircraft spotter's hut. Harry caught a glimpse of the motor torpedo boat (MTB), amazed that it was still recognisable after all this time, as the aircraft settled onto the water, and then it was gone as the pilot turned the plane and water-taxied it slowly to the beach. He stopped about 10 meters short, cut the plane's engines and deployed an anchor through the cabin door.

'Looks like we're going to get wet then girls,' said Harry grimly. Rising from his seat he talked briefly to the pilot, who didn't appear to understand a word of English.

'So much for English being the international language of the air,' he said, and then lowered himself into the waist-deep water.

'No, no,' shouted the pilot as Laura made to follow Harry who was half way to the beach. 'You wait see.'

The women watched as he opened a box behind the pilot's seat and lifted out one of four orange packs. He threw it out of the door and pulled a toggle on the side.

With a loud hiss the CO2 canister fired and a small dinghy appeared. Reaching under the passenger seats he produced a paddle.

'Right, who first?'

Laura looked out at the dripping, bedraggled form of her husband standing on the white sand and burst out laughing.

'Oh yes, very funny,' said Harry with a long face.

'Yes, very funny,' echoed the pilot. 'Very funny.' He and Lucy joined Laura in her laughter, the pilot actually hooting like a monkey. Harry watched them for a moment, and then he too saw the funny side of it, realising he would be the subject of many tales told in the bars around the airport.

Once they had all settled down, although Laura would still get a sudden giggling fit every so often, the pilot transferred the ladies to the beach one at a time. Finally he went back for the supplies and in very broken English told Lucy that he would remain with the plane and do a little fishing. He also gave her a walkie-talkie so she could let him know when they were coming back.

In the meantime Harry had stripped off his wet clothes and changed into some heavy jeans from his pack. He wandered over to the MTB, unable to believe that his dream had given him so much detail. It hadn't changed much in 55 or so years. The gunner's body was gone of course and so was what had been left of the machine gun; no doubt a trophy somewhere in a bar or someone's house. The shell of the vessel, though, was very similar to how he remembered it and he felt his stomach turn as he recalled how ill he'd been after seeing the rear gunner. Time and moisture had both taken their toll causing the whole structure to decay but the basic shape of the hull was intact, though the wood was soft in places and had started to decay in others. Harry found that he could just pull sections of wood from the wreck and crumble them in his hands. He noticed that a bird had at sometime used the gunner's seat as a base on which to build a nest, but that too was abandoned as if the environment was unsuitable for bringing new life into the world.

A cold hand descending onto his shoulder made him jump out of his skin.

'Jesus...' he hissed turning to see Laura at his side.

'I'm sorry darling. I didn't mean to startle you.'

'It's OK,' he said. 'I was miles away.'

'It's amazing Harry, it's exactly how you described it.' She paused, looking around. 'I can't see the jetty though.'

Harry held her hand and slowly walked along the beach. 'This is about where it was,' he said. As if to corroborate his claim he bent down and dug at a disturbance in the otherwise smooth sand. Before long he had exposed six inches of rotten wood, smoothed by the action of the sea.

'This must have been one of the supports,' he said. 'I suppose the rest got washed away by storms or whatever.'

'Where's the path to the hut?' asked Laura, looking towards the tree line.

'It should be straight up from here,' he said.

They both looked up to the line of jungle that appeared to be completely uniform. Walking up they found a few more pieces of wood far above the high tide mark, but could not find any entrance into the forest. Lucy came up to join them, linking her arm through Harry's. She too had a pack on her back, insisting that she carry it herself. Harry had no idea what was in it but by the weight he assumed it was just a change of clothes.

'It's here somewhere Brad,' she said, not even realising that she had spoken using the name she'd called him so many years ago.

Harry opened up his pack and unsheathed a large machete, much sharper than the one he'd used back in 1942. He took a few tentative swings at the heavy undergrowth, got a feel for the tool and then walked along the face of the jungle swinging the heavy blade at regular intervals. As he went he checked his bearings on the wrecked boat at the water's edge. After a few minutes he was satisfied he'd gone far enough to the left and returned to the ladies who had planted themselves in the sand. Checking his bearings again he set off from his original position moving to the right. Twice he came to what appeared to be areas of less density but as he concentrated his efforts he was foiled by the shear weight of greenery just behind the edge. At the third spot he made easy work of the vegetation and soon disappeared from view.

'I think this is it,' he shouted back to the girls, and they quickly joined him in the forest. The pathway was in quite a clear condition once they moved away from the beach. Although the path had probably not been used since the war the thick canopy above them had cut out most of the light and thus resisted the growth of new plants. There was a certain amount of spreading by established bushes but the main obstructions came from decaying branches and trees fallen from the canopy high above.

Ten minutes later they were standing at the edge of what had once been the clearing around the spotter's hut. Here the ground had been unprotected from the sun and over the years many plants had taken hold; the quicker-growing trees reaching up high and forcing the slower ones to spread across the ground forever searching for the light they needed to manufacture energy. As Harry hacked his way through the dense growth he saw that the forest had all but reclaimed even the burnt remains of the hut. All that was left were some main timbers that had been spared by the fire and the scorched metal fittings and nails. Harry kicked at the wood and felt it disintegrate under his boot and as he looked down at it he saw uncountable insects of varying size and colour scurry away.

Harry was sweating heavily by now and accepted the canteen of water offered by Laura.

'I think we should take a rest here and consider our options,' he said between gulps of tepid water.

'We don't have any other course of action but to press on to the area that I buried Brad,' declared Lucy.

'Are you sure that's such a good thing Lucy?' asked Laura softly.

'Why else are we here?' she replied matter of factly.

'Harry?' said Laura turning to her husband.

Harry looked back at the two concerned faces. Lucy was right of course, why else *were* they there? As he looked at her he saw the need in her eyes. All the years of waiting were about to come to an end one way or another, all her questions answered. He switched his attentions to Laura. A different concern was written on her face; she could see the next few days tearing him apart. He gazed deep into her beautiful brown eyes and saw love reflected in them. They were begging him not to go on but at the same time offering support if he decided that was the route to take.

He turned away from the two women to enable him to sort out his own turmoil of emotions. He could not begin to assess the psychological damage he might be doing to himself on this crazy quest, but could he live at peace with himself if he turned back now?

He turned back and looked Laura full in the face. 'We must go on,' he said.

She looked back at him and for one moment he thought she was about to burst into tears, and indeed she felt like it, but deep down she knew he was right.

She smiled back at him. 'Yes,' she said softly. 'We must.'

Chapter Forty-Eight

Three hours later they were approaching the beach from along the small river. They knew it would have been easier to return to the beach and skirt round to the river but Harry felt that they needed to retrace their steps of fifty years ago. Harry was amazed at the changes in the stream. Years of rainy seasons, typhoons and high tides had broken down the pools where Brad had caught fish, and the stream now meandered all the way to the ocean. Laura had noticed that the spirits of the other two had dropped the closer they got to where the final chapter of their strange story had been played out. They dropped wearily to the forest floor, clearing as much of the undergrowth as possible.

Laura quietly prepared a snack of bread and cheese as the other two sat staring at the water. Lucy suddenly let out a shrill laugh.

'I was about to say you're buried over there,' she said, and her pointing hand flew to her mouth to stifle the groan that threatened to escape. The other two said nothing; both lost in their own thoughts.

They ate in silence and continued to sit long after the meal was finished. It was Laura who broke the spell: 'I'm going down to the beach,' she said for no reason. 'Come with me Harry.'

Lucy nodded when Harry looked over to her and he jumped up and helped Laura to her feet. Walking on the white sand hand in hand they both fought for the words needed to break the silence that had fallen over them since arriving at the clearing by the river. Laura was the first to speak.

'Does any of this really alter anything?' she asked him.

'Not for us, maybe, but for Lucy this thing has been with her for over fifty years.'

'But what do we do even if we can find the grave?'

'Dig him up I suppose,' he said.

'Dig him up,' she shouted, and then in a quieter but no less urgent voice. 'You can't just go round digging up fifty year old corpses. Just think what it might do to poor old Aunt Lucy, not to mention that exhumation without a permit is illegal.'

'To be honest,' he said slowly. 'I was more worried about the implications of finding an empty grave.'

Laura stopped in the sand as a shiver went through her body. Her mother would have said that a goose had just walked over her grave, but that didn't really seem appropriate at the moment. Instead she turned to Harry and said:

'Harry, let's go home.'

'I can't,' he replied. 'You could ask me anything else in the world and I would do my best for you. You know I love you, more than anything, but this is something I have to do and if I didn't do it, because you asked me, it would always remain something between us. I hope you can understand that darling.'

'Yes I do understand,' she said. Harry pulled her to him and hugged her as if he were trying to break something. He released her slightly and she struggled to find his lips with hers. Kissing long and strong they dropped to their knees in the sand, their passions aroused. Thoughts of Brad having done this with Lucy flashed briefly into his mind and he paused to look into her face. She opened her eyes and smiled and all thoughts of Lucy were gone as she joined her hands around his neck and pulled him down onto the warm sand.

Their lovemaking was slow and sensual, just what they needed to reassure each other and strengthen the ever-growing bond between them, at this difficult time. As they lay back on the sand when it was over they were both quiet, deep in thought and feeling much closer to each other than before.

Suddenly Harry jumped up,

'Did you hear that?' he cried. As Laura sat up she saw him scanning the horizon.

'What is it sweetheart?' Harry cocked his head and listened. 'Oh, nothing,' he said and then looked at his watch. 'Christ, we'd better get back to Lucy; she'll be worried about us.'

Hand in hand they ran back to the river. They found Lucy asleep in the shade of a tall tree. Around the base of the tree were small chippings of wood and they could see where Lucy had carved into the bark. A heart about three Inches Square contained the words Brad & Lucy beautifully cut into the wood in an ornate scripture. Bending down Harry could see the penknife was still in her hand and he shook her gently.

'What is it?' she cried, pulling herself nimbly to her feet whilst waving the short blade in an arc in front of her waist. 'Is it the Japs?'

'No, no it's me, Harry,' he said jumping clear.

Lucy brought her eyes to focus on his rugged face. 'Oh Brad. I'm sorry I was dreaming,' she said relaxing back onto the ground.

'I think it's time to find the grave Lucy,' said Harry, and helped her to her feet.

'Yes of course – lead the way.'

'Well I don't know where it was,' said Harry. 'I wasn't there for that bit.'

'No you weren't were you?' she giggled. Harry looked back to Laura and registered the look of disapproval on her face. He smiled and took hold of her hand as Lucy walked around to try and get her bearings.

It took over an hour to find the final resting-place of Lieutenant Bradshaw and four abortive sorties into the dense undergrowth. Just when Harry was about to give up at the fifth attempt he swung the machete into the soil in frustration. Instead of the soft earth he'd expected there was a metallic clang as the blade deflected off rock. Harry pulled his hand back in surprise as the shock was transmitted through the handle and into his fingers. He let out an explosive expletive, turned to apologise to the two ladies and then dropped to his knees to investigate the find.

Pulling back the lush vegetation he cleared an area to expose a small pile of rocks not dissimilar to a cairn.

'That's it, that's it,' cried Lucy excitedly. She all but pushed Harry out of the way and started scratching ineffectively at the ground.

'Hang on Lucy, this isn't necessarily the grave,' said Laura, though it did seem unlikely to be a coincidence. Lucy had moved a few of the stones and turned round with a look of triumph on her face.

'Then explain this,' she said pushing a small object into Laura's hand. Laura clasped the cold article in a balled fist. Even before she saw it she knew what it was. Harry had told of the mysterious piece of jewellery he'd remembered wearing in his dreams and sure enough, as she opened her hand she saw the gold band. The ring was dulled by fifty years subject to heat and moisture but as she rubbed it the delicate pattern of woven gold was revealed. Turning it in her fingers the inscription on the inner surface was plain to see. She read aloud:

'Te amo Madre ....'

'RM,' finished Harry. All three stood in silence as the enormity of their find sank in. Up until that moment Harry had thought there would be no evidence to link him with the happenings on the island in 1942. He reached out and took the ring from Laura's open palm and was about to slip it onto the ring finger of his left hand when he paused and turned to Lucy. She was staring at the ring with tears welling up in her eyes and Harry knew that she was reliving the moment when she had slipped it onto the finger of Brad as he was dying. They had since found out that the inscription was Spanish and meant I love you Mother, though they had found no clues to the significance of the words.

'Lucy I think I understood Brad well enough to know that he would want you to have this.'

Without saying a word she accepted the ring from Harry's out-stretched hand, held it to her lips and kissed it before slipping it into a pocket. Harry turned abruptly and stumbled from the graveside not wanting the women to see the tears forming in his eyes. Laura followed. Once they were out of earshot Laura stopped and pulled Harry around.

'You can't open the grave sweetheart; you'll kill her.'

Harry didn't know what to say. He had to know yet the last thing he wanted was to upset Laura at this difficult time for both of them. Lucy, who had followed them from the grave after securing the ring on her crucifix chain, saved him from the situation.

'Of course you'll have to know whether there's anything in there or whether it's just the silly ranting of a senile old woman.'

She held her hand up to hush their protestations. 'I would have to do it if I were in your shoes.'

She smiled and walked past them towards the beach. Harry chased after her and gave her a kiss on the forehead. 'Thank you Lucy,' he said and turned back to Laura. 'Come on, let's get this over and done with.'

They walked back to where they'd left their kit bags and Harry pulled a collapsible spade from his.

'You were pretty sure then,' said Laura.

'Oh this,' he said. 'I got this in a fishing tackle shop while we were waiting for the plane.' Laura followed him back into the clearing and stood and watched as Harry moved the remaining rocks marking the grave. The earth underneath was cool and damp and Harry had no problems digging into it. Laura stayed and watched though she would like to have left. A morbid fascination, not to see the remains if any, but more to see her husband's reaction and to be there to help him if necessary, held her. Harry had only been working for about five minutes before he felt the spade come up against something more solid than the earth. He stopped and laid the spade to one side and dropped down onto one knee to have a closer look. Brushing the loose soil away he uncovered a large bone that even to his untrained eye was obviously a human femur. There was a fair amount of decaying fabric across the brown stained bone but thankfully there was no evidence of decayed flesh; that had been broken down by the forest and it's animals long ago.

'I really don't think there's any more I need to see here,' he said, replacing the bone in much the same position he found it. 'As for how I came to dream the life of a World War Two fighter ace I guess I'll never know.' He paused for a moment to reflect on the find. 'One thing we can be sure of now is that Lieutenant Charles Bradshaw, United States Navy, died and was buried here in 1942 and that I am no more part of him than you are.'

Harry carefully filled in the grave and rebuilt the small pile of rocks that marked it. 'Come on then,' he said as he finished. Let's get back to Lucy and get off this island – it gives me the creeps. He packed away the tools he'd used and put his arm around Laura's waist. 'Mind you, it still leaves a lot of questions unanswered.'

'Like how I felt I'd been here just from your description,' chipped in Laura.

'Yes, and how Lucy reacted when she first set eyes on me.'

'But I'd heard that you affect most girls in that way,' said Laura in an effort to lighten the mood.

'Well I didn't notice you swooning in the school when I walked in with Pete Hancock.

Harry tried to tighten his grip on her waist but she squirmed free and burst out of the newly cut passage into the clearing by the stream. Expecting to see Lucy waiting for them she came to a stop and looked around the empty clearing. Harry cannoned into her and nearly took her off her feet.

'Lucy's not here,' she said as Harry fought to keep them both upright.

'Probably gone down to the beach,' said Harry. He was feeling much better having completed the gristly task that had been hanging over him for the last few days. Pulling Laura round to face him he kissed her and she responded at first but then pushed him away.

'No Harry, I'm worried about Lucy. Let's go down to the beach and find her.'

'Yep,' he said. 'Your right I suppose.' They set off together towards the beach; Laura calling Lucy as they went.

Arriving on the beach they could see no sign of her. The sun was still reasonably high in the sky and they had no trouble seeing their own footprints in the sand from earlier that afternoon. They couldn't see any other prints that might have indicated the presence of Lucy. Laura called her name a few more times and turned to Harry when there was no response.

'Where can she have got to?' she asked, the first signs of consternation showing on her face.

'I'm sure there's a logical explanation,' said Harry. 'She's probably bedded down somewhere by the stream and is fast asleep. She is getting on a bit you know, and this has been a long day for all of us.'

Harry only wished that he were as convinced of this as he hoped he sounded. Arriving back at the small clearing they carried out a methodical search of the area. Like the beach it was entirely fruitless. After a few minutes Laura commented that her pack was also gone, along with it the walkie-talkie. Harry had picked up on those facts as soon as they had arrived but didn't say so for fear of upsetting Laura further.

'Harry, I'm really worried,' she said. 'I've got a bad feeling about this.'

'Don't worry. You know what old people can be like. She's probably gone off exploring; reliving the past, that sort of thing.'

'But it'll be dark soon,' said Laura. 'We're never going to find her once the light has gone.'

'And we're not even going to try,' he said and held a hand up to stop her protests. 'If we leave here there's a good chance we'll miss her as she returns, and as you say, the chances of finding her as the light drops are next to nothing.'

In her mind she admitted he was right, but she couldn't just sit still and wait. 'I'll go and have another look on the beach,' she said. 'You wait here for her, I won't be long. While she was away he went through his pack and pulled out the things necessary for spending a night out in the open. When Laura came back after 15 minutes or so he had arranged the camp into an orderly fashion. She found him over a portable gas heater warming a tin of noodles. Behind him a mosquito net was spread over a thin cord between two trees. Under this he had built up a mattress of undergrowth over which he'd spread a couple of space blankets

'No luck?' he asked, looking up at her worried face. She shook her head and dropped down onto the soil beside him. He climbed off the tree stump he'd found and offered it to her.

'She'll be fine,' he said. 'She can get in touch with the pilot if she gets into trouble and besides, she seems to be a fairly robust character.'

I suppose you're right,' she said, but she was still worried.

They ate the noodles; taking it in turn to use a pair of chopsticks to extract them from the one tin. They finished off the meal with some chocolate bars and then Harry put on some water to boil for tea.

'Tell me about your Aunt Lucy,' said Harry after they had sat in comfortable silence for a while, listening to the night creatures of the jungle waking up and setting about their foraging.

'There's not really a lot to tell,' she said. 'As I told you at the wedding, I found a reference to her in one of old Grampa's diaries that were left to me when he died. It was very vague; I think she was regarded as the love child of one of his brothers, Donald I seem to recall, and was adopted by him and his wife.'

'What, by your Grampa?' asked Harry.

'Now that's one of the things I had trouble understanding,' she said. 'She was adopted by her true Father and his wife, though whether she knew Lucy was his child I'll never know. I heard they were killed during the war when she was quite young but I never put two and two together until I heard your story. After that no one really knew what happened to her until I found the address when I was going through the diary. Where she's been since the war nobody seems to have any idea. The address I wrote to was in Belfast,' she finished.

'Where Matthew came from,' added Harry.

'Oh God, I hadn't thought of that,' cried Laura. 'I guess he might still be alive.'

'If he is he would be very old. Though I suppose not impossible I think it unlikely. On the other hand the Lucy I knew in my dreams liked Matthew; saw him as a replacement for her father. I wouldn't be surprised if they lived together in Ireland after the war.'

'But none of this is helping with the current situation,' she said. Looking out towards the beach they could see that the sun had set and it was almost completely dark.

'Well whereever she's got to she's staying there for the night,' said Harry. 'No one can travel safely through this.' He motioned to the forest with both hands. 'Come on darling let's get an early night, no one knows what tomorrow may bring.' How little did he know!

Chapter Forty-Nine

Laura was the first to wake in the morning though the sun was still trying to struggle above the horizon and it remained quite dark under the canopy of trees. She lay still in the makeshift bed so as not to wake Harry. She had been surprised to find that the space blankets were quite warm, especially when she was also wrapped around her man. Gently she pulled herself from him a little way and pushed herself up onto one elbow. In the early morning light she looked into his peaceful face, noticing that he was in REM sleep. I wonder what he's dreaming about, she thought. He looked so happy and calm that she secretly hoped she was a prominent figure in the storyline.

She may have been disappointed; Harry was flying again and due to the dreams he'd had whilst in the coma he recognised the machine as a Wildcat. Looking around through the glass canopy he saw that he was on his own and that he was over a pure blue sea. He made a few small inputs through the flying controls to give him an idea of the handling. The aircraft responded immediately. It felt like it was a wild animal waiting to be unleashed onto some unsuspecting prey. Looking around again to ensure the coast was clear he checked the engine instruments. Seeing nothing untoward he pulled the aircraft up into a loop. She went over the top like a dream and Harry pulled her out of the dive into a second loop. Instead of finishing the manoeuvre he rolled off the top and settled into straight and level flight. Something had caught his eye as he was starting the second loop and so after orienting himself he looked to his left and saw a small island.

Harry put the aircraft into a steep dive in order to get a closer look though he already knew what he would find. He was surprised then when everything went black. Harry was still in the plane, still flying it, but he couldn't see any of the instruments or the outside world. He started to ease back on the stick conscious that he was in a steep dive. He felt the G come onto his body and at that moment the blackness cleared as quickly as it had come on. He was skimming over the tops of some trees and his first instinct was to pull up, however as he started to make the input something stopped him. The plane was flying perfectly happily and he found that he was enjoying the sensation of flying dangerously low. Instead he scanned the skies to ensure there were no threats from other aircraft. Happy that he was alone he briefly looked in to check his instruments.

Anyone watching from the outside would have seen a 'wiggle' in the flight path. Harry didn't see it but he felt it as the tail wheel just brushed the treetops. He stabilised the plane and tried to analyse what he'd seen in the cockpit. He was no longer in a Wildcat, though the instruments appeared to be of the same vintage. He didn't have any more time to think about it as he was fast approaching the end of the tree line. He roared across the boundary between land and sea and just caught a glimpse of two people standing on the white sand looking up at him. Harry pulled the aircraft into lazy climb then rolled and pulled to fly a hard teardrop manoeuvre, dropping back down to the same height over the sea but facing the other way. He could clearly see the figures on the beach jumping and waving. As he got closer Harry could see the man was dressed in American flying gear, though the woman with him was dressed in civilian clothing. Harry tried to wing rock (a universal sign of recognition) but instead found his fingers curling round the trigger on the control column. In a moment of inspiration he looked out onto the upper wing surface. In the middle of the mottled surface he saw a large red circle.

'No,' he shouted out loud, but at the same time he felt the recoil as the guns started to fire. Harry saw the figures sit down just in time, and the sand thrown up behind them as his bullets crashed harmlessly into the beach. In a flash he was over the tree line but not before he'd seen the astonished faces looking up at him. It was like looking in the mirror and although he didn't get a good look at the woman he knew it was Laura.

'No, no it can't be,' he cried, but even as the words came out he was already thinking about his next attack. He knew the figures on the beach would make a run for cover under the trees, but he also knew that they would jink hard right at the last moment. As Harry turned in towards the beach he saw them running but instead of lining up on the pair as they headed straight for the trees, he offset a little to the right.

'No,' he cried again. 'That's not fair. That's not how it happened.' All this time Harry was fighting with the controls but his flight path stayed steady as a rock. He felt, in horror, as his finger tightened on the trigger and just as he squeezed it the people on the beach jinked right as he knew they would.

'Harry wake up, you're dreaming,' shouted Laura as she shook him by the shoulder. In the eerie blue light of the dawn she could see the beads of sweat glistening on his forehead. Harry woke quickly, jerking upright. Laura soothed him, running her fingers through his damp hair.

'What was all that about?' she asked in a concerned yet authoritative voice and Harry gave her the gist of what the dream was about.

'It's this place,' she responded. 'It gives me the creeps so Heaven alone knows what it's doing to your confused mind.'

Harry pulled himself to his feet and looked at the dial of his luminous aircrew watch. It read 4.30am but Harry knew that he would not be able to get back to sleep. Instead he collected together the items he would need and set about making a brew of tea. Laura lay down on her back and watched Harry working in the early morning light.

'What do you think our next move should be?' she asked.

'Back to the aircraft, pick up Lucy and then back to Tokyo and home.'

'What if she isn't there?'

Harry gave the question some thought and then answered carefully. 'I'm sure she will be there, but if not we'll contact her on the short-wave radio and go and pick her up. The only other place she could have got to is the village; she never did get to see it in 1942 and she may want to see the place that caused so much trouble for Brad.'

He finished making the tea and handed a mug to Laura. Next he rummaged around in his pack and produced some eggs, carefully wrapped in cotton wool and wedged into a box. Taking four out he put them into the remaining water and started the stopwatch on his wrist.

'You never cease to amaze me,' laughed Laura.

'In those immortal words 'you ain't seen nothin' yet.'' he said, delved once more into his pack and produced a vacuum pack of bacon. Laura couldn't contain the laughter that bubbled up through her throat and spilled out into the quiet morning. In response a startled monkey screamed high in the treetops and set off a chorus of calls.

Ten minutes later they sat together eating eggs and bacon. Harry hadn't got his timing quite right and the eggs were a little over done; however the meal was going down extremely well. After breakfast Laura went to the water's edge to wash the dishes and Harry broke camp packing everything carefully into his seemingly bottomless backpack. As Laura returned they both stood and watched night turn into day. It happened very quickly once the sun had broken the seemingly inpenetrable barrier presented by the horizon and so loading the last of the implements they set out upstream; the direction from which they had arrived.

Four hours later they arrived back at the beach having followed the path down from the remains of the spotter's hut. Arriving at the waters edge they both dropped the packs they carried and walked straight into the sea. The water was relatively cool and very refreshing after four hours walking in the jungle. The going had been much easier due to their recent journey in the opposite direction, but they had moved slowly in order to check for any signs that Lucy may have come that way. They had seen none. They looked over to the floatplane and failed to see any activity. They turned to each other and their hearts sank. As they stood they heard a low rumble of thunder and out to sea they could see the high clouds of cumulo-nimbus storm clouds across the horizon.

'They've probably taken to the tree line for some shade,' said Harry. 'Or failing that they could be in the aircraft.' Laura gave no reply but started walking over to the plane that was sitting half in and half out of the water. Harry followed at a trot and soon caught up with her. Arriving they tried to peer into the body of the plane through the empty cockpit. They both called out Lucy's name almost in unison. There was no reply. Walking round to the blind side Harry found the pilot asleep on the port float. He idly held a small fishing rod between his crossed legs, his right arm wrapped around it in order that it would not be dragged away if a fish took the bait. Harry called out as he waded out to him. For a moment he thought the man was dead and quickly looked around at Laura on the beach.

Reaching out he gently shook the pilot's leg and jumped back as he reacted by striking the rod. Failing to feel any resistance on the line he began to wind in still not opening his eyes.

Harry gave an exaggerated 'Ahem,' and the small Japanese man opened his eyes. Harry suspected the pilot had been aware of him all the time.

'Is the lady here,' he shouted.

'No need shout, I no deaf,' the pilot replied.

'Sorry, I didn't think you spoke English.'

'I speak velly good English, thank you,' he said indignantly, and Harry could see that they were not getting off to a good start. 'Now what you say?'

Harry used a soft tone and consciously slowed down his speech: 'Is the lady here?'

'Yes, she behind you,' he said, pointing at Laura and giggling to himself as if he'd made some brilliant joke.

'No not her,' Harry snapped. He quickly realised he would get nowhere if he lost his temper and as if to echo his thoughts the pilot began to re-bait his hook and prepared himself to make a fresh cast.

'Sorry,' said Harry. 'I mean the other lady, Lucy. Is the older lady here?'

The pilot turned back to Harry with a confused look on his face. 'Other lady?' he asked.

'Yes, the older lady we were with yesterday.'

'No other lady,' said the pilot, and cast his line into the blue ocean.

'Yes,' said Harry starting to loose his patience again. 'The lady that hired you; Lucy Fairbrother.'

'No other lady; me hired by man on phone from England.'

Harry was filled with a feeling of dread. He could remember Lucy distinctly saying she had lain on the light floatplane when she had outlined the trip. He drew a deep breath and said as clearly as he could: 'When we flew from Japan there was me, my wife,' he indicated Laura with his right hand. 'And Lucy, a much older woman.'

'No. Only you and wife.'

Laura had come over to join Harry in the water when she realised there was a problem. As it was she ended up holding her husband on his feet as his knees started to buckle.

'No,' he shouted, grabbing the pilot by the front of his faded red checked shirt. He pulled the frightened oriental face to within a few inches of his own. 'There were three of us.' He turned to Laura for support. All he could read in her face was doubt mixed with a little fear.

'You gave Lucy the walkie – talkie, the radio.' He said as he let the pilot regain his seat on the float.

'I no have walkie – talkie,' he said, and then disap peared into the fuselage through the side door. Harry thought he'd frightened him off but was proved wrong as the pilot re-appeared in the doorway. He held out a grubby piece of paper in his hand.

'The sheet,' he said. 'The man...the...'

'The manifesto,' Harry finished for him. The pilot nodded furiously and handed the paper over to Harry. It was all in Japanese but in the bottom left hand corner was a small drawing of the inside of the cabin. Two seats were crossed and there were some crude drawings in pencil that Harry assumed were representative of some cargo. Harry turned and gave the manifesto to Laura who looked at it with a blank expression.

'May I?' he said. He indicated that he wanted to have a look inside the aircraft. The pilot nodded and backed into the cabin from the doorway. Harry easily pulled himself up into the aircraft. He immediately saw the two seats he and Laura had occupied on the starboard side, but the place opposite was taken up with cargo strapped to the floor. In fact there were no seats at all on the port side of the aircraft.

'No this cannot be,' he said to no one in particular. 'This is impossible.'

The pilot just shrugged his shoulders as Harry looked at him hoping for some answer. Fearing the worst he backed into the cockpit holding his hands up on thin arms. 'Just you and wife,' he said. 'You and wife, no one else.'

Harry looked at him for a few more seconds, then turned and jumped into the water. Laura had walked out of the sea ahead of him and was walking up the beach peering at the sand. Worried that he may have put the fear of God into the pilot he shouted through to the cockpit. 'You stay here until we come back.' The pilot put his head through the cockpit window and showed Harry one of his best smiles revealing the yellow teeth with two missing at the top. He gave a thumbs up sign and so Harry set off after Laura.

Joining her at the MTB he realised that she was searching the sand for footprints. They followed their tracks up to the palm trees where Lucy had joined them, but the sand was such a mess that regarding the question 'was Lucy ever there', the results were inconclusive.

'Harry this is madness,' said Laura. 'Of course she was with us.'

'I know, but why would the pilot lie?'

'I don't know,' she said and started to cry. Harry held her close and whispered in her ear: 'It's Ok sweetheart, there's a logical explanation to all this. If only we could find some evidence to show that she was with us.'

Laura pulled herself away from him. 'What about the tree?'

'What tree?' he asked.

'The tree she carved the heart on – in the clearing by the grave.'

'Yes, of course. Once we've checked it and convinced ourselves that we're not going mad we can confront the pilot and find out what's going on and why. He grabbed her hand and they ran back down to the floatplane.

'Can you wait another day?' he asked the pilot who had taken to fishing again. 'We have got to go to the other side of the island to check something.'

'One hundred American dollars,' he replied grinning at them.

'Fifty,' said Harry who was used to bartering after visiting foreign ports in his time in the Navy. They finally agreed on eighty Dollars and Harry gave him forty with the promise of the other forty on their return. Happy, the pilot once again turned his attentions to the fishing rod that started to jerk about in his hands. Harry and Laura left him as he pulled a large multi-coloured fish from the ocean and quickly dispatched it ready for a lunchtime meal.

Chapter Fifty

It only took them about three-quarters of an hour to get back to the clearing by Brads grave. There was no need to make their way through the jungle and they made good time following the beach round to the small river. As they got closer they started to hurry until they were at a full run as they neared the entrance to the forest. They both stopped as they reached the dry riverbed. They looked at each other, Laura with uncertainty written all over her face. Harry did not allow his doubt to show.

'I love you,' he said and gently took hold of her face and gave her a soft kiss on the lips. She wanted to respond to him but her mind was elsewhere and she pulled away. Holding hands they walked slowly into the jungle. For some reason Harry knew what they were going to find and it filled him with foreboding. As if to confirm these feelings the air was suddenly filled with a terrific boom as an electrical storm out to sea was triggered. Laura pulled him as she ran to try and reach the cover of the trees as if in protection from the weather.

Walking up to the tree Lucy had carved they stopped and stared in horror. The bark of the tree seemed to be completely normal. Laura dropped to the ground and started to weep softly. Harry on the other hand rushed up to the tree and started rubbing at the moss and lichens that covered the trunk. After a couple of minutes he sat back on his heels and just stared at the tree in disbelief. He had not found the fresh-carved heart he'd hoped for. Instead he had revealed the heart with two names that had obviously been cut into the bark in the long distant past. The edges of the carving were weathered; no longer clean cut edges as they had seen yesterday. The body of the letters and the outline of the heart were filled with dust and dried moss. They were looking at the work that Lucy had done in her despair and loneliness shortly after Brad had been killed in 1942.

Laura came up behind him. 'Are we dreaming?' she asked.

'I don't know,' Harry replied in a subdued voice. 'I just can't understand any of this.'

Harry stood up to join her and brushed away the tears from her cheeks. Without a word being said they both walked towards the opening leading to Brad's grave. It came as bit of a surprise to find the grave as they had left it yesterday not as it would have been if left undisturbed for fifty years.

'Well at least this proves that we were here,' said Laura, not realising how bizarre that would have sounded to an outsider. Harry walked up to the grave and made a readjustment to one of the top stones and as he went to get up his ankle twisted as a stone under his left foot moved. Cursing he looked down at his boot and noticed that the stone was one of a pile next to Brad's grave. Clearing the undergrowth he revealed what was obviously another grave. Harry seemed to lose any grip he may have had on reality and began clawing away at the pile of rocks.

'Harry stop,' cried Laura, and seeing that had no effect she shouted with authority: 'Harry!'

He stopped and looked up at her with crazed eyes and seemed to suddenly come to his senses.

'Sorry Laura,' he said and smiled his appreciation as she helped him to repair the damage he'd done to the grave in his frenzy. As Laura was putting the final stone to the top of the pile her fingers felt something on the surface. Brushing the dried moss from the smooth surface she could just make out carved letters.

'Harry, look at this,' she said feeling a tremble run through her body. She handed him the stone and he rubbed at it and tried to decipher the words. All he could make out in the poor light available was 1942. Leaping to his feet he said to Laura: 'Quick lets get down to the beach and clean it off in the sea. It may be an answer to this confounded riddle.'

Together they raced to the beach. As they approached the water's edge they were conscious of the surf that was building up and looking out to sea the dark black clouds were much closer, threatening a storm in the near future. Harry knelt at the waters edge and rinsed the stone in the sea. Bringing it back out he rubbed the rock dry with the bottom of his tee shirt and they both saw that the writing was clearly visible.

'*Here lie the two bodies of*
Lieutenant Charles Bradshaw USN
and Lucy Fairbrother.
Both killed in action
15 March 1942.
Smidt.

They both stared at the writing in silence until the spell was broken by a tremendous crash of thunder. They felt the first spots of rain and rose together to get to the shelter of the jungle canopy. As they ran to the tree line Harry suddenly stopped and cocked his head. Hearing the sound of an approaching propeller plane he scanned the skies assuming their pilot had come to look for them to get away before the weather turned really ugly. Another bolt of lightening accompanied by more thunder left an orange/green glow in the sky. Silhouetted against it Harry saw the small plane approaching them from the sea. He waved his arms in the air and Laura joined him as she too saw the aircraft. As it came closer Harry stopped waving and watched the plane's approach. It was going too fast for the seaplane they'd arrived in and as he stared the sudden realisation that he'd seen this picture before came to him. Grabbing the surprised Laura round the waist he pulled her to the ground just as the sand started to dance up around them and they heard the clatter of the of the twin 0.303 inch wing mounted machine guns of the Mitsubishi Zero that roared over-head.

Chapter Fifty-One

Harry was the first to recover; he knew what was coming after all. Grabbing Laura by the hand he roughly pulled her to her feet and made a beeline for the trees. He'd lost sight of the Zero as it thundered over the tree canopy, barely pulling up in time, but he knew the pilot would be reversing as quickly as he could. Sure enough the scream of the plane reached them before they'd covered half the distance to the jungle. Laura was screaming in fear but Harry took no heed and dragged her up the sand as he sensed rather than saw the Zero fly a teardrop turn to end up facing them once again. Harry had flown this in his dream and knew the pilot would be inputting fine adjustments to the flying controls drawing them into his sights. He chanced a glance over his shoulder and saw the Zero yaw right as if anticipating Harry's next move. He looked back just in time to see Laura jink in the same direction, following what she remembered from his account of the incident in the rehab unit in Truro.

'Nooooooo,' he cried, but he already knew he was too late and sure enough he heard the harsh report as machine guns opened up behind them. He dropped to his knees and waited to hear the bullets smash into Laura's vulnerable form, the sound of guns already silenced as the pilot reached minimum range. Instead he heard the Zero scream overhead, its engine struggling as the nose was pulled up too late to stop the tail wheel smashing through the fine branches of the forest roof. Moments later he looked up in disbelief as another shadow howled overhead, its guns opening up a second time as the pilot dragged the Zero into his sights

'Come on darling,' he cried as he reached her sprawling form and pulled her once again from the fine sand. 'It didn't happen like this before but let's get the hell out of here just the same.'

Laura quickly came to her senses and hand in hand they ran along the trees to the relative safety of the river-bed. Entering the forest they turned just in time to see the Zero flying straight out to sea with the Wildcat close on its heels.

'No it can't be...' mused Harry.

Brad was quietly cursing himself in the cockpit of the Wildcat. He'd missed the chance of an easy kill as he'd dived onto the unsuspecting Zero. He glanced nervously at his engine instruments but saw nothing amiss. It had been a momentary flutter in engine tone that had caused him to mess up his first attack, only just recovering in time to heave the aircraft out of its shallow dive. He wouldn't make the same mistake again and only hoped that engine would behave long enough for him to complete the task. It had been running hot a while ago but since turning back for his ship she seemed to have settled. He had stumbled across the Zero whilst trying to ascertain his position and didn't really have the fuel for a prolonged engagement, but he had watched as the Japanese fighter lined up for a strafing run to the beach and decided to take the quick kill. In his mind he felt it would make up for aborting his mission but now he was regretting the decision as the Pratt and Whitney coughed again and spewed a small puff of white smoke from the exhaust.

As he watched, the Japanese pilot pulled the Zero into a steep climb, rolled off the top and presented an inverted plan form to Brad. Pulling back on the stick Brad felt his aircraft respond and anticipated he would soon achieve a firing solution from which there was no chance of escape. The Zero was low on energy and without forward flying speed would be helpless when Brad brought his guns to bear. Brad tightened his finger on the trigger as the Wildcat's nose relentlessly crept towards his foe, who realizing his fatal mistake was desperately trying to force the nose of his Zero below the horizon in order to build up enough speed to give him flying control.

On the ground Harry had left the shelter of the jungle, realizing that they were no longer a target. Laura followed cautiously and stood beside him shielding her eyes from the sun as she watched the dogfight.

'He's got him now,' said Harry. Not an expert in air combat by any means he was interested in every form of flying and could see that the Zero was in a hopeless situation. 'He'll tear him apart before the Jap has any chance to evade.' A short burst of gunfire punctuated the air as if to confirm Harry's appraisal of the situation, but instead of the Zero showing any signs of distress he watched as a huge plume of white smoke burst from the cowling of the Wildcat.

Brad was inching the Zero into his sights and silently thanked the Lord that he'd been given this second chance. He could see the pilot throwing his head from side to side as he desperately tried to manoeuvre his stricken aircraft, and felt a tinge of regret for a fellow airman as he gently increased pressure on the trigger. He'd opened fire a fraction too early and the stream of lead disappeared harmlessly into space behind the tail. He pulled a little more and was aware of his airspeed washing off as he went just past the vertical. The engine coughed momentarily and recovered just as quickly causing a shock of relief to flood through Brad's adrenaline-charged body. Tightening up on the trigger for the final phase of the attack he was interrupted by the Pratt and Whitney finally letting go. The cockpit was suddenly shrouded in white smoke and Brad felt the last of his speed decay as the aircraft fell helplessly onto its back. He struggled to roll the aircraft right way up already realising that his fight was over and he would have to abandon the aircraft. The white smoke had cleared only to be replaced with a sinister trail of black smoke and oil streaming from the right side of the engine. Even as he watched, the first licks of orange flame curled up through the smoke, twisting in the airflow towards the cockpit.

Sliding the canopy back Brad tried to locate his harness release and felt the first judders through the airframe as .303 shells started to smash into the tail plane and wings. He reversed the flying control attempting to regain inverted flight but found that he no longer had control over the aircraft. Suddenly the Wildcat flicked right and Brad was thrown hard against the left side of the cockpit. He looked in frantically trying to locate his safety harness release before the aircraft went into a full spin and make escape virtually impossible. The canopy was starting to slide back into place when suddenly it burst into a thousand pieces as a shell thudded through the bottom of the aircraft, narrowly missing Brad's thigh and smashing through the glass on the left side. He was hardly aware of the pain in his wrist as flying glass sliced through the flesh but blood splashing into his face further obscured his view. Centripetal force was pushing him further onto his left side as the spin of his incapacitated plane tightened, and he was aware that time was running out as his arms flayed helplessly around the smoke-filled cockpit.

Laura threw one hand across her mouth to stifle a moan and the other gripped Harry's elbow, tightening until the knuckles went white.

'No...oh no,' moaned Harry as he watched the helpless Wildcat spin towards the sea in a cloud of black smoke that rapidly lengthened into a trail as the doomed aircraft picked up speed. 'Bail out...for God's sake jump out,' he shouted.

They watched in horror as the Zero continued to close, spraying the wrecked frame with bullets whilst the pilot kicked the rudder one way and another to enable the widest spread of the death spitting cannons. At the last moment the pilot pulled away; white vortexes forming at the wing tips as G was applied. A second later the Wildcat disintegrated; torn apart by an explosion they saw before they heard. The bulk of the 14 cylinder engine flew clear of the wreck, carried by its inertia, as the rest of the aircraft, but for one wing that spun away like a child's kite in

312

a wind storm, broke into small pieces or burnt away in the ensuing fire ball. Laura dropped sobbing to her knees but Harry continued to stare in morbid fascination with the image of the blast imprinted upon his retinas, the small spec tumbling clear of the carnage missed as he turned to comfort his wife.

Something finally went Brad's way and his right hand floundered into the harness release at his waist. No sooner had he released the harness than he was sucked from the cockpit only to feel the windrush of the tail as it careened past his face. Then he was free - and just in time as he was tumbled end over end as the force of the remaining fuel igniting at close quarters reached him. He was well aware that the clearance from the sea was minimal and he expertly located and pulled the D ring of the ripcord, allowing the chute to billow above him. Only moments later and before the chute could complete his retardation he crashed into the sea.

Winded and half drowned Brad clawed his way to the surface, struggling out of the parachute harness as he did so. His first action was to scan the sky to check the Zero wasn't coming back to finish him off, but he was pleased to see a small spec out to sea and correctly assessed that the Japanese pilot was content with downing his aircraft. As it happened the pilot thought he'd never got out before the Wildcat exploded and would report the American pilot as killed in action. He turned in the water and looked toward the shoreline about a mile away. He took some time to blow some air into his life vest before rolling onto his back and kicking out in a lazy breaststroke, glancing over his shoulder occasionally to keep his bearings and ensure he took the shortest route to dry land.

'What do we do now,' asked Laura 'It's not supposed to happen this way.'

'I really have no idea,' sighed Harry. 'This is as new to me as it is to you now.'

Harry pulled himself to his feet and slowly walked to the water's edge. Picking a small stone from the sand he tossed it into the blue sea and watched the ripples expand from the point of impact. He turned as Laura walked up behind him and softly stroked the back of his neck.

'Sweetheart I've just had a thought.' He paused whilst he considered how to put across what was bothering him and Laura didn't interrupt his train of thought. 'When I was here before...well...'

'I know what you're thinking,' said Laura, realizing his difficulty. 'You were in a coma.'

'That's right. So logic would say that something bad has happened to us in the real world, if there is a real world.'

Nothing was said as they both considered the implications until Laura leaned against him on tip-toe and lightly brushed her lips over the nape of his neck. 'Don't worry darling, there is a real world and we must still be alive. Mike will sort it out.'

'I'm sure you're right,' he said, turning to kiss her gently on the forehead. 'I'm sure you're right.'

Hand in hand they wandered back to the opening into the jungle. Both were deep in thought. Both had reservations about the assumptions they'd made. Both were scared.

Chapter Fifty-Two

Hours later Laura sat leaning back against Harry who idly ran his fingers through her soft hair and was deep in thought. He was mildly surprised to find that they still had their possessions from 'the real world' and they had dined quietly on his meagre rations of chocolate and hot tea. For the thousandth time he tried to make sense out of what was happening to them.

'I'm scared to go to sleep,' muttered Laura reading his mind. 'In case we wake up as someone else.'

'Do you know how crazy that sounds?' chuckled Harry, leaning forward to gently kiss her hair. 'But just in case we do I want you to know that I love you and wouldn't want to travel back in time to a desert island with anyone else.'

Laura pushed back against him feeling safe though still scared. 'Well as honeymoons go this has got to take the biscuit.'

Harry chuckled again and leaned over to pull a space blanket from his pack. Suddenly he froze and at the same time felt Laura tense. Without moving he strained his ears. Nothing happened for about 30 seconds and he was just about to return to his task when he clearly heard another stick break down towards the beach. Gently pushing Laura away he leaned and stared toward the beach but in the failing light he couldn't see a thing. Slowly getting to his feet he considered his options and softly crept away from Laura toward the opening in the trees. He glanced over his shoulder and saw he didn't need to indicate for Laura to hide as she was already out of sight having crawled into the opening they'd cleared earlier in the day to view the graves.

Looking forward again he stood stock still and watched as a crouched lone silhouette carefully made his way toward him through the gloom. Shortly the figure stopped and after a minute Harry was starting to think that his eyes had been playing tricks. He could feel his heart beating in his chest and was amazed at the sound it was making. Surely if there was anyone there he would be able to hear it and Harry was about to give up and go back to Laura when the tree that he was watching slowly started to creep forward again.

'Stand still or I shoot,' Shouted Harry, his voice deafening the silence and causing a cacophony of noise to start in the forest above.

He saw the figure drop to his knees. 'I said stand still...and drop your weapon.'

He could feel his quarry trying to penetrate the darkness from his position but Harry was hidden against the backdrop of trees and other vegetation.

'Last chance or we open fire,' he blustered, and became aware of Laura making an awful din behind him, helping to give the impression that he wasn't alone.

Harry watched as the figure slowly pulled himself to his full height and heard as his service revolver was tossed onto the hard earth.

'Identify yourself.'

There was no reply and so Harry took a couple of paces forward. 'I said Identify yourself and place your hands on your head while you're at it.'

Harry continued forward and watched as the man slowly raised his hands in a gesture of surrender.

'Last chance. Identify yourself!'

'Ok, ok,' came the reply. 'Lieutenant Charles Bradshaw, United States Navy. Jeezus but I'm having a bad day. And who do I have the pleasure of addressing?'

'Oh thank Christ for that - Brad its Harry, Tony Harrison - we thought you were dead.'

'Do I know you?' Brad started to walk forward trying to peer through the gloom.   'And who's we?'

'Now that's a long and interesting story,' Harry laughed as he too began to move. When they were about 2 yards apart they both stopped. The light was too bad to make out features but they could see they were facing men of similar build and height. 'And the 'we' is my wife Laura,' he continued, turning as she came up behind him.

'Come on back to our camp and I'll try to explain, but I warn you that some of what we'll tell you is going to sound a bit far fetched.'

Together the three of them walked back to the tree where they'd made their base and settled down. Brad was wet and tired and they helped him out of his wet clothes and dressed him in the slightly damp set that Harry had removed after his 'dip' disembarking from the plane. The light had completely gone now and not daring to light a fire meant that the task of making Brad comfortable was completed in total darkness. Laura cleaned and dressed the cut on his wrist as best she could using the first aid kit from her pack, and soon they all sat in silence wondering where to begin with their stories.

'We thought you'd bought the farm back then,' began Harry. 'We watched the whole thing from the beach.'

'You saved our lives Brad, thank you,' murmured Laura squeezing his hand gently, but the only reply was the rhythmical breathing from the exhausted airman as he drifted into a well-earned sleep. She gently laid his hand onto his chest and as it slowly rose and fell with his gentle breathing she caught the glimpse of a twinkle on his finger. Reaching down she felt the fine weaved effect on the ring and knew immediately that on the back would be the words "Te amo Madre. RM".

Chapter Fifty-Three

Laura was the first to wake in the morning and busied her-self around the site as the darkness slowly gave way to a dim light. She looked at the two men sleeping, both so alike and yet of course hugely different to her. As she watched they both started stirring, slowly climbing out of a deep dreamless sleep. Harry was the first to surface and climb-ing up he stretched languidly, trying to shake off the stiff-ness of two night's sleeping rough. He gave Laura a hug and a soft kiss and slowly made his way down to the shore for a refreshing dip in the blue, calm ocean. Removing his clothes he dove straight into the water and swam parallel to the beach keeping to the shallows, and even without goggles he could see fish moving in his wake through the clear water. Walking out of the sea he lay down on the hard damp sand near the water line and quickly dried in the ever-increasing heat of the sun.

When Brad made it down to the beach Harry had rolled over to give his back some sun and had just about drifted back to sleep.

'Ok so you gonna tell me what this is all about,' he asked, standing over Harry's prostrate form.

Harry sat up and looked into Brad's face, shielding his eyes from the hot sun that had quickly risen above the horizon. He was prepared for what he saw, unlike Brad who took two steps back, his face a twisted mask of confu-sion.

'It's...it's like looking in a mirror,' he stammered. 'We could be twins. Hell we must be twins!'

Harry watched his reaction and once again wondered how he was going to explain what was going on. He came to a decision.

'Brad, sit down,' he said. 'I've a hell of a story to tell you; a story that you're not going to believe, but I will be able to substantiate everything I tell you as we go along so please just try to listen, ok?'

Laura walked up to join them and together they sat down with Harry who had turned to sit with his knees drawn up to his chin, deep in thought.

'There's no easy way to say this so I'll start with what I know about you. You're Charles Bradshaw, born just outside Lorain, Ohio in 1917.' And so Harry related the story as Brad sat there in stunned silence. Laura filled in when she thought he'd missed out important facts but on the whole Harry was able to continue to the end without interruption. He expected Brad to laugh and dismiss the story out of hand but instead as he finished Brad just sat in stunned silence, unable to comprehend what was happening.

'So you're saying I'm captured, right, tortured by the Japanese and a German Officer. That this island is a secret base for missiles hidden in a village?' He looked into their faces in turn, hoping to catch some hint of mischief or humour, but instead saw the stony faces of two very serious young people. 'Ok so how did I, or is it we, get off the island?' he asked with a sardonic grin.

Brad had purposefully skipped over Brad's demise at Frank's hand and now bluffed by saying he wasn't around during that bit, but was back in his own time.

'So you're time travellers...and you expect me to believe this do you?'

Harry climbed to his feet and started to walk away gesturing Laura to join him. As she did he looked back round to Brad who had remained sitting, deep in thought. 'Brad, you've never told anyone this but you told Lucy, or rather you will tell Lucy.' He pondered the statement and decided it didn't really matter which was true. 'When your sister Beth was killed you cried just about every night for two years.'

Brad flung himself round and climbed to his feet, an angry retort at his lips, but Harry and Laura had turned away and were walking back up the beach hand in hand.

'So what now?' asked Laura, as they walked into the cool air beneath the jungle vegetation.

'Give him time love,' said Harry. 'He's got a lot to take in. Imagine yourself in his shoes.'

To their surprise it was only about half an hour before Brad joined them in the shade. He sat down with his back to a large tree and appeared to go to sleep. Harry glanced over at Laura and smiled; he could see a lot of himself in Brad.

'Ok,' he said, without opening his eyes. 'I really don't begin to know what this is all about but for the time being I'm gonna have to go along with your story. That is until I can figure out some other way of you knowing so much about me, so much of my private thoughts.' He thought for a minute and then continued. 'So, what now? By my reckoning the next thing that should happen is we get shot at again and meet the mysterious Lucy.'

'Right,' said Harry. 'But I wanna try to make it to the spotters hut without getting seen by the Zero. Things have got to be easier if they aren't all over the island looking for us.'

'Couldn't agree more buddy, mind you I'm still trying to sort out in my head if you two are just wackos or if I'm dreaming, but for the time being we'll do it your way.'

'Well maybe it'll put more credence to our story once you meet Lucy,' said Laura picking up her pack. 'Shall we go?'

The two men looked at each other and laughed. 'She wasn't here the last time,' whispered Harry confidentially.

'I heard that buster,' she retorted and pushed her way between them and set off towards the beach.

Chapter Fifty-Four

They made good time along the tree line and as they went Brad continued to quiz Harry and Laura about their story.

'What are we going to do when we meet Lucy?' asked Brad finally, happy to let Harry take the lead.

'We tell her nothing. Let her think that we've just met,' said Harry. 'She's been through so much already and she could come unhinged if we lay this on her.'

By now they were rounding the corner and in the distance they could see the MTB smoking on the beach. Following Harry's lead they dropped to their knees in the sand. Harry looked at the position of the sun and guessed he'd arrived at least a couple of hours earlier than on his last visit, and he tried to remember what Lucy had been doing before he arrived on the scene. Laura pulled out a canteen of water and they all took a long swig before she tucked it back into her pack.

'Ok, by my reckoning Lucy is either burying the spotter or she's aboard the boat gathering stores,' said Harry. 'Either way she'll welcome an interruption.'

Laura considered the two grisly tasks and a shudder ran through her body. 'Let's get there as soon as we can then, I can't bear to think of that poor girl alone and frightened.'

Harry thought for a moment and then led the group forward, hugging the tree line and scanning the sky for any unwelcome intruders. As they neared the MTB the sweet, sickly smell of death hung in the air and Laura felt her stomach turn over as she thought of the burning remains on the boat. Harry again dropped to the sand as they heard a crash from somewhere in the burning wreck and before long Lucy's petite form could be seen moving about near the stern. Throwing a bundle over the side onto the sand she quickly followed and began to drag the blanket of provisions she'd collected along the beach towards the forest. She didn't so much as glance up the beach and was completely oblivious to anything but the task at hand.

Harry stood and started a tuneless whistle as the three moved along the beach toward the struggling girl. Harry had hoped she would hear them as they approached, softening the shock of finding other people alive on the island. Instead they were nearly upon her when she noticed the movement and looked up. There was no reaction, not even on her face. Indeed she appeared to be in a trance-like state as she stared briefly at them, her eyes dark and cold; uncomprehending. She turned back to her sack of provisions as if the others didn't exist. Brad trotted over to her and gently removed the blanket from her resisting fingers. She didn't even look up; just tried to get the blanket back from Brad, feebly grabbing at the air as he swung her collection toward Laura and Harry. Realising she wouldn't achieve her objective she dropped to the sand and slowly covered her face with her filthy hands.

Laura rushed forward and knelt down in front of her. Gently pulling her forward she cradled Lucy's head against her shoulder and together the two girls wept, drawing comfort from each other. Harry and Brad looked at each other sheepishly and started to busy themselves recovering the tinned supplies that had spilled from the blanket. Harry wondered over to the MTB and climbing aboard began to scavenge whatever he could find, before joining the others back on the beach. It hadn't taken long as he knew exactly where he would find the small group of objects he had stuffed into the pockets of his jeans. Arriving back he found the others had retired to the edge of the jungle and Lucy was just finishing her story of escape from Java.

'We need to get off the beach and into some shade,' said Harry, scanning the horizon nervously.

Lucy looked up and smiled for the first time. 'There's a hut just inside the jungle; I was taking some food I found on the boat.'

'Great, lead the way Lucy.'

Lucy smiled up at them again and her face was transformed to the beauty that Harry remembered. Pulling back some heavy vegetation she indicated the opening into the jungle that Laura and Harry knew was there. Laura smiled at her husband, proud of how he had let Lucy show the way and thus regain some of her composure.

'Brad would you come and help me with the supplies?' said Lucy, and then to the other two. 'Just follow the path and you can't miss it.'

Laura took Harry's hand as he opened their way to the path. They quickly found the hut and entered the small room that Laura saw was exactly the way he'd described it. Laura was thankful that Lucy had already removed the body of the spotter, though the unmistakeable smell of death still hung heavy in the enclosed environment of the dwelling. Leaving her to await the arrival of the other two Harry slipped out and quickly returned with the rusted machete from the back. He found Laura close to tears in the centre of the room and quickly crossed to take her in his arms. He pulled the hair back from her face and stared down into the depths of her eyes.

'I love you Mrs Harrison,' he said softly, and gently kissed her as the tears spilled over and ran down her cheeks.'

'Oh Harry, where will this end?'

They both jumped at the softest of coughs from the doorway and turned to find Lucy beaming at them.

'Sorry you two,' she said bashfully. 'Brad tells me that you're newlyweds.'

'That's right, nearly a month now.'

'So how did you come to end up in this stinking hole?'

Harry turned to look at Laura, his face completely blank. She smiled at him and continued easily. 'We represent a family in Ireland who engaged us to track down a relative who came here as a missionary. Father Matthew Golding is his name; I don't suppose you've come across him?'

'No I'm sorry, but as I said I've not long been here myself.' She thought for a while then added. 'That must mean the island's inhabited. We can get help, maybe even get rescued.'

'It's not that easy I'm afraid Lucy,' said Harry. 'You see when I'm not tracking down lost preachers I work for British Intelligence. The only reason we were able to undertake this mission was as cover to an information gathering assignment. It is believed that there is enemy activity within the village not too far from here, where Father Golding is working, and that activity is prejudicial to the allied war effort.'

'And you brought your new wife along as part of your cover,' gasped a shocked Lucy.

Laura smiled at the young girl. 'I'm an intelligence operative too Lucy, its how Harry and I met.'

Harry squeezed her hand and smiled to himself. If he was surprised by her inventiveness he never showed it. The 'cover story' was brilliant. It gave them reasons for knowing the layout of the island, for knowing Matthew and would even pave the way for treating Frank with suspicion when they came across him. She's better at this than me, he thought.

'And are you and Brad brothers or twins?' asked Lucy.

'No we're not,' replied Harry. 'In fact it's uncanny; we only met yesterday and...'

He was interrupted by the sudden ear-splitting roar as an aircraft flew over low and fast just above the jungle canopy. Harry looked meaningfully at Brad as if to say 'more proof of my story'. Instead he said to the group as a whole.

'Good job we got off the beach, I'd rather the Japs didn't know we are here yet. If something is going on here that may just have been a regular patrol, or it could have been to check there was no activity around the MTB. Either way we're gonna have to be careful and I suggest we move out of here inland first thing in the morning.'

No one argued and so the two women started to sort out the supplies, splitting them equably between the packs that the men would carry; the startling similarity in appearance of the two men seemingly forgotten. Laura was careful to keep any evidence of their own time hidden from view, as she and Harry had discussed the night before. They were going to have enough difficulty pulling this off without the added complications of late 20th century technology. Meanwhile Harry led Brad outside clear of earshot.

'Ok Harry, you're calling the shots. So far you've hit the nail on the head.'

Harry smiled grimly. 'From now on in it gets a little more difficult. Tomorrow we're gonna meet Frank and he really is a nasty piece of work.'

'Well with us two looking so much alike how about he meets just one of us and the other can have a free reign.'

Harry thought for a while. The idea had its merits; one of them would always be loose to cover the others if things turned nasty. On the other hand it would be difficult to pull off unless the same one was always on the outside and with the habit of nightly wanderings Frank had, things could very quickly go wrong.

'It's a good idea Brad but I think we'd be better off pooling our resources. Maybe if we had more time to plan it out carefully it would work to our advantage but as it is let's stick together so we can keep a wary eye on our friend Frank.'

'Fine by me buddy, you're the boss; being an intelligence agent an' all.'

Harry chuckled. 'We made that up off the top of our heads. I know about as much about intelligence gathering as I do about crochet!'

Brad joined him in a deep laugh, a rare commodity in these times of war. Sobering quickly they went on to discuss how best to handle Frank and decided that they would not allow him to take the offensive.

'As I remember it I was in the water with Lucy when they appeared on the far bank and Frank challenged us with his rifle. This time I want to be lying in wait for him; let us be the ones to put the fear of God into him instead of the other way round.'

'Tell me about you and Lucy,' asked Brad. 'Or should I say me and Lucy?'

'Oh no, you can work that bit out for yourself as we go along.' Harry turned back to the hut. 'Come on Brad, let's get back and see if the women have rustled up anything to eat.'

Re-entering the hut they found Laura heating a small bowl of meat stew over Harry's camping stove. The one 'modern' possession they had decided to make use of was looking a little worse for wear; Harry had dented and scratched it before rubbing damp earth into the metalwork giving the new stove a look of something that had been dug up in a trench somewhere on the Western front. The two backpacks sat on the table ready for the morning and there was little else to do but eat and get some sleep. Harry sat down after the meal and gave a thumbnail sketch of their intentions for the following day. Lucy appeared perplexed and looked around at the group.

'Why do you need me to come with you, wouldn't I be better off just waiting here?'

'I think you should come with us for three reasons Lucy,' explained Harry. 'Firstly I think that the Japs may send a patrol this way just to check the Boat over. In fact I'm surprised they haven't already. Secondly we can't leave you here alone and although Brad is only here by accident of circumstances, he has agreed to accompany us and help with the reconnaissance of the village.' He paused for a few moments before delivering the carrot Lucy would not be able to resist. 'But thirdly and more importantly we need your help.' Watching her reaction Harry saw her eyes light up and knew he'd been right; she needed to feel wanted and with that and her feisty spirit he knew he was onto a winner.

'I'll do anything I can,' she said with feeling. 'Anything to get back at those murdering bastards.' She flushed a deep red; embarrassed by her own savagery and at swearing openly in front of them all, but even so they could still clearly see the fire in her eyes.

'It won't be direct action against them Lucy, I cannot take that responsibility, but we intend to take Father Golding out with us and he's gonna be scared. We need someone to take responsibility for him while we go on to complete our mission.'

Lucy looked a little disappointed at not taking part in whatever action was planned against the enemy and Harry continued quickly. 'Can you use a gun Lucy?'

'Yes I can; my father taught me the day after Pearl Harbour. Since then I've kept in practise and I'm quite a good shot.' She looked round the table and then smiled and added. 'Even if I say so myself.'

'Good,' smiled Harry. 'Because we are gonna need someone to protect our backs – a rear guard action if you like and though I hate to ask I was hoping that maybe you could fill that role.'

Harry had the sneaking suspicion that Lucy could see right through him but she smiled anyway and accepted what he'd said without further discussion.

'Ok,' said Harry. 'If no one has anything else to add I suggest that we all get some sleep; it's been a long day for all of us.'

Chapter Fifty-Five

Laura woke early in the morning and gently eased her way out of the cot bed she'd been sharing with Lucy. Careful not to tread on Brad's prostrate form she made her way to the door and found Harry surveying the clearing as the dawn light slowly lifted the dark blanket that enveloped it. Running her hands around his waist they stood in silence; both lost in their own thoughts. High in the trees birds started to move and the ever-present primates began to chatter, running amongst the towering limbs as a new day greeted them.

'A penny for them,' said Laura eventually.

'I'm just thinking about what might have happened to us in the real world,' he replied. 'For all we know we may have been killed and in fact this is our real world from now on.'

'As long as we're together we can face whatever happens.'

Harry turned and smiled at her, kissed her on the nose, something she found a little strange but tolerated, and then made his way back inside where the other two were starting to stir. They had a quick breakfast of dry fruit high energy bars from Harry's pack and then, taking a final look round the hut to ensure they'd not forgotten anything, they left with Harry taking the lead. He located the path into the jungle and started to proceed inland. The going wasn't as tough as Harry remembered but then the machete he'd brought along was a much better tool than the rusty implement he'd found and handed over to Brad.

Harry paused and Laura watched him looking around trying to get his bearings. The forest was getting thicker and the going was much tougher but Harry knew this was because they were approaching the river. He turned about 45 degrees from their track and started to hack his way through the deep vegetation. About 30 minutes later the jungle growth gave way to the river and Harry held up his right hand indicating for the others to stop. Turning round to face them he squatted down and addressed them quietly.

'Let's take a rest here,' he said. 'I've taken us off the path in case any patrols come along for water.'

'You seemed to know the river was here,' commented Lucy.

'Yes I did, the intelligence service supplied us with the basic layout of the island. From here there's a track leading to the village but I don't know what condition it's in or whether it's been used lately.'

'What's next then Bud?' asked Brad.

'I want to lay low here for a while; see if anything or anyone comes along.'

Lucy turned to help Laura prepare a simple snack and the two men wondered down to the water's edge. Looking downstream they could see that the watercourse wound slowly round a slight bend. They had a good view of the eroded banks on both sides worn by countless trips to fetch water over the years. Their position offered them good cover and taking the pistol that Brad thrust at him Harry sighted it along the water towards the cut in the stream. Happy with his position he told Brad to go back to the others and then made himself comfortable for the wait. How long that might be he wasn't sure, but he knew that Matthew and Frank would be along just as he had known everything that had happened since Brad had joined them.

Over the next hour his mind wandered but kept coming back to the same problem: what was happening in the 'real world'. He had reassured Laura, saying that Mike would sort it out, but he wasn't so sure. If he and Laura were still alive in the present then they must be in comas similar to the one he had been in following the crash. If that was so then they might just be left lying in a hospital somewhere with no one really having any idea as to how to treat them. Harry hoped the simple precautions he'd taken in the 'real' world would suffice and as he mulled these thoughts over in his mind he unknowingly lowered his guard.

He nearly leapt out of his skin as he became aware of a presence behind him and he quickly rolled to his right bringing the revolver up in one swift movement. Expecting the worst, his face broke into a sheepish grin as her saw Laura tumbling back from him. He lowered the gun and sat up to help Laura as she hissed at him. As he reached up for her he suddenly became aware of a voice coming across the water. Quickly he pulled her to the ground beside him and twisted to bring his weapon to bear.

'...for goodness sake, there's no one here and I need a drink.'

Harry recognised the soft Irish voice of Matthew and sure enough his short rotund figure appeared at the water's side as he lay down to scoop a handful to his lips. Harry strained to see Frank but he was nowhere to be seen.

'Come on down here,' said Matthew between gulps. 'You must be thirsty after that long slog.'

Frank slowly came into view and Laura saw he was exactly as Harry had described him. Holding the rifle to the front Frank slowly approached the water looking this way and that. He watched Matthew and licked his lips in anticipation, but he never lowered his guard. Even as he lowered to one knee and took a mouthful of water from his left hand Harry could see that he continued to scan the area, his finger steady on the trigger of the cradled weapon. Harry knew he couldn't afford to get into a firefight with Frank and he certainly didn't want to shoot the guy without provocation. Suddenly an idea came to him and he wracked his brain trying to think of the right words to say.

'Laufen hallo Leutnant, Sie noch herum mit Jenem stupit Priester?' he shouted in his best German accent.

'Ja muß jemand anschauen...' Frank trailed off as he realised his mistake and jumped up swinging the rifle in the direction of Harry's voice.

Harry loosed off a shot that smashed into a tree a few feet from Frank's head.

'Drop it Frank or the next one doesn't miss!'

'W w what the...' stammered Matthew as he crawled clear of the water looking around in fear.

Harry watched as Frank froze. Even in his confusion Frank had just about got the rifle pointed in his direction and Harry knew that if Frank so much as twitched he would have no choice but to squeeze the trigger sending a bullet to the point of aim in his adversary's chest.

'Ich habe es gesagt fallenläßt oder macht nicht Sie Englisch verstehen?' barked Harry.

Frank let the weapon slip from his fingers and slowly raised his hands in a gesture of defeat.

'Father would you kindly pick up the rifle and walk with it towards me.' Harry rose to his feet, the revolver held in both hands and levelled at Frank. 'Don't walk between me and our friend Frank here,' he continued as Matthew recovered the weapon.

As soon as Matthew had the rifle Brad appeared on the near bank and waded across the chest-deep river to retrieve it. Soon Harry, Laura and a surprised Lucy joined him.

'Now just what in the blazes is going on?' asked Matthew as Brad relieved him of the weapon.

'Yes pray tell,' responded Frank arrogantly.

'Well let me see Frank,' began Harry staring into Frank's dark eyes. 'Or should I say Lieutenant Hanz Muller. Born in Berlin to German parents in 1920 and later educated in The United States. Now assigned to the secret German/Japanese missile project in the Pacific.'

If Frank was surprised to hear what Harry knew he didn't show it.

'Is this true?' asked Matthew.

'Of course it's not true,' spat Frank angrily. Harry ignored Frank and continued.

'Yes it is father; I work for British Intelligence and we have a dossier on Frank here about so thick.' He held his finger and thumb about an inch and a half apart before continuing. 'Tell me Matthew did you notice anything strange going on in the village before you left a couple of weeks ago?'

'I take it you have a dossier on me too.' He looked thoughtfully into Harry's face and continued. 'Well now that you mention it the locals have been a little subdued for some time now.'

'I think Frank and his friends might have had something to do with that,' said Harry. 'And what about building; any construction of any kind been going on?'

'No not really...Well...'

'Anything father, anything out of the ordinary?'

'Well the meeting hall that I used to teach in was closed up about a month ago. The Elders told me that it had become unsafe and would need to be refurbished, something to do with the roof. It looked Ok to me the last time I was in it but since then parts of the roof have appeared to collapse inwards' He thought for a moment and added. 'Quite a few of the men have left to visit a neighbouring island to get the necessary raw materials.'

Things were starting to fall into place and Harry thought out loud:

'So the Japanese visited the island some 5 – 6 weeks ago and threatened the village if they did not co-operate. To make their point they abducted a number of men to hold as hostages and at the same time lay down a plausible cover story for the sake of outsiders. Under that cover construction began on the meeting hall to convert it to a surface to air missile sight.'

'And how do I fit into all this?' asked Frank idley staring at the back of his right hand that he'd lowered during Harry's supposition.

Harry jerked the revolver at him and as Frank replaced his hand on his head he continued:

'Well that's fairly plain; you are heading up the scientific team. You are ideal for the job as you have military training and probably more balls than the rest of the academic boffins. Once it was realised that Matthew had left the village you were sent to track him down and keep him out of trouble. I've no doubt you were ordered to execute him if he proved to be a problem.'

Matthew looked at Frank, his thunderous mask quite comical on a man of his stature.

'How come you answered in German Frank?'

Frank just sneered at him and said nothing, but of course his silence was an admission of guilt. Matthew backed away from him and turned to talk to the girls as Brad set about tying Frank's hands behind his back.

'What now?' he asked Harry as he finished.

'Let's talk about that out of earshot,' said Harry. In reality he had no idea where to go from here. Things had not gone to plan and he needed time to consider their options before deciding on any plan of action.

'First we need to get as far away from here as possible, we have no way of knowing who might have heard that shot,'

'Didn't you say that Frank had fired at you when you were last here,' asked Brad.

'Yes he did but we changed things last night when the Zero didn't see us on the beach, so who knows what else might have changed. For all we know there might be a patrol just behind Frank making their way to the spotter's hut.'

'So back to my original question; what next?'

Harry thought hard trying to retrace his steps in his mind. They had two options as he saw it.

'Ok, we can either make our way to the temple by the village and from there plan some sort of mission to sabotage the missile base, or we make our way down to the beach and await the arrival of your countrymen. Either is fraught with danger; I don't even know where the Americans came ashore, but I do know that there was a Japanese patrol in the area that saw them and reported back to the village.'

Harry remembered clearly how Frank had ambushed them as they sat in the clearing by the beach. He had been working independently but had soon been joined by Schmit and the Japanese patrol, according to the account given by Lucy. If he remembered her story correctly they had marched a fair way back to the village before they were engaged by Lt Branson and unfortunately Harry had no idea which way the Americans had come from. He came to a decision:

'Ok Brad, I think the chances of us rendezvousing with your countrymen before bumping into the Japs are fairly slim so let's press onto the old temple and see if we can't put a spanner into their works and maybe set up some sort of signal to bring the ground forces to our aid.'

Brad's face lit up at the thought of direct action and quickly agreed with Harry.

'And what about our friend Frank here?' he asked indicating over his shoulder with his thumb.

'He comes with us,' answered Harry. 'And if he causes any trouble we shoot him.'

Harry smiled and winked at the two girls as they spun round with protests written across their faces.

'Harry, you can't,' cried Laura quickly picking up on the charade.

'I can and I damn well will,' he responded. 'He would shoot you as soon as look at you and I mean to make sure he never gets the chance.'

'You haven't got the guts,' started Frank, a sneer slowly spreading across his face. 'You and your two little whores don't...'

Frank never got the chance to finish as Brad brutally slammed the butt of the rifle into his midriff. He dropped heavily to his knees and vomited onto the hard earth. Still retching, he slowly raised his head to look Brad straight in the eyes. As he started to speak Brad raised the rifle again ready to bring it down into Frank's upturned face.

'No Brad, please.'

Brad turned slowly to look at Lucy and gradually the mask of hatred fell from his face. He lowered the rifle and turned once more to look at Frank.

'She's right,' he spat. 'You're not worth it.' He turned and walked away. Lucy followed and took hold of his hand.

'Thank you Brad, I know you're not like that.'

He looked into her pretty face and smiled. Her eyes were brimming with tears and he lightly brushed them aside.

'No Lucy, Thank you,' he said, and bent to kiss her forehead before turning to walk back to the river for a drink.

Within the hour they were ready to move out. Harry led the way with Matthew and the two women behind him. Brad came up the rear with the trussed up Frank ahead of him, and although to begin with he was difficult and dragged his way along, the frequent jab in the back with the rifle barrel soon had him keeping up with the rest. Despite getting lost on several occasions they made good time and were not disturbed by any patrols. The jungle was quiet.

It was dark when they arrived at the statue and Harry stealthily eased his way into the clearing whilst the others laid low. Quickly scouting around he made his way back and gave the others the all clear. The girls started an evening meal from their rations and Matthew made himself useful collecting soft foliage from the forest floor. Carrying them to the hut he spent some time fashioning beds which would prove to be far more comfortable than they looked.

'So what about him?' asked Brad, as he finished tying Franks feet securely together.

'Guess it's me and you taking turns in watching him,' said Harry. 'We need to keep a watch anyway so it won't be any added burden. How about 4 hour shifts?'

'Fine by me Harry, I'll take the first stint.'

And so they settled down for the night. Brad was restless and got up to walk about the clearing at regular intervals. As he walked round he frequently glanced at Frank's prostrate form but never saw any movement, just heard the regular breathing of a man fast asleep. The night was clear and muggy and finally he lay back to look at the stars and to think about Lucy. He liked her that was for sure. What did she think of him? Had he blown his chances with his uncharacteristic behaviour back at the river? He shut his eyes briefly to picture her in his mind; her chestnut hair, her hazel eyes. Yes, I really do like her he thought as he slowly drifted off into a deep sleep.

Brad jerked awake. He looked up into the moonlit face of Frank towering over him. His lips were curled back in a vicious snarl and his eyes, as black as night, seemed to smile too. Brad could see the large boulder held above his head, could see the fresh wounds around the wrists where his antagonist had laboured against the bonds that had held him, and knew at that moment that he could do nothing to stop the crushing blow that Frank would soon deliver. Even as he began to roll to one side he could see Frank begin the down swing that would snuff him out. Resigned to his death he rolled back down where he had lain.

'Goodbye Lieutenant,' sneered Frank, and from that moment everything appeared to move in slow motion. Brad watched the sneer turn to an evil grin as Frank's eyes narrowed slightly. He saw a thin line of spittle run down his chin as the boulder resumed its arc. He heard the ecstatic groan as Frank anticipated the effects of what he was about do. Brad wanted to shut his eyes but couldn't. Slowly, so slowly the boulder moved towards the zenith of its journey and at that point the groan was cut off abruptly to be replaced by a rushed intake of air. Frank's eyes opened wide in disbelief and the line of saliva on his chin was replaced with a surge of dark bubbling blood. Brad's gaze was drawn to Frank's bare chest where a shaft of metal had appeared. As he watched the machete was slowly withdrawn and a dark mass frothed from the wound. Slowly Frank's body crumpled as the weight of the stone he was holding brought it down to form an untidy heap at his shoulders. Brad was now staring into the shocked face of Harry who held the machete in trembling hands. Brad recognised the look of someone that had killed for the first time and jumped to his feet to relieve Harry of the weapon that had fallen limply by his side.

'Harry I'm so...'

'Let's just go to bed Brad; we'll take our chances with the Japs,' said Harry in a shaking voice before turning and walking slowly back to the shelter of the hut.

Chapter Fifty-Six

Nothing was said the following morning. After Harry had left, Brad dragged the body into the undergrowth behind the hut and concealed it as best he could. Returning to the hut he'd found Harry rolled up in one corner, apparently asleep, and the two girls whispering in the darkness. He'd given them, and Matthew who'd woken up at his entrance, a brief outline of what had happened and then they'd all tried to get some sleep.

'Ok, time for a council of war,' stated Harry as they finished their breakfast of cold bully beef. 'We have no real way of knowing when the American ground force will be on the island, so what should we do?'

He'd talked to Laura, and between them they couldn't work out the time scale between him landing on the island and 'bumping' into the Americans.

'As I see it we have two choices,' he continued. 'We either sit it out here until reinforcements arrive, or we take some sort of action to disrupt the Japanese in the village.'

He looked round the group and did a mental inventory of his assets. He had Brad, a seasoned veteran albeit in air combat, a priest, two women and himself. As far as weapons went they had a revolver, a rifle and two machetes. Not a lot to be taking on an unknown force of Japanese soldiers presumably armed to the teeth. Given that, their choice seemed to be very one sided. He looked from face to face but gained no inspiration.

'Has anyone got anything to say?'

In face of the silence that greeted him he was just about to announce the only sensible decision when Matthew stood up and cleared his throat.

'You all know I am a man of God...' He looked skyward before continuing. 'And I hope He will forgive me, but I know the people of the village.' He returned his gaze to those before him, his face grim and full of doubt. 'They are a proud people and must detest living under the rule of these barbaric Japanese. If there is anyway we can liberate them, any way at all, then we must do so as soon as possible.'

He sat down with head bowed and waited for the reaction from the others. Harry looked round the group and saw he wasn't going to get any help. He considered the unexpected input from Matthew.

'Well if we do decide to take some sort of action there are some points we have to consider. Firstly, we must assume that the Japanese have hostages hidden away somewhere; what's going to happen to them?'

'The same as if we wait for the Americans,' said Laura.

'Ok,' said Harry conceding that issue. 'Secondly, if we are not completely successful in what we attempt, what reprisals will the Japs take on those in the village?'

'Harry, if we are going to act we can't afford to think about what happens if we fail,' said Brad. 'Whatever we do must be assured of success, or so subtle as not to give the Japanese cause to think it was attempted sabotage.'

'Which brings me nicely to my third point,' said Harry. 'Just what in the hell do we do?'

The silence was complete. Looking at his comrades all he saw was fear and apprehension and he knew this was reflected in his face also.

'Ok we'll have to put some thought to that, in the meantime Brad and I are going to trek to the village, reconnoitre and spy out the lay of the land. The rest of you get some rest and lay low.'

'I'm coming with you,' blurted out Laura.

'No Love, we're not gonna get into any trouble, just have a quick look see. We want to be able to move fast and not cause any disturbance.'

Laura knew better than to argue the point any more and regretted that she'd mentioned it and shown her concern, for as she looked at Lucy she saw her resolve starting to break.

'Come on then Lucy; let's see what we can do about getting this place more like a home.'

Harry smiled at her and reached over to give her a kiss on the forehead as he and Brad Climbed to their feet.

'We'll be about 6 hours but don't worry if we're a little longer,' he said. 'Here Lucy, you can shoot; look after this.'

She accepted the rifle and expertly checked the chamber before making the weapon safe.

With a final look and a wink at Laura he led Brad to the forest wall in the direction of the village.

The going was harder than he remembered; even taking into account that he now had a new machete. He and Brad took it in turns hacking their way through the thick undergrowth and despite the tough going they made good time. As they progressed Harry described the layout of the village and surrounding area as best he could. Brad asked questions at intervals until Harry was happy that he had the picture as well as he did. He had no real way of knowing when they would reach the village but after about an hour and a half the hackles on his neck warned him they were getting close. Edging their way with more caution now they soon moved into a position from which they had a reasonable view of the village. There was no evidence of the Japanese presence and all was calm and quiet. Harry began to wonder if this part of his 'dream' were true, until after about 15 minutes a soldier appeared from the side of a building to have a crafty cigarette.

Even at their range they could see the man was nervous, puffing rapidly so that he had finished in about 2 minutes flat and once again disappeared into the village.

'So,' whispered Brad. 'You've been right on all counts so far, I don't suppose you have any bright ideas in your crystal ball.'

An idea was forming in Harry's head but he decided to keep it to himself for the time being.

'No such luck Brad. I think we've seen enough to confirm our position, let's get back to camp.'

Backtracking was much easier and Harry was content to let Brad lead the way as he thought about the plan formulating in his head. He tried to recall the layout inside the missile room, particularly with regard to the operating station. He remembered the binoculars and the steering joystick but were there any other controls? He thought there must be the means to fire the missiles from the station but he couldn't be sure and there was no way of getting in to check without their entry being discovered. Even if the missiles could be fired locally, would the blast from the missile incinerate the console and the operator? As he thought about it further he realised that he didn't even know the state of development of the missiles, and considered that they may not even be ready to fire. The plan, if he could call it that, was rapidly crumbling and he was back to square one.

Fire was his next train of thought. On the surface it seemed a good idea but again as he thought about it a lot of negatives came to mind. Was there enough flammable material in the hut to make it effective? The walls were concrete and most of the roof had been removed, so what was there to burn? How would the missiles react to heat? If they were armed any resultant explosion would devastate the village and kill a lot of innocent civilians, mostly women and children.

Before he knew it they arrived back at the hut and Laura came running up to him and threw her arms round his neck. As she smothered his face in kisses he was aware of Lucy walking up to Brad, taking his hand and smiling up at him.

Later that day, just before the forest put itself to sleep, Harry called them all together for a pow-wow. He started by summarising their situation, their firepower if you could call it that and a brief description of what was happening in the village. The others all sat in silence as he spoke, and finally he finished by throwing the floor open to ideas for their next move. He looked into their shadowed faces as the light started to dim. Laura looked beautiful as ever in the poor light, her proud face deep in thought causing her brow to wrinkle. Brad stared at the back of his hands, his vast knowledge and experience as a fighter pilot not really helping him in the current situation. Matthew had his eyes shut and Harry could see his lips moving as he prayed silently. Finally his eyes rested on Lucy; her pretty face looked quizzical as if she were juggling an idea in her head. Rocking her head to one side he saw the white of her teeth as they bit down on her lower lip, and then her face relaxed as she discarded whatever scheme had been vexing her.

Harry paused for a moment or two hoping she might volunteer her thoughts to the group, but she remained silent.

'Have you got something to say Lucy?'

'No Harry, it was just a stupid idea,' she said, smiling at him.'

'Well at this stage a stupid idea is better than none,' he coaxed.

'Well,' she began hesitantly. 'We know the Americans are coming but we're not sure when. I must say I'm surprised your intelligence service hasn't co-ordinated their effort better but that's by the by. It seems to me that you've been trying to think of some way to disable the rockets but we don't have to do that. In fact the American scientists might want to get their hands on them intact. We need to create a diversion so that the Allies can take the village with the least resistance.' She paused for thought and continued. 'In fact it might be best if whatever we do is as far away from the village as possible; try to draw the Japanese away. That way hopefully we will get the least number of civilian casualties.'

She looked at Harry and blushed a deep red. Slowly a smile broke out on his face and as it spread to an enormous grin she relaxed and looked around the group.

'You've done it Lucy, we've been blinkered by wanting to take out the missiles.'

Suddenly everyone was talking at once, immediately coming up with plans and ideas. Harry sat back and let them exchange ideas as he thought about the implications of what they intended to do.

'Ok, ok listen up!' he shouted. The room went quiet and he continued. 'By taking this route we will be putting ourselves into far more danger than by just trying covert disruption in the village. We need to come up with a plan to give us the best chance of survival.'

He stood up and walked out of the room leaving the rest subdued and deep in thought.

Much later Brad found Harry and Laura deep in discussion.

'What gives you guys?' he asked.

'Harry and I have been trying to work out time scales and it's proving difficult,' said Laura looking up at the new arrival. 'It seems there is a fairly large discrepancy between the times things were happening here and in the future.'

'How do you mean?'

'Well,' said Harry. 'What took about 3 to 5 days here seems to have taken months in the hospital in England.'

Brad didn't even try to make sense of it.

'Well what's your best guess Harry?'

'Taking into account that I was confused and injured my gut feeling points at the day after tomorrow, possibly the day after.'

'That could make a big difference,' said Brad. 'If we do this too early then the chances are we're gonna end up dead. Too late and it will be pointless.'

Brad picked up a straight stick and rooted around on the ground until he had a handful of pebbles. He laid the branch in front of Harry and gave him the stones.

'Ok,' he said. 'Above the stick is now and below is the last time you were here. Start matching the nights off using the stones as markers.'

Harry immediately put 2 stones above and 2 below the line.

'That's the night by the pool and the night in the hut; those I'm pretty sure of.'

Brad winked at Laura and the two of them left Harry to it. Half an hour later they returned to find him sitting cross-legged with a smile on his face.

'Should' a just gone with my gut feeling – the day after tomorrow it is,' he said, beaming up at them.

Sure enough there was one stone below the line with no matching counterpart above. He started relating the nights to Laura, his hand moving along the line of pebbles as he went. Laura watched carefully, mentally ticking off each night from what she could remember of his story. Arriving at the single stone he picked it up and tossed it in his hand.

'So this is tomorrow night,' he said. 'And the Americans should be here the day after.'

'Harry,' began Laura slowly. 'I think you've lost a night.'

As Harry froze the pebble grazed his forehead and dropped to the ground. The men both looked at Laura.

'Remember the night you escaped and Lucy 'speared' you?'

'Yes.'

'Well you spent the whole night asleep in the jungle and I don't think you've placed a stone for that one.'

Harry counted through the stones again wracking his brain to remember.

'I think your right darling,' he said. 'Yes you are right, thank God for the women on this little trip eh?'

'So that gives us two full days then,' said Brad. 'Plenty of time to think of something.'

'Well an idea is forming in my head Brad; what do you think to this...'

Laura left the two of them talking deep into the night and when they finally retired the others were fast asleep and had no idea what faced them over the next two days. If they had known none of them would have been able to get a wink of sleep.

Chapter Fifty-Seven

The next morning found Harry and Brad up early, jogging along the beach. Both men were fit and although both felt the urge to race ahead to see who would 'win', they realized the need to conserve their strength if they were to pull Harry's ambitious plan. They had left the others at the hut and although there had been some concern most were happy to rest up until they were needed. Before long the MTB came into site and the two men hugged the tree line and surveyed the scene. Harry looked up; the rain that had started in the night seemed relentless as it fell from the grey overcast sky. If this keeps up, he thought, it might mean a change of plan, and for the better. Though early, the temperature was already rising sharply and they were sweating profusely despite the deluge. As they watched for any movement in the boats vicinity they took the opportunity to take a long drink from their canteens.

'I think it's all clear,' whispered Brad, referring to the beach and not the weather.

Harry agreed but continued to watch for a few minutes and then led the way from the cover of the trees. Silently they approached the burnt-out hulk, the scene of destruction still playing on Harry's nerves.

'So what do you think?' asked Brad.

'Well from what I remember the hull was intact but the whole plan rests on whether we can get her running and off this beach,' replied Harry.

They both instinctively walked to look at the port quarter where much of the damage had taken place. Harry waded into the water and ducked down to inspect below the water line whilst Brad pulled himself aboard. Minutes later Harry joined Brad on deck and they both had the same story.

'Well the hull looks ok but the left screw has completely had it,' reported Harry. 'The other two look ok though and two of the rudders are mercifully unscathed.'

'It's not just the left screw,' said Brad. 'The left engine is completely burnt-out and the shaft is distorted. There's a bit of a leak where it exits the hull but nothing we can't handle.' On a more positive note he added: 'The others look great though. If we can get them running this old tub just might have one more mission in her.'

'Ok, let's get to work. I'm not too good with engines so if you can start some sort of overhaul on the good ones I'll take a look at what armament we can get together.'

Brad grinned back at Harry. 'And what makes you think I'm any good as a mechanic?'

Harry just gave him a sour look and Brad shrugged his shoulders and dropped down below into the engine compartment. Harry's first task was clearing away the remains of the crew. He hadn't wanted to ask Brad's assistance as it proved to be the thankless task he'd imagined. He realised that with his war experiences Brad would probably have been better placed for the grizzly task but the type of man that Harry was meant that he'd prefer to do the dirty work himself than ask others. The rear gunner or what was left of him once again proved to be the worst, and the catalyst for loss of the light breakfast that Laura had prepared for them before they had left the hut that morning. As he cleared away the remains he saw that in fact there had been two guns, one on each side. The left gun had been completely demolished, presumably with the gun crew, and it was just the right gun remaining, though damaged beyond any slim chance of repair. It wasn't too long before he had cleared up as best he could and he got down to checking what weapon systems they might be able to salvage.

Firstly he checked the fire control system on what remained of the bridge.

'Well that lot's out,' he mumbled to himself as he threw a bloody rag onto the torpedo firing station. Most of the controls were burnt beyond recognition and the firing button was bent upward and seized solid. He even swung at it with some scrap metal that was once perhaps a chair, and still couldn't budge it. He wondered out to look at the torpedo tubes and got more bad news. All four were damaged and the left two looked like a 10 storey building had fallen on them. He moved to the starboard side and saw with some pleasure that the forward tube was intact, though empty and the after tube was loaded but with some fire damage. Closer inspection revealed that the system might be viable if they could rig up some way of firing it.

Satisfied he made his way below to look for the magazine and possible reloads. He scrabbled around what were mainly living quarters and store rooms but found no evidence of torpedoes or indeed anywhere they might have been stored. Had he studied US naval history at all he might have known he was aboard an ELCO 77 footer that only carried 4 mark XIV 21 inch torpedoes on the upper deck, pre-loaded into the tubes. Giving up his search he quickly checked out the 30 calibre machine gun mounted on the bow only to find the same story as the other guns; unusable. A little dejected he made his way aft just in time to see Brad appearing from below.

'How's it going buddy,' asked a black-faced Brad.

'Not too good on the weapon front,' he answered. 'Basically we have one torpedo that we may be able to rig up, the rest are all knackered.'

'Well some better news here then; I recon the right should run no problem and the centre is about 50 / 50. Give me a couple of minutes and we'll just about be ready to try turning these babies over.'

'How you gonna start them Brad, the bridge has been destroyed.'

'I'm ahead of you on that one buddy; I've just wired the starting circuits straight up to the batteries. All I have to do is connect the last terminal and they should start. What you should be asking is how I'm going to engage the screws.'

'So how are you gonna engage the screws?'

'That I'm still working on,' he said, as he disappeared from sight once more.

Harry sauntered round the boat wondering what he might be able to do to help. Making his way back to the bridge he tried to identify the engine controls in the vain hope that they would still allow them to engage the engines. The main panel was twisted and buckled beyond recognition and it wasn't too long before he gave up all hope and started to make his way aft. The next moment, without even the hint of a splutter he heard one of the Packard 4M-2500, Super Charged engines burst into life with a throaty roar. A billow of black smoke burst from the small narrow exhaust and then settled down to a healthy stream of white vapour as Brad brought the engine back to a comfortable tick over. Seconds later the second engine burst into life and Harry couldn't help but grin, as their luck seemed to be on the change for the better.

'She's all yours Skipper,' grinned Brad as he once again popped up like a meercat on the Masai Mara plains.

'All astern,' shouted Harry above the idling engines.

'Aaaah, there you have the problem in a nutshell Harry, have you checked the controls on the bridge?'

Harry nodded but gave a thumbs down.

Brad cut power to the engines and they were left in an eerie silence. 'Well we'll get over that hurdle soon enough,' he said, optimistically. 'Hopefully the others will be here soon and we can look at re-floating her.'

They took a break, sitting in comfortable silence in the steady rain, on the back of the boat. It was still hot and the cool rain on their skin gave them some relief, though they could feel the humidity rising by the minute. Neither really knew where they would go from here but they both had absolutely no doubt that they would come up with a plan and that it would work. Soon they became aware of the others approaching and jumped down to meet them. Sitting in the shelter of the boat Harry gave a quick report on the state of the hull, the engines, props and rudders, and finished with a quick run down of the weapon system, or rather, the lack of it. At the end he was left facing three blank faces, along with Brad grinning through his oil-stained face.

'But why does all this matter?' asked Laura.

'Because we're going to refloat her,' grinned Harry. 'And what's more we're gonna take her on one last victorious voyage.'

Harry spent the next 15 minutes outlining his and Brad's plan. Some of the details were a bit sketchy and he was even making up parts as he went along. Brad chipped in with a few points here and there, and when he did all three faces turned to him in unison. As they approached the end of this initial brief they saw three shocked faces staring up at them as if they were from a different planet.

'Have you gone completely stark staring mad?' demanded Matthew.

'It's crazy,' mumbled Lucy.

'Yes crazy,' repeated Laura. 'But so crazy it just might work.'

Harry and Brad left the three of them talking the plan over; trying to see a good side to it. Making their way back onto the MTB they split up, with Brad going back to the engines and Harry making his way to the one serviceable torpedo. After 15 minutes tinkering Harry decided that all he had to do was provide an electrical charge to the launching circuit to simulate pressing the fire button on the bridge and the torpedo would go. As to what settings; depth, range, speed, heading etc, he had absolutely no idea. However if everything went to plan then those settings really wouldn't matter. Satisfied, he made his way to the engine room just in time to hear a long list of expletives thunder out of an upturned Brad. He appeared with blood pouring from a deep wound on his thumb.

'Let's take a break,' suggested Harry.

'You're the Boss,' the instant reply.

'I wish you hadn't said that; if this all goes to shit then I'm to blame,' responded Harry. 'Mind you if it does then there won't be anyone left to blame me.'

'Blame you for what?' asked Laura.

'Oh nothing you need worry your pretty head about sweetheart, what are you lot up to anyway?'

'Lucy and Matthew have gone in search of some strong timbers to help lever the boat into the water when you try to refloat her.'

'Good thinking,' replied Brad. 'Lucy's idea?'

'Yep,' said Laura. 'And Matthew was only too pleased to help; to take his mind off things I think. So what's the news with you guys, not too good if the language was anything to go by!'

Brad blushed deep red: 'Sorry Mam,' he mumbled. 'I had a few setbacks and then this.' He held his thumb in the air and Laura saw the steady flow of blood pouring from the wound. She made her way over to him and gave her attention to his thumb as he continued.

'Well I can engage the engines easily enough, by brute force, but disengaging them may be a different story. For the transit to the hot spot I'll only use one of them and if I damage it then at least we will have one good engine for the final phase. Mind you I have to find reverse first and if I can't disengage, and we do get off the beach, then we'll be transiting backwards!'

'And what about you darling?'

'Well I reckon I can fire the torpedo,' replied Harry. 'Though whether it will go off armed or not, I'm not really sure.'

They all sat in thought for a moment.

'We've done about as much as we can for now,' said Harry, getting to his feet. 'Let's get back to the others and come back in the morning to try and float her.

'Maybe we should do it now,' said Brad. 'Tomorrow night is the night and if we have any snags we won't have a lot of time to sort them out in the morning.'

'Yes, but if you can't disengage the engine then we have to go now and that's too early and leaves us unprepared.'

Brad conceded the point and the three of them jumped to the beach and went in search of the others. As soon as they joined up Brad led the way back to the spotter's hut where they found the meagre pile of provisions that he and Harry had transferred earlier that morning. The two girls prepared a light meal; little more than a lumpy drink in reality, whilst the others went over the finer points of the plan.

'Well it all seems simple enough,' muttered Matthew.

Harry joined them from the window where he had been watching the steady rain splashing down through the canopy.

'Well there may be a little change, and it may work in our favour if this weather keeps up,' he said seating himself next to Brad.

He spent the next few minutes outlining the changes to his earlier plan and watched as the smiles grew on the faces around him as they filled with refreshed hope. For the first time in 24hours they began to see an alternative to dying in this lonely part of the Pacific.

When the others had turned in for the night Harry and Laura took a stroll along the beach. The rain had stopped for the moment but the sky was still a dark, angry red as the sun set beyond the horizon. They stopped and kissed under the clouds.

'What's going to happen to us?' asked Laura.

'I don't really know,' he replied. 'But I think our future has something to do with Brad's ring. It seems to have been cropping up at regular intervals throughout this whole saga'.

'You're right; I hadn't seen it before but now you mention it, its usually been at fairly critical points too. Have you spoken to him about it yet?'

'No,' he said. 'In fact I really have no idea how to breach the subject.'

'Well if the time is right the situation will present itself,' Laura said confidently.

I hope so thought Harry. In fact he didn't have any real confidence that they would see a future in either their time or now, but of course he didn't speak these thoughts aloud to Laura.

'I won't ask to hear your thoughts darling, I have a feeling I'd rather not know. Come on let's get some sleep; we have a long day tomorrow.'

Harry smiled at her astuteness and wondered if indeed they would have a long day or if it would be cruelly cut short at the hands of the Japanese army.

Chapter Fifty-Eight

The sky brightened slowly as the sun rose above the thick even layer of cloud that had been constantly precipitating throughout the night. The bird's morning chorus was subdued and the occasional chatter of a monkey high in the branches sounded forlorn in the quiet of the morning. Brad slowly rose from his makeshift bed, thinking that he was the first to rise, only to find Matthew knelt in prayer in the dim morning light. Careful not to disturb him Brad made his way to the exit and slowly slipped out in the muggy air of the forest. The rain felt cool on his skin as he made his way down to the beach to carry out his ablutions as best he could.

'Had a bit of a lay in then?' whispered Harry, causing Brad to leap out of his skin as he pushed through the sodden foliage onto the beach.

'Jesus Harry, what are you doing up and about? You nearly scared me to death!'

'Same as you probably. I couldn't sleep anyway; never really could before a big mission.'

They fell into silence as they watched the last of the increasing light from the sun's vain efforts illuminate the MTB. Without talking they both strolled down to the water's edge through the torrential downpour, ridded themselves of their clothing and immersed their bodies in the warm water. As Brad lazily breast stroked parallel to the beach Harry powered out to sea with an almost perfect crawl action. After about 200 yards he dove down and swam as deep as he could but did not reach bottom. With a strong kick he made for the surface, rolled onto his back and powered back to the shore line and drew himself up the beach. If it wasn't for the circumstances he thought, this would be paradise. The feeling was further enhanced as he saw Laura appear at the tree line. She was absolutely perfect and he hoped that he had not brought her this far only for their lives to be snuffed out. Worse still he thought, if something should happen to her and he survived how would he ever live with himself?

Pushing these negative thoughts from his head he dragged on his wet clothes and made his way across the sand to meet her. She melted into his arms and just hung on, shaking slightly. Neither was aware as Lucy crept past them and walked down to join Brad at the waterline. As if following suit, she fell into Brad's open arms and held him like there would be no tomorrow. All four were trying not to think that indeed there might not be a tomorrow for any of them. Lucy and Laura were both failing and wept into the chests of their respective partners. Lucy and Brad were the first to break and wandered off hand in hand along the beach. Laura noticed them and smiled.

'I hope this works out for them,' she said, drawing Harry's attention to the couple who had stopped and were kissing gently in the persistent rain.

'Me too,' said Harry, though his mind was a million miles away running the forthcoming mission through his mind, trying to iron out any wrinkles.

Once again all four of them were lost in thought and eventually it was Lucy and Brad who walked to the forest and led the way back to the hut. Matthew had finished his prayers and greeted the others solemnly. Not much was said as they wolfed down the last of the provisions and got ready for the task ahead.

Arriving at the beach Brad and Harry had one last swim around the water line and declared the boat fit for the sea. Next they spent an hour of brute force and cursing as they worked to perfect a jury rig to the rudders to steer the boat from the stern. It was then a 2 hour wait for what they deemed would be the height of the tide. They used the time making the final preparations; loosening the sand around the bow as much as possible with the machetes. At two points set a little back from the bow they had dug two deep holes in the sand angling under the boat. In these they positioned the levers cut the day before and after a short rest they were ready to float her; Brad scuttled to the engine bay and quickly fired up the starboard engine to a muted round of applause from the shore.

'Now the tricky bit,' shouted Brad above the din of the engine. 'I'm going to put the engine into reverse, hopefully, and when the water starts churning at the stern that's your signal to try to prise her off the beach.'

Harry gave a thumbs up and turned his attention to the task. He and Laura manned one of the levers whilst Lucy and Matthew gripped the other.

Brad took one final look to judge if all was right. He noted that the water was about as high up the beach as he'd seen it and he got a thin-lipped nod from Harry, who with the others was starting to take the strain.

Brad increased the revs on the starboard engine and left it to settle down. Once satisfied it was running smoothly he peered into the stripped-open gearbox and tried a subtle shove to engage reverse. Nothing happened and so with ever-increasing brute force he started hammering at the centrifugal gearbox. Just as he started to think he was going to fail at this early hurdle there was a terrific metallic crunch and the revs fell rapidly. He quickly gunned the engine and as the revs picked up he started to feel movement under him. Leaping up he looked over the stern to see the outboard propeller churning the sea to a frothy green mess. Transferring his gaze he saw the others heaving with all their might on the homemade leverage system.

Harry was shouting something to him but he could not hear above the din of the engine; however he rightly assumed he was calling for more revs and immediately dropped below and gave the engine all he could. In the confined space the screaming howl of the supercharged engine was deafening and he was relieved to jump up again to check on any progress. Nothing. Dropping below he throttled the engine right back and then slammed it back into full reverse. Once again he felt the propeller bite and once again looked out to see if he was having any effect.

Harry was gesticulating madly and Brad again correctly guessed that he was calling for more stop/start action. Stooping once more into the noise he started rocking the revs up and down in a regular fashion and soon started to feel the boat rocking on the beach.

Outside Harry grimaced as he braced himself against the wooded lever. In unison with the others he soon picked up the rocking motion and as a team they matched their efforts to increase the action. Slowly they felt the boat start to ease backwards, and not before time as Matthew was starting to look like he was on his last legs. Laura didn't look much better but as they started to see the fruits of their efforts their strength momentarily picked up and with a gargantuan push the MTB started to slide out to sea. Brad obviously felt the movement and set the revs to a middle position and jumped up to see the coastline slowly drawing back as the boat gradually picked up speed. He looked at the others jumping in the shallows and could hear the cheers even over the smoothly running engine.

Ducking down he appraised the spinning gears and decided the easier option to stop the boats motion would be to stop the engine. This he did by cutting power from the batteries and with the shaft still engaged the engine jerked rapidly to a stop. Rushing forward he released the anchor and was relieved to see the boat quickly rest on its cable; all motion other than the rocking in the light waves stopped. Already he could see the others swimming out to meet him and he made his way aft to help them clamber over the stern.

Brad shook Harry's hand on a job well done and they made their way with the others onto what was left of the bridge.

'What are those tubes either side of the gun,' asked Brad, pointing forward.

'Oh did I neglect to mention those?' grinned Harry. 'They look like some sort of retro rocket fit, and...'

'And?' urged Brad.

'...and they're all loaded.'

What Harry was referring to were in fact twin 8 tube, 5 inch rocket launchers which were retro fitted to some of the Elco boats later in the war.

'Will they work?' asked Laura.

'I don't see why not,' said Harry. 'I've wired up a firing circuit direct to the batteries and it should just be a simple case of completing the loop to fire them. Much like the torpedo really.'

Brad chuckled. 'And how long were you planning to keep those a secret?'

'It wasn't a secret; I just failed to mention them but they were there for anyone to see. What it does mean though is a vast improvement in our fire power; enough to grab the Jap's attention and perhaps take us seriously.

As the team relaxed and explored the boat a little further, Harry and Brad lashed up a mix of tarpaulin and space blankets to give some respite from the rain. The girls knocked up a small meal from the provisions they found in the galley that Lucy had missed during her initial scavenge and took it up to the bridge.

'Where's Harry,' asked Laura looking around.

'Just gone over the side to check the hull and to take a rough measurement of the draft; anything over 5 – 6 feet might throw a spanner in the works this evening.'

As the others sat and ate in silence Harry once again took a deep breath and ducked below the surface. He was satisfied that the hull was sound, and relatively undamaged. The two remaining screws appeared to be in good order as did the rudders. He progressed down the side of the boat taking rough measurements relative to his body length at various points and after another couple of dives he reckoned he had a good idea of the maximum draft. He swam back to the rear of the vessel and pulled himself aboard. Making his way amid ships he reported back to the others.

'I'm guessing at about 4 foot 6 inches at the deepest part of the draft.'

'Ok that should be fine; much more than that and we could be in trouble,' said Brad.

'Right lets go over the plan and individual responsibilities one last time. We have to be in position before total darkness otherwise we might miss our mark. Remember that intelligence suggests there will be an American Marine force in position just after dawn tomorrow. Given the time it will take for the Japs to reach the ambush point in the dark I think we need to start our action at about 0300. I only wish we could contact the Marines to let them know we're coming; the last thing I want is to get taken out by them before the trap is set.' He paused and then continued. 'Brad, engines; anything to report?'

'Well once the right had stopped it was an easy job to get it out of gear and so we should be going in on 2 engines, however ...'

And so the final planning went on well into the afternoon; all wrinkles were ironed out, each individual went through their responsibilities in fine detail and by the end of it Harry reckoned they had a good plan, and what's more, a better than 50/50 chance of pulling it off and coming out the other end alive. With nothing more to do at this stage they all tried to get some sleep though Matthew was the only one to achieve it.

As the sun began its downward path toward the horizon the crew galvanised themselves into action. Lucy, Laura and Matthew went forward to raise the anchor; not an easy feat without the winch mechanism. After about 10 minutes hard labour they gave up and reported to Harry. In the meantime Brad had started the right engine and left it ticking over awaiting the signal to engage the screw. After a little discussion Harry came up with a plan for the anchor and gave the nod to Brad who deftly, this time, engaged the propeller in forward. Using the homemade tiller system Harry kept the revs at low and manoeuvred the boat over the anchor. Matthew tied it off on a cleat as Harry carried the boat into deeper water. With the anchor now free and with a bit of team work Lucy,

358

Laura and Matthew managed to lift the anchor to just below the waterline as the boat transited the coast towards the river inlet.

'Let this rain have put enough water in the river please God,' whispered Harry.

'Amen to that,' replied Matthew as he sidled up beside him.

Harry was still worried; not only about the depth of the river, but also the width. He estimated the boat at about a 20 foot beam so he knew it was going to be touch and go in places, depending on how much water a combination of tide and rain had put into what was little more than a stream earlier.

Brad kept the engine at low revs, and with the mufflers doing their job they travelled up the coast at about 2 knots in 'silent mode'. Even at that slow pace it wasn't too long before they could make out the opening in the tree line that indicated the position of the river bed. Harry pointed the boat at the gap and Brad throttled right back on the engine and they glided silently until they stopped in the current about 50 yards off shore. Harry could make out the turbulent boiling on the sea's surface as the fresh muddy water of the river spilled into the sparkling blue ocean. It looked like the river would be navigable in the MTB and hopefully the strong flow would have cleared out any fallen debris that had collected in the dry days preceding.

As planned Brad stopped the engine, knocked it out of forward, restarted and engaged reverse. Harry silently thanked the long afternoons he'd spent on the river Dart during his officer training learning to manoeuvre 45 foot picket boats in all conditions, as that experience now aided him in moving the boat into position. Carefully he backed the boat against the current and into the river. As he crept under the canopy of the forest the light dimmed noticeably and he shouted to Brad to reduce speed. Eventually the engine was at its lowest sustainable revs and still it felt too fast for Harry. As his eyes began to grow accustomed to the dim conditions, Harry relaxed a little and edged the boat upstream confidently but at the back of his mind was the awareness that he would have to drive back out at a considerably higher speed and in the pitch black of night.

Harry was pleasantly surprised by the change in the river. It really was a raging torrent now and apart from the occasional piece of foliage or rotting wood that crashed into the stern as he carefully navigated backwards, it appeared reasonably clear of debris. At the back of his mind was how long the river could sustain such a flow. Shouldn't be a problem as long as the rain holds up, he thought, but if it stopped too soon they could find themselves grounded and that would be the end of their action. Soon they were in almost complete darkness with just the occasional break in the canopy above allowing the dim light of the moon to penetrate and light their way. Harry was edging back as slow as he could; navigating by feel as much as anything else, and even at this slow pace they were still taking on a little water as the coursing river met the flat stern of the boat. Even so, it was not enough that they should worry; in fact it was probably the least of their worries considering what lay ahead.

As they approached a particularly dark spot heavily surrounded by thick undergrowth Harry gave the signal to cut the engine. The silence in the air, interrupted only by the howl of some creature disturbed in the canopy, was the signal for Matthew to let the anchor go and soon after the boat hung on the current. The stern swung round and came to rest against the deeply overgrown bank but Harry was happy that it wouldn't be too much of a problem when they set off again. Happy that the boat was secure Harry and Brad decided on watches and the others made themselves as comfortable as possible and surprisingly fell straight into deep sleeps. Brad sat in the stern and listened to the jungle settle down once again. The last of the moonlight was gone and the evening creatures bedded down for the night leaving the quiet broken only by the occasional screech as a night predator took its prey.

'Well Brad, whatever way this goes I reckon it will be our last night together,' said Harry, who could not get any sleep and had made his way over to join his friend.

'Reckon you're right Bud.' Brad fiddled with his fingers and then reached over and placed his ring in Harry's hand. 'I guess your story has proved to be true, and I can't even start to understand it or comprehend how you are going to get back to your own time, but I think it may have something to do with this. It's been a common thread throughout and just maybe it'll get you and Laura home safely.'

'Thanks Brad, I think you're right. Laura and I have discussed it a few times and we never really knew how to broach the subject.' Harry put the ring away in a secure pocket. 'If we all get through this and Laura and I get home maybe you could come and see us in the future.' Harry stopped, realising how unlikely his last statement sounded.

'Maybe I will,' muttered Brad. 'Maybe *we* will,' he continued looking over at the sleeping form of Lucy.

Chapter Fifty-Nine

'Wake up sweetheart,' said Harry as he gently shook Laura's arm. 'It's 0230.'

Laura was instantly awake and reached up to stroke her husband's face. He bent down and kissed her gently and they held each other tightly for a few minutes before Harry drew back.

'Brad's given me the ring'

'Did you ask him for it?'

'No,' said Harry. 'He just thought that we may need it to get home.'

Laura hugged him tightly again and then slowly got to her feet. The others were rising around her; each quietly going about their predetermined tasks set at the numerous briefings and discussions over the last 24 hours. All of them were scared, some more than others, but each had something precious to loose in the next few hours and that heightened their fears. Soon they were ready and Brad started both engines, proved them and then cut the starboard. With the ease of an expert car thief he selected reverse on the centre engine and Harry guided the boat upstream and over the anchor, which had been unshackled on the boat so that they didn't have to faff about trying to raise it. Let's face it they weren't going to need it again. As they continued backwards the anchor chain rattled through the cleats and awoke a troop of monkeys high in the tree tops. The noise seemed to explode into the night and set off a chain reaction, which to the frightened participants below seemed to last forever and to be loud enough to wake the dead. The cacophony did eventually settle down and the boat made slow progress backwards up the river. The crew listened apprehensively, convinced that the noise would bring the Japanese raining down on them, but after 15 minutes they came to the conclusion that they had been too far away from the village.

As they eased their way upstream Harry tried to picture the river in relationship to the village, from the time he and Frank had floated into the village on logs. This time the tide was not really making any difference; there was so much water in the river that it was flowing quite quickly towards the sea and overcoming any tidal influence. Harry had not even felt the boat brush the bottom and was happy there was plenty of water for the four and a half foot draft. He didn't recognise any of the water way which, given the flooded conditions, was not surprising. He heard a dog bark in the distance and automatically signalled Brad to reduce the revs. They were getting close.

The MTB was still making way astern, but only very slowly now. Timing was going to be important, if not critical. There was no sign of light yet, however they were under the canopy and Harry assessed that it would only be a matter of 30 minutes or so before the sky started to brighten. He knew that if they went ahead with the plan too early they would not be able to get the boat safely back to the coast, too late and they would miss their chance with the US Marines and the Japs would 'dig in' in the village with the resulting consequences for the local population.

Looking down Harry could not see, but could feel his hand shaking on the homemade tiller. He was really scared, not so much for himself but for the others. His mind took him back to the beginning of this adventure; to the crash, the dream, to waking up and finding Laura by his side. He remembered their wedding and honeymoon and how their situation changed once they'd found the graves; and so to their current predicament. They all looked to him as the natural leader of their little group, even Brad, and that's what scared him most. They were all relying on him; his plan, his ideas, and if anything went wrong it was down to him.

And so his thoughts turned to Laura. He loved her so much and knew he couldn't bear it if anything happened to her. And as he thought of her so his resolve grew. This would work, they would get through it and what's more; they would get home. He looked down again and saw in the dimmest of light, that his hand had stopped shaking. He smiled and looked up to his motley crew standing there in the dull illumination of the breaking dawn. The rain had finally stopped.

'Alright,' he called just above the quiet noise of the muffled engine. 'Let's do this.'

In the time it had taken for the night sky to lighten they had approached until they were almost on top of the village. Thanks to the quiet of the engine no one had yet been disturbed. At a nod from Harry, Brad started the starboard engine and knocked the centre into neutral. He looked at Harry.

'Good luck,' he said, and gunned the right engine. The noise was deafening and at least three dogs went into a mad frenzy of barking. High above the tree dwelling animals took up the chorus and soon the jungle was alive with sound. The light was still poor but Harry could make out some movement upstream and shouted to Lucy. She immediately let off a couple of shots with rifle, adding to din. This was the signal for Laura who made the necessary connection to the battery. The next moment the air was shattered with a howling screech as the starboard rocket battery let loose all eight rockets high into the canopy off to the starboard side. They flew from the launcher in rapid succession streaking through the sky at supersonic speeds like wailing Bansees, leaving a trail of smoke in their wake. They burst through the lighter foliage but as each struck more substantial trees the warheads ignited and the jungle was momentarily lit up like bonfire night. The blast was thunderously loud at such short range and Harry was blown off his feet by the concussion wave that accompanied the roar. Luckily he had ducked at the moment the rockets were fired, to protect his night vision, and felt the air move as shrapnel crashed into the superstructure, where his head had been just milliseconds before. Matthew was not as lucky and cried out as a piece of burning white hot metal buried into his calf, missing the bone and passing clean through.

The domino effect continued, with the rockets being the signal for Brad to engage the engines. They could by now hear the manic shouting of the Japanese as they tried to ready themselves for an assault on the 'invading army'. A few shots rang out and they clearly heard one of the rounds thudding into the hull just above the water line. Brad threw the Starboard engine into gear and was dismayed to hear it splutter a few times, catch and then die completely. The boat juddered as the prop bit but then returned to the gentle drift downstream as the engine quit. More shots rang out from the direction of the village as the enemy became more confident; realising that instead of a massed attack, they were only under threat from the one patrol boat they could just make out in the dim light. Orders were shouted and soon the boat was under a concentrated hail of gunfire. The crew took cover behind whatever they could and all looked towards Brad in the engine compartment.

Brad had realised his error; in the excitement of the moment he had engaged the engine with far too many revs on and the shock force of the load of the propeller had stalled the engine. He didn't waste any more time on the right, but throttled back on the centre, engaged the prop and then cagily brought the revs up. The engine gobbled up the 100 octane aviation fuel and the MTB surged forward. Harry was momentarily thrown off balance, but recovered and took control of the vessel in the narrow water way. Happy with the centre engine Brad turned his attention to the right and quickly got it going. Successfully engaging the screw he gave a thumbs up to Harry in the increasing light. Had all three engines been serviceable the boat would have reached 40 – 45 knots and Harry was thankful they were a fair bit slower.

'Back off a little on both,' shouted Harry.

'What?' demanded Lucy, thinking Harry had gone mad. 'The Japs are close behind us.'

This statement was punctuated by a powerful explosion in the water behind them. Harry looked back with water dripping from his face.

'A rifle launched grenade I think,' he shouted. 'But we have to slow down so they don't lose us.' He didn't add that at their current speed he was likely to crash at some point and they would be sitting ducks.

The firing had become much more sporadic now and the others saw the truth in what he was saying. Brad throttled back to idle on the right engine and Harry silently thanked him as it removed part of the yawing movement and made the vessel much easier to steer.

'I've been hit,' said Matthew, in a conversational tone.

All eyes but Harry's, who was watching the river and steering the boat, turned and saw Matthew sitting on the deck holding his left leg. He looked a bit pale in the early light and his best efforts could not stem the flow of blood onto the wooden planking. Lucy rushed over and assisted him as best she could though there wasn't too much she could do at present.

Another explosion ripped through the relative quite, though this time much further behind. It was followed with a few random rifle shots and then nothing.

'We're getting too far ahead,' shouted Brad. 'Just as you predicted.'

'Ok, bring the other back to idle as well; we'll let them catch up.'

As Brad throttled back the jungle suddenly seemed impossibly quiet. They continued to move gently downstream on the current but the pace was well below that of a foot soldier on the well-worn path paralleling the river. Brad climbed up and knelt next to Harry in the stern. Laura, in the meantime had left her station to help Lucy with Matthew. They managed to stop the bleeding by crudely plugging the wound on both sides with a clean handkerchief, much to Matthew's discomfort, and then bound the leg with a ripped up blanket.

'Well what do think Buddy?' asked Brad. 'Have they called off the chase?'

His answer came in a shocking form as a bullet tore into his right shoulder. He was thrown backwards and ended up in the engine bay where he gunned the first engine he came to with his left arm. A rapid fusillade of bullets followed but all harmlessly hit the boat or the water off the stern as the MTB shot forwards.

'Brad, are you OK?' cried Harry as he fought to control the boat. 'Brad, answer me!'

Lucy had seen Brad go down and was running aft as fast as she could, tears welling in her eyes and spilling onto her dirt-streaked face.

'Brad, Brad...oh please no,' she cried as she all but fell into the engine compartment. Brad was lying on his back with his eyes closed and his left hand holding his right shoulder.

'Brad, talk to me, please talk to me.'

'I'm ok,' he mumbled. 'I'll be ok.'

Lucy prised his hand away from the wound and gasped as blood bubbled up from the ugly looking hole. Even in the dim light she could see splinters of bone clinging to the sides of the wound. She started ripping at the remains of the blanket she was still holding. She examined the shoulder carefully and could not detect an exit wound, so she placed a large pad directly over the point of entry and bound it as tight as she could. Brad groaned throughout the procedure but didn't object.

Another explosion rocked the boat and she threw herself over him as water rained down on them both.

'How does that feel?' she asked recovering surprisingly quickly.

'Bloody awful,' grinned Brad.

Lucy finished off her first aid by strapping his right arm across his chest in an attempt to immobilise the shattered shoulder joint. She was happy that no major blood vessels had been compromised and his breathing indicated that his lung had not been punctured. Brad sat up and fought through the dizziness. Noting once again that there were no sounds of gunfire outside he reached over and throttled back on the engines. The boat slowed but this time they were all careful to keep some form of cover between them and the estimated position of the enemy.

After ten minutes Brad eased himself out of the engine bay and wormed his way over to Harry.

'It's very quiet.'

'Yep,' replied Harry.

'Maybe they've gone back to the village.'

'Or maybe just regrouping; getting in some heavier fire power, who knows.'

'How about the other rocket battery?'

'I'd rather save that,' said Harry after giving the idea some thought. 'We have no idea what's around the corner.'

At the thought of what might be ahead Brad dragged his eyes from peering astern and looked forward. He saw that they were about 100 yards from the cut where they had come across Matthew and Frank. As he was turning back to Harry a movement caught his eye on the left bank where the path approached the water.

'Ambush,' he shouted, and made for the engine bay.

'Laura standby on the rockets; on my word,' shouted Harry, and ran forward to the port side rocket pods. With no time for finesse he stamped the launch pods down to a near horizontal position and dashed back to the steering mechanism just as Brad brought both engines to full capacity. The boat lurched forward rapidly accelerating to around 30 knots. As if on cue a machine gun rattled into action and rounds came scything across the water and into the port bow. The gunner then marched the impact point up and across the boat towards the stern. As the boat closed the ambush point, the rapidly changing angle was giving the Japanese marksman some difficulty. Had they drifted past on the flow of the river the gun would have cut them to pieces, probably killing all on board. As it was their sudden action caught the Japanese off guard and their ambush was ineffective.

The MTB was rapidly approaching the gun emplacement and as Harry peered over the side he could make out a force of about 6 soldiers; two on the machine gun and the others bringing rifles to bear. Harry just made out a grenade launching rifle swinging in a steady arc towards them.

'NOW Laura!' he shouted at the top of his voice.

Laura made the connection and all hell let loose; six rockets screeched from the launcher towards the enemy. A huge explosion erupted on the bow. The epicentre, a bright burning white. An orange and blue pyrotechnic display burst high in the air only to come raining down on and around the boat. Shrapnel blasted about; splintered wood and twisted metal thrown around in all directions, but thankfully most confined to the bow area. Matthew was the only one forward and luckily most of the blast was deflected upwards by the remains of the bridge superstructure. Though temporarily deafened by the blast, Matthew stayed unscathed this time, safe on the deck of the bridge. The deck around the launcher burst into orange flames, but they failed to get a good hold before being extinguished in the rush of air as the boat flew forwards.

Harry assumed that the grenade launcher had got his round off and silently thanked their luck that it had not hit an occupied part of the boat. Later inspection would show that in fact two of their own rockets had ignited and detonated in the launcher due to the damage caused by Harry's impromptu re-aiming. But it was what happened on the shore that held their attention. Six rockets had ploughed into the small Japanese force at point blank range. Harry watched the scene unfold in front of him as if in slow motion. The soldier with the grenade launcher was hit first; a direct blow to the face. Harry watched in horror as his head disintegrated, the rocket blasting straight through it and detonated on the bank behind him. As he started to crumple to the ground he was engulfed in the explosion, his body shattered by the force of it and blown out toward the patrol boat. Five more explosions followed in quick succession and the remaining soldiers were cut down by the flying shrapnel; sliced limb from limb in the bloody conflagration that followed. Harry's lasting image of the incident would be the unidentifiable body part flying over the stern, leaving a trail of blood as the boat roared past.

Harry kept the speed on as long as he dared, not knowing if there were any more Japs, and if so where. He swept the boat smoothly round a right hand bend and immediately came under a hail of bullets. This time there would be no counter attack, just speed to carry them past the unknown force as quickly as possible. He heard shells smacking into the hull on both sides and though he was keeping as low as he could, he felt the burn as a round grazed his forehead and was aware of the trickle of warm blood into his right eye. Noting the river ran straight for the next hundred yards or so he held the tiller steady and ducked well below the twisted metal around him. He could only hope that the others were doing the same, and were safe. Suddenly the boat jarred and veered to the right as an explosion ripped through the port bow. Another quickly followed and Harry fought to maintain control. Brad instinctively throttled back but not before the hull hit a glancing blow on the right bank, rocking the craft and throwing it back into midstream. Harry steered hard right and just managed to avoid the bank on the other side of the river before getting things back on course.

As quickly as it had started the gun fight was over; quickly left behind by their speed.

'Bring her back to dead slow,' shouted Harry.

He realised that their attackers had been foolish, concentrating their force in one place, or two if he counted the machine gun. Had they spread the remaining units downstream they would have maintained a much longer period of concentrated fire and would have more than likely crippled the boat and its crew. As it was they limped on toward the open ocean, smoke billowing from the impact of two grenades on the port bow. As they slowed Harry shouted for a roll call and was pleased to hear everyone answer.

'Cut the engines Brad.'

'Aye, aye skipper.'

Harry could see just up ahead, a fallen tree was blocking half the river. He steered the bow into the obstruction and was satisfied to see the stern swing round and rest against the opposite bank. He hoped they would be able to get moving again when the time came, but right now he needed to take stock of the situation and check his crew. Wiping the blood from his face he saw that it was already congealing and was happy it was not a serious wound. Nevertheless, Laura was quickly at his side peering at the crease in his head.

'That was too close sweetheart,' she murmured as she cleaned the blood away and assessed the wound. Harry just laughed and pulled her to him, overjoyed that she was not a casualty to add to the ever-growing list.

The rest were not so lucky. Lucy helped Brad to his feet and Harry and Laura saw that her right eye was all but closed as a livid red swelling grew from the cut just above the eyebrow. She had been thrown against the bulkhead as Harry had hit the bank towards the end of his charge.

'Are you Ok Lucy?' asked a concerned Laura.

'Well my eye's not too bad,' she replied. 'But this I'm not so sure about.' She held up her right hand and Harry's stomach turned as he saw where a bullet had passed clean through, taking most of the knuckle of the forefinger with it.

'Oh my God,' screamed Laura, running to assist her.

'Oh it's not so bad,' she replied, lifting it to her face for inspection before collapsing onto the deck. Brad did his best to catch her on the way down but grimaced as her weight pulled on his injured shoulder. Laura arrived and took the load cushioning the last part of her fall. As she attended Lucy's hand as best she could Brad made his way back to Harry.

'You Ok?' he asked.

'Yeah, just a graze. How's your shoulder?'

'Painful, but I'll live.'

'Looks like my Laura was the only one to get away unhurt,' said Harry. 'You, me and Lucy all got hit.'

'And Matthew of course,' said Brad.

'Oh Christ I forgot about him.'

Harry eased his way past Lucy and Laura and made his way to the bridge. He dropped to his knees as he surveyed the scene. Matthew was sat in a pool of blood, leaning against the grey metal of the bridge structure, his strapped leg out in front of him. His other leg was bent at an impossible angle and protruded to the left of his body as if twisted by a child that had become bored with a toy.

Harry guessed that the blood was from a wound that had broken his leg and thrown it to its present position.

'Matthew?' he queried, looking into his serene face. 'Matthew, are you Ok?'

Matthew didn't move, didn't blink, didn't anything. Harry knelt down in front of him and pushed two fingers against the jugular artery in his neck. As he did Matthew toppled over sideways leaving a smear of blood down the wall. Harry stared at the metal of the bulkhead. A bullet had passed through pushing jagged metal into Matthew's scalp. He saw with disgust that some flesh with thin strands of grey hair was hanging off the distorted metal, but it was the bullet that had done the damage. Though slowed by the bulk head there was still enough momentum for it to enter Matthew's skull and kill him instantly as it passed through the soft brain tissue. He never knew what had hit him.

Harry gently laid Matthew on his back amongst the wrecked remains of the bridge. He arranged the body such that the others would not see the devastating damage to the back of his head. He tried to cross his hands over his chest but it was not like in the films and they just kept flopping back by his sides. As they fell his right hand opened to reveal the crucifix he'd been clutching as he prayed during the gun battle. Finally he covered Matthew's face with a blanket he found on the floor and then made his way back to the others and gave them the sad news. There were no hysterics, just gentle weeping as Lucy and Laura held each other in the growing heat of the jungle.

Chapter Sixty

Harry expected a mutiny. He was crushed by Matthew's death and thought it might cause the others to admit defeat and turn themselves in. Just the opposite. It strengthened their resolve if anything and they were soon sat planning their next move.

'Nothing's actually changed,' said Harry. 'The plan is the same. We must assume that they are waiting for us on the beach by now so the intention is just to go hell for leather and try to make it to the open sea and pray that the Japs are distracted by the Marines.'

'How far do you think it is to the beach,' asked Lucy, who was quickly recovering from the shock of her bullet wound.

'Quarter of a mile, maybe half at the most,' answered Harry.

'Well by my reckoning the Marines should be approaching this area of the island anytime soon so lets get the show on the road,' Bolstered Brad, anxious to impart a positive attitude to his frightened comrades.

'What about the torpedo,' asked Brad?

'I've been thinking about that,' replied Harry. 'But I don't really see any way we can usefully employ it unless they block our exit to the open ocean with something, and I don't think they've had time for that. Even if we tried I'm not sure it will actually fire if I'm perfectly honest.'

'Ok then, let's get to it.'

Their game plan was frightening in its simplicity. They would rush to the ocean hoping to draw as much fire as possible from a concentrated Japanese force on the beach. This would in turn attract the attention of the US Marine force close by, at least if Harry's 'dream world' was still running correctly. It had been accurate up to now so they saw no reason to doubt it would continue and that their luck would hold. When asked what they'd do once they got out to sea Harry had said just two words: "Wing it"

Brad started up the engines with relative ease and signalled to Harry that he was ready. Lucy gave him a kiss and a tight hug and then lowered herself as far below the deck as she could. Laura repeated the process with Harry and joined her. Looking forward Harry could make out a turn to the right in the rapidly widening river and hoped there were no added obstructions since their passage this morning. He tried to brush away the thought that jumped into his head but failed; had the Japs blocked the river? He flashed Brad a tight-lipped grin and nodded. Let's hope not, he thought as the boat lurched forward past the tree, eagerly on its way to oblivion.

Harry did his best to keep the boat in the middle of the river as he eased it around the tightening right hand bend. The light was improving as the sun rose but the thick canopy still subdued it and kept most of the detail in shadow. As their course straightened Harry adjusted their path as the water narrowed; trees encroaching on both sides, and almost too late Harry recognised it as the place where he'd caught the fish on his first day on the island. He shouted to Brad who gunned both engines and the small boat leapt forward.

'Heads down,' he shouted needlessly as the boat shot from under the canopy into a hail of gunfire.

Strangely enough it was the very first bullet fired that took him just on the lower jaw line, tearing the lower mandible from its rightful position as it passed through to lodge deep in his neck. Everything from that point slowed down for Harry. He felt the tug of the tumbling bullet as it ripped through his body, yet he felt no pain. His head was pulled down by the impact and he watched in amazement as the second round from the stream smashed into his left collar bone splashing blood and shattered bone into his face. The third thudded into the meat of his shoulder, the sound registering yet still no pain, and finally the fourth just grazed his left arm. He looked down at the torrent of blood cascading down his front and knew at that moment he was dying. He tried to shout for Laura but the air just rushed out of his fractured larynx, bubbling to a stop as he realised it was futile. He tried to breathe in but felt blood gurgling into his lungs and he looked up and thanked God that it would be quick.

Harry closed his eyes, but not before he noted with some satisfaction that they had reached the open sea and that the Japs were far behind them. He gratefully sank to the deck as he felt the revs fall from the engines below him. He was vaguely aware of a gun battle going on in the distance behind him and but for the state of his face would have smiled at the fact that their plan had worked like clockwork. His final thoughts were of Laura as he heard her scream and felt her hands in his. He did not have the strength to open his eyes but felt the searing burn of her hot tears as they fell silently onto his face. Just before he slipped into the black void that beckoned him, he heard her final words.

'Not now Harry, I love you...'

Chapter Sixty-One

Harry opened his eyes and raised a hand to shield the bright light that seemed to pierce the very flesh of his eyes. Failing to make out any features of his surroundings he cautiously looked down at his body, afraid of what he might see. In retrospect he wasn't sure if he would have been more disturbed to find bloody clothes and homemade blood stained bandages, rather than the clean pyjamas and seemingly total lack of wounds

'Guess I'm dead then,' he said out loud.

'Not quite but it was a close run thing,' laughed a familiar voice.

'Brad...Brad is that you?'

'Good guess. Lucy, go and get Laura and Mike.'

'Brad what happened, where am I, what...?'

'All in good time Buddy, just relax until the others get here.'

Harry lay back on the soft bed and closed his painful eyes, which try as he might failed to penetrate into the room. He felt a warm hand grab hold of his, the skin thick and wrinkled. He looked up and noted that the light was dimming allowing him to make out a silhouette leaning over him.

'Brad is that you, I can't see properly.'

'Yes buddy, but you gotta be prepared for...'

Brad was interrupted by the sound of a door being thrown back against its hinges.

'Harry, oh Harry,' squealed Laura as she burst into the room almost tripping in her eagerness to get to the bed.

Harry fought back tears as the kisses rained down on his face from the woman he thought he'd never see again. He hugged her tightly returning the kisses before he remembered they had other company. He held her face on both sides and peered to make out her features. His sight was returning quite quickly now and he smiled as he looked into the deep brown eyes of his beautiful wife.

'I love you.'

Laura burst into tears and hugged him tight once more.

'Hello Harry,' said a quivering female voice.

Harry looked over Laura's shoulder and saw an old couple standing at the end of the bed.

'Do I know you?' he asked.

'As I was saying buddy, you gotta be prepared for a shock,' responded the old man.

'Brad, Lucy?'

He looked into Laura's face as she nodded.

'Yes it's us,' said Lucy

'But...'

'You left us in 1942 and we have returned to now; your own time.'

'But what happened? The last thing I remember was...' Harry paused as he tried to think.

'Oh God,' he cried as his hand flew to his face.

'It's ok Sweetheart,' soothed Laura. 'You're not hurt.'

'Ok you lot, let's not scare the poor man to death.'

'Mike – now that's a voice I definitely do recognise,' said Harry

Mike made his way to the bedside and sombrely shook Harry's hand.

'I wasn't expecting you back so soon,' he said. 'Let's check you over and then between us we should be able to answer all your questions.'

The medical was fairly cursory; Mike knowing that Harry would be in good health and, apart from some tiredness over the next few days, would be raring to go in no time. As Mike finished, Laura fussed around the bed trying to get Harry as comfortable as possible.

'Enough Woman, just tell me what happened,' he growled with mock ferocity.

And so Laura picked up the story...

'Not now Harry, I love you, don't die, please don't die.'

Harry just stared back into her tragic face as the tears tumbled down onto his. He tried to say something but the words were lost in shattered throat and as the last picture in his mind began to grey at the edges as he spiralled towards a black pit he was vaguely aware of Laura scrabbling about in his clothing.

Laura's glazed eyes focused back onto Harry as he lay back on the bed; 'I knew I'd lost you and in doing so had lost myself as well. The last act I remember was slipping the ring onto your finger, holding you tight and rolling us both into the water.'

She looked over her shoulder to the others. Brad nodded.

'That's about as we saw it Laura; we ran to the stern but there was no sign of either of you in the water. We just guessed that you'd gone to a watery grave.'

'So what happened next?' asked Harry.

'Well I guess you would find it rather anti-climatic after that,' said Brad. 'We were intercepted by a US Navy picket boat shortly after, and taken aboard a destroyer. We eventually flew home to the states from Australia and lived happily ever after.' He smiled and hugged Lucy.

'Until Mike tracked us down,' Lucy responded, setting an exaggerated grimace on her face.

They all looked over as Mike started to speak.

'My part's really simple; I received a call from Heathrow concerning two passengers that had collapsed on a flight from Australia. I immediately had you transported here where experience told me that if I waited you would recover.'

'But how did they know to call you,' asked Laura, echoing the thoughts of the others.

Harry smiled and revealed an SOS bracelet on his right wrist. Opening it he read aloud:

'In the event of illness or mystery unconsciousness please contact Dr Mike Phillips on 07766057003. Looks like my little insurance policy worked'

'So,' said Laura slowly. 'It all revolves around the ring.'

'I reckon so,' said Mike. 'And talking of which....' He reached into the pocket of his coat and pulled out the ring on the end of a gold chain and handed it to Harry. 'I think

379

that, as long as you were still alive in the parallel world when you put it on, your injuries don't come back with you to this world. Had you passed away before Laura got it onto your finger it may well have been a different story.'

'But why didn't Harry come back the first time like he did this time, rather than spending months in a coma?' asked Laura.

'Search me,' said Mike. 'Maybe he would have eventually got back under his own steam, or maybe a precedence was set and now it just happens as he slips the ring on and off; I guess none of us will ever know as, let's face it, we're dealing with forces beyond this world.'

'I Guess so,' replied Harry, looking at the ring as he accepted it from Mike.

'Just keep it safe,' muttered Mike.

Harry held the ring between his thumb and forefinger. He looked through the centre into Laura's beautiful deep brown eyes. A small smile broke across her mouth as he winked and she slowly looped her arm through his.

'Hold on tight,' he said quietly.

Then looking at each face in the room, he said quite clearly: 'I wonder where it will take us this time,' and slipped the ring onto his finger.

THE END